PARANORMAL

Charles Hays

Trafford rev. 06/19/2012

 www.trafford.com

North America & international
toll-free: 1 888 232 4444 (USA & Canada)
phone: 250 383 6864 ♦ fax: 812 355 4082

Contents

DEDICATION

This book would not have been possible without my gorgeous wife,
Dorothy R. Hays (1937-2010) and my dedicated
Mother, Sallie Ann Hays (1910-2002).

Foreword

M Y FAMILY NEVER really embraced the concept of television. Believe it or not, we each favored the old fashioned way of telling or imagining stories. And, in each family, there was always one relative who would qualify as a World Class Storyteller. To be specific, my Mother Sallie or her two sisters, Mina and Canzallia would provide the evening's entertainment.

The genre that we all liked best was that which concerned the telling of ghost stories. Of course, such stories were frightening to young children but, each tale would allow us the privilege of having to go to bed early. But, a full stomach after an all-day session of hoeing corn or pulling weeds would, eventually, win out and force us to retire sooner than we desired. As you might expect, we would resist the 'sandman' for as long as possible.

This book is based on ghost stories that those three sisters told me when I was in my youth or young maturity years. I have wrapped the storyline of those tales around a fictional organization known by the acronym of PESO which stands for the Phenomenological Event Study Offices. That fictional organization has the assignment of studying ghosts and capturing their images on special infrared cameras that work so well at night.

His type of camera is a modification of the model used by the military to observe enemy soldiers at night when visibility and fog is such a problem. Dr. Paul Gray is my protagonist who provides unequivocal proof of the fact that these reported ghost sites are properly documented and described. His Final Report goes directly to a fictional Governor for the State of Kentucky who wants to manipulate the unsuspecting ghosts by building new State Parks around their locations for profit. In other words, the Governor is my antagonist who wants to squeeze more money from the tourist traffic by using a new approach. He wants to combine a bed and breakfast operation with an outdoor theater that features no actors and actresses, only a cast of qualified ghosts.

Names, characters and known incidents within the State of Kentucky are modified as a product of the author's imagination to enhance the story's presentation and, to protect the innocent people, places or local histories. Any suspected resemblance to actual persons (living or dead) and all associated events at any specific location are strictly coincidental and completely unintentional.

Chapter One

ORIENTATION

DR. PAUL GRAY was sitting at his new desk in the squad room of the Phenomenological Event Study Offices (PESO) and, he was not a happy camper. He considered himself to be a detective who was held in high esteem and honored for his successful solution of many murder cases dealing with unique turns and twists or overly complex plots. He did not consider himself to be a follower of the supernatural cult.

He was staring at the lettering on the front door when he realized that the Mexican painter may have had money on his mind when he labeled the glass as 'PESO'. These four letters seemed larger than would be expected on a normal basis. He may have been driven by thoughts of monetary rewards but, who knows for certain? Acronyms can be very misleading on certain occasions.

In addition, Paul was very angry because his former boss at the Metropolitan Police Department (MPD) had transferred him to this PESO outfit from his true love of solving complicated murder cases. Maybe, that's why he was still so angry about the transfer. He had not been given a choice in the matter. For Gray, it was either of two options; go to PESO or go through the back door at MPD.

Gray firmly believed that it was all because of that cute little red-haired girl that his former Captain was chasing. All right, chase away, Captain. One day soon, I will let him know that I had shagged her first, not him. Maybe it is best that I won't be around when the Captain discovers that particular fact. Gray's old Captain was a man who liked to inflict punishment on some of his most dedicated Staff members. His favorite place to settle issues was at the boxing gym which exists just down the street.

Then, Paul's mind wandered to the question of what does the word 'phenomena' really mean to these PESO people? What do these employees do to justify their paychecks? Does this new job involve cases that are hypo-normal or hyper-normal, or both? Will I be given the opportunity to evaluate both extraordinary and supernatural assignments? Will they be challenging or boring? Oh heck, time will tell and truth will out. I'm just getting a little hyper wondering about what my job description will tell me about my unknown future. Where the hell is everybody? It's late already.

He looked at the wall clock and he realized that he had reported early for the first time in his working career. He imagined that he probably did that to impress his new boss, Captain Mira Mirren. He shuttered at the aspects of working for a female but, in this case, he had no control over that. When a transfer is ordered, you have to live with what you get. The rumors about her reputation as an administrator were all good even though she was known to be a lesbian. Silently, he said, "I have never taken one of those to my bedroom, not ever. Maybe Ms. Mira swings both ways. I'll have to check her out later, after we have gotten to know each other a little better."

He browsed the surrounding area to see how each nameplate was photoengraved for every desk that was located near his own. It was an easy guess where the Chief's office was located. That was the largest office of the squad room. Next to the entrance for Mira's room, there was a Gold-plated desk sign which read, Joan Lake, Assistant to Chief Mira Mirren. To his left, there were two desks, one for Herb Moore, Engineer and another for Shirley Hooten, Detective.

In his own row, there was a freshly made plastic nameplate that read Dr. Paul Gray, Chief Scientist and another desk for Lola Bryce, Laboratory Technician. He summarized the PESO Staff in the following manner; two men and four women. If Herb Moore truly was a '*Senior*' Detective then it meant that there could be one man versus four women, what a glorious day!

In other words, it might be 'Heaven on Earth with Paul Gray pitted against Shirley, Lola, Joan and Mira. At least, he was hoping that it go in that particular direction. He was reminded of that old adage which states the view that one cannot get too much of either love or education. And, at first glance, PESO seemed to offer favorable probabilities for both attributes.

At the precise moment of 0800-hours, Captain Mira Mirren and her Fellow workers entered the front door to begin their work assignments of the day. They each glanced at him as if to say, "Something new has been added and it's probably none other than Dr. Paul Gray, our new Chief Scientist."

Herb Moore slowly slipped into his desk chair which contained three soft foam seat cushions before saying, "Welcome aboard, mate. But, he didn't bother to shake hands or say anything else. Perhaps, he resented the competition of another male in his erstwhile group of lady hens. Men who are not too far from retirement are very possessive, aren't they?

Shirley, Lola and Joan sat down on their respective chairs but, the latter young lady said, "Chief Mirren will be calling for you in just a few moments, Dr. Gray. Just give her a chance to get settled in and, then, she will take you through your orientation meeting, Okay?"

I replied, "Fine with me Joan. Then, I will have more time to adore your charming appearance." And, immediately, Joan's face turned as red as her beautiful hair. Privately, he gave thanks for her presence. Joan would make a fine replacement for the girl that he left behind with his former Captain back at MPD. He thought that some things never change; lose one red head but, find another. In that respect, women are like busses. Miss one but, catch the next one!

Then, Dr. Mirren wiggled a forefinger that apparently meant, Come hither 'you hunk'. So, I went in that direction but, as I passed Joan's desk, I gave her a cute little wink which was my own way of saying that I admired her lovely appearance. As I passed her desk, she blushed a second time and, this time, her face was redder than before!

With my best Rufus Sewell appearance and my favorite John Wayne swagger in full tow, I entered the Chief's private lair where I sat down on one of her guest chairs that faced her attractive thirty-ish appearance. Suddenly, her formal and explicit disapproval became more obvious since she no longer had a smile on her face.

Angrily, she said, "Any time that you enter or leave my Office, You must open or close my door. That's my number one rule. I try to maintain a closed-door policy as much as I can and that's my number one rule. He laughed and said, "Isn't it supposed to be the other way around? At the MPD my former Chief always used to say that he ran an open-door policy. This isn't the MPD. While you are here, you will do as I say. So, shut up and listen to what I have to say. Close that damned door."

Quickly, I got up to close her office door but, this time, I chose a different chair in the hope that another chair might bring me better luck but, as it turned out, changing chairs didn't help me very much at all. She proceeded with an irate lecture about me and what my Personnel Record File said about my strengths and weaknesses. She said, Mr. Gray, you have the reputation of being an incurable romantic and I won't allow that to happen, not on my watch. Joan Lake belongs to me and only to me. That's my number two rule. Is that well understood, Paul?

I responded by saying, "Yes Ma'am, it is. But, if you and Joan ever fancy a threesome, I am both available and interested." She was extremely flustered by my remark but, she did manage a quick reply. She said, "If we ever do need your services, don't call me. I will call you, OK?"

Then, she changed the subject to say, "Gray, do you have any idea why I asked for your '*scientific*' services?" I replied, "No Ma'am, I have not been properly informed. I just showed up, so to speak. But, I would wager that I am here because of my problem solving capabilities. They were very helpful skills in making me a World Class Detective, Ma'am.

She said, "Close but, no cigar. Our new Governor is proud of fact that Kentucky has more miles of running water than other States do. As a result of that fact, Kentucky also has more reported paranormal events than any of the other States. And, we have more State Parks than most of the other States. So, in a nutshell, I wanted you here in this Office because of your established investigative skills. Gray, you are the only detective that I know who has *zero* unsolved cases. I find that to be amazing and that is what I need for my Department.

As a scientist, you would probably measure our overall mission in terms of Boolean Logic Parameters. Here, there are three interactive variables; (1) Investigative Skills, (2) Unequivocal proof that Ghosts do exist and (3) The building of New State Parks. Gray, I expect that you have the necessary skills to greatly assist PESO with respect to items (1) and (2).

Basically, I need your help. None of my previous employees have been able to handle this job position but, you appear to be more promising. I think that you have the ability to do well at PESO providing that you can adjust your attitude in a positive manner. If you stop viewing women as your own private sex slaves, I think that you might be more than successful.

Our Governor wants to use Kentucky's running water and our high incident rate for ghost sightings as a means to increase our State income." I asked, "How so?" She replied, "His plan is sheer genius in certain ways. He has given us a State-of-the-Art Laboratory to characterize all known supernatural events which occur within our State boundaries. I will give you a theoretical example which explains his plan. Dr. Gray, you will be asked to evaluate a given phenomenological event (PE) location.

You will visit your assigned ghost site and carry out your own investigations where verification and characterization will be your main concerns. You will take physical samples for your assistant Lola to evaluate. She will try to prove both authenticity and recurrence percentages. Afterwards, the Governor will build a new State Park around the site that you have evaluated. His motivation will be to develop an overnight lodging facility for attracting more tourist dollars to visit the area. He is growing tired of locals taking all of that tourist money when Kentucky needs cash injections so badly during this awful recession of 2012.

Our Governor is a strong believer in paranormal events and he wants to earn a monetary profit from each of them, especially if they are feasible according to you and Lola. He needs your back up for both reliability and recurrence frequencies.

"I asked, "What roles do Herb and Shirley play in this study of rumors about these reported paranormal activities?" She said, "Herb is busy with the State Park side of things; e.g., The construction aspects of building new edifices and their required highways, parking lots, et cetera.

Shirley is his assistant that keeps old Herb on the straight and narrow relevant to records, reports and efficiency."Those two will also scour the entire State of Kentucky for finding new and likely locations that you and Lola might have to evaluate in the near term future." He asked, "Besides taking care of Joan's needs and priorities, what is your contribution to the sum of total knowledge at PESO?" She smiled and said, "I will present all findings to our Governor and I will make all required recommendations that will lead to the development of a new State Park. Beyond that, I will handle the budget and keep track of my people. One wrong move by you and these already prepared termination papers will be signed and processed. Do you read me Dr. Gray?" What could I say except, "Yes Ma'am, I do."

Then, 'She who must be obeyed' asked, "Any questions, newcomer?" I responded in a semi-aggressive manner by saying, "These are my requirements or, I refuse to accept this position:

- I want an operating budget for my own requirements. My associate Lola will be your responsibility, not mine.
- I want reasonable travel expenses to cover all of my time while I am on the road and in the field. If I am in my office, this budget item does not apply.
- I want an unrestricted petty cash allowance of $5000.00 dollars per month.

I want a marked police car for my own personal use. That Cruiser must be a chase car suitable for high speed runs; e.g., an 8-cylinder engine with 450-horses under the hood. I insist on having a Ford vehicle and, absolutely, no damned Chevrolets or foreign imports of any make or model. Unless it is imported from Detroit, I don't want it.

- I expect complete electronic support with a smartphone, a laptop computer and an I-Pad. I also want a radio unit that will transmit across one end of Kentucky to the opposite end; viz., from my car direct to your office.
- I expect my first case file to be submitted to me within 24-hours or I resign my position.

Do you read me, Chief Mirren?" My new boss responded in the following manner, "Here are your car keys and your new vehicle is parked next to mine in slot number one. My third rule is this: don't ever park in my parking space. Inside your new automobile, you will find all that you will need in the way of electronic support. I accept your terms and this file will be your first assignment."

She handed me a storage box that was heavily stuffed with evidence and related material. She added, "This case came to us directly from the Governor's Office so, don't screw it up. In fact, it would be very wise for you to always support your Governor's choices when it comes to any assigned cases. He is quite an authority on the subject of the supernatural. In other words, we do need a positive result from you on your first case outing. Do you read me loud and clear, Dr. Gray?"

I looked her square in the eyes and said, "Ma'am, you will get a positive conclusion from me only if one exists. I won't play politics with anyone about any of my cases or my final reports. Understood, Ma'am?"

She looked somewhat surprised but, she quickly answered, "I do reserve the right to edit your final reports before they go to the Governor's Office. And, that will be enough talking for today. Read your first case file over very thoroughly. And, by tomorrow morning, tell me how you want to proceed.

Otherwise, I will have to find a suitable replacement for your darling face and cute buns. If you decide to accept this first case on behalf of PESO, I will be pleased to have you aboard as my Chief Scientist. And, I am certain that all of my women are very anxious for you to stay here for several years. But, Paul, know this and know it well. If you make anyone of my Staff pregnant, you will be terminated or reassigned to some place much lower on the ladder."

With a wicked smile on my face, I replied, "I promise that I will not impregnate Mr. Herb Moore." Her smile was more wicked than mine as I left the office. In the process of leaving, I closed her office door very tightly with a short burst of noise.

Then, I went to my new apartment to study my first case file without any disturbances of any kind. It is difficult to study important files when there is so much feminine pulchritude just a few feet from your desk. My new case was entitled 'School Girls' and the subject of young girls was to Dr. Gray's way of thinking, fundamentally enticing.

He felt that way because they all grow up to be beautiful women and they become God's best creation for making men happy.

Chapter Two

SCHOOL GIRLS

C HIEF SCIENTIST PAUL Gray was lounging at his new apartment when he opened his first case file which was simply identified as 'School Girls'. At first, he let his large ego control his reactions. Something of this sort went flying from neuron-to-neuron inside his skull, viz., "Why am I wasting my time on something as trivial as this particular Case?

I am an internationally known detective who is famous for solving complex criminal cases. And, here I am sorting out details about what happened to three little girls during a flash flood that occurred back in 1937. He asked himself, who really gives a damn about those three girls, anyway? The year of 1937 lies too many years in the past for most people to even care or remember. Isn't that the reality behind this assignment?"

Then, he saw something that changed his entire outlook completely. One of the girls in the case was named 'Pauline Campbell' and that made a difference. Paul's nanny was also named Pauline Campbell and he was reminded of how his Pauline played her guitar and sang songs to him when he was just a little boy.

For that reason, he became more riveted to the file and its players. Suddenly, he was motivated to try and solve the reason that Pauline left the bridge and drowned in the raging creek below. As he continued to read more about this little girl and her three sisters, he began to realize something that was very important to him and his egotistical opinions.

This PESO business is not too much different from that of my old job at MPD. And, Pauline is not too much unlike my other victims that I evaluated while I served the City's finest, the Lexington Police Department (LPD). Plain and simply stated, Pauline and her sisters lived and they died.

It isn't necessary that I have to determine the cause for their deaths and I don't have to search for their killer. It's nice that I don't have to solve the mystery of their demises. All I need to do is to explain these reported sightings which have been repeated over the past 74-years. There have been thousands of sightings for the girl's images but, why do they continue to exist over such a large span of time? Why do they refuse to go into the bright light and disappear forever? Is Pauline trying to tell us something? Suddenly, he seemed to be more attracted to the challenge of it all but, he couldn't explain why. He needed to dig deeper so that he might learn more.

He decided to make random notes on the more important aspects of this particular file. He typed the data into his laptop computer as he lifted records from that storage box. Later on, he would merge them into some logical order but, for the present, he would try to determine the ranking order for both worthiness and relevance. The following list summarizes his initial reactions to the case file contents about this apparition.

- Three girls did drown but, all reported sightings have been silent ones. Usually, there are associated screams or noises that can be interpreted by experts of the kind that work for PESO.

However. this is not the case for these girls. Their case is about phantom images only and nothing more.

- Allegedly, this drowning incident occurred on Leatherwood Creek in Perry County. At or near the Letcher County line and due East of Delphia. He estimated that the ghostly figures made their appearance at a point which is about eight miles from Cumberland, Kentucky.

According to weather experts, the initial 1937 flooding was classified as a 'flash flood'. These occur primarily during the afternoon-to-evening hours of the day when there is an abundance of atmospheric moisture and very little vertical wind shear. Flash flood waves, moving at incredible speeds can roll big boulders, tear out large trees, destroying buildings and bridges to create new water channels and new stream branches. Flash flood waves can easily reach a height of twenty feet or more.

- Leatherwood Creek runs into the North Fork of the Kentucky River which feeds the Ohio River. The 1937 flood stage at Cincinnati, Ohio crested at a record depth of about eighty feet or so. In brief, that flood was classified as a 100-year event.
- Their cause of death was, obviously, drowning but, the root cause for their demise was blamed on their school teacher who did not send the children home quick enough to save their lives. She released them from her two-room school at 3-PM when classes should have been dismissed no later than by the lunch period.
- The failure of that swinging bridge was attributed to heavy debris being carried along at a very high velocity. Of the thirteen children that were to cross that bridge on that fateful day, only ten made it across to safety. Pauline Campbell and her two sisters helped the others to survive but, they forfeited their lives for their valiant act of bravery.

In summary, he felt sympathetic about poor Pauline Campbell and her two sisters, so he decided, then and there, that a trip to the headwaters region of Leatherwood Creek was now mandatory. He needed to interview the locals, any relatives or survivors of the incident. And, if he got lucky on this first trip he planned to document field images at the actual site.

He had a hunch that his crystallographer, Lola Bryce, would be required to solve the factual causes for this apparition. For that reason, he decided to take several specimens back to Lexington because the geology of this region is quite complicated. In other words, his Final Report to his gay boss and that smart but, money-hungry Governor needed input from Lola.

Next morning, he called in at about 4-AM to say that he was going on a field trip to Leatherwood of Eastern Kentucky for the purpose of characterizing young Pauline Campbell's ghost imagery. He left his new boss a message because he had no desire to debate his reasons for going out of town on travel status. She, being a typical woman, would want to discuss the pros and cons for going on travel status during the second day of his employment at PESO.

'She who must be obeyed' would surely ask detailed questions of where, why and how, et cetera. He imagined what he really wanted to say to her and it went something like the following:"I'm a professional, girl so leave me be. I know what I am doing and I will bring you up to date when I have something significant to report.

As an added touch he would like to say, "Ma'am, I don't give a damn about keeping you so well informed about my whereabouts and my detailed activities. I will bring you up-to-date when I have something more significant to discuss." Until then, you will have to wait your turn and wonder. Then, he went undercover by turning off his radio and his cell phone.

As he drove silently toward his hometown of Hazard, Kentucky, his thoughts were about his childhood, not the Case File. He surveyed his own personal case file by remembering his family, his nanny, his school years, his buddies and his former girlfriends. He was going to try and locate one of his former sweethearts before he did much of anything else. Is Doris still there in Perry County? Would Doris be available on such short notice? Would Doris care for him once again? After all these years will she still like me well enough to go to bed with me?

He was hoping for the best when he checked into his favorite Motel, the La Citadel which rests on top of Town Mountain with that fabulous view of the valley below. After I check in and get unpacked, I will call her and we will get together for an evening about lost love and lust that's recently found.

For now, he would take a short nap on his bed because that high speed driving had made him very exhausted. He would call Doris Pratte a little later in the evening and they would think of something to do to each other's body which they would both greatly enjoy.

He woke up next morning and he was amazed to discover that he still had the same clothes on that he wore to the check-in desk that previous evening. His reaction was, "Wow, I gave up good sex with Doris for just a good night's sleep. For me, that's definitely not my customary behavior.

Gray ate his breakfast at what used to be called 'Maw Comb's Restaurant near Bridge Street and the L&N Railroad Depot. He said, "Excellent food for a fair price." His memory of Maw Combs went back to the days when he was a juvenile and delivering papers for the Hazard Daily Herald.

When he was hungry, he would stand at her window at stare at the prepared food until Maw would motion for him to come inside where she would give him a free bowl of pinto beans. All he could say about her was, "God, how I loved that old woman. She made the best pinto beans that I have ever tasted. In return, I would always give her an extra copy Of the day's newspaper and she would be reading the news before I could get out of the front door. She was an ugly old woman but, she was very well enlightened by reading the current events of her newspaper.

After Paul's customary breakfast of eggs, sausage and several cups of hot java, he motored-up for a trip to Leatherwood Creek. This time, he turned his radio and cell phone on so that you-know-who could give him some private hell about communication and his apparent desire to avoid team play. After a few moments of driving, she did just as he predicted. She began with, "Where in the hell are you? Report in to me, Dr. Gray or I will have the Highway Patrol arrest you. And, don't think that I won't because I surely will."

He decided that he would give it five more minutes before he reported in to Miss Mirren, the control freak that just started being his new boss. Man, was she in for some new experiences about how to manage a free spirit of the Paul Gray type. He steered his car over to the road's shoulder for safety purposes before checking in with his new boss.

She did just as he had predicted. She ranted, raved and vented her rage through his cell phone connection. She was several decibels above her normal voice but, after a few minutes of wild frustration, she simmered down enough so that they both could have a decent conversation.

Her pertinent point was a simple question that either one of the two could have answered in a 'New York Second' had they been so inclined. She asked, "Do you need back up with Herb and Shirley?" To which he replied, "No Ma'am." Then she asked, "Just what do you expect to achieve with this unauthorized visit to Eastern Kentucky?" He replied, "Ma'am, I am looking for stronger evidence to support some of the conjecture that I found in the evidence box about this case. I have to begin somewhere and, for me, this is where I want to begin.

Quickly, she said, "Do you have an open mind or are you biased against what we women wrote?" Paul replied by saying, "Ma'am, I am an incurable womanizer. Of this, there can be little doubt. I know that you would like me to be different but, it's hard for an old dog to learn new tricks. I could never be overly biased by what any woman says or does. Provided, of course, that there is some likelihood of intercourse in my near term future.

At that moment, our connection went dead and, it didn't sound like an interference problem. 'She who must be obeyed' was obviously very angry. Our second conversation and it fell flat on its face, oh woe is me. I was probably talking to an audience or on a conference call without my knowledge. If that be the case, she should have forewarned but, she didn't.

Gray returned to his car and drove toward his final destination, a small grocery store near Leatherwood Creek that was run by the Campbell family. This new information was fished from the Hazard Telephone Directory and he was convinced that this might be a good place to begin his relevant interviews.

Because there was no mention of this family's connection to be found within the PESO evidence box. Previous writings from the evidence box were based on invalidated rumors which were not supported by actual fact. Sorry, Mira but, that's the way it is. I will try to separate fact from fiction for this case from this date forward.

Gray located that little store and he went inside to speak to the owner. He presented his shiny new Police ID badge to the clerk, an old man who was at least 80-years young and quite well preserved. This is to say that he looked much younger than his actual age.

Paul started his first interview by saying, "Mr. Eldon Campbell, I represent PESO and the Governor's Office. I am here to talk with you about the strange images that these three 'school girls' present somewhere near this area. Can you help me, Sir?"

The old man looked Paul right in his eyes and said, "Yes, I can help you but, the real issue is why should I help you? I can't see any reason for helping the Governor's Office. What has he ever done to help us country folks?"

Paul answered by saying, "I am not responsible for what the Governor does or doesn't do. But, I will say this much. I didn't vote for him in the past election. And, I will bet you a hundred dollar bill that you did." Old man Campbell managed a big grin before saying, "You are right. I did make that mistake. What do you want from me, young fellow?"

Paul answered him in this manner, "Close up the store for the rest of the afternoon and take me to the site where the girls still perform their haunting sessions. In return for that valuable service, I will give you that 100-dollar bill, okay?"

In almost total disbelief, the senior Campbell said, "We have a deal young man. I'll get my grand-daughter Mabel to take over the store so that you and I can transact some business. That location is not very far from where we stand. He went to the back of the store to inform Mabel as to where he was going.

Young and beautiful Mabel came up front to stand behind the counter and say, "Grand Dad, I see that you have another tourist on the hook, right?" Her grandfather grinned and said, "Mabel, this one is paying his own way. He is not like all those others that wanted something for nothing.

And, for certain, he isn't like the ones that came down here from Frankfort, Kentucky. We ought to be back in less than two hours or so. Isn't that about right, Dr. Gray?" I said, "Yes Sir. That should do it for today. But, I may need to return tomorrow or, perhaps, even more often. Gray couldn't help but notice that attractive smile on Mabel's face. So, like General McArthur, I muttered those historic words, "I shall return."

We rode in my police car for a short distance so that the old man would not have to scale those near-vertical walls of Leatherwood Creek. After about one-quarter mile or so, Mr. Campbell said, "Stop here, this is the place." In that short distance between his store and the actual search site, he had asked me all sorts of questions about my engine, radio, computer, cell phone and electronic equipment. This man was not a typical mountain man. He had a very inquiring mind which meant that he enjoyed learning about new things. Almost immediately, I liked him. He and I had one thing in common, we both liked Mabel.

After we got out of the Police Car, the old man started talking about the drowning incident. You could tell from his tears that he didn't enjoy talking about the story of their demise. "I walk over here about twice a week to pay homage to my dear departed sisters. Pauline was the oldest followed by Marie and Inez Campbell. I loved them dearly and I still regret my actions on that fateful day."

I asked, "What did you do?" He answered, "I have never admitted this to any living soul but, you do look like a trustworthy person so I need to confess something to somebody. I've got a lot of guilt that has been riding on my shoulders for almost 74-years now." Paul noticed that his tears had been transformed into outright sobbing so, Gray was patient and sensitive to the needs of this old-timer. He waited until Campbell's outpouring of grief had subsided.

Then, Paul asked, "Did you do something bad to your sisters?" He answered, "At the time, I was only nine but, I did give them a playful push while we were crossing the bridge. Pauline had a firm grip on the other two so, all three of them fell off the swinging bridge and went into the raging waters below. I have regretted that move ever since. I am so sorry for killing my three sisters. Please forgive me, God."

"So, if this was a simple accident between four very young children, How do you explain the hauntings over all of these years? He replied, "I have always assumed that to be God's way of punishing me for pushing poor Pauline as we crossed the bridge." Paul said, I doubt that very much, Mr. Campbell. God, in all of his greatness is into forgiveness, not punishment."

Paul tried to change the existing mood by saying, "Mr. Campbell, please point to the place where the sightings have been witnessed. There might be a simple explanation for this observed phenomena." He pointed at the creek and said, "Right here, where the water turns slightly toward the West. On a foggy night with light winds, clearing skies, wet ground, low visibility and strong moonlight, Pauline appears to haunt my tormented soul. I used to come over here more often but, I just can't do it anymore. It hurts me too much."

Dr. Gray said, "Relax and be comfortable in my air conditioned car while I go down to the water's edge for some sampling purposes. I will have to take soil, sand, water and rock samples to try and determine what is fueling this chemical reaction." Campbell smiled and said, "Thank you. I really didn't want to go down there again.

But, Dr. Gray, when you do get to the water's edge, keep your eyes pointed toward the right door window of your car. I will motion for you to go either North or South to exactly where the images always appear." Gray said, "Thank you. I need your help in that regard because homing in is sometimes the hardest part and, especially, during the daylight hours." Then, Paul began his climb down the stream wall to the exact position where the haunting were routinely observed. He slipped a couple of times so he gave thanks that the old timer was not descending that tenuous climb.

His first reactions came as a big surprise but, he decided to withhold all comments until Technician Lola Bryce had completed all of her analyses. He needed absolute proof to support his suppositions before he announced them to the general public. Next, he gathered his specimen jars or vials and stored them in protective containers. He sealed his sample envelopes as well. Then, he started climbing those steep creek walls for a return to his parked car and old man Campbell.

He was happy to see the old man again but, he was happier to breathe the cool refreshing air coming from his very efficient air conditioning unit. After a brief pause, he asked the old man a very important question,

"Who owns this property?" Campbell's answer was exactly what Gray had hoped he might say. He said, "I own this property and over 1000-acres that surround the spot where my Pauline haunts me."

"Mr. Campbell, I have to return to my laboratory in Lexington to drop off these samples of mine for analyses. But, before I make any official decision about Pauline's appearances, let me say that I think that your sister is trying to make you a rich man. Just promise me one thing. Don't sell this property to anyone no matter how much money they might offer. And, that applies especially where our Governor is concerned. He wants this property pretty badly but, I plead with you, don't sell any land to that bastard.

I will return in a fortnight with all of my papers, my proofs and my Final Report. Please do not make any decisions that might affect your ownership in part or in total without talking to me and only to me. There are too many people out there in the flatlands who might want to make a fast buck at your expense.

Of course, Mr. Campbell was elated about everything that Gray had intimated or implied. His greatest joy was that, perhaps, he had misunderstood his Sister's intent. Maybe they were trying to reward him rather than to punish him. He hadn't been this happy for ages. As they neared his store, Campbell asked, "Why are you being so nice and protective of me? We hardly know each other yet I now refer to you as my good friend."

I could see that he was becoming overwhelmed by all of this good news so, I felt that he deserved an honest explanation about my involvement and motivation. "Eldon, how much do you remember about the rape of the Cumberland? In the beginning, it began with the salt mines of Eastern Kentucky. That was followed by the deforestation of our trees. Then came the coal business where smart Yankees like President Roosevelt robbed us of our mineral rights. Well, this is no different. Your Governor is trying to steal away your destiny and your personal rights.

And, I will not be a part of this unfortunate situation. Our Governor should not be allowed to cheat you out of what is rightfully yours, not on my watch. And, if you will allow me the ability to remain invisible to our common foe out of Frankfort, I will make you a rich man.

Eldon had tears in his eyes when he said, "Men like you are so rare these days. You would put your own life in danger so that mine will be a better life to live. Paul, you deserve a medal and, the sad thing is that I have none to give you. No one will ever know about our secret meeting and, neither Mabel nor I have ever seen you. God bless you, Paul Gray. May your happiness always be with you wherever you may go and may God grant you a safe passage way."

I explained my loyalty to him in another way by telling him about my nanny, Pauline Campbell. I said, "From the first moment that I read this file about your sisters, I felt somehow connected with your Pauline and I have made every effort to better understand her presence and its relevance from that aspect angle on Leatherwood Creek. I dropped him off at his grocery store and I resumed my return to Lexington toward the Northwest.

He made record time in going back to his apartment at his home base in Lexington. That Ford police vehicle, with its big 450-HP engine, was a pleasure to drive. And, he exceeded 118-mph on every straight stretch of the highways. Tonight, he would rest but, tomorrow, he would face the wrath of Miss Mirren and some of the others who really envied his ability to get out of the office while they could not.

She would not allow them to visit their bathroom without signing out on her 'Duty Change Board' that adorned the wall near the front entrance to PESO headquarters. He had plans for that damned board but, not just yet. Later on it would soon meet its fate.

He arrived early to work on the next morning because he wanted to catalog his samples and specimens. He had to log them onto another one of Mira's forms so that Lola's schedule might be better monitored. What a waste of paperwork, he thought. Lola is a big girl who can handle it if Mira would allow it to happen. But, control freaks are like that, aren't they?

He had just finished assigning laboratory test numbers to each of his test samples when Lola Bryce came through the front door to begin her day's work. We exchanged greetings before she said, "Man are you in deep shit today. All the 'Queen Bee' has been talking about for the past few days is how you seem to abuse her rules. She demands teamwork and, she is planning your termination unless you change your ways. In case you haven't noticed it, Dr. Gray, she is one of the most dedicated control freaks that I have ever seen. Sometimes, that can be very stifling and, I am happy that you are trying to change things for the better."

"Lola, I know that Miss Mira is very insecure and feels the need to know everything that is going on in the Department. But, thanks for the 'heads up' tip. I will try to keep my job but, if not, I will go into private practice to paddle my own canoe."

Lola nestled her body up next to me and pressed her large tits against my chest before saying, "I hope that she does not fire you because I don't want you to leave. Where you are concerned, I have plans." All the while she was saying that, she was also stroking my male plaything. I told her, "Why don't we continue this conversation at my apartment tonight?"

And, after she withdrew her affectionate touch, she said, "I was hoping that you would say something like that. Is 8-PM acceptable?" I said, "Most certainly." Privately, he thought, "Let the games begin and Lola shall be the first one to discover my bedroom. Appropriately, Paul began to hum that old song, *Whatever Lola wants, Lola gets*."

Before I left her Laboratory in the basement, we discussed very thoroughly all of the details about the samples which I had extracted from the haunted site. And, I also explained the urgency. I said, I have promised the land owner that I would have a finished report within the next fourteen days. Is that suitable to your schedule, Lola?

She smiled and said, "Only, if we can have our intercourse on a regular basis, my dear handsome hunk. If you can promise that then, I can work miracles with your test specimens. Consider it done, Paul because fourteen days is no real problem. I was flattered so, I quickly agreed to the union of our bodies. And, I did lovingly anticipate the evening hours that were in our near term future.

Reluctantly, I returned to my upstairs desk to face the wrath of our local man-hater, Ms. Mira Mirren. After a short while, I saw the curled finger that meant come hither, Dr. Gray. Thereupon, I entered the lion's den for what I knew would be an unattractive experience. But, first, he winked at Miss Lake and, as expected, she blushed again.

As he entered her office door, he said, "Good morning, Chief." However, she failed to return his greeting. Instead, she ranted, raved and recanted her memorized speech about teamwork by team players. He paid special attention to the part where team players are rewarded while 'soaring eagles' are not rewarded for anything. Privately, he thought, this bull shit tells me that another year will pass before I get any pay increase.

Finally, she got off her soap box and allowed him to make his trip report. She interrupted him only once when she said, "There is nothing in Shirley's Report about any Campbell family. Good work, Dr. Gray. Then, she asked him about the samples that he had collected and, their pending schedule.

When he told her that everything would be wrapped up within about fourteen days, she seemed very pleased. Finally, she said, "Dismissed Dr. Gray. Now I have to brief the Governor." As she reached for her telephone, he quietly left her office without closing her door and he did that for reasons that related to pure meanness. He muttered, "To hell with rule number one."

Sex with Lola was monumental to say the very least. She was something of a tomboy but, that woman certainly knew her way around the bedroom. What she lacked in facial beauty was to be ignored in view of her capabilities while she was hard at work under his coversheet. In that respect, she was a true champion at the performance of face fucking. You could tell that she truly enjoyed doing that for Paul. She stayed all night and he was satisfied in a way which he had not experienced for several weeks now. Not, since the red head of his previous assignment at MPD. By this time, she was probably being screwed by his former boss, the Chief of the Metropolitan Police Department.

In between cuddling, caressing, kissing and screwing, Lola Bryce kept him busy and well informed. She said, "Paul, I was very surprised to discover such large amounts of Fluorspar mineral deposits in almost all of the samples. And, Paul was elated by her findings and her speedy work. However, he pretended to be unimpressed by Lola's laboratory findings. He dismissed her discovery by saying, "There is no reason that Crittenden County should have all of the Fluorspar deposits that exist in the State of Kentucky. Perry County deserves its share as well as any other area does."

Next day, when he reported to work, he found about twenty new case files piled on top of his desk. And, this made him realize that it was Mira's move to slow him down. So, he decided to read the upcoming files while he was forced to remain at the Office. However, he would only read them to give the false appearance of being quite busy. It was evident that she, as a supervisor, wanted to reel in his reins and ride the horse as much as may be possible. More control tactics and that is for certain.

He promised that he would try and learn the business of 'ghost hunting' without ever leaving his desk. And, he was dedicated to his promise that he had made for Eldon Campbell. He would not elevate any of these training cases to a field status until the fortnight was over, a promise is a promise and Mr. Campbell deserves redemption.

After Pauline's presence was explained by Lola's findings, he decided that he would return to the field but not just yet. During this fortnight, a certain wall chart was to vanish in plain sight. The Duty Change Board would not continue to exist after tonight. He felt that when a man has to pee it should not involve a public disclosure. This is to say that one should not have to sign-out for visiting the urinal bowl.

He also vowed that he would not elevate any of those twenty case files to the status of a formal field investigation. He wanted to finish the Campbell file before taking on any other assignments. In other words, he would complete the Campbell haunting before he undertook any additional field examinations.

He would handle his work in this matter no matter what the 'Queen Bee' had to say. His preferred style was to wait until Lola had finished her findings on the field samples from Leatherwood Creek. Then, he would write his final report, advise the landowner, present a finished copy to Mira and allow her the grand privilege of informing the Governor on status and significance.

It gave Gray considerable pleasure to realize that Mira and the Governor would the final link for this particular communication chain.

And, he gave thanks that he would not be involved. Eldon said it best when he asked, "What has that bastard done for Perry County?"

In order to make his job more enjoyable, he planned to write his Final Reports from the comfort of his own apartment. That procedure would allow him the pleasure of privacy and more efficiency. This would also offer an opportunity to escape the eyes and ears that wanted so badly to know everything that the good doctor was doing. So, his first major purchase was a new computer, printer and monitor. He was old fashioned in that he demanded a tower system in lieu of a laptop. Then, he added the necessary software, Wordperfect X5 and Microsoft Word.

He loved to write and create good reports so, his major objective was quickly becoming that of arriving at work early but, leaving work as quick as possible. As long as Lola did not betray his home office plan, he was free to write his reports exactly as he wanted them to be.

The only problem with this plan was there would be nights when Lola would not be allowed to stay all evening. This was not really attractive to either one of them but, Lola did admit that she could get used to the idea of more sleep and less sex. Paul supported their part-time celibacy agreement on the basis that absence does seem to make the heart grow fonder.

On the thirteenth day of his stated fortnight, he told everyone that he was going to visit his family at Hazard for the weekend. But, actually he was going to visit with Mr. Campbell to give him a personal copy of Gray's Final Report on the subject of 'School Girls', on time and as promised.

Perhaps, Paul might have violated one her Majesty's rules but, he had little choice in the matter. He needed to intervene to keep that damned Governor from cheating a nice man like Eldon Campbell. When he arrived at the headwaters of Leatherwood Creek, he was warmly greeted by the entire Campbell clan. He presented his findings to that Leatherwood audience and he accented these major conclusions:

- "You have a great fortune of Fluorspar on your property. The current price of Fluorspar is $400.00 per ton so, for you people, coal is no longer the king. Just remember this, every Country that makes steel has to have a lot of Fluorspar for a favorable slag reaction in their steel-making process.
- In my opinion, I believe that Pauline's apparition was to help the family and, nothing more. She appears exactly where the primary vein exists for this great discovery. And, her images reveal her pointing right at the main deposit. Without her help, we would never have discovered the wealthy deposit that lies underground.
- If you allow the Governor to build a State Park on your property, one of two things will happen. Your sister's apparition may disappear from abuse and the lack of proper maintenance. Secondly, the State will take all the profits that are rightfully yours, not theirs. It will be another prime example of how the Cumberland was raped of their salt, wood and coal. You can't let that happen again, enough is enough already."

I strongly recommend that you create a Fluorspar mining operation. Get a lawyer involved and trust no one. A lot of people will try to cheat you but, persevere and each of you will become a very wealthy person. I ask for one thing only, absolute anonymity. My boss doesn't know that I am here and she would not approve of me giving you this insider information. That is because she is working for the Governor and not for you. I'm a born and raised hillbilly so, I want for you to have the best that life can offer. The audience clapped their hands rapidly while Mr. Eldon Campbell promised that I would always remain invisible to the Governor or any of his Staff.

Young Mabel asked the best question when she inquired, "What makes the vision work?" I was pleased to give her the best answer that I could muster. I said, "As your grandfather stated, the necessary ingredients are clearing skies, light winds, wet grounds, low visibility and, most of all, frontal fog accompanied by strong moonlight.

This type of fog occurs when warm raindrops evaporate into a cooler, drier layer of air that is nearest the ground. Once enough rain has evaporated into the layer of that cooler surface, the humidity of the air reaches 100% and a dense fog follows. The Calcium Di-fluoride of the fluorspar minerals reacts with the water to form bubbles that rise to create the apparition, your Great Aunt Pauline.

The contrast of Pauline's image is dependent upon the fog density. Some nights, the fluoride bubbles will cause Pauline to be more active than on other nights. In that respect, it is like reading faces in the globular clouds on any summer afternoon." For a successful result in the clouds or in the Creek, a vivid imagination is your greatest asset.

Mable thanked me and said, "Gee, I wish that I was as smart as you. I replied, "Mabel you are young and there is still plenty of time. Take some of this Fluorspar money and enroll at the University of Kentucky. In the short period of just a few years, you will be a scholar for each of us to admire and respect.

Then, I left for my weekend visit with my own family. But, that was the happiest trip that I have ever made to the Upper Leatherwood region. Mabel would now be able to get educated and, that made me feel ever so productive and, inwardly, blissfully happy. Helping her and her Grandfather certainly warmed my heart ever so much.

Chapter Three

STUDENT GHOST

TODAY WAS THE day that Dr. Paul Gray was ordered to select a second case file entity for his dedicated study and subsequent analyses. He had just finished his assignment on the 'SCHOOL GIRLS' apparition and that management pair of control-freak Mirren plus the money-hungry Governor were not very satisfied. They were convinced that Paul Gray had taken some sort of bribe or kickback from the Campbell family but, they were unable to prove anything.

Mira and the Governor were very suspicious of him because the Fluorspar mining operations actually began before Mira had finished studying Paul's Field Report. They looked furiously for a connection but, they were unable to find any evidence that might link Paul Gray to the Campbell Family.

It was logical that the Campbell's would choose great wealth over the sale of a little plot of land for a new State Park. But, how did they know about the massive Fluorspar deposits? Did they have help from the inside of PESO? Was Paul or Lola involved? There were many questions that went unanswered. If bribes or kickbacks did exist, what happened to the money trail? They had seized the bank records for both Lola and Paul but, nothing unusual had been discovered.

Paul Gray or Lola Bryce, may have crossed a line or two so, both Mira and the Governor would now have both of the two under close surveillance until further notice. Perhaps, the appearance of cranes and augers at the Campbell Farm, at or near the same time that Mira was still reading Paul's Report, may have been a coincidence But, 'She who must be obeyed', could find no proof of any wrongdoing by two of her best employees. But, Paul knew that someone would always be looking at his ass so, it might soon be time for him to seek a change of venue.

In other words, it was time for Gray to get out of 'Dodge City' and to take on another case, decidedly one that contained less heat content. In Lexington, too many eyes were watching every move that he made and, moreover, everything that he purchased. He was under the magnifying glass so, he would be unable to live outside of his means.

He had to be a model citizen until the Governor's bullies we called off. They seemed to follow every move that he made. His private thoughts involved this question, What ever happened to the good old days when everybody trusted everyone else?

Yes, his friends at the People's Bank and Trust Company told him that the Governor's lawyers had seized his deposit records but, they found nothing unusual. And, Paul didn't seem to mind. He concluded, "Let them look because I am clean and I don't give a damn. As far as I am concerned, that stuff is purely 'sticks and stones' activity.

Mabel Campbell is now enrolled at the University of Kentucky Community College in Hazard and, that's the driving factor for everything that happened at Leatherwood Creek. I bear no regrets for anything that I did for the Campbell's. Young Mabel was my underlying reason for most of my actions because lovely young maidens deserve both education and love and, in that specific sequence.

He needed a more typical problem. One that did not involve a great wealth or the possibility of anyone amassing a huge fortune. He decided on an unsolved 20-year old cold case about a small Jane Doe that was sexually molested and murdered without the unidentified killer ever being prosecuted. This was the stuff that he had built his career on while working for the Metropolitan Police Department at his previous position. It was his livelihood prior to working for the gay queen or her buddy, the Lord Governor. While at the MPD, he was restricted to solving only murders. This PESO case was different in that both murder and spiritual hauntings were each involved. And, he was determined to enjoy working on something old and something new, old meaning murder and new meaning paranormal.

It has been too long since I solved a murder plot. I am going to enjoy this case no matter what Miss Mira might say or do. She might want to choose my assignments for me but, at the end of the day, I am the master of my own destiny.

Once again, he left Lexington with his siren blasting away at a maximum noise level and he was running silent without any radio or means of communicating with the Queen Bee and/or any of her associates. He was heading South and East toward Hyden of Leslie County where this particular apparition always appeared. His rudimentary plan of attack included the following tasks:

- He needed to interview Mrs. Stella Warfield, the last teacher to actually observe the student ghost.
- He needed to visit the graveyard where the Jane Doe's remains were interred.
- He needed to take DNA samples of Jane's bodily remains for the student ghost and compare those results to a person of interest. He had a hunch who the killer was but he needed more evidence.
- He also had to characterize the haunting site so that he could cover both goals of this investigation, the murder and the apparition.

In this manner, he hoped to find sufficient cause to close this case and put an end to the ongoing controversy about what happened to this little girl. He was pleased to discover that Mrs. Warfield was still alive and more than willing to discuss her own experiences about her young Jane Doe. He called her on the cell phone and they made an appointment to meet for a joint discussion of what Jane said and what she did.

In an interview with Dr. Gray, Stella Warfield stated for the official record that the ghostly image appeared during one evening while she was staying late to grade test papers. Suddenly, she felt a cold chill and she sensed an atypical awareness that someone else was in the classroom with her.

As she surveyed the room, she saw a small child at the back of the room who had her hand raised high. As she stared at the pretty little girl with such beautiful hair, she heard the poor child say, "Please Ma'am, show me my lesson in my Primer. I'm getting to be too far behind the other students. And, teacher, I can't find my little teddy bear. Have you seen my teddy?"

Mrs. Warfield walked toward the back of the room to confirm that an earlier edition of McGuffy's Primer was held in the child's small hands. But, before she could get any closer, that vision just abruptly vanished.

Next morning, Stella talked with her Principal about the sighting. He told her that this apparition was not new. He said, "The ghost of that little girl has haunted this school for more than twenty years. And, uniquely, the girl's speech pattern never varies. She always asks for help with her lessons and she always wants to find her teddy bear before vanishing away in the atmosphere."

The odd thing that the Principal mentioned was that the little girl always appeared before a new teacher and never in front of a seasoned veteran. This made Gray believe that the girl's spirit was seeking help from the new and uninformed instructors but, when no help was given, the young girl apparently gave up and disappeared, leaving behind a small lock of her hair which was apparently a gift for her new teacher. Quickly, Gray asked, "Did you keep that lock of her hair?" When she said, "Yes, I mounted it behind a glass lens of a gold broach which I seldom wear anymore. Would you like to borrow it, Dr. Gray?" He quickly requisitioned the broach and gave her a signed document for the associated transfer of DNA evidence.

After that, they had a cup of coffee together and they talked small talk for a few more moments. Then, he thanked her for her enlightening assistance and he left her house to travel toward Cigar Tree, Kentucky for a meeting with the Warden of Kentucky's best prison system. It would be a long drive with a stop at some cheap motel before he could visit with the Warden but, it was worth it since he needed her assistance very badly.

He had asked the Warden for an appointment to take place on the following morning and he was grateful that she agreed to have an unscheduled meeting with him as a 'walk-in' visitor. Gray had sent her more inmates than anyone else in the Lexington area so she was always willing to help him whenever she could.

He was excited because of his gut-feeling that he knew who the killer was but, he needed the kind of proof that only the Warden could provide. His gut was telling him that he was closing in on his prime suspect and it reminded him of the good old days at MPD.

His suspect was a despicable human being by the name of Frank Minton who was a known serial killer and child molester. Paul had been a member of the team that convicted him so, he knew the bastard quite well. Unfortunately, Minton had recently been killed by inmates at the prison where most of the prisoners hated any and all killers of young children.

But, where DNA is concerned, dead men can still offer undeniable and strong legal evidence. Gray badly needed to obtain a DNA sample from Minton's body remains or from Minton's autopsy records. He was interested in a sample of Minton's hair but, he was willing to accept whatever the Warden could provide.

Next morning, he checked out of that fleabag motel and he ate his 'free' breakfast entirely too fast. Stuffed with several cups of Java, he hurried to the visitor's entrance at the main gates of the State Prison at Coffee Tree, Kentucky. The Prison still looked very much like a new building so, his thoughts wandered to his past where he was a regular visitor to these familiar surroundings.

He signed in as a short term visitor who needed about one hour of the Warden's time. He thought that 60-minutes would be enough time but, he knew that his visitor's pass could always be changed if the Warden was in full agreement. After his sign-in, he was escorted to her Office by a former football player that weighed at least 300-lbs.

I asked him what his hobby was and he gave me a two word response, "I like to break bones."

The Warden greeted Gray at her open Office door saying, "Hi, long time, no see, Dr. Gray. I had begun to think that, perhaps, you had met with some sort of foul play or been killed by some angry husband. I am glad to see that you appear to be in the best of health. Do you still work out at the YMCA gymnasium?"

Before he could answer that question, she had another one. She asked, "Are you still having fun with your red haired girl friends? It had been quite a while since I had seen her last and she was always a woman of many words so, I was wise to let her continue. She could get pretty pissed if someone dared to interrupt her.

She looked at me with those sultry eyes and said, "What do I have to do to convince you that black girls give better sex? If you want proof of my statement, just make a date with me and I will prove that particular point beyond your wildest dreams, I promise."

I looked at her with a longing desire and I said, "I have a 60-minute pass if you care to demonstrate your prowess in that back bedroom of yours." She kept that little room a secret from most people but, I had been there previously.

She wisely said "Let's get our business started and, we will play later. How can I help you Dr. Gray?" Then, he began to apprise her of his official needs and priorities. He said, "I need a DNA comparison between my Jane Doe victim and one of your dead scum-bags. I have a gut feeling that they might be connected.

She asked, "What's the inmate's name?" I told her that his name was Frank Minton and that he was originally from Leslie County. Then, she shivered with obvious fear. She said, "You can sure pick out the meanest of my prisoners. That SOB caught an ice shard in the heart on a hot, sunny day in the exercise yard. and, all the witnesses clapped their hands in full approval. My guards were also elated to observe his demise.

With a wicked little smile, she asked, "At your Laboratory or mine?" Gray answered, "I have the Jane Doe sample in my Lab at PESO so, I would prefer to study your Minton sample at Lexington if that is all right with you. "But, before Gray could finish his sentence, She started laughing in an uncontrollable manner.

I asked her, "Why are you laughing at me so hard for?" She con continued laughing for a little bit more but, soon, she became calm enough to ask me this question, "Why is a hunk like you working for a dyke like her?"

I told her that somebody has to work for Mirren and I was the unlucky bastard who drew the assignment. In order to boost my morale and display my self-confidence, I said, "I bet you a 100-dollar bill that I can turn that broad." The Warden said, "That's a bet that I will take. I know Mira Mirren better than you do and she is too infatuated with that Joan Lake person.

Mira will never cross over to the side that enjoys sex with a man.

That is a sucker bet. Man, are you one dumb ass." Gray said, We will see if you are right but, I need some time to work on her switching over. Give me one year to get her in my bed and then, we'll see which one of us is the loser of our wager. The Warden said, "Fine with me but, in twelve months, you will be 100 smackers poorer."

Next, she picked up the telephone and made a call to the resident physician who had performed the autopsy on Frank Minton, inmate number 91111. She asked that a hair sample be hand delivered to the Warden's office as soon as possible. Then, she hung up, looked at her watch to say, "We have 32-minutes left for our morning exercise. Are you ready, white boy?" Paul said, "Damn right, I am. Lead the way, boss lady."

We worked fast because we were fighting the clock. She gave me some head and I licked her clitoris before my penis entered her vagina and anus. It was a furious exchange of bodily fluids between two hungry participants. Our intercourse became the ultimate personification of both horizontal integration and lust. Her beautiful bronze colored skin was like a strong magnet, drawing him closer and closer to her perfect breasts. The Warden was an adorable woman who was designed for giving outstanding sex. Truly, one of God's best creations.

She looked at her watch and said, "That's the best 32-minutes of sex that I have ever had. I have a feeling that, if you can ever get Mira in your bed, I'm going to be 100-dollars poorer. Paul, another thing, when I come to Lexington next month, can I stay all night at your place? I want some more of this, white boy." I replied, "Yes Ma'am and anytime. I would love to have you over for an all-nighter and that's for certain."

Next, I collected my Minton hair sample from the Warden who said, "You are one lucky guy. We keep these samples for help with any unsolved cases like yours. But, we were about to deep six these samples because none of my employees cared one iota for that miserable soul. His official known kills totaled sixty-three victims and, most of them were young girls of the pre-puberty stage. Frank Minton would have gotten the death sentence but, the Governor intervened. Our State leader was hoping that Frank might admit to more killings so that additional bodies might be found. But, that did not happen. Inmate number 91111 knew that his life expectancy depended on him keeping his mouth shut. That was his so called insurance policy."

I gave her a goodbye kiss and I told her what a great sex partner she was. And, it wasn't just bull shit. The Warden was truly one outstanding black woman who did give great sex. A lot of white girls could learn from her if they would ever adjust their attitude problem. Can you imagine any white girl taking any sexual advice from a black woman? Typically, the ego of a white woman is too large for them to submit to such a situation.

Once again, I drove from Coffee Tree to Lexington at breakneck speeds to visit with my laboratory assistant, Lola Bryce. I wanted a DNA comparison of two hair samples in record time. Further, I told her that there would be no sex until the DNA testing was completed. Accordingly, she moved faster than ever before.

However, her price was high. She agreed to do the two resemblance tests and percent difference comparisons ASAP but, in return,

She would expect an entire weekend of sex, wine and caviar with little old me. I felt more than lucky because I was aesthetically pleased about her beautiful body and her excellent choice in men.

Lola found that the two hair samples were familial positive. They were brother and sister samples so I was able to cross-check the birth certificates to determine her real name. Officially, her given birth name was none other than 'Angel Anne Minton'. Frank Minton had killed his young sister and Paul had developed unequivocal legal proof for that hideous crime.

It was very flattering to realize that he had not yet lost his intuitive logic. Paul was very pleased that he had solved this old cold case but, moreover, he would greatly enjoy sharing his data with his former Captain at the Lexington Police Department. And, he would make certain that his previous boss knew exactly what he no longer had. The 'Great Gray' now belonged to another outfit called PESO.

Mad Mira was at her worst when she read his Final Report about little Angel Anne. The first words out of her big mouth was, "Who told you to take that case over some of the others?" I replied, "It was one of the twenty case files that you placed upon my desk for me to read so that I could learn more about the ghost business and I enjoyed the challenge."

"You know that the Governor wants to build new State Parks for a profit by taking advantage of these phenomenal spirits. And, there is no way that this Angel Anne person can fit into any of our profit making schemes."

I interrupted her angry tirade with a suggestion. "How about building a Taj Mahal type shrine on Interstate 75 where, for a price, tourists could see and hear the whole story about poor little Angel Anne. I would have two shrines at the two places where North and South tourist traffic stops to pee on Kentucky's best urinals. I would call it a mini-museum. And, eventually, the Taj Mahal attraction would more than pay for itself."

Mira looked at him and, shook her head in total disbelief. Privately, she wondered how any man could be so creative. But, all she could say was, "Dr. Gray, you are dismissed. Now, I must keep the Governor informed about your suggestion of mini-museums on I-75 and other roads. Please close the door as you leave my office."

Again, I left her office door open while she dialed the Governor on his very private cell phone number that he carried everywhere he went. Those two deserve each other. A woman who will not love men and a Governor who cheats everyone that he can. Later on, I will press Miss Mirren to call off the wolves that were tailing each of my separate moves. I felt that two-months of having to look over my shoulder at the State Highway Patrol agents is sufficient. After all, one of their unsolved cold cases had been finished at record speed.

Queenie, give me a break, please. I need my freedom and this is America. So, go watch somebody else, like your lovely protégée, Miss Joan Lake. But, like leaves of three, leave me be.

Chapter Four

LANTERNS

D R. PAUL GRAY and his associate Herb Moore were having a coffee break together at the nearby Starbucks Café when Herb asked him a personal question, how do you like working for our dyke Commander-in-Chief?" Paul considered that Herb could be a snitch for Ms. Mirren so he answered that question carefully. He said, "Believe it or not, Herb, I have worked for worse managers elsewhere."

Then, Herb confessed, "That, at one time, he had planned to take early retirement just to get away from that woman and her control freak style of management. He added, "Before you arrived, she used to make us sign out whenever we needed to use the toilet. Now, it's somewhat improved because she spends most of her time trying to keep up with you and your whereabouts.

Dr. Gray, myself and the other Staff members are so grateful that you have elected to join PESO. It's great fun to watch the antics that you two are providing for our daily entertainment. Welcome, aboard mate." This time he did shake my hand with a strong grip as if he really was glad to know me. Paul replied, "I truly believe that best way to cope with a typical female supervisor is to keep her guessing."

Herb said, "I really can't argue that point because I have four ex-wives. I couldn't get along with any of them because they each wanted to be the boss. It was maddening." Then Paul shocked him with this inquiry, "Is that why you and Shirley are playing house together?"

Herb was almost speechless but, he managed to ask "How did you know? Is it that obvious?" Paul replied, "The eye doesn't know how to tell a lie, Herb. The body language of both you and Shirley tells me that there is some chemistry between you two. How does it work for a man of your age?"

He hesitated and said, "Please don't mention this to our dyke supervisor or I might lose my retirement privileges." Paul promised his silence while Herb continued, "When poor Shirley was young, she was molested by her father and she developed into a lady that loves only older men. I play the role of being her dad and she pretends to be my daughter.

It's great sex and there are no bosses involved. Our union is based entirely on mutual consent. You need to consider that when you become my age." Paul said, "Perhaps that will be helpful in the future but, not just yet." They finished their coffee break and both of them returned to the pussy pit.

She who must be obeyed was at my desk and going through my personal stuff when we arrived at the squad room. She said, "What have my two little boys been up to this morning? Both of you are late for work again. I will have to write you up for your delinquencies."

I moved my head to a position where my nose almost touched her nose and I said, Here is my ink pin. You will need this if you are planning to write any fiction about Herb and I." The entire Staff of PESO snickered and, they wondered if I was going to kiss a lesbian in public view.

Then, I withdrew to report that Herb and I were using our coffee break to compare notes and discuss lanterns. She said, "Why lanterns?" I responded by saying, "Because that is my next case, Chief dearie." She stiffened to say, "Dr. Gray, I will tell you what your next case file shall be. Around here, employees don't select their assignments, I delegate them."

I said, "Go ahead and delegate if you like. But, don't expect me to do everything that you ask me to do unless it's a threesome between myself, you and Miss Joan. Then, both of the red heads blushed together which was, by itself, a beautiful image to enjoy.

Angrily, she stormed back into the safety of her office without giving me back my favorite pen. Now, she was stealing my stuff so I pondered the possibility of writing her up for theft. But, I didn't have the balls to do that, not yet anyway.

Mira didn't know it yet but, that sweet little scene was Act One for winning my Coffee Tree wager. I would proceed with caution but, I wasn't worried because I still had almost a full year to turn the lesbian manager of PESO.

Lanterns have always been a favorite interest of mine ever since I was a youngster. Our front porch on Combs Street faced the Yard Office of the L&N Railroad where my father worked for forty-eight long years. I used to sit in our porch swing and watch the train traffic moving back and forth during the late evening hours.

It was interesting how those train men would swing their lamps to generate all sorts of signals to the locomotive engineer at the head of the line. The lanterns also served as a swell mood enhancement device. Who needed sleeping pills when a flickering light from about one-quarter mile away would produce the same result?

Many times, I remember my Mother coming outside to the porch swing to carry me to bed because I had been watching too many lantern signals from afar. Those flickering signals were the fireflies of my imagination and, they also served as my own personal catalyst for better sleep.

One of my favorite locomotive engineers was a man by the name of Buster Townes. He was the older brother of Paul Townes, a former Mayor of Hazard Kentucky. Buster grew up in the neighborhood on Eversole Street which feeds into Combs Street and we became the best of best of friends. When Buster walked to work or returned from work, he would always stop and talk to me about the adventures of riding the rails between Ravenna and Leatherwood.

I fell in love with railroading because of his stories. And, like my Father, Buster could tell short-short stories in less than three-minutes total time. They were brief stories but, they were expandable and quite enjoyable.

We would walk and he would talk. But, moreover, I would listen very closely. If I had anything to say about railroading, he would always listen, even though I was just a kid. Mind you, he never treated me like a dumb kid. In fact, he was quite proud of the fact that

I was stringing occasional columns for the Hazard Daily Herald at the tender age of six. We were more like two brothers. I valued his friendship and I still do after all these years since his death which was caused by that horrible derailment.

Buster Townes died of suspicious circumstances and his story needs to be documented by one of the PESO detectives, namely, me. Don't tell Mirren because she would argue the point. But, in my heart, I want to avenge his death in any manner that I can. And, like the poet said, "Let us sit upon the ground and tell sad tales for those who are underground."

One day, when Buster was walking home. I stopped him to say that trouble was brewing. He asked, "What trouble, Paul?" I said, "Last night, when I was sitting on our porch swing, I saw the Riley gang put a small tree trunk on one of the outbound tracks."

He laughed and said, "Not to worry, my little friend. Our forward end cow catcher will remove any obstacle that the Riley gang might place in our path. With our speed and momentum, we can cut through almost anything, even large tree trunks.

I felt silly until the next run that Buster made. That was the night when the Riley gang derailed poor Buster's engine near where the Jack Lott Hollow intersects the L&N property. I watched the Riley gang do their dirty sabotage during the sunset hours of that ugly day. They used a steel rock chisel as a fulcrum to roll a very large tree trunk to the exact position that would cause derailment of Buster's engine.

That large tree trunk was placed on the blind side of a sharp curve such that Buster would not be able to stop in time. His destiny was to hit that big tree trunk at top speed. And, he was a fast driver who held the speed record for the run from Leatherwood to Ravenna. So, when I first saw the accident developing, the Riley's were still rolling the tree down toward Jack Lott Hollow and the L&N tracks.

Quickly, I left the vantage point of my front porch and started running to tell the yardmaster that a huge obstacle was being placed on the outbound tracks. I didn't make it in time. I got as far as the middle of the L&N Swinging Bridge before I heard that awful collision. The engine was derailed and Buster was trapped underneath his locomotive. Like all other locomotive engineers, Buster Townes had been taught to stay inside of the cab during a rollover event. But, Buster panicked.

Both he and his lantern tried to jump away from the derailed engine.

And, to this day, I can still see the image of his flickering lantern which landed very near to the exact point where he died. Buster was crushed by several tons of heavy steel as the rolling vehicle pinned him against the ground.

In the years since his death, other people have heard his dying screams and seen his glowing lantern. I am grateful that those people did testify about what they saw. Otherwise, I would have guessed that I was going bonkers by the supernatural aspects of this closed case. Because I strongly felt that Buster was sending me a paranormal message from afar, I decided to re-investigate his accident.

And, like Clark Gable in 'Gone With The Wind', I promised to give the boss lady this anticipated terseness: "Frankly, Mira, I don't give a damn as to what the Lord Governor might say. I am doing this case because Buster Townes was one of my L&N friends. He was like an adopted brother to me.

That awful night, I was the first person to arrive at the scene but, nobody would believe my story about the Riley's involvement. They assumed that I was just a little boy who had some grudge against the well-known Riley gang. And, in a way, they were right because I did have more than a few disagreements between myself and some of their gang members.

I liked to visit the coal tower and share a hot lunch with my dad.

It was great fun to climb that tall tower where one could see for miles in all directions. My magnificent obsession was to go where no other Hazard kid was allowed to go.

Those years were still of the Great Depression era where most everyone was always hungry and the Riley's were no exception to that rule. They would try to steal my two lunches from me while I was walking toward the Coal Tower location from the L&N Swinging Bridge exit area.

In order to protect myself from their thievery, I would carry a nail-loaded mast, a large hunting knife and Mom's 32-Caliber purse pistol. But, mostly, I would just outrun them. I had plenty of baseball muscles but those simpletons had fewer muscles than I did. They never caught me even though they tried on numerous occasions.

During my last investigation of Buster's death and his associated paranormal activity, I went to where he died during the daylight hours to look for additional clues that were so difficult to see at night. I studied the area as closely as possible without seeing anything of interest. Then, my exponential search pattern took me toward the outer fringes of his rollover limit boundary.

There, I found the broken glass fragments from Buster's lantern. That would certainly explain the flickering images that were reported in many of the observed sightings. I took a few specimens of those fragments for Lola to examine. I needed to know what kind of glass was used to fabricate his lantern lens. I was hoping that she would discover it to be Favrile glass, one of Tiffany's greatest creations and, one that was used in certain lamps of the 1930's, including railroad lanterns.

Low and behold, I next discovered a bundled array of small white limestone gravel rocks that were spread about to form the image of, 'TR' which I assumed was a reference marker that meant just one person, the infamous Tom Riley of gangster fame. Before he died, Buster Townes was trying to tell us that Tom Riley was involved in his derailment. Perhaps, he saw Tom and his gang in the moments just prior to the train wreck or soon afterwards.

After I crossed that railroad bridge for the final time, I used my radio to put out a 'BOLO' on Tom Riley's whereabouts. My quest was over before it really had a chance to get started. My bronze beauty at Coffee Tree reported that convict Tom Riley was serving a life sentence without any parole for the premeditated murders of several young men.

With this information, I was able to close the case file on Buster Townes of Hazard, Kentucky, a life-long friend and a good railroad buddy. Buster's apparition of flickering lights and eerie screams ended with my solution of his cold case. No other sightings have been reported since that time.

I did keep the glass fragments of that Favrile composition as a souvenir after Lola had confirmed that they were, indeed, lustrous glass compositions. It makes my day when I look at them and remember Buster Townes reciting short-shorts on our strolls up and down Eversole hill. He was one of the kindest men that I shall ever know.

Plus, he was the first man to teach me the art of being a fair storyteller. And, I will always love him for that. If we could talk with each other again today, we would not speak typical words about the weather or the latest news events, et cetera. Instead, we would share short-short stories together. And, that would be much more fun than the dull stuff about the Hazard Bulldogs or Cincinnati Red Legs. A life that is cut too short is a terrible loss to the community-at-large.

Chapter Five

TROUBLED

WHEN THE LEXINGTON Herald newspaper featured a special article on PESO and its mission, the reviews by its readers were not very friendly. Most readers wrote in to say that the PESO operation was a terrible waste of tax dollars. And, they demanded to know why it was to be tolerated by the Governor during these persisting recession years.

Dr. Paul Gray enjoyed seeing the Governor get roasted but, he had no idea what was in store for him because of that expose by the local newspaper. And, he didn't have to wait very long for Boss Mira to pitch in her two-cents worth of criticism.

She who must be obeyed flashed her come hither finger again and he, reluctantly, strolled toward her office. He wondered, "What have I done now? I haven't been in the field for several weeks so, I couldn't have done much of anything wrong. He reasoned that she might be inviting him to participate in a threesome with Joan so, he closed her door in dutiful fashion, honoring rule number one.

He sat down in what looked like her most comfortable chair as he waited for her to start chewing his ass. That maneuver was her specialty and she could do it better than any of his previous supervisors.

Her deriding wasn't long in coming when she asked, "Why did you release this harmful insider information about PESO to the local press?"

Immediately, he replied, "Ma'am, I am not guilty of such a stupid move. Why would I take such a chance? This is the best pussy pit that I have found in recent years. It's a bachelor's dream with you, Joan, Lola and Shirley being omnipresent.

If I had talked to Editor John Mills of the Herald, I would be long gone already because you would have already processed those previously-prepared termination papers, correct?" "You damned right, hunk, you would have been history, if you were the culprit and if I had known of your involvement."

But, she called me 'hunk' and that made me feel pretty good about myself. So, I made a mental note to keep that in mind for later usage, if needed. I had fleeting thoughts about the fact that my year is just beginning and, so far, I haven't lost or gained any strategic ground in winning or losing my Warden's wager.

She continued her denunciation of the Herald's editorial and all of the reader comments, except for one. She asked, "Did you or Herb read the comments section?" I said, "No, Herb and I briefly considered only the editorial itself at our coffee session this morning. Neither he nor I care very much about what the crazies have to say about anything. Tis' a fool that criticizes without having any facts."

She asked, Do you know Editor John Mills very well?" I answered, "I know him like a brother. He and I went to school together at UK. Why do you ask?" Bluntly, she said, "I want you to take him to lunch and pump some information from him." I followed with the question, "What information?"

"In the comments section that you and Herb failed to notice, there is this challenge by one of Peso's unnamed critics. It seems that several sightings in Breathitt County are bothering the residents and they want us to get rid of the offending spirits."

Quickly, I said, "Dr. Gray does not give professional services as a 'ghost buster'. We offer solutions for spirits that are seeking a release via the glowing light. We also try to analyze why some spirits resist all opportunities to fade away into the abysmal darkness. And, we even select which spirits would make good perpetual actors or actresses for the Governor's new State Parks. But, what we don't do is to assassinate troubled souls. None of those twenty case files that you gave me as my reading folder says anything about killing any spiritual beings."

She asked, "Not even for a threesome with Joan and I?" I was shocked by that particular question and the first thought that came to my mind was, "Hot, dog, I have won my Coffee Tree bet!" In humble fashion, I said, "Ma'am, Editor Mills and I will have lunch tomorrow and I will be motoring to Breathitt County on the following day."

Mira said these encouraging words, "Both Joan and I will look forward to your return and then, my handsome hunk, you can collect your reward. It will be a long night that neither one of us shall ever forget."

After that monumental promise to perform, he hurried to his desk to call his old friend, Editor John Mills but, out of respect for Mira, he had remembered to gently close her office door upon leaving. He had dutifully remembered rule number one; i.e., her door had been lovingly closed.

Editor Mills gave him the name and contact information over the phone because he was tied up for a week and couldn't help Gray before another week had gone by. Paul appreciated John's speedy response for the contact information so he decided to travel to Breathitt County today instead of tomorrow. Gray would waste no time on this assignment because he was more interested in a return to Fayette County rather than a departure from Fayette County. That threesome was a promised fantasy that would not leave his cranium, not once.

And, as you might expect, his siren was at its loudest setting and he did 120-mph on the straight stretches. He was a man who was in a big hurry to quickly do this dastardly deed so that he could return to his office as fast as humanly possible.

Wow! Two glamorous women in one bed at the same time. Hallelujah! My prize awaits me and I am more than ready. First, there is just one obstacle in my path; How does Paul Gray slay the dragons that people in Breathitt County no longer want?

To his way of thinking, the banishment of a spirit would require cause and effect logic. For example, if the cause of death is known, then, banishment or expulsion requires a fault tree analysis. That is where and how he decided to begin his plan of action for a new acquired skill called 'Ghost Busting'.

Since the Civil War, families in Eastern Kentucky have had numerous feuds that are based on one or more of the following:

Acquiring greater wealth or property, political disagreements, misguided loyalties, revenge activity and, outright hatreds where brothers fought brothers and families fought families.

It is not something to be proud of but, nonetheless, feuds have always existed and many men and women of the highland region have lost their lives because of improper reasons and a lack of reliable information. Unfortunately, too much moonshine has fueled plenty of these feudal issues. We refer to those as being homebrew-based hatreds.

Gray's 'impossible mission' involved two such feuding families, the Henry's and the Tate's. And, all of their ruckus began shortly after the Civil War had ended, according to records that originated from the Breathitt County Sheriff's office.

John Henry was a merchant who operated a small country store about ten miles from Jackson and up the South Fork, toward Quicksand Creek. The closest location for obtaining fresh supplies was the County seat of Breathitt County, Jackson. That trip for new supplies would require about one day's journey, depending on how many beers he drank while he was in the big city. On a muggy evening when fog was abundant, someone shot and killed John Henry with a 12-guage shotgun. That sound spooked his horses and they became run-aways, spreading his supplies for more than a mile over the countryside.

Naturally, everyone blamed the Tate family because of ongoing arguments about joint property boundaries. These two families have never been truly good neighbors. So, when one squabble was settled, another followed shortly thereafter.

The body of John Henry was taken home for his funeral services so, between all of the wailing and weeping, the men of the Henry Family planned their revenge. An eye for an eye and a tooth for a tooth was the operating rule for life in those Kentucky mountains. Fortunately, for the Tate's, the local Sheriff talked the Henry's into a few more weeks without any subsequent retaliations. He told the Henry's that he needed more time to investigate the matter more thoroughly.

Just when it seemed that a feudal war might become a reality, strange things began to happen near the site where John Henry was murdered. This all began when another neighbor, Tom Stevens, was riding his wagon down that old road. There, he saw the apparition of a man walking next to his horses and his wagon. Although it was quite dark and still damp from rainstorms that had passed this way, there was enough moonlight filtering through the clouds to allow an excellent resolution of the ghost sighting through the not-too-dense frontal fog.

As Tom watched, the walking man seemed to be unaware of the close proximity between Tom's horses and his wagon. At least the ghost paid them very little interest until, suddenly, he climbed aboard and sat down in the wagon seat beside a frightened Tom Stevens.

The apparition rode along with Tom for about thirty yards before pointing down toward the approximate area where John Henry was murdered. After that the signal ghost just vanished into the damp night air.

For reasons which should be apparent, Tom Stevens wasted no time in getting back to where he lived. Members of the Stevens family said that Tom's mind was never the same after that particular wagon ride. He vowed that he would never again outside on a foggy night.

After Tom's sighting, it became almost impossible for anyone to pass that specific spot without seeing the pale silhouette of a man standing near the site of John Henry's demise, especially, if it was on a damp and foggy night. As always, the signal ghost would be pointing down to a spot below the road just a few yards from where the 'bush whacking took place. The sightings became so numerous that Sheriff Horn was petitioned to re-examine the area.

Although John Henry had been dead for about six months, the Sheriff and his men did search the area thoroughly for a distance of about one mile in each direction from where the killing took place. One of the deputies found a pocket knife with the initials 'WT' carved into the bone handle. This discovery was located at about ten feet away from where John Henry was hit by shotgun pellets. And, relative to the plane of the roadbed, that knife was found 'downward and below' just as the signal ghost was always pointing or looking.

This discovery caused the two families to prepare for an all-out war because one son of the Tate family was named William Tate. Hence, the initials of 'WT' were apparently his undoing. Naturally, the Henry family assumed that the knife belonged to him and no one else.

But, once again, Sheriff Horn bargained for more time so that the knife could be investigated further. He reminded everyone that, on each Saturday morning at the Breathitt County Courthouse 'Knife Trading' was a very popular activity. On that basis, the subject knife could have belonged to almost anyone. That would be the second time that Horn had been able to postpone a killing spree. Inspector Gray paused to think that Sheriff Horn deserved a medal for his peace-keeping endeavors.

Unknown to the Henry clan, John, the father, had killed a man named Oscar Tabor in a bar room fight over in Harlan County about thirty years ago. Wilson Tabor, a son of Oscar Tabor, was a seven year old boy at the time of his father's demise. He vowed to avenge his father's death after he reached manhood and located the John Henry that he was searching for. He ended up buying a farm at a safe location several miles away on Troublesome Creek where he lived quietly while he was planning an opportunity to kill John Henry.

His true identity would have been difficult to unearth because no one had made any inquiries on Troublesome Creek and because nobody knew that Oscar Tabor had a son named Wilson. However, Sheriff Horn was a very intelligent man and a lucky guy.

Routinely, it was his practice to mail circulars to all the nearby County Courthouses with this kind of enquiry. "Got any Court Records that can be associated with these names: John Henry vs. Oscar Tabor or any combinations of both W's vs. T's? I need help on a murder case that I am trying to solve. And that's how he learned about the Henry-Tabor trial in Harlan County. They sent Sheriff Horn a complete file about the Henry-Tabor matter.

During the trial of John Henry for the killing of Oscar Tabor, the jury gave a verdict of not guilty because of self-defense. Subsequently, John Henry, being single at the time, moved to South Fork of Quicksand, where he married and started raising a family of his own.

After Wilson Tabor's incarceration and when he was confronted with the evidence of his lost knife, he broke down and confessed to the revenge shooting of John Henry. As for the punishment phase, several angry vigilantes broke into the jail and hung him on an oak tree not far from where Henry had been killed. Storekeeper John Henry was a man that was well liked so, lots of people in the town of Jackson took their own revenge.

At this point, Investigator Gray was struggling to place all this information in proper context because his unproven theory was that, before he could banish any spirits, he had to know what turned them into spirits in the first place.

For example, what was the original reason for trouble between the Henry's and the Tate's? That required some dedicated research since it happened many years previously. Interviews and official records told him that a Henry male had raped a twelve year-old Tate girl; and, for revenge, she had killed him with a shotgun shell. Ever since then, the Henry-Tate feud has been on again and off again through the ensuing years.

After the Oak Tree incident and the hanging of Wilson Tabor, each family has softened their views through intermarriage and mutual friendship. That is the status at this time, except for the sightings which every citizen wants to be eradicated by miracle worker Paul Gray. He was wearing the carpeting out on the floor of the Jackson Motel while trying to figure out how he was going to annihilate so many evil spirits. Pacing back and forth and, sometimes, throughout the entire night.

At least five people are here involved and there two teams of crazy horses to worry about. This is a complex scheme of troubled spirits and, most certainly, the greatest challenge of his young PESO career. He decided to make a list so that he might better understand everything that is bothering him.

And, there was the additional stress of Mira and Joan as a threesome. He wanted so badly to get back to Fayette County where he could realize his sexual feast and personal fantasy. In order to manage that return to Lexington, Paul needed to take care of business in Jackson first and foremost. But, for now, back to his list of salient observations.

- The ghost of John Henry took the form of moaning and groaning. Everyone who went up and down that road at night was sick and tired of hearing the noises that his troubled spirit made. Those people wanted that ghost removed.
- William Tate committed suicide because he was unable to convince anyone that the 'WT' knife was not one of his possessions. Even his girlfriend, Lisa, doubted him and that was too much for him to stand. But, after his death, he haunted

her by always moaning for her affections. Bill Tate's moaning and groaning was driving her crazy. Therefore, she wanted that troubled spirit to disappear and, forever so.

- Wilson Tabor was hung to death on that big Oak tree but, people could still see his image on foggy nights and, worse, they could hear his screams of torment. Sheriff Horn said that he had five-hundred signatures on a petition to get rid of Wilson's ghost. Even the vigilantes who strung him up were tired of seeing and hearing poor Wilson's pain and suffering. Obviously, they were victims of a rather large guilt trip.

- The death of Oscar Tabor was in another County so Paul Gray was not concerned with getting rid of that particular spirit. However, the owner of that saloon did ask Paul for advice on how to proceed. He said that Oscar's appearance was bad for business and that he would like to get rid of that ghost ASAP. They agreed to meet at a later date which was left as 'TBA', to be arranged.

- Tom Stevens became mentally deranged over his encounter with the signal ghost that was seen pointing at Tabor's knife. Now, he was foaming at the mouth and afraid of his own shadow so, his wife pleaded that Tom's 'old-self' be re-established, if possible. Their farm was deteriorating badly without Tom's help so her request was more than justified.

- And, the crazy horses who weren't worth a damn since their exposure to those unworldly spirits. But, how does one exorcize eight horses? He reasoned that curing eight lame horses might be his most difficult task of the lot.

Then, Tom devised a plan based on cause and effect logic. He reasoned that he might be able to remove each troubled spirit by getting rid of its original cause; i.e., For a given sighting, he planned to remove the one thing that precipitated the entire haunting event.

He conceived this approach by being mindful of details that other men might overlook. For example, when Lisa Atkinson grew tired of William Tate's amorous hauntings, she moved herself to Ohio without giving poor William any forwarding address. And, that single event forced William to stop pestering her. In that manner, the annoying ghost no longer had any one to annoy.

He received permission from Sheriff Horn to remove the firing pin from the weapon that Wilson Tabor used to kill John Henry. And, on the next foggy night, he went hunting for the image of two men fighting, Henry versus Tabor. And, after his arrival at the killing ground, there was no fighting to be seen. Thus, cause and effect was in play. The root cause being the firing pin and the end effect being two men fighting. He was elated to have sent two ghosts into the bright light. And, in the process, he destroyed an unwanted sighting.

Next, Paul Gray chased the haunting of the Wilson Tabor sightings where a strung corpse was regularly seen dangling from the oak tree and screaming frightening sounds that must have terrified every child in the neighborhood. In view of what he had learned from his previous ghost removals, he cut the large limb that Wilson was hung from. As a result, there was no ghost to be seen on any subsequent nights. He was elated because it was working. He would soon be with Joan and Mira so, he was excited about that, as well.

Then, he tackled the problem of the eight demented horses who were mortified by the John Henry killings and the wild Stevens ride. They were crazy horses that were practically impossible to manage. Paul had those eight animals sold at the State Fair in Louisville.

And, he used that profit to buy new horses for both outfits, the Henry Farm and the Stevens Ranch. Amazingly, Tom Stevens cured himself by handling his new horses who were healthy and compatible with Tom. In this case, Tom's love of horses was all he needed as a cure to his own health problems. His normal health returned after the crazy horses vanished.

Paul Gray didn't fully understand the principle that allowed him to banish undesired ghosts but, he adored the results. And, yes, he was more than elated because Mira and Joan were anxiously awaiting his return to Lexington. He paid his large Motel bill, jumped into his car and sped to Lexington where he hoped to collect his reward, a threesome with Mira and Joan.

Mira greeted him with mild enthusiasm and she even hugged him loosely in public but, it was not a hearty hug that might turn a person on. In fact, Paul felt that for some reason, Mira was being frigid toward him and impervious to any of his advances. She said, "Paul, the good news is that the Governor is delighted with your fine work in the Jackson area. He now refers to you as his resident ghost-buster.

But, the bad news is that Joan and I have both changed our minds.

Neither she nor I are interested in having a threesome with you."

He felt devastated but, he tried to hide his inner feelings. If that's what it takes to turn this dyke, then so be it. All that I need is some more time. Until then, I have to be patient because she is fighting some real tough issues at this time. It's not an easy task to stop being a Lesbian.

And, it doesn't really matter at this time. I've got Lola on a steady diet of healthy sex and my Warden friend is truly amazing. She will be at my apartment in record time if I ask her to be. All is right with Paul Gray's world, at least for the present.

Chapter Six

EERY MUSIC

A T THE NEARBY Starbucks Café, Herb and Paul were having their 100% Arabic coffee with a conversation about mountain music as played by an all–string band. Herb defined a string band as one which should include only the following instruments: a fiddle, guitar, banjo, mandolin and zither.

Herb asked, "What is your favorite old time mountain song?" Paul answered, "My favorite is a religious one and, it's called The Great Speckled Bird. I like it best if it is played using only a single guitar with a solitary vocalist. A singer named Roy Acuff made that song famous.

He asked Herb if he remembered that old song but, Herb said, "No, I do not." "Herb, here's the part that most people remember best so, see if it jogs your memory, OK?

"I'll be joyfully carried to meet Jesus,
On the wings of that Great Speckled Bird."

Do you recall any of those words? They are taken from the Bible and a lot of people place great significance to their meaning." Herb replied, "Nope, it doesn't ring any bells for me. But, you know that I am not too strong on the Bible or religion, in general.

Paul was disappointed that Herb did not remember his favorite melody but, he understood, especially since Herb was reared in dear old Tennessee. After all, Roy Acuff was a Renfro Valley singer who was popular during the 1930's and 1940's. Now, that's a long time ago to remember one song.

Then, Paul asked, "Herb, what is your old country favorite?" Herb did not hesitate one bit as he said, "Mine is older than yours and it's called 'Fire On The Mountain'. Here are two lines that I remember best.

"Fire on the mountain, Lightnin' in the air.
Gold in them hills and its waitin' for me there.

"Does that ring any bells, Paul?" I'm sorry Herb but, I have to say that, no, it does not. It is a catchy thought, however." Then, Herb changed the subject to ask, "Have you ever attended a barn dance?" I said, "Just once. I didn't know how to dance and I ended up stepping on the toes of my date. I never tried dancing again, not once. Herb laughed and said, "Paul, that is so unlike you. I would have expected you to be a ladies man when it comes to the dancing business."

Then, they went back to the pussy pit of PESO. 'She who must be obeyed' was waiting at the front entrance door for the two of them. She asked, "What have you two been up to? Do either one of you know what 'office hours' really means? Herb was speechless but Paul had a comment. He said, "It is a far, far better thing to have been promised a 'threesome' once than to have never been promised a threesome at all."

Mira's face turned a lot redder with her associated anger but, she did return to her office without saying anything else. He winked at Joan but, this time, she didn't blush. Actually, she winked back at me! And, Paul was elated. He reasoned that, perhaps, there was an opportunity for a threesome through Joan rather than through Mira. He thought about that old cockney verse of "Truth will out and time will tell, so, what the hell?" Paul liked the way that his day was beginning.

Later in the morning, she curled her finger once again to signify that she wanted to talk to him in her office. He was hoping for good news about a certain triangular tryst but, that was not to be. Instead, she merely wanted to hand him his next assignment. Not a single word was exchanged between the two of us. And, after she handed me that folder, her other hand waved me back toward my own desk.

I wondered, is this the level that we have sunk to? I didn't like it one bit. I need to be more aggressive or I will lose her. So, before I left her office, I whispered to her these words, "Your perfume is driving me crazy. It makes me want to possess you." Then, I left her office very quickly because I knew that she was going to throw something at me and she did, a very large book hit the wall and made a sound that woke everyone up, especially old Herb.

I placed the new assignment down on my desk while I considered a gift of candy or flowers. I don't like it very much when any woman rejects me and that goes double for gay women. I like for the lesbians to feel what they are missing.

Then, I picked up my new assignment to read what it was about. It was entitled, "Fire on the Mountain." Immediately, I laughed. And, when I showed it to Herb, he also laughed. Suddenly, the entire office was laughing with us. Their laughter was like a virus that spread with amazing velocity. Then, poor Mira came over to my desk and asked, "Why are you all laughing at me?"

Quickly, I answered, "No Ma'am, we are not. Herb and I were laughing at the coincidence of having coffee and singing the chorus of an old country song called 'Fire on the Mountain'. And, hours later, I am given an assignment with the same title. Then, the others laughed at us because they had never heard us laugh before. And, a good laugh is like a good yawn, it's contagious. Mira looked at me and said, "Somehow, I can't bring myself to believe you but, I guess that will have to do for now. Go home and get your gear and stay out of my office for a few days. When you are around here, you are too disruptive. Give me a break so that I can finish the writing of my monthly report to our mutual friend, the Governor."

I replied, "I am sorry, Mira but, I do have that effect on a beautiful woman such as yourself." And, as I left, she was smiling right at me and no one else. Two points for the home team or was I imagining things again?" "It is very difficult to read Miss Mirren. Perhaps, in her case, it will require both lovely flowers and lots of Fanny Mae candy on a regular basis. So, I placed an order for both candy and flowers before I left Lexington.

Gray's visit to Harlan began with two important phone calls. One to Sheriff Billy Smith announcing his late arrival. The other phone call was for a sleeping room at the Holiday Inn. Because of his late arrival, Paul needed an appointment for the following morning. They agreed on 0900-hours as a good time to meet over some steak and eggs at Mom's Eatery on Main Street.

When Smith inquired about the reason for their meeting, Gray told him that he was here to do something about that perpetual music that someone named Robert Holgrave was making. Smith laughed and said, "It's about time. That damned music has been played over and over for more than 160-years. It's high time that the State of Kentucky has decided to do something about our problem. What took you so long, Dr. Paul Gray?

He pulled into the Holiday Inn Express parking lot and he felt nearly exhausted from his drive. The route to Harlan from Lexington is tiring because there are insufficient straight stretches that will allow high speed driving, Paul's favorite way to travel. There are also too many hills which exist as obstacles. Before he fell fast asleep, he thanked God and Dewey Daniels for the Hazard Express Highway. His only wish was that more roads like that one could be built. But, good roads require a lot of money and, at this time, Kentucky was almost bankrupt.

Next morning, when we met for the first time, we had breakfast together at Mom's Eatery. It was my treat, of course, because I had an expense account while Sheriff Smith did not. Paul was most astonished to see that Smith bore a strong resemblance to some of his own family.

In fact, he and Smith could almost pass for brothers. It was unnerving to sit there and wonder if my Dad had ever traveled to Harlan for some clandestine love affair. I quickly dismissed such thoughts as being purely coincidental because my Father was totally married to his Sallie, my Mother.

After that surprising shock of being such strong look-a-likes, we both got down to some serious talk about the open case that was our business for the day. Nell, our attractive waitress was feeding the two of us coffee faster than anyone else in the restaurant.

When I asked Bill why she was giving us such nice treatment, he replied, "I think that she wants a threesome. We are two good looking dudes so why shouldn't she be impressed with us? Do you want me to book an appointment for tonight? Your room after 9-PM and her rate is $1000.00 for an all-night party. She will bring her virgin sister along for $500.00 more. Do we have a deal?"

Paul said, "No, because that's too much money for me to pay and, I don't do virgins." Smith countered with another offer. He said, "I'll do the virgin and we'll call it a foursome for $1250.00, ok?" I was unwavering with my final decision since my answer was still the same, negative. After that, Smith gave Nell some kind of signal and our empty coffee cups stayed empty.

That didn't matter too much because, when we moved our bodies, you could hear the sloshing of coffee in our stomachs. Which meant that it was high time to quit drinking so much Java anyway. Then, I asked for Sheriff Billy to fill me in on the highlights of the Holgrave matter.

Thereafter, he began to talk me about the musical haunting which he described as,'Eery Music'. He said that the haunting began after the first year of the California gold rush in about 1850. It started from an old log cabin off of Wallins Creek near Watertown Road where a married couple by the name of Holgrave lived and died.

For your first visit to that cabin, I'll give you an escort to the site if you wish. But, for all subsequent visits, you will have to be on your own. Or, I can give you maps of the area if you prefer them. He explained, "My only Deputy is on sick leave and my Dispatcher is a sixty-eight year old woman. I need to stay as close to my home base as possible. I'm sorry, Dr. Gray. It's just bad timing for you and I."

"Bill, I will go by myself. It seems to me that you have enough on your mind at this time. If I get lost, I will just activate my GPS locator. Don't worry about me because I will be just fine. It's you that I am more worried about. If you need an extra Police Car to assist you, just send me your SOS. I'll be glad to substitute for your missing Deputy, if need be. In other words, I'll be your backup if you need one."

Bill seemed visably impressed with my offer of assistance so, he gave me a final tip about that log cabin area. Smith said, "When you do arrive near your target zone look for that log cabin as a marker. It is the only log cabin that is still remaining in that region so, you can't really miss it. But, remember to lock your Police Car and pack some iron. There are some dangerous gangs who live in that area."

I thanked him for the insider tip as I departed for Watertown Road and points nearby. Smith left for his daily assignment of handing out traffic tickets and taking care of other miscreants such as drunks and disorderlies. I felt sorry for him because today, the City of Harlan would have only one policeman on duty and, from what I have heard about the 'Bloody Harlanite', they could use more than just one. Oh, well, if Jesse Stone can handle it in solo fashion, so can Sheriff Billy Smith.

My trip was uneventful except for the lovely scenery. And, I got there in record time. My 450-HP engine hardly labored at all. The cabin was easy to find since it was practically dilapidated from having no occupants for more than one-hundred years. The last known person to have lived in that cabin was a fiddler named Robert Holgrave.

According to his case file, Holgrave was an excellent fiddle player who was in great demand at all of the local square dances. The PESO data presented him as being an authority on old mountain tunes like 'Fire On The Mountain', among others.

He was an interesting man who had played at Renfro Valley, the Grand Old Opery House and movie theaters along with other regional stages of renown. But, his favorite stage was his front porch where he would play for his lovely wife Barbara.

After a lengthy Saturday night dance at a neighbor's house, the Holgraves were very tired so, they slept late on the following morning. When the Sun was about twelve o'clock high, he got up and was observed to be tuning his fiddle. Then, he played his favorite song, 'Fire On The Mountain' and sung the words that he loved so well. Before Barbara could finish preparing his breakfast, Bob fell from his rocking chair, and he was stone cold dead.

But, according to the Peso File, Barbara could still hear him playing that old tune, over and over again. His performance was repeated again and again. And, it became maddening to her. After her husband's funeral, Barbara moved to Middletown, Ohio to live with her daughter Betty until she died of old age and natural causes. Her latter years were quiet ones because the haunting melody remained in Harlan at the old log cabin which remained unoccupied because no one else could stand Holgraves's incessant noise either.

On misty evenings, some sightings included visionary evidence of an old man playing his fiddle and singing his favorite tune. On certain occasions, his music had a pulsating sound as if it were coming from far, far away and, being carried by the wind. At other times, that 'eery music' would seem to be all around the listener but, in no permanent place. In other words, those sounds would be here and there but, not for long.

A stanza or two from the North and, then, a brief silence before starting up again from a different direction. Gray concluded that the fiddler was probably searching for his wife. And, at other times, there would be no sound at all. This problem of inconsistency made it unfit as one of the Governor's new State Park projects. Were it a recurring event with more favorable probabilities regarding predictability, the Governor might be interested in acquiring the property. But, in this instance, he could not risk the selling of tickets for a ghost that refused to play.

Therefore, this particular madness was left for the Wallins Creek residents to deal with. And, because they had petitioned the State of Kentucky to get rid of that 'on again, off again' music, Gray had been asked by the Governor to apply some of his recently acquired 'ghost busting skills.

He canvassed each of the neighbors to make certain that no one would object if the old music was banished into oblivion. Paul was concerned that, perhaps, one stoned hippy might object to its removal on the basis of "It's groovy, man. I like it." Fortunately, he found no such person. All of the stoned hippies in the area wanted their own music, not Holgrave's.

Each of the non-hippies that lived in the area gave a similar response. They said something like the following: "After all of these years, you dare even ask? We are sick and tired of that old haunting being played over and over again. We would prefer to have some peace and quiet, for a change."

So, he returned to Harlan to ask Sheriff Smith to proceed with condemnation proceedings against that property. This action would not be difficult since no land taxes had been paid for many long years. He also asked for fire engines to be made available on the date that the cabin was be razed. He was concerned that the fire might be spread toward other properties along Watertank Road.

Further, he asked Billy Smith to call him whenever he was ready to torch the old log Cabin. At that time, he would return to Harlan to witness the event on behalf of PESO and the State of Kentucky. He also told Billy to set up a foursome for no more than $1000.00 dollars. He hoped that Nell and her sister would agree to that sum of money. After all, our Country is in the midst of a horrible recession. Billy could steal the virgin girl's cherry and I would take Nell, the fully grown and well developed woman.

The ashes of that old cabin were monitored for a period of six months. And, after 'Fire On The Mountain' was never heard again, Ms. Mirren declared the PESO case to be, officially closed. She told me that I had done a good job and I told her that my second visit was more enjoyable than the first. But, I never told her why. Man, that foursome was, in a word, awesome!

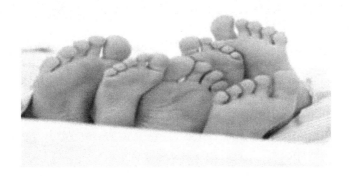

Chapter Seven

RETARD

SCIENTIST PAUL GRAY was enjoying an apparent lull in his work schedule but, it was also becoming a little boring. He liked it best when he was hard pressed to find a solution for a complex case or when he was having trouble in eliminating a spirit that did not want to enter the bright light. Paul didn't realize it then but, his boredom was about to end.

Privately, he was hoping that some nice females like Nell and her sister would call him on his telephone and invite him to come and take part in the night life of Harlan, Kentucky. During one of his inspection trips to monitor the ashes of Robert Holgrave's cabin, he had sampled both of the two sisters. And, he was especially impressed with young, Maybelle, who was no longer a virgin. He said, "Maybelle has one of the tightest vaginas that I have ever entered. But, I'm thankful that Billy Smith broke her hymen. Paul had no desire to have his own penis bleed for a solid week."

At that precise moment, the telephone did ring and he almost ran to where it was located. He answered the ring with an excited voice but, sadly, he soon realized that it was 'She who must be obeyed' on the other end of the line. Mira said, "You must come to the office. I need to talk to you about your next assignment." Paul argued that it was Sunday and he didn't want to work on the Sabbath. She countered with this reply, "If you want that threesome with Joan and I, you will be here in fifteen minutes or less.

And, if you don't report for work now, you will be dismissed from the ranks of the gainfully employed. And, that's a promise." "Mira, I haven't shaved yet and I need a shower." She said, "Never mind that, come as you are." With a grin, Paul said, "But, Mira, I sleep in the nude." She said, "In that case, I will make an exception. Be here in twenty minutes flat and not one minute more. And, the clock is ticking as we speak."

He drove fast and made the deadline with two minutes to spare. She said, "Thanks for showing up, Dr. Gray. I really thought that you might not appear. Not, with the way that you like to flaunt my authority. May I offer you some coffee?" He said, "No thanks. I don't drink any of that watered-down stuff. I will drink only 100% Arabic Coffee from Starbucks. Let's go there for brunch. It's within walking distance and I'll pay."

Surprisingly, she said, "That's fine with me." She grabbed her Sun bonnet and we walked together as lovers do. Along the way, Gray asked, "Why do you wear that silly little hat?" She replied, "Because I am a redhead and, with my fair complexion, I sun burn much too quickly." He said, "Oh" but, then he had visions of a naked Mira with her extremely white skin and no blemishes." At least, none that he could see.

After a large Danish pastry, several doughnuts and plenty of coffee down her throat, she started talking about Gray's next assignment.

She said, "This case comes to PESO directly from our Governor and the highest level in Washington, DC." Paul was surprised and he interrupted her to ask, You don't mean the President do you?" She was so happy about the honors that she was crying with joy. "Yes from the Commander-in-Chief, himself."

Obama asked for help from our Governor and, it was pitched to him on this basis: "Work this case or I'll withdraw all of your unrestricted funds for the entire fiscal year." She said, "Paul, we badly need that money because of this damned recession."

Paul replied, "What you are saying is that this assignment is important but, it's also vital to the entire Commonwealth, correct?" She answered with a sincere "Yes, it is." Paul grabbed her hand, kissed it and said, "I will do my best to help you, Mira." Then, they left

Starbucks and headed back toward their offices at PESO. And, they went there, hand in hand, as young lovers do. He had a file to read and she had some office work of her own that was long overdue.

After a few minutes, she did an uncharacteristic thing. She closed her window blinds, took off all of her clothes and wiggled her forefinger for him to enter. He stopped reading about the President's paranormal interests and he hastily entered her lair or should I say pubic hair?

She was already wet so, there was no reason for any initial foreplay. Their orgasms for that first exchange of body fluids were truly huge. For most of that memorable Sunday, those two would have several sexual encounters and romantic interludes of caressing, kissing, touching and feeling. At one point, Paul asked her why she was doing this and her response was simply stated, "Our liaison is long overdue and, I can't get you out of my mind."

Paul thanked her for that entire day of fantastic sex before heading out to Letcher County. First, there was that breakthrough with Mira's penchant for women only but, now there was something of national interest, to serve the President's needs and priorities. He told himself that this PESO job isn't so bad, after all.

And, he would smile all of the way there saying over and over the following:"That's progress. Mira does know how to please a man, after all. He was hoping that there would soon be a sequel but, something in the back of his mind said, don't count on it Dr. Gray because Miss Mira is wound pretty tight and she is under a lot of stress. He would have to be very patient with this one."

His objective was Blackey, KY but, it was impossible to find a decent place to stay in that town. Therefore, he decided to stay in Cornettsville, about five-miles due west of Blackey on Highway 7. He arrived, checked into an old motel and, immediately, began his interviews with the locals of Cornettsville.

He would ask of them the following question, "Do you know anything about a retarded kid and his dog that are haunting the town of Blackey?" He measured their responses according to these different age groups: 21-40, 41-60 and 61-80. The category of 21-40 did not produce any significant results since less than ten percent stated that they had witnessed the apparition.

The middle aged category of 41-60 wasn't much better because only about 15 percent of them had reported that, yes, they had seen the ghostly haunting. But, the wonderful news was that nearly 75-percent of the old timers did report that they had seen the vision and, on multiple occasions.

One old timer's testimony was, especially, pertinent. He said, "That poor boy and his dog always appear inside of their cave on foggy nights." So, these interviews did confirm the PESO records. This sighting had been active for fifty years, or more and, he was going to have to locate their cave. Soon, he would have to go hill-hopping in the Blackey neighborhood.

Paul was elated since seventy-five percent 'affirmative' from a single age group was enough to justify a new State Park near Blackey. He was also relieved because of the Presidential pressure that was here applied.

And, other pressures were in play. The Governor was pissed because there were too few parks and too much ghost-busting. Nobody wants to incur the wrath of two politicians but, poor Mira was caught in the middle once again. But, Gray now had some valid reasons to go the 'extra mile' for Mira. She had recently given him some of the best sex that he had ever received.

Next on his list of 'things to do' was to find a suitable guide. He wanted a stout man from the 61-80 classification who could climb the Town Mountain around Blackey with ease and without the risk of a heart attack or any other debilitating issues. On the basis of good health and stout muscular tones, he chose Henley Duff to lead the way to that cave and back again. And, for the sum of $500.00, Henley said that he would gladly serve as his guide.

They agreed to start their journey on the morning before frontal fog was predicted for the hills around Blackey. But, bad luck prevailed. The TV Weatherman said, "No fog to be seen until three more days have passed." He could make a quick return to Lexington but, that would not be cost-attractive. He decided to do more interviews until the fog returned.

But this time, he would approach the subject from a new aspect angle. He would do a quartile experiment where twenty-five people of the 61-80 group would be asked, "Tell me the story of that teen-ager and his dog." He would receive comments from both men and women of both cities, Cornettsville and Blackey.

He would record their voices and save them for transcription purposes back at PESO Headquarters in Lexington. For the present, he would ask them to talk for a fee of twenty-five bucks each. Surprisingly, all twenty-five people gave, essentially, the same version of that sad old story.

It seems that a man named Don Crowe was badly hurt in a coal mine accident and, thereafter, he was unable to work for a living. Crowe did own his inherited family farm but, that was about all that he possessed.

As a result of his accidental injuries and the associated, unrelenting pain, he became an embittered man where nothing seemed to please him. And, as time marched forward, his personality deteriorated even further. Neighbors stopped dropping by and none of his relatives would send him any mail, not even a Christmas Card. Eventually, the mailman stopped all mail deliveries because no one wanted to face the angry Mr. Crowe. And, he was always mad about everything, even the weather.

After about twenty years of such anguish, he traveled to a neighboring village and asked Miss Cassie Edwards to marry him. She said "Yes" and, for two reasons. One motivation was to get away from her father and her two brothers who raped her regularly.

The other reason was that Mr. Crowe was about twenty-five years older than Cassie was. And, it was her desire to have only a few years of sex to endure before Don Crowe could no longer perform. It was a grand scheme to escape from her family and to have a life of her own but, that plan of action didn't last very long.

Don was of the old school who believed in wife-beating. The theory for his generation was to whip their wives often in order to keep them honest and productive. In this case, productivity meant serfdom, from dawn to dusk. Don started beating Cassie after a few short weeks of apparent marital bliss.

When Cassie became pregnant, she honestly believed that the beatings might cease but, they did not. In fact they became worse. Especially, since Crowe targeted the lower abdominal region where his child was being formed. His prenatal son was subjected to many hard blows from his father's fists.

When the midwife came to help with the delivery, she informed all of her friends that there were multiple bruises on Cassie's body.

Her water broke early and that atypical delivery cost poor Cassie her life. She died right after Jed Crowe was born. The midwife tried to reshape his skull to make it more rounded but, to no avail. Jed Crowe would be forever burdened with an extended, oblong skull. It gave young Jed an abnormal and ghoulish appearance that was more than frightening.

The death of his young wife seemed to make Don Crowe become more of an introvert than ever before. He blamed young Jed for Cassie's demise and, if it wasn't for the neighborhood women, that ugly little baby would have soon perished. They brought excess amounts of Mother's milk or goat's milk and they took care of Jed until he was about three years old. After that, the neighborhood women stopped coming by the Crowe house and, for two good reasons. One, Don was overly rude to them and, secondly, it was apparent that this child was badly abnormal.

So, at the tender age of about five, Jed entered the unkind realm of serfdom. He would serve his demented father with pure hatred until he was about fourteen years of age. Then, one day, a German Shepherd puppy wandered onto the farm. Jed named him 'Rocky'.

For the first time in his miserable life, the retarded boy had found something that he could love and, in his own way, the dog returned an equivalent demonstration of genuine love and loyal devotion. That partnership of Jed and 'Rocky' was, most assuredly, designed in heaven.

And, Jed really needed something to cling to because he had only hatred for his father and the neighborhood children who taunted him constantly in an unkind manner. That bad treatment by those horrible school kids caused Jed to completely stop attending classes. After all, he was fifteen years old and, still, in the second grade. So, he left.

Crowe's addiction to moonshine whiskey became much stronger and, as a result, he beat Jed more often with a stiff leather strop that was used to sharpen his razor blade. As his brain began to deteriorate further because of too much drinking, he would whip both Jed and Rocky for the slightest provocation.

With time, the young man became more withdrawn from his father and, as a result, Jed spent as much time as he could with his dog. Acceptance and tolerance for his dad's errant ways eventually eroded to a severe hatred for his whippings with that damned leather strop.

He could not understand why his father would punish poor Rocky. From Jed's point of view, Rocky never did anything to deserve such harsh punishment. And, when two bad tempers clash, big trouble is just around the corner.

On one very cold night, during a winter of uncharacteristic freezing temperatures, Jed brought Rocky inside of the cabin to try and keep his dog alive. If he had been left outside, the dog would have frozen to death. But, his drunken father would have a decidedly different opinion. He said, "Get that mangy mongrel out of this house. I have told you, time and time again that your dog can't sleep in my house. It's for humans, not for animals."

And, in a drunken rage, Don Crowe started beating poor Rocky with his hardened leather strop. Rocky took the first few swings in a very courageous and submissive manner but, suddenly, Rocky's mood changed. And, as dogs of his kind do, he retaliated.

Rocky assumed his killer stance, growled in a killer mode and he leapt for Crowe's throat where he locked his jaw and held it tightly until Don Crowe was lifeless. Poor Jed didn't know how to react or what to feel. He was happy that his cruel father was gone. Those long years of parental abuse brought no tears or cheers.

Jed was also thankful that Rocky had saved him from another harsh beating. But, he was also very worried. He remembered from last year when the Sheriff hung a man from a tree for killing someone. And, he definitely did not want to see his dog be hung by his neck until he was dead. He shivered in fear at the very thought of that consequence.

He hugged Rocky for a few minutes before saying, "Rocky, we will bury Dad in the morning and, then, we will leave this horrible place. We will take what we can carry and we will go where no Sheriff can ever find us. And, that will become our new home. We will be free of all this hatred and meanness that surrounds us."

They did bury Don Crowe in a shallow grave which was situated as far from the house as they could manage. Then, Jed Crow took the shotgun and everything of value that he could carry or stuff into his back pack. And, he even strapped a few things onto Rocky's back.

Next, the two of them left that house of pain and suffering. Their goal was to be 'foot-loose and fancy-free' for as long as they could survive in that wilderness of about 800-feet above sea level. One eye witness was reported to say that he saw a man and a dog climbing up Town Mountain on one of the coldest days that he could remember. His reaction was, "What crazy person would go mountain climbing in this cold weather?"

Otherwise, it would be several months before any sightings of Jed or Rocky were observed or reported.

Even though intervening search parties were well organized and planned, all searches failed to find any evidence of Jed and his dog. Young Crowe was certainly a crafty lad in his own environment of the outback. And, he was dedicated to the avoidance of the hanging tree for his dearest pal, Rocky. His purpose in life was obviously that of being Rocky's best friend and strongest ally.

After about one year of losing food and vegetables to a raider which they thought was either a raccoon or a mountain lion, the neighborhood mobilized a hunting party to find the guilty culprit. Their forays up and down all of the nearby mountains were carried out at night and under the cover of darkness plus frontal fog. Also, they used hunting dogs so, the citizens were quite determined in finding their thief. It was only a matter of time before Jed's hiding place would be discovered. What they did discover would alarm each one of the hunters.

In one of the mid-elevation caves, the hunters found the two culprits who had been stealing for survival purposes. Both Jed and Rocky were sighted. He had his shotgun cradled over his chest while Rocky was in his killer stance and fiercely growling. Each of the hunters backed off when they took a good look at that viscous German Shepherd. Rocky would have given his life for his best friend, Jed.

All around the cave entrance, the intruders saw empty food cans and bones that were spread about as garbage and unwanted litter. It was obvious that Jed Crowe was dead but, his dog was still alive and moving about in a defensive demeanor. The hunters tried to encourage Rocky to leave his mountain abode by using bait. They would leave tidbits of meat down the mountainside but, when the meat was gone, Rocky was gone.

He would always return to his master and their cave.

And, to this very day, the apparition of both 'man and dog' still appears. But, only if the valley is covered with a dense fog. During an evening when there is no fog, nobody could ever see anything that was either abnormal or from the fourth dimension.

Paul Gray was somewhat surprised to observe that all 25 people from the quartile experiment told, essentially, the same identical story. So, when Henley Duff did appear for the trek up and down Town Mountain, Paul asked Duff what he thought about those experimental results. Henley said, "I'm not too surprised. The people from around these parts are honest folks who don't make it a practice to stretch the truth. I have seen the apparition myself and, I can swear to their honesty."

It would take the two men, Gray and Duff about one hour to scale the mountain and the dense underbrush before they could make camp near the cave's entrance. They unpacked the PESO gear and they staked out logical locations for Paul's night vision cameras. Next, they placed PESO's equipment around the cave's entrance area. Then, they patiently waited for the fog to rise. Henley wanted to talk but, Paul said, "No, we don't want to spook the spooks, do we?"

When the fog did settle in and, after the spirits had materialized, Paul was overwhelmed with their vivid contrast. He told Duff that their pictures would probably be the best that he had ever taken with his night vision cameras. Duff exclaimed, "I told you so, didn't I? Aren't they a great looking pair?" Jed was resting his shotgun on his right shoulder as if he was prepared for a defensive action, should it be required. Rocky was curled around his Master's feet but, his eyes were menacing. He appeared to be ready for a fight, if necessary.

We tossed Rocky some soup bones and he actually wagged his tail. We also left some food for Jed and he nodded his head with guarded caution. It was obvious that Jed was still unable to trust strangers. But, among all of this, I was quite impressed with the clarity of this scene.

I wondered if the salt crystals and schist rocks had anything to do with the excellent contrast that was apparent. I took some samples for Lola to evaluate because I wanted to know what caused their outstanding preservation.

However, Gray was most impressed with the serenity of this vision and the associated happiness between this young man and his dog. It was both clear and evident that a state of well-being and contentment had reigned supreme in this little cave of theirs. That entire scene reminded Paul of a Norman Rockwell print that featured a boy and his dog, Americana at its best.

To his way of thinking, this would be an ideal panorama for the Governor to capitalize on. This is to say that it would make a lovely new State Park. What is more heart-warming that the affection that is here so perspicuous? He took picture after picture until his supply of film was exhausted. He wanted to capture every aspect angle for his final report.

And, with each exposure, he hoped for a successful print that would be better than the previous attempt. That old salt cave with its sparkling schist reflections was an excellent background for great photography. He was elated about the trip and, its associated rewards.

When the early morning hours started to appear, he and Henley packed their gear and returned down the mountain to Blackey. He thanked Mr. Duff for his help and he tipped him a few extra bucks for being such a valuable guide and good companion. They had a good breakfast together and they said their goodbyes. Paul told him that he might make some more guide money by working with a man called Herb Moore who would be responsible for building the new State Park at Blackey.

Then, he located a gift shop where he could buy some Dolly Pardon souvenirs and related paraphernalia. Dolly was born and reared in Blackey and he was a most dedicated fan of hers, along with Marilyn Monroe. He wanted Dolly's body but, that he could never possess because she was such a well married lady. He also planned a side trip to 'Dollywood' if he was unable to buy what he needed at Blackey.

He wanted to buy a full-body cut-out of Miss Dolly, if he could find one. Paul needed one of these so that his seamstress could make him some new sheets for his bed. He preferred Egyptian cotton and silicone implants where they were needed. He also wanted to do a little research on her while he was in this area. He wanted to find out if one rumor about her was true. "Did she get pregnant without being able to see her belly?

Some people swore that her boobs were too large for her to see her feet.

If that be true, how could she ever see if her shoes matched her dress? Or, if one sock was red while the other was not?

With a full-body cut-out of Miss Dolly lying on the rear seat of his Police Car, he drove toward Lexington where 'She who must be obeyed' reigned supreme. Most of the way there, he had one unsolved question on his mind; viz., "Why did the President get involved in this haunting about Jed and his dog?"

- Was it because Jed was black?
- Was it because Crowe was his Uncle?
- Was it because he liked dark German Shepherd dogs?
- Was it because he wanted a Park in Blackey?
- Was it because he liked the name of Blackey?
- Or, was it because the Governor needed to be controlled?

Of these six possibilities, Gray's own preference was the last one. He strongly felt that the Governor was running out of control because he even fancied himself as the next Presidential nominee. And, taking away his unrestricted funds was one excellent way of bringing him back into the fold and, under Presidential control. That seemed to be the most logical answer to Gray's question. Politics never dies. It merely transforms into other manifestations, some good but, others bad.

Chapter Eight

WARLOCK

A LL OF THE employees at PESO were absolutely elated about having been responsible in justifying a new State Park for Blackey, KY. Thanks to their own hard work and, Dr. Gray's tireless tenacity. His 'ghostographs' of both Jed and Rocky were touted as being breakthrough images for the entire scientific field to marvel at and envy. In brief, the praiseworthy quality of their images was believed to be a unique function of damp salt air and moistened micro-particles of schist.

And, all of the expenses for this Park were paid for by the President who swore that all of the money came from personal funds.

No one knows why he spent all of that money but, rumors did suggest that he wanted to do something nice for his Uncle, Don Crowe. In any case, they were also delighted that the Governor did receive his unrestricted Federal Funds, on time and exactly to the penny that had been budgeted. This meant that all PESO salary checks would continue to arrive as scheduled and, that each PESO employee could keep their job.

None of them enjoyed working at PESO more than Paul Gray did.

On this particular evening, he had invited Herb and Shirley over for a foursome with himself and Lola. He gave thanks for 'triangles' and 'squares' since they had become such a stable item regarding his sex life.

On this evening, his personal goal was to convince Shirley Hooten that younger men are okay even though she has always preferred the older men.

Paul had run this event past Herb and he was supportive of our intentions. In that regard, Herb said, "I can't keep up with Shirley's demands on my body. Please cut me some slack at this party or I will have to take early retirement just to get away from that female. Shirley is the hottest woman that I have ever known." But, I did warn him, "Just wait until you tackle my Lola. She is like a jungle tigress when she is in my bed." Herb didn't return any comments. He only groaned.

After a very tiring night of new positions and two busty babes, Paul really had to struggle just to get out of bed and go to work. He knew that he was going to be late for work because he had only one shower for three bathers. But, it was worth it since everybody had a good time. Herb had a great time with Lola before he fell asleep, that is.

She reported that Herb was snoring during their act of intercourse. And, Lola laughed about that because she didn't think that such behavior was possible. And, I agreed by saying, "I don't understand how Herb does that. I know that I couldn't snore with a beautiful woman pounding her tits against my chest." Shirley said, "Oh, Herb does that all of the time when he is with me. And, I find it to be very annoying. I want him to be enraptured with me. But, instead, he just says that good sex is the best sleeping pill that was ever invented."

When Paul did finally arrive at work, he found Mira wiggling her finger as he entered the outer door. She wanted to talk to him before he even had a chance to sit down at his own desk. Gray had another thought, that, perhaps he should not have had so many cups of coffee at Starbucks.

Now, she is going to chew my ass for being so late.

But, that was not the reason for her 'come hither wiggle'. She was so angry that she could hardly speak. He muttered a concerned question, "What is wrong, Darling?" She said, "Joan and I drove by your apartment last night and all we saw were other people's cars. Namely, Herb's and Lola's.

Joan and I were planning to give you that threesome which you have been wanting so badly. But when we saw evidence that a foursome was in effect, we just drove on by." How could you do that to us, Paul. Both Joan and I wanted you so badly. Our bodies were aching for your touch so, we went home very disappointed. She was starting to cry but, she held her tears back because she didn't want Paul to witness any of her crying.

Paul told her that he was very sorry that he missed the 'big event' threesome but, could he please have a rain check? And next, he tried to inform her that last night was just meaningless fun for that foursome party. He said, "I would try to jump over the moon for you and Joan or, mostly, for you and only you. I will never forget that fabulous Sabbath of ours. And, I sincerely apologize for not being available when you needed me."

She patted her eyes with a soft Kleenex and she looked him straight in the eye to ask, "Do you really feel that our Sunday meeting was important for you?" He replied, "That was when I fell in love with you, Mira and I will never be able to thank you enough for that glorious day."

Then, she said, "Here is your next assignment and go home for some rest. To me, your eyes resemble a Kentucky road map. I don't want to see you again until after this new case is completely solved.

And, I don't want you to send me anymore candy or flowers. After you do return, we will have ourselves a little meeting. At that meeting, we will have to agree on some new rules dealing with the problems of 'no Shirley and no Lola.' Paul, I want it to be just us, only you and I."

Paul was torn by his different emotions. He was happy about going one-on-one with Mira and, he was sad about her almost crying. In some respects, he did not want to lose Lola but, some things are inevitable when you have to settle down to live with just one mate.

He vowed to take this position. "If I have to give up 'triangles' and 'squares', she has to split with Joan and that lesbian business. Oh, hell, that foursome of ours was caused by an extended celebration of that new State Park at Blackey. Surely, she will understand that and, I certainly hope so because Mira is one lovely red head that I don't want to lose.

That woman is a keeper."

He returned to his apartment so that he could read his next assignment file without being bothered by anyone. Paul's new case was entitled, 'A Housewife's Unusual Disappearance'. His first reaction was that he would have to change that title because of its excessive length. It is much too long for a PESO Final Report and, don't most housewives disappear on a regular basis anyway?

Paul Gray felt he was an authority on that subject because he had charmed several of them using his male magnetisim and irresistible appeal. And, those wives made it easy for him. What manner of a woman needs to go shopping for groceries seven days a week? He would go to Walmart's where they would meet and the rest would be romantic history.

This episode would require a visit to Viper, KY on Highway 1165. By going in that direction, he would be forced to drive past the 'House of Pratte' where Doris, his high school sweetheart lived as a young maiden. He wondered, "Is she still alive? Is she still available? Even the remote possibility of meeting Doris again thrilled him because she was, without a doubt, the hottest girl that he ever dated during his early manhood years.

But, back to this current investigation because that is what pays the bills.

Paul would give this task the name of 'Warlock' because that is what it is all about and, this new name would remove even the slightest hint of adultery.

A young couple named Edward Burns and Canzallia Pendleton moved into the area to marry and settle down. Edward had gotten a new job in the coal mines and they were trying to avoid an older man named Jonathan Pondle. For several months prior to her marriage to Ed Burns, 'Can' had been pestered by Mr. Pondle who wanted her for himself. He argued that 'Can' was the reincarnation of his former wife who had died more than forty years ago. Several attempts had been applied by the Pendleton family to discourage Mr. Pondle but, he ignored all such attempts declaring that Canzallia belonged to him, not Edward Burns.

Therefore, their move to the Viper area was an attempt to get away from Jonathan Pondle who seemed quite determined to steal her away from her lover, young Edward Burns. Finally, the family agreed that if,

'Can' would marry Edward and move to another town, perhaps the stalking by Jonathan would end. At least, they hoped so. Every member of the Burns-Pendleton families regarded Mr. Pondle as a 'dirty old man' who was unworthy of their young and beautiful Canzallia. Hence, the relocation and marriage proceeded as planned.

After their wedding ceremony was completed and when the dancing was over, the young couple headed toward their new home to consummate their marriage. Suddenly, Pondle appeared in the middle of the road trying to block their passage. Edward slammed on his brakes to avoid hitting the old man while 'Can' screamed as loud as she could. It was very frightening to see that old man near the middle of that dark night.

Then, Pondle strolled to the passenger side of the car to talk with his beloved 'Can'. He said, "I have found you and I know where you live. I will die in a few days but, I will come back for you. And, this time you will come with me because that is your legacy. You belong to me and, not to that country bumpkin." Before Edward could get out of the car to settle matters with his fists, Jonathan's image had already vanished into the dark night air.

A few days later, Pondle was found in his house in faraway Clark County and, as predicted, he was dead. The Coroner and the attending deputy waited three days to pronounce Pondle as being legally dead. They were confused because of the following:

- There was no breathing.
- There was no rigor mortuus.
- His body temperature remained at 98.6 ° F.

So, his death certificate was uniquely modified to read 'Apparently Dead'.

Pondle's last will and testament provided enough money to cover the expenses of being buried near where his lovely Canzallia lived. His final wish was to be buried in the local cemetery that was about one mile from the Burns residence. No one in Perry County knew Jonathan Pondle but, a few church officials did oversee his burial. 'Can' had no warm feelings for the man yet, she felt drawn to his grave site and his tombstone. She adopted the site and placed wild flowers on Pondle's grave each week following his interment.

Her philosophy was that Pondle was a man who had once stated that he loved her and, because he had no apparent kinfolks to decorate his grave, she decided to commemorate his passing. Wild flowers are not very expensive and she felt that it was the right to do.

And, for awhile, things seemed to settle down in old Viper town. No more Pondle appearances, just peace and quiet for approximately one year. On the night of her first wedding anniversary, Canzallia was reading a book in the comfort of her living room while her husband and a couple of his beer buddies were in the kitchen and opening a new keg of draft beer. There was a pounding at her front door and she said, "I'll see who it is Edward. You don't have to bother."

All three men heard 'Can' open the front door but, they heard nothing else thereafter. They waited for the guest to make his appearance in the kitchen but, nothing happened. Their living room was all too quiet. So, after a few seconds more, the three men pushed their way into the living room area to see what was going on. To their amazement, the front door was left wide open and the snow had stopped falling.

Husband Edward and his two beer buddies, grabbed their Mackinaw jackets and their gas lanterns to step outside and search for Mrs. Burns.

She could not be seen anywhere in any direction so, all they could do was to track her small footprints in the snow. Those marks led down the front yard and toward the County Road. The three men continued their search in workmanlike manner but, they made no discoveries, grim or otherwise.

After about thirtysome minutes of additional searching, they arrived at the front gate of the local Cemetery. Her small feet had passed by that open gate and they had proceeded toward the grave of Jonathan J. Pondle where, mysteriously, they ceased to exist. Canzallia's small foot prints had just vanished into thin air.

While his two best buddies stood guard over Pondle's grave, Edward went to get some helpers and additional witnesses who were not kin to the Burns Family. He also sent one person to awaken the local sheriff but, he had serious doubts that he could be aroused at this late hour of the evening.

It was just past mid-night and, terribly cold when the ten men began the serious task of opening Pondle's grave. Their lighting problems were solved by ten lanterns so, that they could monitor any weird occurrences that might come their way. Nothing unusual happened as they continued their digging. When they were able to observe the casket lid, they called for Edward Burns to pry the casket lid open for inspection. Rightfully, it was his honor to verify where her footprints had ended.

Edward used a rock chisel as a fulcrum to open the casket lid. To everyone's dismay, that coffin was empty. It contained no remains for either Jonathan or Canzallia. So, there was no logical explanation for the disappearance of Mrs. Edward Burns.

Gray concluded that this particular scenario was a physical impossibility. It was also a documented fact that Pondle's interment had been witnessed by a majority of the Church membership. They also observed that Pondle's coffin was covered with a hard clay soil which made penetration more than difficult. And, as usual, the undertaker had packed that clay soil down very tightly using a heavyweight compactor. In those days, that was the procedure so that grave robbers might be discouraged by the extra soil. It was our best deterrent for those who would steal from the dead.

Yet, when 'Can' disappeared, Pondle's grave had not been previously disturbed. And, the men with their shovels testified to that observance when the Sheriff took their testimony for the Official Record. So, Paul Gray questioned this issue, "How is it possible for the remains of Jonathan to have gotten out of his casket and broken the hard clay deposits that sealed his tomb? He had been declared 'apparently' dead and buried for over a year when this most recent tragedy of Mrs. Burns occurred.

Gray continued by asking, "What unearthly influence or paranormal power could have caused Canzallia to leave her young husband whom she loved for an old man that she had, repeatedly, rebuked?" 'Can' had a happy lifestyle and a lovely little home to enjoy. Yet, she chose to walk barefoot in her evening gown through a heavily-packed blanket of a three-inch snow deposit? That one mile trip to the graveyard would have been taken in the dark and, without any lanterns to guide her path. And, then, to have vanished without leaving any tell-tale signs behind?

All this about her disappearing act didn't make much sense to Gray as phenomenal-like events sometimes do. A thorough search for the whereabouts of Mrs. Burns and Jonathan Pondle was made by the authorities but, no trace of either one was ever found. It was concluded by some mystics that both Canzallia and Jonathan were re-united again somewhere in their world of spirits. Unfortunately, Gray could make suppositions about this case but, he had no facts to prove anything.

While back at his motel and during the writing of his Final Report, Gray became a little concerned. In this specific case, there were no sightings for the Governor to wrap a State Park around. And, that situation could prove harmful to someone's wealth; namely, his own. So, Paul was hard-pressed for relevant recommendations to place in his Final Report. He had no facts to work with except for her freakish disappearance. So, he changed the title of his Case File to read, 'Warlock' while he imagined the rest.

He reasoned that Warlocks do exist and they do seek Witches as soul mates. Further, he concluded that, maybe, 'Can' was Pondle's duly appointed and spiritual Witch. If that be true, then their first kiss would lower his age to hers and, they would be happily in love with each other for their assigned eternity. There was nothing wrong with their getting together as Warlock and Witch except for causing the Earth bound husband Edward Burns some grief and despair. But, Edward would just drink more beer and find a replacement wife within about 90-days.

His Final Report would characterize Warlocks and Witches as being good people from another spirit world that is deep within our Galaxy or somewhere in Brooklyn, NY or, maybe in Hoboken, NJ. Who knows where such spirits go? Wherever they do go, I am certain that they are happy with each other. And, they almost have to be satisfied with each other because an 'assigned eternity' is a very long time, believe me.

What Paul appreciated more than anything else was the great love story where poor Pondle overcame so many issues and obstacles to locate his true love and to be reunited with her again. Now, Jonathan's greatest concern is how to fight reincarnations and to run the risk of losing her once more to another earthling or a beer drinking bumpkin. Paul imagined that Jonathan would be very protective of 'Can' around Memorial Day on May 30th when such reincarnation events usually occur.

Now, that is a Warlock story that fits like a fine glove. Our Governor could build 'A Theater Under The Stars' to commemorate the love story between Jonathan and Canzalia Pondle. That drama would demonstrate how hard Jonathan struggled to find his spiritual mate and how difficult it was to take her to a place of safety, unlike Brooklyn, NY, et al. But, remarkably, to transport her to an indefinite region or expanse that was far removed from her first husband and his beer drinking buddies who molested her whenever they became overly intoxicated.

Paul reviewed his Final Report and he tagged it with a 'POST-IT' note which read, "Mira, this is a play worth doing. Daniel Boone and the Harrodsburg play isn't the financial success that it once was so, we need to produce something that is totally different. What say you?"

That being the end of this assignment and, because Paul was unable to locate Doris Pratte, he motored to Lexington as fast as he could to meet with Mira for some fabulous sex, if possible.

Chapter Nine

HAUNTED HILL

THE GOVERNOR LIKED the concept of 'A Theater Under
The Stars' for the Warlock-Witch story involving Jonathan
Pondle and his new bride, Canzallia Burns (Pendleton). That couple's
struggle to find true happiness was something that Mira really enjoyed
and, as a woman, one that she could relate to; i.e., her favorite novels
were of the romantic genre.

Mira was also elated to know that the engineering drawings for
this new theater were being completed at this time. And, she had
been advised that actual construction was scheduled to begin after
the Spring rains became history. So, things were moving along fast
for this Project and, she was so happy that the Governor was in full
support for everything that was connected with this Theater Project.

The Governor was also happy about the fact that his Kentucky
would soon be elevated to the same status that was already enjoyed
by NY, CA and TX. Those states have outdoor theaters and, soon, KY
would enjoy the same luxury. Old Governor was really proud of that
being an eventual reality.

But, Mira didn't like Paul's hard work well enough to forget
about the foursome incident. While he was on location, Mira made it
tough on Herb, Shirley and Lola. There were an excessive number of
Staff meetings about trivial subjects that seemed to go in great circles

without any real substance or relevance. Mira was keeping her Staff on a busy work schedule.

As for Paul, Mira was giving him the silent treatment. It appeared that she didn't want him to ever be near her office again. Proof of point was established when Mira sent him his next case file while he was still working on the Warlock Report at the Viper Motel. Paul truly felt that he was being shunned.

Perhaps, Mira is being pressured by a real strong demand for a completed report concerning his latest assignment, including art work and field photography. It might also mean that Mira is treating the perpetrator of 'squares' and 'triangles' events as if he had leprosy. After much consideration about her feminine logic, he thought he knew what Mira's real intentions were. And, there was nothing wrong with her acting in that manner. She was simply practicing what a lot of women try to accomplish when they are falling in love with someone. They resort to the old adage that "Out of sight is out of mind."

His mode of operations was to do this new case file as quickly as possible. Then, he would return to PESO at Lexington where he would pretend that nothing unusual had ever happened. If games were going to be played at PESO, then he would introduce Mira to the Master of Gamesmanship, namely himself.

Then, he analyzed his next case very thoroughly. Since it did appear to be a simple affair, he checked out of that Viper Motel, waved as he passed Doris's old house and headed for Barbourville, KY where the townsfolk were complaining so much about the damages caused by a certain haunted hill. He wondered, "How could a 'pile of dirt and rock' cause so much trouble? There must be a simple scientific explanation for all of this.

He checked in at a small motel in Barbourville and began his interviews at the front desk where the question of the day was, "Have you or your vehicle ever been damaged while on a certain hill in the neighborhood?" If, he was interviewing on the streets of Barbourville, he would inquire, "Which hill? "What kind of damages?" And, with witnesses, he would say, tell me about that hill, what were your own experiences?"

Almost every person that he talked to said the same thing. "Yes, I have been on that mountain top and, yes, I have received mechanical damages. Is PESO going to do anything about that damned haunted hill?"

In terms of probability theory, more than 96-percent of the town's population was familiar with the hill's reputation and, practically every one of them were absolutely furious about the situation.

Some of the citizens who possessed the greatest angriness did admit to having signed a petition which they had previously forwarded to the Governor's offices in Frankfort. Suddenly, Paul Gray understood one need for Mira's apparent urgency. She was catching heat from Frankfort, the State Capitol.

Therefore, it was logical that Miss Mira wanted her best investigator on the job and, quickly so. She knew that Dr. Gray would do whatever was required to solve the problem. Remembering that Mira didn't like heat of any kind, Gray told himself that he needed to move fast and solve this matter as soon as possible.

If he could quickly solve this case, perhaps she would forgive him for his foursome with Herb, Shirley and Lola. And, if he could not solve this case, the Governor would be inclined to blame Mira for losing a pile of voters in Knox County.

Next, he would review the accident complaints and, after that, he would investigate the field site. Dr. Gray and that haunted hill were about to become adversaries. And, his new motto was, no ghost messes with my Mira or me. But, the ghost(s) on the mountain couldn't see this one coming. He reasoned that the advantage was his.

There appeared to be no common link to all of the different damages which were reported in the Sheriff's Logbook. Instead, the only thing that was apparently in common was the fact that everything occurred at the top of that hill. Nothing ever happened on the slopes or approaches. And, there were a large number of incidents dating back to the 1930's. So, these two observations would be of considerable importance to Dr. Gray.

He asked himself, what was going on in the nineteen thirties and why was it restricted to the top of that mountain? At the time, the entire Country was under the grips of the Great Depression. Yet, it was also the time where great advances were being made by the transportation industry.

For example, automobiles, trucks and tractors were replacing mules, horses, carriages and wagons. Henry Ford had something new to offer and everybody wanted one. Those early reports in the Sheriff's Logbook described a typical encounter as being of this form, "When we reached the top of that hill something invisible would follow them. We felt the presence of another being, human or otherwise."

Travelers on foot have reported that they could hear footsteps walking beside them. Some have also said that they felt the touch of a hand on their shoulder even though nothing or no one was in sight. Why at the top of the hill and no place else?

Horseback riders have complained that something unseen has spooked their horses while others have felt someone or something to jump on their horses with them, as if to hitch a ride. A few of those riders have reported that they even felt arms around their waists after the invisible ghost mounted a position just behind the rider's saddle.

There were a few recorded events where the horses bolted and ran out of control for several miles before being halted. After automobiles and trucks made more horses obsolete, the actual intensity of reported damages seemed to increase in size, frequency and severity.

Folks who drove gasoline-powered vehicles along this small stretch of the mountain's crest have reported many involvements. For example, some have complained about incidents where something heavy either jumped or fell on top of the hood and sheet metal portions of their vehicle. Occasionally, portions of the cars, trucks and tractors were badly damaged as if a collision had occurred. But, there was never any evidence of another party or parties being involved. There were no fallen rocks, tree limbs or other such debris on the roadway surface.

One driver said that he hit something unseen in the road at the top of the hill. He saw nothing on the roadbed but, he did get out of his vehicle to see if he had accidentally hit a person or an animal. He searched the area carefully but, he found no evidence that he had hurt anyone or anything. However, his grille had been badly sabotaged.

In another incident, a Patrol Car was investigating the phenomena when something jumped on top of his Cruiser and broke both of his flashing spotlights. The policeman reported that nothing unusual was to be seen in the area and, accordingly, he never learned who or what caused his damages.

The ghost behind all of this hatred rarely makes an appearance. And, when he does show himself, it is always on a foggy night when a very dense fog rises to unusual heights. The mountain's elevation is 985-feet above sea level so, there is a dead zone for a good sighting of this angry spirit. In other words, if a dense fog is at about 1000-feet high, then the spirit might be seen and evaluated. But, if the fog reaches only 900-feet said spirit will not be seen. A mere difference of just 85-feet can make a big difference.

Gray decided to camp out on 'Haunted Hill' to see if he could get a decent image of this angry spirit using his infrared camera and similar devices. Fortunately for him, a dense fog was predicted to reach a level of 1050-feet that very evening.

Paul had developed his own wild opinion that this haunting was caused by an angry spirit who didn't want progress to advance or the times to change. Perhaps, it was a spirit who loved horses. Or, probably, someone who wanted Detroit to go out of business. And, feasibly, someone who wanted the Ford Family to be exiled to Liberia. Who knows exactly why?

He waited and waited some more until the image suddenly arrived to verify that his theory was correct. That image was one of a horseman who carried a wooden mallet to strike objects in his path. Gray saw his polo swing coming so he was able to avoid being hit. Paul's foe was a strong spirit so, if he had made contact with his skull, Gray would have been badly hurt.

After repeated efforts, this ghost gave up his attempts to hit something human and, he left the scene, leaving behind several dents in Gray's Police Cruiser. But, not before Paul was able to capture several sharp images. Gray was very disappointed that the other polo ponies of the area failed to show because he fancied a polo match. He thought that it might be fun to watch. But, on this evening, nothing like that occurred.

Tonight's observations explained a lot of things about the hatred that his polo player held for gas-powered vehicles. What about the other ghosts? The ones who pestered only foot travelers, the horseback riders, or others still unnamed and not yet identified. These thoughts led him to believe that there are different species of ghosts that thrive on this haunted hill area.

The governor might like this area as a new State Park candidate but, it would be one that would be very expensive to build. Kentucky would have to quarantine and close the old existing road so that a new by-pass could be built to go around the polo player's kingdom. If a new State Park was to be built on that old mountain crest, Knox County could be sued to cover any damages that occurred as a result of a stray hit by a polo mallet.

Because of that possibility, Paul voted negative for a new State Park on the hilltop area. However, he did strongly support the closing of that old road and the building of an expressway by-pass for Hill 985. His buddy Herb had given him an insider tip that the Governor owned several construction companies, one of which builds roads and expressway by-passes. Paul was hoping that if, the Governor was creating heat for Mira, a new fat contract for an expensive expressway might soothe his pea-picking heart.

And, because he knew that Mira and her Staff were always receiving heat from Frankfort, he decided to expedite the delivery of his Final Report which he had just written while he was a prisoner of the Barbourville Motel. He quickly published the file to a PDF format and uploaded it to Lexington in less than a New York minute. She would be reading the Haunted Hill story before he could pay his bill and check out of the Motel. God bless computers.

He headed in the direction of Lexington as fast as possible because he had a red head on his mind and he wanted to see her as soon as he could. He needed to eat something but, he decided to wait until after mid-morning before he had brunch at Jerry's Restaurant in London, KY.

But, that was not to be the case. As he approached London, he received another assignment that was sent to him by his red headed girlfriend using his e-mail collar of docgray@hotmail.com. He had selected that particular address because he considered himself to be a hot male.

Now, he had more than justifiable cause to think that Mira was trying to wean him from his apparent addiction to 'triangles' and 'squares'. Absence does make the heart grow fonder but, exile has the opposite effect. Didn't Mira know that too much of this stay-away business might cause him to stray-away on a permanent basis?

His latest assignment via e-mail was named 'Obsession'. The title was attractive but, he didn't open the attachment because he was growing so tired of too much field work. He wanted to sleep in his own bed for a change.

He decided that he would view the attachment later but, not before brunch. He was very hungry so he pulled into the Jerry's Restaurant on Interstate 75 for some eggs and sausage, mountain style. He liked to eat at any of Jerry's places because, while he was studying at the University of Kentucky, Jerry's hamburgers and coffee had kept him alive and alert.

After he had finished his meal and drunk several cups of Jerry's best Java, he paid the waitress and left the joint. While he was in his car and still on the restaurant parking property, he became curious about his next assignment. So, he uploaded her attachment to find out what that was all about. The attachment took him by complete surprise.

The voice of Cher was singing 'Burlesque' in the background and Mira was miming her words. Paul assumed that Joan was the camera person because her appearance was never evident. One by one and piece by piece, Mira removed all of her clothing and she never missed a bump or grind movement with the beguiling sounds of that sexy music.

He was surprised to see that Mira performed as well as any professional might have done. Paul became convinced that, somewhere in her past, she must have studied dance and, she had learned her lessons very well. 'Burlesque' was a song to be remembered. It was a catchy tune that was designed to appeal to every bachelor that listened to those enticing words. Paul was very good at lip reading and this is what Mira sang:

"Show a little more, Show a little less.
Everything you dream of is yours to caress."

She was dazzlingly beautiful and, with her more than ample equipment, she was both gorgeous and irresistible. So, out came the handkerchief which he used for emergencies. There, in Jerry's parking lot, he masturbated. That was his best defense against the pain of stone ache and the astonishing requirement for some gonadal relief. Some of his pipes were cleaned and he was happy again.

Afterwards, he tried to figure out why Mira was doing this to him but, the only logical explanation that he could come up with was that Mira wanted to be missed by him and him alone. Considering the subject of 'body beautiful' she was truly magnificent. He referred to Mira as his personal Aphrodite, a God of love and beauty.

Near the end of her DVD performance, the camera zoomed in on Mira's vagina while she sang this personal challenge,

> *If you cherish something nice,*
> *These lips will surely suffice.*

At that time, Mira was stark naked and this fantastic woman was begging for a bump of another kind. Paul couldn't wait until he could see here again and hold her in his arms. He might have to buy his own copy of 'Burlesque' and, she might have to teach him how to dance but, he knew that both activities were in their near term futures. He thought of nothing else while he ran his Ford in hot pursuit at maximum speed.

But, once again, that was not to be the case. Another e-mail message had found its way to his web address before he could achieve his arrival at Lexington. He was angry as hell and swearing that this would be the last assignment that he would accept. He wanted no more e-mails or DVD's to be sent by such an impersonal procedure.

She would cut him some slack and keep him in Lexington for longer periods of time or, he would resign his position. Being in the field too much was, in his opinion, cruel and unusual punishment. He needed that little meeting with Mira that she had suggested. The one about new rules and 'no Shirley or no Lola'.

Chapter Ten

AIRPORT

THE GOVERNOR WAS a man of widely variant interests. He loved the 'Warlock' concept because of his vanity. Now, the Commonwealth would have what every large State already had, a 'Theater Under The Stars'. He likened his latest development to that of New York, California and Texas.

Now, his Kentucky had some real class in the form of a new theater activity. His other theater at Fort Harrod was losing some of its patrons so, perhaps, Warlock's love story would see more success or, at least, pick up some of the slack.

He hoped that this new play would be successful for another reason.

His wife would be the Official Sponsor of the new theater and, while she is away, he could play with young girls of his own choice. Our Governor suffered from a post mid-life crisis.

If you readers think that 'Warlock' would be the Governor's favorite, then you should give 'Haunted Hill' a second study. Kentucky's highest administrative official would like 'Haunted Hill' best because of all the bribes and kick-backs that were coming his way. Closing one road and replacing it with an expensive expressway by-pass would be very costly to the Commonwealth.

And, his current rate was twenty-percent in cash money using untraceable bills or bearer bonds. Herb told Gray that the 'topper' was worse. The request for quotation (RFQ) covering the building of this new road was hand-delivered to the two construction companies which the Governor already owned. No matter how you look at that situation, 'Haunted Hill' was about to make the Governor a very rich man.

What did Dr. Gray like best? That would be his apartment in Lexington which he had not been permitted to visit for several weeks at the latest count. Mira was still sending him superfluous assignments that wasted his time but, these tasks were sufficient to keep Paul on the road and away from PESO in Lexington.

He was growing very tired of her current procedure and he wondered why it had become what appeared to be her standard operating procedure or 'SOP'. Paul thought that it was related her apparent belief of the theory that absence makes the heart grow fonder but, he wasn't buying that crap anymore. Then, he had a thought. If Lola had no samples to work on, then, her job position could be eliminated.

And, that would be one way that Miss Mira might have exacted her revenge for the unapproved foursome. He would test that theory by sending Lola more samples than she could possibly process in a reasonable time. Keeping Lola busy and watching what Mira does was the plan of action for the next few days. It was time to go collecting rocks for Lola to analyze. After that, he would begin his latest assignment called 'Airport'. He developed his own plan which was based on these controlling factors:

- This new assignment was familiar turf for him.
- As a child, he was a regular visitor to the airport.
- As a teenager, he was called an airport junkie.

As an adult, he became an international authority on the subject of airplane crashes.

Therefore, he felt quite confident that he could easily solve this assignment and move on to better places; hopefully, his apartment at Lexington. Paul was sick and tired of buying more underwear than he needed. He was also tired of washing dirty underwear and soiled handkerchiefs in the motel sink. He decided to finish his current report and take it to Lexington where he would personally present said report to Miss Mira without telling her, in advance, that he was heading for his home base. And, he would not tell her that he had arrived until after he became re-acquainted with his own bed.

If she tried to contact him by radio, telephone or computer, he would go to an evening response schedule where she had already gone home for the day. He would answer her previous questions or instructions but, he would do that only on a once-a-day basis, offering appropriate communication skills for his boss but, at a much lower frequency rate. That seemed to be the only proper approach to this 'Wall of China' that she was building between the two of them.

He checked in at the La Citadel Motel at Hazard. Then, he visited his Mother for a few hours before beginning work on his latest assignment. He was going to enjoy this case because it was like a page torn from his own book.

His experience with the old Hazard Airport began when he was just five years old. His Father had taken him there so that they could have a weekend outing together. As they walked, hand-in-hand together, Paul said to his Father, "Dad, there is something wrong with that man's engine. And, he pointed upward and toward the sky to identify which plane was experiencing trouble." The subject airplane was flying at about 1500-feet high with an orbital heading of North-to-West-to-South-to-East.

In other words, he was spiraling downward toward the airstrip where he was trying to make a safe landing. But, with a misfiring engine, he didn't make it. He crashed and burned not fifty yards from where Dad and I were standing.

During the 1940's and subsequent years, the Hazard Airport was rated by the FAA as being the most dangerous landing approach in all of America. Pilots would fly in from other States to test their skills against the toughest path that had to be made by an airplane if a successful landing was to be achieved. The approach was known as a 'corkscrew' or 'cyclonic' maneuver where the 'spiraling down' was mandated by the nearby hills and trees which the pilot had to avoid if he wanted to make the runway safely at the valley below.

On that day in 1937, I was introduced to the risks of flying heavier than air equipment. My first visit to an airport featured a terrible crash and, worse, a fatality. Experts claim that the hearing of a child can be far superior to that for an adult. In this case, I heard the sputtering engine while my Father did not.

A few years later, the Perrini Corporation of Boston came to Hazard for the purpose of doing contract work for the local Coal Mining Companies. They offered giant mechanical augers which represented the formal onset of modern-day surface mining technology. That Boston Corporation also had several nice airplanes at the Airport and I was privileged to examine each of them, thoroughly and regularly.

The Perrini Family lived on Combs Street and I played with their three children who were about my age. Mrs. Perrini took a special liking to me so she took me to the Airport on numerous occasions. And, I appreciated her for other reasons, she had the prettiest tits that I had ever seen during my pre-puberty days.

After Mrs. Perrini 'adopted' me as their fourth son, there were plenty of trips to the Hazard Airport and more engine failures or other tragedies for me to observe and learn about on a hands-on basis. And, this trend did not end until after they built a new Airport in the 1980's. The advantage of this new airstrip was that 'corkscrewing' was no longer a deadly threat to pilots since it was no longer required.

The elevation of this new airstrip was at 1253-feet above sea level so, a headlong landing was feasible. As a result of this new construction, Perry County relinquished its inglorious title as America's most dangerous airport.

Later, when I was in Graduate School at UK, I would visit the new airport to observe an engine being overhauled or other such repairs being made. I was a lot like my Father, a man who never met a stranger. I would visit the airport to mix with the pilots and their mechanics. They called me their favorite 'airport bum'.

All of this background information is to convince the reader that Dr. Paul Gray is more than qualified to participate in this new assignment.

In fact, Mira included a 'Post-it Note' to say, "Have fun with this one, Paul. Based on what your resume says, "This one should be right up your alley."

The dangerous days at the old Hazard Airport were, in a word, awesome. Just about every pilot who flew out of there had a unique story to tell and each of those stories was quite fascinating. The

Country's most dangerous airstrip also had the most dangerous skies or, so it would seem.

The stories that Dr. Gray liked best involved the business of time warps and those associated paranormal events.

So, when Doc Gray first received this new case file from Mira, he felt as if 'déjà vu' was in full force. In fact, he also wondered if it was a story that he had heard before while he was working his way toward becoming an 'airport junky'. Looking back, he remembered that 'time warps, seemed to be a common occurrence at the old Hazard Airport.

Do all of the yesterdays and every tomorrow really exist someplace? Are they trapped somewhere in time and space? Is it possible that previous times might be visible to a selected few who have actually gone back to participate in events that occurred previously?

And, by the same token, is 'back to the future' still in vogue? Is it possible to visit the future to examine events that have not yet occurred in the present? Imagine the pleasure or discomfort if one could see how his unborn children have lived or died?

As impossible as it may seem, this Peso Case File contains documented evidence about time warps at the old Hazard Airport. The one story that Gray liked best involved a young pilot named Arthur Foley who would, at a later date, become a decorated war hero during WW-II.

This soon-to-be Army Air Force Colonel had this to say about his experiences at that airport. He told this interesting story. He said, "On that particular day, I was corkscrewing to a peak altitude of about 1500-feet when I entered a very dense cloud. Immediately, I lost all of my instruments and I was flying blind.

To me, everything seemed to be haywire as I developed an instant headache where my brains seemed to be boiling. I was in trouble to the point that I didn't really know what was best for me to do. I distinctly remember hearing and feeling my heart beats pounding so, I must have had several spikes in my blood pressure, as well. I was facing big trouble but, there was nothing that I could do. I wasn't controlling my machine but, I felt that it was controlling me.

When I did emerge from that dense cloud into to a fair weather region that was so much clearer, I saw that the ground below me had been transformed into a totally different world. I saw virgin timber, a Kentucky River that was much wider and deeper and I saw no indication of any coal mines in any direction. In fact, there was no indication of any civilization, either.

I decided to buzz the area at near tree-top levels for a better view. When I did that, I saw a hunting party of Indians who were spooked by my airplane. They shot their arrows at me but, I was able to avoid all such attacks. The Indians had the advantage of distance but my speed was too great for them to harm my airplane. I was flying a Piper Cub so, I did receive a few 'hits' but, none of them brought me down.

I figured that the actual date must have been around the Daniel Boone era because I could distinguish wagon tracks on the ground. Therefore, I was several miles off of my intended course. I looked toward the Southeast where I saw Cumberland Gap which Boone would have used on a regular basis. After that particular shock, I did a 360-degree turn-a-round and high tailed it back to the Hazard area. I used the North Fork of the Kentucky River as my guidepost.

When I saw that particular cloud again, I verified its position and elevation by a calculated guess. Again, the river spoke the truth because its meandering bends had not changed that much with time. Of course, there was no Thacker's Garage or Elmer Davis's Service Station to assist me because I was flying blind and in the past, not the present.

After I reached Combs Mountain, I went for a steep climb and started a circular path until I reached the proper altitude. Then, I crossed my fingers and busted that damned cloud to start corkscrew-ing my way to ground, and my ultimate safety.

I was exhilarated to have survived that particular run to Cumberland Gap and back again, safely. However, my photographs of the scenery that I did see were classified as 'fakes' by experts at the FAA and the US AAF. But, no one would make any criticisms of the hunting arrows because they were classified as being genuine. So, the arrows supported my claims but the terrain photographs did not. Foley gave Gray some sage advice when he said, Experts are not always honest people."

Another pilot named Wilford Jones also testified that he had a similar flight to the one that Foley talked about. With this one exception, Jones flew into the future, but, not the past. Gray pulled

Jones's sworn testimony about his flight from the case file to read it again. These are the recorded words of Wilford Jones who said, "I was busting clouds near Hazard when I lost my bearing and watched my instruments go crazy. He had to land his airplane on a mountain-top airport in Northern Tennessee.

Jones reported seeing something called TV and it frightened him some.

That television in the Tennessee airport building was featuring a black President that was speaking from Washington, DC. Quickly, he finished his snack, filled-up with the gasoline that he needed and left the Tennessee skies in a big hurry. He flew back to his home base in Hazard using full throttle on his single-engine Cessna. He was frightened by the fact that a man named Obama could ever replace a gentleman like FDR.

The best scientific study on this problem of time warps at the old Hazard Airport was documented by four pilots, Margo Eblen, Gwendolyn Combs, Bobby Adams, and Les Wilson. In a planned experiment, they proved that the entire problem was a strong function of directionality involving the North, East, South or West.

Their mission was to spiral upwards to initiate a precise circular route near the underside of that densest cloud. They were instructed to hold that pattern until all four planes were stabilized in the same orbital circle. When they were given the go-ahead signal by the lead pilot, Margo Eblen, all four planes were to exit the target cloud at four distinct points on a large great circle.

They were flying blind on the inside of that target cloud but, they were able to maintain both altitude and speed to keep holding a circular path within a great circle. After thirty seconds of flying that circular path, Margo touched a button that sent a powerful sound signal to each cockpit and, immediately, all pilots heard the signal which meant, exit this cloud, now. Immediately, all four pilots departed from the target cloud on a linear path which was crudely ninety-degrees apart. They each turned to their right side to avoid any possible collisions.

Margo ended-up flying toward the apparent South and she held a steady heading of 180-degrees, Gwendolyn flew toward the apparent East and she held a steady heading of 90-degrees, Bobby exited his great circle position and he flew toward the West at a heading of

270-degrees and Les departed from his position to venture toward the North at a heading of 360-degrees. After emerging from the target cloud, they had been previously instructed to take as many photographs as possible before returning to their own air field. In other words, this experiment was to confirm or deny the previous sightings of one Arthur Foley.

Except that, in this case, there would be four witnesses, two women and two men, so the Army experts would be challenged by whatever these heroic pilots might discover. The de-briefing sessions were a formal affair that were presented to a panel of experts but, the photographs which were taken created the most interest.

Margo's mission was of paramount importance because her flight path was the only one that was exactly identical to the one that Foley had taken, a due South direction. Her pictures were sufficient to reveal that Foley was not lying or exaggerating. The Army experts even measured some of those giant trees and compared them to Foley's results. Lo and behold, those huge trunk diameters were identical in size. Margo had been time-warped to an earlier time when the forests were still virgin and had not yet been devastated by the profiteering class from Yankee-land.

Gwendolyn's pictures were also solid proof that the time warps of Hazard were genuine. In her flight toward the Eastern sector, she took some photographs of a Civil War skirmish. A Southern General saw her plane and, when he waved his hat to her, she recognized General John Hunt Morgan. It was strange how Gwendolyn was always able to locate promising men. At the last count, she had survived five different husbands.

Bobby Adams, who was flying his big plane toward the Western sector, flew over a village of red-headed women in white dresses that were so beautiful. He took a lot of pictures of those girls and swore that, one day, he would marry a red-haired woman and he did, a beauty named Chloe Ann Spicer out of Winchester. His other pictures fully characterized boat traffic on the Mississippi River. And, as you know, trade boats going up and down the Mississippi have been virtually non-existent for several years now.

Sadly, Les Wilson's plane never made it back to Hazard and his disappearance was not explained by subsequent investigations.

Perhaps, he was a victim of unfriendly skies, stormy weather or engine malfunction.

Or, maybe he met a woman that he could not resist so, he stayed where he was, as close to her as possible. The exact root cause will always remain a mystery.

But, if you knew Wilson as well as Dr. Gray did, then you would accept the latter explanation over the former. Les was one-hell-of-a pilot and a special friend to all of the ladies. He had an addiction that was close to what Gray suffered from. He tried to bed every young woman that he met. In any case, there were no available photographs for the Northern sector. But, if Les ever does re-appear to the present time, I am certain that his pictures would be entirely of beautiful women that he left behind in the good old days. Les was a 'love them, leave them' type of guy.

Gray's interest in the loss of his friend Les would motivate him to fly a similar pattern to see what Wilson saw. As he corkscrewed out of that dense cloud over the Hazard Airport and turned toward the North, he saw no civilization just some terrible flooding of the Ohio River near Ashland, KY. Paul concluded that the time warp studies were not similar for all pilots unless they were done at precisely the same time. In other words, what Margo, Gwendolyn and Bobby saw were unavailable for Paul to see because he was flying at a later time and date.

Paul was unable to explain any logical reason for the photographs but he did have a strong hunch that Radon gas was somehow involved. That would explain why the instruments went crazy and it would also cover some of the hallucinations that were reported. However, he knew that most of those delusionary sightings were caused by too much moonshine.

As to whether or not this old airport could be used as a new State Park location, forget everything about that possibility. That old airport has been transformed into an exemplary Perry County High School and also as a Retirement Home for the elderly citizens of Hazard and Perry County. There is no way that the Governor would have his way for this Project. Imagine the furor that would result if 100 elderly people were forcibly displaced. And, worse, consider the madness if several hundred children had no place to attend any of their classes. If enacted, either one of these two events would cost the Governor too many lost votes in Perry County. For that line of reasoning, Paul voted 'negative' on the aspect of having a new State Park for this location.

Having finished the Report called 'Airport', he decided to detour a few miles so that he could take a look into the rumored hauntings at the old Miner's Memorial Hospital (MMH) in Hazard. Numerous sightings have been reported for that location yet, none of them had been examined by any PESO scouts or field investigators. He would tell Herb Moore about this 'hotspot' location and he would suggest that he and Shirley become more involved. In other words, Paul was making a preliminary inspection that might one day bring a new State Park into Perry County.

Gray decided to check this source out for another reason. This was where his Father had died and he was just plain curious. As he entered the abandoned MMH building, he felt a strange presence as if someone had grabbed his hand to walk with him while he inspected the old hospital. He felt that it was someone he knew and, of course, he hoped that it was his Father. It was an uncanny feeling but, also a soothing one.

Paul felt that the ghost of his Father Courtney was giving him a grand tour of the facility. These are the sightings that his Father hosted and apparently wanted his son to see or hear.

- There were footsteps to be heard in the stair wells.
- No security men were present because each of them had previously resigned because of on-the-job fear.
- A man in a gray suit was seen walking the steps.
- You could hear doctors being paged yet, there was no pager.
- Attempts to install new light bulbs failed. New or old, they still flickered.
- A typewriter was overheard and going at full speed in the Emergency Room.
- Voices called your name when no one was to be seen.
- An inflated balloon is floating in the Maternity Ward.
- People have been attacked by some 'black thing' near the Mental Ward.
- An elderly woman can be seen looking out one of the second floor windows.

- Crying babies are heard near where they were first born.
- Two men have been observed while fist-fighting on the tarmac of the parking lot.
- Running water can be heard but, never seen.
- Naked men and women have been seen dancing on the waiting room floor.
- Angry nurses are yelling the word 'NO' over and over again.

With 15-sightings to talk about, Gray felt that this was enough to impress both the Governor and his right-handed enforcer, Mira Mirren.

At least, he would try to sell the concept to his bosses because Hazard badly needed more tourists and, especially, Hazard needed the cash money that tourist traffic can bring to the table.

His initial thoughts were to buy the MMH property for conversion to a medical nightmare show place for his paranormal followers. He said goodbye to his Dad's ghost and loaded up his Police Car with his possessions to start his trek toward Lexington. But, he didn't inform Mira that he was coming.

His belongings now numbered two large over-stuffed suitcases and four boxes of dirty laundry. He left town wondering if he could con sweet Mira into doing his washing for him but, then he said to himself, "Silly boy, surely you jest."

Chapter Eleven

REVENGE

HE ARRIVED BACK at Lexington very late that night. His detour to Miner's Memorial Hospital had consumed too much of his daylight hours but, he did enjoy feeling those stout hands of his Father once again. Dad's presence was, without a doubt, priceless. But, upon his return to Fayette County, he had a gut feeling that something was wrong with Mira so, he decided to buzz by her house to see if she needed his assistance on anything.

When he turned into Mira's Cul-de-Sac, he was shocked to notice that the Governor's car was parked out front. That big limousine was empty so this meant one of two possibilities; namely, the Chauffeur was inside doing a foursome with Mira, Joan and the Governor. Or, the Governor had driven the car to Lexington by himself.

Suddenly, Paul became enraged. What about that sexy DVD attachment that Mira e-mailed me? Does my beautiful 'love card' mean this little to her? Why is she doing this? There was a high risk of being seen but, he decided to take a peek anyway.

It was a good thing that he was running low on clean laundry because, tonight, he was wearing his old Police uniform from his days of serving on the Metropolitan Police Department. So, if any of the neighbors did make any inquiries about him being there, he would just politely say, "Ma'am, this is official Police business. Please go back inside your house and stay there where you will be safe."

Even though Paul considered it to be inappropriate behavior, he decided to have a look because she could be in trouble. Lovely Mira could have a gun pointed at her face, who knows what that low-class Governor was capable of doing?

Luckily, Boss Mirren has wooden shutters on her windows and, as everyone knows, those shutters have small slits through which a lot can be seen if one will look with his eyes partly closed in just the right amount. He walked toward her illuminated bedroom window to give it the old college try.

When he arrived at her window, Paul witnessed a shocking sight. Mira was deep-throating the Governor. On the other side of the room, Joan was having her pussy licked by that seven foot chauffeur. She seemed happy but Mira seemed distressed so, he wondered, "What should I do? Should I break the door down and try to save two damsels in distress?"

No, that would be the wrong thing to do because the neighbors would hear the loud noise and they would call 911 to summon the real Police. As a result of their involvement, the fallout would be irreparably destructive, impossible to repair, rectify or amend. My friend, Editor Mills of the Lexington Herald would have the expose of his lifetime but, PESO would subsequently cease to exist. After the Governor would be finished with them, none of the PESO people would be numbered among the ranks of the currently employed.

Fortunately, Mira's neighbors did not bother to call 911. They did look out of their windows but, all they saw was a Policeman with a flashlight who had parked his Patrol Car and was doing his apparent duty.

Paul returned to his Police car and, he left the area driving as silently as he could. He would drive to his apartment because there was nothing that he could do to help Mira. At this late hour, he still was worried why she would ever participate in such an event. Which one was the aggressive one, the Governor or my Mira? Thinking about that brought tears from his eyes.

But, Gray was enraged at the Governor's entry into his private world. He would pay for that unwanted intrusion. But, how could it be done.?

He needed a good plan and, in the worst way. He knew that sleep would not be easy on this particular night. But, he did have a rudimentary plan that needed much refinement. He began the planning phase for that undertaking.

He couldn't wait until next morning when he would savor his five cups of good coffee at his favorite coffee bistro. Hopefully, she would notice his car in the Starbucks parking lot and join him for a breakfast treat of Danish or doughnuts. He needed to see her privately, but not at PESO Headquarters.

After he had downed cup number three, he looked up and there she was and her beauty was almost overwhelming. He got up from his chair to give her the royal treatment that she deserved. Paul chose her favorite chair and he scooted it along the floor to give her a formal setting as a gentleman would do. She was impressed and he could tell that she was somewhat titillated about him trying to be a gentleman.

Then, she reverted to form when she asked, "Are your coming to work or not? Both of us are already late so, what will the others think?"

Paul replied, "I don't care what the others think. I have to talk with you so, have a pastry treat with me and hear me out, please." She said, "Wow, you actually used the word 'please'. I am all ears, Paul. Go ahead, please."

Paul began by saying, "Mira, I am really pissed off about something and I am seriously thinking about quitting my job." She interrupted to say, "I don't want you to leave PESO. I will accept your resignation if you want me to but, I don't really want for that to happen. Not when things are looking so much better between the two of us. What is bothering you, Paul?"

He told her about his drive-by of the previous evening and said, "That's why I am so pissed." Inwardly, she was shocked that Paul Gray could be such a 'peeping Tom' or 'voyeur' type of guy. She paused further to think about punishing him for trespassing on her property but, she cut him some slack seeing that he was still in apparent dismay. His sad eyes made her believe that Paul was in denial about the images of the previous evening. And, she likened his present state to that for a little whipped puppy.

After another round of coffee, she grabbed his hand, caressed it softly and asked, "What did you see, Paul?" He replied, "I saw you trying to be Linda Lovelace with that bastard the Governor. You were deep throating him and, I want an explanation. How could you?"

She brought out the Kleenex to wipe away a few incipient tears but, she whimpered softly and said, "I do wish that you had not seen that demonstration of 'face-fucking'. I don't like to perform that particular sex act because it hurts my throat so badly.

But, believe it or not, he made me do it. He threatened to shut down PESO if Joan and I didn't respond to his demand for a foursome. And, there is likely to be more rapes of Joan and I because his wife has quit giving him any sex. I'm scared, Paul and, I don't know what to do. I have spent the whole night inducing vomiting spells to try and destroy that man's semen. That's why I am late for work."

Paul interrupted to say, "Both you and Joan were raped against your will and, with that big seven foot chauffeur being present, you really had no option except to submit. Unfortunately, you can't ask for help from the Police Department because you did willingly allow him access to your home. But, not to worry because I have a plan which will stop the Governor from repeating his actions of last night. That sort of behavior by his highness will never happen again. I promise you Mira.

Paul gave her a warm hug before saying, "Thank you for saving my job but, that bastard governor has to go. At this time, he is embarking upon a direct path that will cause him to become one of my dead spirits unless he changes. I will kill the bastard if I am forced to use blunt force. However, I do have a plan in mind that should work. But, I do need more time to set it in motion.

She kissed him lovingly on his cheek before saying, "I do love you, Paul. You are such a nice person and a good care giver that I would like to marry someday. There needs to be something solid in our future, don't you think?"

Her question went unanswered as he said, "For the present, you go do your work while I go do my ton of dirty clothes which require washing.

I will be in the Office tomorrow to discuss my final input on both 'Airport' and 'Hospital'. One of those two offers great potential as a new State Park candidate while, the other offers much less. But, we can talk more about all that tomorrow morning. Paul went his way and Mira went her way and nothing more was spoken about that damned Governor.

He would design his 'payback' plan all day while thinking about Cher's voice and Mira's seductive dancing. At the same time, he would regret the fact that he was using so many of his treasured quarters. Paul had a thing about twenty-five cent pieces, particularly, the older ones which were not the modern-day sandwich types.

Gray still had a lot of anger in his system and he needed to exorcize his memory of that sickening image where the inglorious bastard was abusing his poor Mira. Privately, Paul was afraid that he might lose his cool and do something stupid like killing the perpetrator. Nothing seemed to work so he blamed his dirty clothes and vented his anger in that direction. He gave them too much detergent and too much Borax in an unsuccessful effort to try and forget last night's memories.

He told himself that, after the laundry was finished, he would try and wash away his sorrows by having too much moonshine. I'll throw myself a party for one and hope that some of Perry's best illegal whiskey will wipe my slate clean. It does work sometimes and, today would be an ideal time to wash some of his anger away.

Next morning, the business of 'going large' with a one-man drinking party had provided him with a horrible hangover. As he arose from his Marilyn Monroe bedding, he swallowed four Advil gels dry and without any water using only saliva. He was desperate for their acclaimed fast-action results. He needed help now and, in the worst possible way.

Then, he went into the bathroom for his morning ritual of a large, long pee to help with the leg cramps that plagued him during the night and whenever he drank too much homebrew. Next, he shaved using hot water from the basin and, afterwards, he took an invigorating semi-cold shower. He felt that he was ready for Starbucks but, he wasn't too sure about being ready for PESO and Mira. He badly needed strong coffee of the 100% Arabic content on this particular morning. He vowed to ration himself on his homebrew intake during the next time that he hosted a one-man drinking party.

He sat on his chair at the Starbucks Coffee Bar and relaxed with his sobering, but favorite coffee. He decided to sharpen his observation skills by attempting to psychoanalyze each of the patrons that were present on this morning. He liked to study people.

- There was one older man who was reading the Wall Street Journal. You could tell that he was the snob of today's group.
- Another man was reading the Sporting News. You could tell that he was an over-aged jock in search of a young woman.
- There was one older woman who was reading Book Reviews from the New York Times. You could tell that she was a wannabe writer.
- There was a young woman who was reading her copy of FASHION magazine. She was a neatly-attired clothes horse.
- Then, there were four tables of University students who were not studying their textbooks. They were each trying to save Mother Earth on a very limited budget.

Since he was analyzing his copy of Mira's most recent assignment, he smiled and said to himself, I am the only eccentric that is doing any constructive work in this entire coffee bar! He paid his bill and left for his PESO Office.

He truly felt that this new file folder contained an unusual storyline which he found to be refreshing, interesting and one with a good twist at the end. 'Revenge' does address a problem that many families have to face if they have disappointing children who refuse to work. Then, Paul decided to reserve judgment until after he had finished the entire investigation.

As he read more of the 'Revenge' documentation, he wondered how and where he could start his writing to give this love story the respect that it deserves. Because it was a love story instead of a frightful ghost story, he had to be more delicate. He wanted to write something that she would like because she badly needed an uplifting experience. Imagine that you had suffered the same forced rape that Mira did. Then, you would understand why she needed his support and a new slant on life with its God-given pleasures and superb sexual entertainments.

Still, he had no special place to begin his 'Revenge' story so, with considerable reservation and much personal concern, Paul chose to start 'Mira's Rebirth' venture near the centermost portion of the entire file. He hoped that this would work because, at the present time, Mira resembled a badly wounded kitten more than the angry dog that she used to be.

She needed to get her groove back so that things at PESO could be normal again instead of her always appearing to be so wistful. Frankly, he said, "I can't wait until Mira starts chewing my ass out again. I want the good old days to return once more. We all prefer the old Mira, not the new Mira. He recalled that Mira wanted something nice in our futures so, let it begin with this, a love story involving the supernatural variety.

Mrs. Inez Callihan was a beautiful widow who lived alone in a small house not too far from Tilford in Letcher County. Her closest neighbors were just next door and they went by the name of the Lincoln Family. The patriarch of that clan was Walter Lincoln, a widower. Walter was a very nice man but, his one fault was that of being miserly which he did not inherit through his genes, it was an acquired fault.

His Family of remaining brothers and sisters plus, all of his own children, were always pestering him for more money but, he passed it out as if it was the very last gold coin that he possessed. And, as it is with other people's money, the clan members would just waste whatever Walter gave them.

Therefore, he learned the hard way. He would give his Family members and his children never enough money and that angered them. They quarreled endlessly about his 'great fortune' which he had collected from all of his coal mines over the years. He had developed his coal mines using his own blood, sweat and tears. He was down to two productive mines and four more mountains so, he still produced large tonnages of his revered 'Black Gold'. Walt had the help of many dedicated laborers that worked the mines but, none of his Family would lose a single drop of sweat to help with their Father's business.

Walter's oldest son was thirty years old and his youngest daughter was a teenager. Yet, no relative had ever entered any of his mines, not one. He was forced to hire laborers using whatever people he could find and train. Walt's Family was dysfunctional to say the very least. And, after trying almost everything, there was nothing that he could do to change their behavior.

More often than not, Walter would come home from work and find them completely stoned as a result of their alcohol addiction. Worse yet, his sons would molest their sisters as could be determined by their nakedness and their bleeding vaginas. That was a maddening experience for Walter so he moved out and took up residence next door with the very attractive Inez Callihan. He had to get away from that crazy Family and those errant kids so, he gathered his firearms and ammunition to swear that he would protect Inez to the bitter end, if need be.

At first, he slept on the front porch while he and Inez whispered sweet words to each other. When winter came, Inez invited him inside to sleep on the couch but, eventually, the couch was replaced by Inez's feather bed. They were in love with each other and, to his way of thinking, Inez was a Saint, totally unlike his deceased wife and those ungracious children of his.

What he liked best about Inez was that she never asked him for any money, not once. She didn't have to because he paid all of her bills, including the many shopping trips that they made together when they visited Hazard, KY. When they did go to that large little city of 8,000 people, he would always buy her a new outfit from Johnson's Clothing Store on Main Street but, near Bridge Street.

Theirs was a match made in Heaven. But, like some perfections, they sometimes fade to imperfections. For these two lovers, trouble started slowly but, ultimately, it all ended entirely too abruptly. How those two coped with life, love, despair and death is the interesting part of this story.

Walter did not believe in banks so, he had hidden most of his wealth near his big house, a large metal building and several other onsite structures. He needed lots of living space because of his large Family and his many dependents. But, having plenty of hiding places on his 1000-acres kept them busily searching for his hidden treasure trove, both day and night.

He wanted to protect Inez from his Family and, so far, his plans had been successful. They were told that if, so much as a single hair on her head was harmed, he would shoot the perpetrator right between his or her eyes. They were warned to leave Inez be and, simply stated, the Lincoln mavericks were fearful of their own Elder. So much so that digging for hidden treasure was always restricted to the Lincoln property but, never on any of the Callihan land. Because the Lincoln crowd could never party enough, they began tearing their own house apart in search of his hidden treasure.

At the current rate of self-imposed destruction, there would soon be no house to be left at all. Walt's own house was falling down around the human termites that Walter had to deal with. The situation had come to a virtual impasse and Walter began to fear that Inez's place might be next.

Therefore, they agreed to move to Lexington so that they could become safely separated from that unkind bunch of sots and whores. Furthermore, Walter reluctantly agreed to depositing all of his Krugerrand coins in a secure vault at the Bank of Commerce which was owned by the Moore brothers, a wealthy farming empire.

Inez argued that her Moore friends would take excellent care of his money. His gold coin collection was now evaluated to be worth more than 300-million dollars. And, he was the wealthiest man in Kentucky but, no one would ever know that by just looking. Outwardly, he appeared to be only the humble husband and devoted lover of Inez Lincoln (Callihan).

Trouble really escalated for Walter when his bad eyesight deteriorated further with his advancing age. After about two weeks of learning how to navigate using his new walking stick for the legally blind, he and Inez went to town on business. He missed a curb and fell down into the path of a passing freight truck which crushed his body and caused a painful death. Inez witnessed what happened and the loss of her husband nearly gave her a nervous breakdown.

She had a difficult time managing his funeral but, Inez was resolute, proud and quite capable. Sadly, no one came to his send-off except the Moore brothers and a few officers from the Bank of Commerce. She didn't invite any of Walter's family to his funeral because she didn't want that pitiful lot to know where they now resided.

When the paranormal hauntings first began, strange sounds of laughter were heard. Inez could see nothing of his human form but, that sound of his guttural laughter was more than familiar. That laugh did belong to the man who had warmed her featherbed so well. After Walt's laughter was heard, all sounds went quiet thereafter.

At first, Inez was frightened by his laughing presence. And, as a widow, she wondered what was so funny that made her Walt want to laugh? This went on for a few weeks before she consulted her Baptist Preacher about how to handle this situation.

Her Pastor advised Inez that Walter's spirit could be exorcised by praying to God while waving a silver-plated Cross that could be purchased from the Church Store for a few hundred dollars. He even advised that he would chase the spirit away for a few dollars more.

She decided that she didn't want to go in this direction because that was not what she wanted. She did not want just laughter. She wanted Walter back as a whole spirit to keep her company throughout day and night. For a few months, time went on and very little seemed to change.

About a year later, when Walter's Will was probated, he left all of his monetary wealth to Inez. To his faithful employees, he donated his two existing mines and the four remaining mountains. But, he left his loving spirit to his wife Inez to be used as she saw fit for the balance of her life. Afterwards, the laughter abruptly ended because his wife bade it so.

The Lincoln relatives were destined to live in abject poverty because of their hatred for all work of any kind. If they could just locate Walter's money, they could party and, big time. According to hearsay, they were currently digging up his cornfields in search of his gold coins.

Supposedly, they knew how much Walter loved his Folger's coffee so they were concentrating on the discovery of Folger coffee cans that were filled with Krugerrand gold but, they never found any. One night, Walter's spirit whispered to Inez that, as of this date, his unworthy lot had worn out more than a hundred shovels. He added, "What a waste of good shovels." And, they both laughed about the crazy antics of his weird Family. And, privately, she gave thanks that they no longer lived next door anymore.

You can still see Inez on Main Street on a regular basis. And, if you look real close, you can see that gloved Lady in Lowenthal's Store clutching the hand of an invisible companion. That would be, of course, Walter and his earthly bride, Inez on another shopping trip in downtown Lexington. Every Saturday morning, he insisted on buying her a new outfit with shoes and the works. Theirs was a love for all time and death could never make those two part.

Paul Gray was fairly confident that Mira would like this Final Report because it was a grand love story about a coal baron and his soul mate.

It didn't have much chance of ever becoming a new State Park but, it did come at a time when she could use her Kleenex tissues for a reason that did not involve the Governor.

But, he was still angry about that rape incident which occurred in Mira's bedroom. His own revenge against that Frankfort goon would soon occur after Paul could put all of the necessary pieces together. At the present time, he still had to buy some more technology and he needed to solicit the services of someone that he could trust, without any reservations whatsoever.

Chapter Twelve

PARTY HOUSE

PAUL GRAY, THE intrepid scientist was back in the Lexington area where he was driven to 'fixing' that damned Governor. It was a matter of principle because old Governor had blackmailed Mira Mirren into doing a 'Deep Throat' procedure or else. And, that contingency meant that if she didn't follow through as he demanded, she would lose PESO and all of her Staff would be terminated. Worse than that, there would be no new State Parks and no increased revenue from additional tourist traffic.

He had thought of very little else for several weeks and, he now believed that he had an excellent plan which was entirely workable. It wasn't exactly perfect, but, it was damned close. At least, it was one that was worth the old college try. It was complicated but, worthy of the cause to save PESO from subsequent blackmail of like kind. His goal in this matter was to protect Mira from face-fucks of the future.

Mira didn't like doing the 'Linda Lovelace' thing and, if this plan succeeded, she would never have to worry about being forced to do that trick again with the Governor of our Commonwealth. If she ever wanted to be more like Linda with him, then that would be her decision, not his.

These were the primary elements of his plan:

- He would rig his bedroom with cameras.
- He would have the capability of both audio and video.
- He would ask Lola Bryce to help him with the plan.
- He would be in the field when Lola and the Governor had their intercourse.
- As a financial inducement to Lola, she would get all of the money that this production earned, from blackmail or otherwise.
- They would send the photographic evidence to the First Lady, not to the Governor himself.
- If a divorce action did develop, Lola could use the evidence as she saw fit. It was her movie so, she held all rights.
- She could become a live-in sex slave for his highness.

Lola was happy about her chances of becoming a wealthy mistress and a new live-in at the Governor's Palace in Frankfort. She had a shot at that end result and she was working hard to achieve its eventual success.

With Paul being out of town so much, she felt that she was 'drying up' and sex is like a foreign language. If you fail to use it, you lose it. He had this new assignment about a haunted Party House and the trap was to be sprung while he was in absentia and apparently working on that assignment.

It was also agreed that Lola would call him after the movie production had been completed. He couldn't wait to leave Lexington so that Lola could get the opening scene started sooner. In the meantime, Paul did hang around long enough to help Lola with the final rigging of the cameras and their control switches, et cetera.

He also did as much as he could about that 'drying up' business. He kept Lola's vagina wet as often as possible so that she might get her groove back before the Governor came calling. After all, he had no idea what was headed his way. If Lola was successful, her valuable services would allow PESO to continue, it would free Mira from a nasty chore and Paul would have the bastard in the corner exactly where Paul wanted him to be.

With everything in place and all that technology being tested and re-tested, Lola was ready for her big scam. Paul's final concern was given to any background noise but, the cameras were running silent so that they would not be heard by either Lola or the Governor. As the astronauts might say, "All systems are ready to go."

With all that being finished, Paul left Lexington looking for the 'Road to Farler' near Wells Fork in Leslie County. He was smiling most of the way and hoping that nothing would go wrong with their plan. He did have some concerns that, maybe, Lola was not the actress that he wanted her to be but, he was darned sure of the critical factor; namely, she was a tigress while under the sheets, remember? So, he concluded that Lola would do just fine and, Paul needed to stop worrying about every little thing.

When he arrived at Farler, KY, he rented a 'bed and breakfast' room from an attractive red haired widow and he got 'settled-in' for some serious PESO business. Next morning, he started by asking the general public this typical question, "What do you know about a haunted house where people do nothing but 'party' about four times a year?"

It was surprising to learn that some of the older crowd had actually been guests at some of those parties. So, this new investigation might be easier than he had previously imagined. In between relevant questions, about the current assignment, his mind was still worried about Lola. Privately, he was thinking, "Why hasn't she called? Hurry up with that telephone call, dearie. I can't go home without it.

'Settling-in' at his new B&B House was a pleasant event for him. Paul used her bed that first time and, she didn't seem to mind. She wasn't the best partner that he had ever had but, she was by no means, the worst of them. On a scale of one-to-ten where a 'ten' meant magnificent, he rated her at about 5.5. Not too bad for a Farler woman who was a little shy and somewhat awkward from lack of practice. He promised to teach her a few tricks during his stay since she needed to get her groove back just as Lola did.

Next, he hired a scout who had watched some of those haunted house parties from a safe distance. Bige Eversole agreed to take him there for the 'paltry sum' of $500.00. And, Paul was beginning to think that 500-dollars was the standard price for guide services in this part of Kentucky. However, it is just expense money from PESO which isn't real money. Isn't that stuff called 'OPM' for 'Other People's Money'?

Bige Eversole told the story of how it all began for him and his Dad while he was a youngster. Elmer and Bige Eversole were having a nice ride in the country, as they often did, on Sunday afternoons. Elmer rode a high spirited stallion named Rex but, the younger Eversole was restricted to his elderly pony called Shitland, not Shetland. His pony got that nickname because his grazing field was so full of manure.

After a good ride on a long road past empty fields and broken dreams, Bige and his dad approached an old house which was brightly lighted in the waning hours of daylight. The sounds of music and laughter were, at first, a surprise to Elmer because, normally, that house was uninhabited. Then, he remembered that such house parties were scheduled on a quarterly basis.

In between parties, that old house was a weather beaten gray with a collapsed roof and loose shutters that were barely hanging thanks to several loose hinges and many rusty, broken nails. The grounds were unattended and, what was a good productive farm at one time, was now overgrown with weeds and bramble.

As the two riders drew closer to the old place, the sounds of revelry became louder and the party lights became brighter. Elmer was impressed because, the last few times that he had passed this way, nothing was going on. Everything was in its usual state of dilapidation and ruin.

Yet, on this occasion, Elmer could see clearly that the house was freshly painted and in excellent condition. Even the grounds around the house were decorated by lovely flowers, the grass was neatly cut and there was no debris or litter which he had witnessed the last time that he passed this way.

His father asked little Bige to hold the reins of both animals while he dismounted to have a closer look. Sure enough, there was a large party going on and the house was filled with people having fun. They were drinking, dancing, kissing and sharing the bedrooms as lovers sometimes do. It was, obvious that a masquerade party was proceeding because each of the men and women were wearing costumes from the Civil War era.

As Elmer Eversole stood there and, while he was looking through a uniform plate glass window, the sounds of the party were suddenly diminished by a high-pitched, blood curdling scream from a woman in distress. That scream was unlike any that Elmer Eversole had ever heard before in his entire adult life.

It was a sobering, agonizing shriek of terror that sent chills down his spine and made the hairs on his neck to feel erect. He continued to hear that horrifying scream for a few seconds more but, later, he heard nothing whatsoever.

Suddenly, Elmer found himself facing a gaping hole in that same window. Most of the solid pane of plate glass had been transformed into nothing but shards. Gone was the music, the people and the screamer. Each of the players and the sounds had just vanished into thin air.

As Elmer backed away from the broken pieces of glass, he saw that the house and grounds had reverted to their normal appearance; deserted, damaged, dirty and crumbling in decay. At that moment, Elmer knew that he had seen enough. He took Rex's reins away from Bige, mounted his steed and, together, they quickly galloped toward home. His pace was limited to whatever the old pony could manage but it wasn't slow because Elmer wanted to put some distance between where they lived and what he had just observed.

Neither Elmer nor Bige said anything about their experience to anyone for a few days. After a week or so, Elmer decided to make a few inquiries because, by this time, his curiosity was rising to the point of much concern and even fear. What mountain men cannot understand is exactly what they fear the most.

The questions that Elmer Eversole asked of the old timers in the district were surprising in some respects and just logical in others. The original deed to the property belonged to a gentleman farmer by the name of Orville Grant, a relative of General Ulysses Simpson.

Orville liked to throw lavish parties at the end of each season, summer, fall, winter and spring. The last party that Grant sponsored was in 1866 just after the Civil War had been finished. It was reputed to be a gala affair and all of the attendees did wear both costumes and masks.

Orville's last party was faulted in a terrible way. It ended with the apparent murder of a young lady who was an uninvited guest at the party. Rumors stated that she was a mistress of Orville Grant. But, the Sheriff of 1866 investigated the matter and he wrote in his ledger that no cadaver was ever found on or near the Grant property.

And, without any evidence of a crime being committed, he allowed Mr. Grant to move away from the area. He didn't want to release him but, his hands were tied by the legal issues of no body, no murder. That agonizing shriek of pain which both Elmer and Bige heard was, without a doubt, that of the dying mistress who came to the party after she was apparently advised to stay away by her lover, Orville Grant. And, she still haunts the seasonal parties which occur each year since.

Paul was elated because such a haunting did have the makings of a new State Park as long as the tourists kept their distance, that is. Parking lots and stadium seats could be built on or near the spot where Bige had held those reins but not any closer than that or the spirits would be spooked and the party images would soon cease to exist and, within a 'New York Second'.

In today's world, tourists could view the party or witness the murder using hidden cameras and acoustical devices that would be positioned in strategic locations; i.e., across the street and inside the house. This State Park would work if the party dates followed some chronological order or a predictable pattern. If the kinetics could be properly tracked, then tickets could be sold on a scheduled basis. In other words, the Park would fail if too many people bought tickets for a wrongful night's showing when no party was in effect.

He thanked Bige Eversole for his excellent accounting of the history that was here involved. He also gave him an extra $100.00 tip and he asked Bige to call him in Lexington whenever one of the four parties was in progress. He wanted to view the house party for himself and, he believed that his visitation was a professional requirement. And, of course, the next big hurdle would be to determine if the sightings were a random occurrence or not. Here, he would ask that a PESO researcher should study all of the Sheriff's ledgers to document both regularity and repeatability.

He still had not heard from Lola about about the entrapment plan and he was beginning to worry that, perhaps, something had gone awry. Maybe, the old Governor didn't like Lola as well as he liked Mira. Who knows what was happening back at home base? However, he did decide to be more patient. And, while he was waiting for that phone call, he would write his final report on 'Party House' and make love to his B&B lady friend who was still too shy and overly awkward. It was challenging work but, someone has to do it, right?

He would stay at her boarding house for a couple of weeks so that he could teach his landlady some new tricks. After the training period of a few days and nights were over, he was amazed by her transformation. His B&B red head became a real success story that attacked Paul every night, each morning and on some lazy afternoons. If Gray wanted a hot, sexy wife, he certainly knew where one fine prospect lived. She resided at Farler, KY.

Obviously, Paul was enjoying this manifestation of ecstatic passion but, he was also stalling while awaiting a certain phone call from Lola Bryce regarding the status of their 'Great Plan'. After about twenty days of isolation with his B&B lady friend, the phone call came through. One night, she left a message on his car phone that said, "He came and I conquered. The 'First Lady Production' is finished. Come home and we will watch an interesting movie together. I am much better than Linda Lovelace ever thought about being. She wore her dress throughout those face-fucking scenes but, I wore what you like best. I wore nothing."

Next morning, he checked out and gave the beautiful red head a monstrous tip for spreading her legs so well and so often. She was crying when he left but, she was also smiling as a happy person would. Paul knew that she had truly enjoyed his 'special tutoring'.

He also said goodbye to Bige, his outstanding guide and the authority for 'Party House'. This trip had been a good one with promising results for a new touring event that occurs just four times a year. Tourists had better book ahead because "Walk-ins are not welcome." This is to say that seating is restricted.

The trip back to Lexington was always boring so he activated the horses that were hiding underneath the hood of his car. When he reached a large straight stretch in Powell County, he was going larger at 148-miles-per-hour. He was flagged down by a State Trooper but, there would be no citation if, he would promise to slow down. The trooper also added, "Stop trying to be like A.J. Foyt."

This Trooper was quite concerned about the local traffic which consisted primarily of elderly farmers and their slow-moving equipment. He asked Paul this question, "What would happen if you had come upon a slow-moving tractor with a trailer load of hay?" Paul pleaded guilty on all accounts but, it was two police cars and what do you expect? They never give each other any speeding tickets.

What he really couldn't say to the Trooper was this: "I'm in a hurry to see the Governor's penis on film. And, I just can't wait. I can hardly breathe from all of this exciting anticipation. Stand aside, Officer and let me commit this crime. I intend to blackmail the Governor's bad ass."

He moved out slowly, but, after he was in Clark and Fayette Counties, he went 'larger' again with sirens blasting all of the way to Lexington town. He called Lola and asked her to spend the night with him but, he also asked her to not tell Mira that Gray was back at his home base.

Lola said that she would be there but, she forewarned him that she was having her menstrual period.

In a way, he was grateful that there would be no sex tonight because he had not yet gotten over that voluptuous red head back at Farler. He badly needed to go celibate for a few days so that he could manufacture enough sperm to support his lifestyle. Or, should he have said that he needs to recover from the B&B lady who learned too many new tricks too well.

Chapter Thirteen

HEADLESS

AS ATTESTED BY his rapid run to his Lexington apartment from the village of Farler, Paul was more than anxious to begin the editing phase for his expose of that idiot Governor. He proposed to 'out' the beast without any collateral damage that might harm his co-workers at PESO.

But, there was some lingering doubts that the Governor might retaliate and try to hurt some nice people at PESO who didn't deserve to be hurt. His short list included Mira, Lola, Shirley, Joan and Herb.

Paul felt assured that he could find another job quite easily. He could also start his own consulting firm if need be but, he wasn't too sure about the others. In this economy, a lot of people live from payday to payday. And, today's wealth cannot be measured by curb appeal. You have to be inside that suburban mansion to know who is eating tube steak and who is not.

After Lola and he had given each other a harmless hug, they exchanged news briefs about his field work and bits of office gossip. Not much had been going on at PESO according to her brief summary. In fact, she intimated that the office was a pretty dull place without Paul's presence. Finally, after listening to her female chatter for entirely too long, he asked the critical question, "Are we good to start or have you finished all of the film editing?"

Lola gave him a beautiful smile and proudly said, "All done my mighty one. I am anxious to see which version you want to see first, the abridged or the full-length copy." Paul said, let's have some of Redenbacher's best gourmet popping corn while we watch both of those two presentations, okay?" So, for most of the evening, they watched both of her two DVD's over and over again. After that lengthy screening review was finished they both talked and arrived at the same opinion.

One DVD was too short and the other was too long. And, as any Hollywood mogul might say, "It's almost where it needs to be but, we are not there just yet." Paul looked at Lola Bryce and said, "You are a pretty good actress, young lady." Before she could answer, he added, "That Governor really surprises me. For an older guy, he has lots of stamina, doesn't he? And, that large plaything of his, wow! How in the world did you and Mira manage to deep-throat that monster?"

She answered, "That's why it hurts women so much, honey. I don't know about Mira but, I was a country girl who practiced on large cucumbers and long sausages. That is why I can give head better than anyone else. Paul, would you like to have some of my face-fucking before we retire for the evening?"

Gray quickly answered, "No thanks, dear Lola. I am too tired now but, I would like to have a rain check." She asked, "In the morning, then?" He replied, "Not for several days, Sweetie. I had too much sex when I was down there in the mountains so I now need some additional time to replenish my low sperm count.

Next, they went to bed on Paul's Marilyn Monroe bed sheets and, the image of Marilyn had no objection to their presence. It was a threesome that only Miss Monroe could approve of but, before you could say 'Booker T. Washington, they were both fast asleep.

Next morning, Lola and Paul were enjoying Danish pastries and coffee at Starbucks before reporting to work at PESO. Suddenly, Paul stopped eating and he told Lola that he might be getting cold feet about their joint venture, the movie that they had just co-produced. He said, "Blackmailing a person is a serious crime that is punishable by incarceration for much more jail time than one would ever want."

She sipped her 'House Blend' coffee and replied, "I know and I have also worried about that same thing. At the end of the day, I have asked myself this one question, should we do this dirty deed? And, in my own judgment, I feel that we should proceed. Our Governor should not have threatened Mira as he did and the abuse that she took to save PESO, that took real courage and bravery. Paul, it is time to right that wrong."

Paul said, "Why don't we let Mira decide? She probably has more to lose than anyone else if this extortion scheme should backfire." And, Lola agreed but, she followed with a question, "Who is going to call her and ask that she comes to Starbucks by herself and, without any other 'tag-alongs'? Paul said, "You make the call and, when she asks what we are doing here instead of being at our office desks, tell her that we are discussing the laboratory samples from Farler."

Lola asked, "What tests?" He responded by saying, "I need you to run some activation samples to carbon date several glass shards and pieces of metallic debris. I have to know how old my specimens actually are. In other words, my Party House at Farler requires greater provenance for my authenticity calculations. Then, she called Mira for our private little meeting on neutral grounds and away from other people's ears. Afterwards, she also placed an order for Mira's favorite breakfast snacks.

When Mira arrived and, after they had both brought her up to date on the proposed expose plan, she was both pleased and pissed. She failed to get aggressive because they were in such a public place. Instead, that gracious lady thanked Paul for his exquisite overall plan. And, likewise, she thanked Lola for going that extra mile on her behalf. Then, Mira went silent and deep because she had some troubling thoughts to consider. After a few minutes of this trance-like deliberation, she wiped the little droplets of sweat from her forehead with a Kleenex tissue before saying, "I want both DVD's for my own usage.

This should be my own battle, not yours or Lola's." Paul handed the two copies over to her as she had requested. He did not tell her that he still had the originals in his apartment for his own usage, if required.

And, then, Mira came up with an excellent idea. She said, "I want cameras to be installed in my home, my office, Shirley's place and Lola's apartment. Neither you nor Paul needs to be in the pornographic and blackmail business. When our oversexed Governor returns for more action, we will acquaint him with the sword that we have hanging over his head.

Then, I will press for some increased wages and a larger budget for our next fiscal year. If he fails to meet my demands, we will proceed with this graphic expose of the dark side that our Governor possesses. Next year is an election year so he should comply with our needs and priorities if, he wants to be re-elected.

Paul, one more thing, I want you to move to another address. If you don't agree to that, then, we need to remove your cameras, paint your apartment and move your furniture around. I want a complete makeover for your place or I want you gone from that address. If the Governor does come back to examine your apartment while you are in the field, I want his highness to be confused by what he sees and, moreover, I want no evidence of any cameras being present in your apartment at any time. Move all of that spy stuff over to my office because I may need it sometime in the future."

Paul was so proud of that woman. She was willing to take the heat so that none of her employees would have to go to jail. He told her that he would gladly comply with her requests provided that, before she did anything else with those two DVD's she would keep himself and Lola informed as to what she was going to do. Surprisingly, our team leader was turning into a born-again street fighter.

After that agreement, the trio went back to work at PESO in a happy mood. Paul had two women, arm-in-arm, and all three persons were overjoyed. They had a plan and they felt protected by each other. That stroll from Starbucks to PESO wasn't very long but, on that morning, it was large, very large. They were the three musketeers who loved being with each other to fight their battles against that naughty Governor. And, loudly, they sang their favorite chant, "All for one and one for all."

Lola would begin her different analyses and Paul would read his final draft for the 'Party House Report'. He wanted to be certain that he had remembered everything that was relevant and significant. Lola would discover that the glass shards were authentic and that their physical shape confirmed that they were, as a minimum, 150-years old.

Most people don't know this but, window glass is a super-cooled liquid that, as a function of time, becomes thicker at the bottom than at the top. Real estate agents use this 'bottom versus top' thickness measurement to determine the correct age of old houses. Lola also did several metallographic examinations to prove that the nails and shutter hinges were of the same approximate age.

Therefore, the 'Party House' was declared to have the provenance that was necessary to justify a new State Park in the Farler community. He wrote his B&B girlfriend that, in about two years, she would be richer than ever before. He warned her that the Yankee tourists were coming, 'Over There, Over There'.

As Paul Gray scanned his newly acquired case file called 'Headless', he kept thinking about Ichabod Crane, Abraham Van Brunt and the lovely 18-year old maiden, Katrina Van Tassell. Katrina was the daughter of a wealthy farmer and huge land owner so she was courted by many young men. Especially, by Crane and Van Brunt who were her two favorites.

Paul loved that old story but, actually, he preferred the silent movie version best of all. One of his favorite movie actors starred in that role for a 1922 movie production. The actor's name was none other than Will Rogers, a great philosopher and a fierce political wit for that day and age.

One of his favorite quips was, "I never met a politician that I liked. They were all too busy taking bribes to spend any time with the likes of me." The Nation suffered a great loss when Will Rogers and Wiley Post died in a plane crash near Barrow, Alaska in August of 1935.

But, back to the story of the original 'Headless' in a secluded glen called Sleepy Hollow near Tarrytown, NY. As Crane leaves a party which he attended at the Van Tassell Plantation, he is pursued by a horseman who has no head! This frightened Crane so much that he left the area and was never seen again. So, poor Katrina lost her favorite lover.

Eventually, she marries Van Brunt but, not until after Ichabod is declared legally dead or relocated to some unknown and distant address.

Actually, Abraham was a person of interest for the investigation of Crane's mysterious and probable death. But, without a body or some other incriminating evidence, the matter was closed so that Katrina might have a proper wedding. For years afterward, there were hints by gossipers that Van Runt was responsible for Ichabod's demise but, nothing was ever proven.

Let us now return to the headless horse rider that roams the countryside near Krypton, KY. Krypton is a famous landmark for another reason. It is the birthplace of Elvin C. Feltner, a well-known philanthropist for the Hazard Community College and Lee's College at Jackson. Elvin made his money dealing with old movies and, at one time, he held the largest collection of old films in the Nation. He had a museum in both Florida and New York. We grew up together as adjacent neighbors on Combs Street in Hazard and, I am pleased to call him an old personal friend.

Within the village of Krypton, there is a straight stretch of an abandoned roadway that travelers like to avoid. They act in that way because of the ghastly apparition that appears and disappears on wet, foggy nights. If the sky, the winds and visibility are cooperating in a favorable way, those who live in the area have frequently spoken of a headless woman who likes to ride side-saddle down that old road. She is always dressed in virgin-white linen clothing and, most people refer to her as being the 'headless bride that rides'.

She is described as being a very friendly ghost that does not try to hurt anyone. But, when she gets real close for an apparent hug or kiss, the other riders run away as fast as they can. They say that they are scared to death of what they see near her throat and neck area. They see fresh flowing blood and lots of it.

It is interesting that this ghost seems to swing both ways. She has been known to try and caress the pretty ladies or young girls, as well. And, if being a lesbian is inappropriate, then she is probably very lonely and just looking for companionship.

The PESO file included one other entry about this headless apparition. One night, when a young man was riding his horse along that particular stretch of this haunted road, his horse saw a moving ghost coming toward them. His animal panicked and he bucked his rider out of his saddle before running out of control in to the dark forest. A few days later, his horse wandered back to his barn but, his male rider companion was never found again. And, the irony for this part of the story was his name. The missing rider's name was 'Ichabod Crane'. Sometimes, history has a strange way of repeating itself, doesn't it?

Over the years, other witnesses have reported that, on damp and moon-lit nights, she would be reaching out as she approached them. But, the ghastly lady in white linen never committed any crimes so, none of the Sheriffs made any real effort to investigate the sightings any further. Of course, they would document the complaint but, that was about the extent of their involvement.

For some strange reason, each observer, except Ichabod, was able to out-distance her and that ghoulish appearance. Paul concluded that, because everyone was able to easily escape from her grasps, she may have been in a protective mode, not an attacking one. But, who was she protecting and why was she defending someone or something? Perhaps, it was Ichabod Crane that she was shielding, who knows?

Everyone who saw this weird specter coming at them confirmed that her arms and hands were always extended outward and toward the viewer as if the headless woman was seeking repentance, confession, satisfaction and, perhaps, absolution.

In the archives section of the Perry County Courthouse, Gray did find some mention of an unsolved crime where a woman's body was found in the vicinity but, her head was missing and it was never located. Unfortunately, no one will ever know who killed her and, subsequently, removed her head. Paul wondered if the headless woman was none other than Katrina Van Brunt? That would be a stretch of the imagination but, it would surely enhance the storyline if a new State Park was ever built in Krypton, KY.

For about two miles, this old road runs parallel with a nearby stream where wet ground, clearing skies, light winds and poor visibility serves to confuse the minds of different observers. In other words, an affinity diagram for such apparitions is entirely favorable for such sightings. If, you are not a student of paranormal science, think of it in this manner:

> *If one happens to be here alone*
> *When it is late at night.*
> *If the fog rises from the water,*
> *And, a breeze stirs the fog*
> *Into grotesque shapes,*
> *Almost anything can be*
> *Seen or imagined.*
> *Paul Gray 2012*

Paul wrote in his notes that if you have a weak heart, stay away from Krypton, KY. It is hardly worth the risk to expire in such a manner. And, in today's world, you need to avoid the expense of an expensive funeral for as long as you can. Gray does have a conscience so, heed my warnings, the search for Kryptonite isn't worth becoming another casualty.

From a financial aspect, this story about a headless woman is a slam dunk for a new State Park and additional income for the Governor's private treasure chest. He was so confident about its chances of success, he recommended that Shirley and Herb should begin their construction surveys and make appropriate engineering drawings as soon as possible.

The success or failure of a new State Park is like that for an Italian restaurant; location, location and location. But, Herb was famous for 'making a silk purse out of a sow's ear'. This is to say that, when those two finish with their architectural design, it will be a fabulous place to visit and enjoy.

Paul was grateful that he wouldn't have to visit Krypton again. Poor Paul was growing tired of seeing just trees, trees and more trees. He considered calling Elvin Feltner to tell him about the windfall of new money for his old birthplace area. But, he hesitated to make that call. If he did leak information about this new project in Elvin's back yard, Feltner would surely want his name to be enshrined on the Park's entrance way in large chromium plated letters, something simple yet, still conspicuously flagrant.

Elvin was too proud of his being the only known multi-millionaire from his birth place of Krypton. And, when he looked into the mirror, he liked what he saw entirely too much. However, I am very proud of Elvin and what he has accomplished with his life.

Now that Paul's part in the 'Headless Woman' case was finished, he would head toward Lexington and the comfort of his Marilyn Monroe bedding for some much needed rest and relaxation. He was tired and he was expected back at work tomorrow. No more breakfast meals at 1100-hours in the day as he had been accustomed to with his red haired owner of the Farler B&B. God, how he already misses that lovely chambermaid.

And, tomorrow is the target date for placing both sound and sight devices in Mira's office and in her bedroom where she lives. After that work was finished on her house, he had the nasty task of moving all of his stuff from his existing apartment to an older home on Clay Avenue, far removed from where his current apartment is located.

Mira wanted him to be protected from any of the Governor's revenge, if possible. And, she felt that way strong enough to personally undertake the redecoration of Paul's house interiors on Clay Avenue. She would take care of the flowers and the interiors but, he had to cut the grass. Oh, how he hated to cut the grass.

This would require about two weeks of very boring work. But, when it was all finished, he would have three bedrooms and two bathrooms. Imagine what he could do with a 3-2-2 playhouse! On that note, he went to sleep dreaming about his new place and its different possibilities for all of his female friends.

All night, he would be disturbed by a different and recurring dream. His house would be a Coliseum of immense proportions and one that contained many different doors. Behind all of the doors, save one, beautiful red heads of all sizes and types were confined. Behind that one other door was a man-eating lion. He was forced to choose only one door but, as he began to make his selection, he would wake up and never know the ending for his dream. It was a night to forever forget.

With everyone's participation and hard work, the blackmailing systems were installed and tested in less than four days. Only an expert technologist could detect that the system was online and awaiting its first victim, the wayward Governor.

The fact that the Farler Lady had drained his pipes so clean was now ancient history which meant that Paul Gray was free to roam again. He was armed with new sperm and he was hunting for any young woman who would allow that to happen. Furthermore, Paul felt that it was the responsibility of the Fayette County Police to erect appropriate warning signs. As a minimum, he expected 'appropriate' to read as follows:

> *Warning Ladies, A great lover is on the loose.*
> *He is well endowed and dangerous.*
> *Continue at your own risk.*
> *We are not responsible for any of his activities.*

So, without those warning signs, he felt that he was free to roam and, roam he did. His first stop was at Coffee Tree, KY to visit with his old friend, the Warden whom he called his own bronze beauty and, his personal icon for horizontal integration.

But, Mira had the final say on any extensive travel plans of his own creation. She wanted him to return to Krypton because Herb and Shirley had turned the new Park Project into a Shangrila-type that they could ill afford. Their plan was truly beautiful and quite exotic but, nonetheless, too expensive.

Paul called Elvin Feltner and they made an appointment to meet in Krypton to view Herb's drawings for the proposed park. Elvin liked the plans so much that he gave Gray a blank check to cover all expenses for the new 'Elvin C. Feltner Memorial State Park'. Elvin was just being Elvin again but the PESO Staff and the Governor were about to become absolutely speechless.

While he was gone to Krypton for that second visit to meet with Elvin, Mira was already working on the interior decorations of his new address on Clay Avenue. Previously, he had left these explicit instructions:

- I want three of the largest king-sized beds that are available for purchase.
- I want Marilyn Monroe bedding on every bed.
- I want three showers to be installed.
- I want no pink colors in my house anywhere.

Mira said, "Leave the decorating to us. It badly deserves a woman's touch and, between all four of us ladies, we will transform your new domicile into a place to admire and enjoy. Don't worry, Paul. Both Joan and I will be sleeping there with you, occasionally, and we will do a great job. You will like the way that it looks and I guarantee it."

She had a request of her own to make. I figured that it would be bootleg whisky but, it wasn't. She wanted me to bring her and her Staff some Kryptonite, a well-known aphrodisiac. She said, "Because of the frequency for my team members to copulate, each of us might need some of that stuff in the very near future.

Buy double doses for old Herb as Shirley has already requested." I told Mira that this would not be a problem so I agreed to make another brief visit to Krypton. However, I knew the real reason why she wanted me out of town. The ladies were not yet finished with the renovation of my house and they wanted to surprise me with what they had done. Women are that way, aren't they?

I met Elvin's Chief Manager at his Kryptonite mine and, I made a huge purchase for no cost at all. The Manager's name was Larry Rice who told me that Elvin had left specific instructions, "Give that man all of the Kryptonite that he wants at no cost. He is a good friend of mine. Then, I understood the reason for his massive fortune. He was the world's leading supplier of Kryptonite which was far superior to Spanish Fly or Viagra. Buying and selling old movies were just a pleasant hobby for Elvin.

Actually, Paul didn't mind being a courier for Kryptonite. He knew exactly where a lovely B&B operation existed. And, he looked forward to getting his pipes cleaned by an expert on intercourse. But, don't ever tell Mira that I said that, please don't. She has an inordinate fear of both competition and commitment as most unmarried red heads do. He stayed at Farler for another week until his pipes went dry again. Then, he motored to Lexington and his old apartment while he awaited his right to visit his renovated home on Clay Avenue. And, he knew that there would be a lot of pink colors on many of the walls. Tell a red head 'not to' and she 'will' anyway, won't she?

Chapter Fourteen

WIFE

ONE OF THE most common paranormal sightings in all of Kentucky involves the two subjects of man and woman as husband and wife, each or both. In either case, they are sighted for one of two important reasons.

They congregate at their specific haunting site to be near their former loved one or to follow through with their own special revenge.

Paul Gray was enjoying a preliminary reading of his latest assignment about numerous milk maid sightings in a place called Thousand Sticks, KY in Leslie County. Her legal name was Mrs. Adele Taylor and she was married to a bad man named Charles Evans Taylor who abused her on a regular basis.

Adele was a very hard worker who spent most of her time in the fields as a crop tender, at the barns taking care of the dairy cattle and keeping the large old house where they lived in an immaculate condition.

All of these tasks, she did by herself because that lousy husband of hers wouldn't lift a finger to help her.

Charley was an irresponsible misfit who spent most of his daytime hours drinking too much moonshine, doing a few odd jobs, a lot of fishing, and knife trading on the Courthouse steps. In brief, husband

Taylor was not worth spit when it came to performing hard work in the bright sun or helping Adele to milking of the cows.

Neighborhood gossip spread the word that Charley had several affairs with other women. When Adele brought up the business of these other women, Charley would always hit her on the head with an iron skillet. After a few more lumps on the head, the subject of 'other lovers' became an unmentionable topic for poor Adele to talk about. She would just try to overlook something that was absolutely detestable to her upbringing and her marriage contract.

However, she refused to leave that bastardly husband of hers and all day long, she would whisper to herself, "For better or worse." She did this even though the iron skillet abuse was increased by a manifold amount. Finally, after one too many bumps on her head, she died.

That last lump involved a powerful right cross to her left temple which badly compressed her brain such that she passed out and died from a massive blood loss and irreparable brain damage. Charles Taylor was not a nice man. He was an assumed murderer and nothing more. But, somehow, he was able to convince the local sheriff that Adele had fallen down the stairs. However, Charley did remarry within two weeks after Adele's burial somewhere on the Taylor farm.

Soon after her death and his hasty marriage to one of those 'other' women, people began to report sightings of strange happenings on the dairy farm. Two farm workers swore that they saw the former Mrs. Taylor walking around the barn carrying an empty milk pail.

People that were passing the farm began to notice strange sounds and, occasionally, they would see a ghost-like figure. On one evening, his second wife said that she could hear the sounds of gravel pebbles being thrown on the metal roof of her 'recently-acquired' home.

On other nights, Charley could hear someone stoking the fire in the cooking stove of the kitchen and making much noise with the pots and pans. When he would get off his lazy ass to investigate, there would be no living person visible but, he could see an image of Adele walking through the closed door frame without opening the door itself.

That vision would continue to go into the outside darkness where it would suddenly disappear. Other people reported that they could hear the sound of milk pails being moved around in the barn that stood closest to the road. Charley and the first Mrs. Taylor would provide a sufficient love-hate relationship that was a likely candidate for the development of a new State Park.

Gray was elated about the prospect of these multiple sightings as being a justifiable argument for grabbing that tourist money. He would leave that decision with Mira and the Governor because, for the present, he was banished to Leslie County for more conformation services about another State Park possibility.

His police cruiser was in the garage for routine maintenance so he had to lease a small, under-powered KIA that sputtered all the way to his destination. He asked, "Why do people buy these things? These disposable cars are a sorry excuse for the 'Yankee Tank' that almost flies whenever there is a straight stretch ahead.

It has to be because these foreign cars are cheaper and Exxon-Mobil is in that loop with their mad desire to maintain $4 per gallon across the Nation. He guessed that their executive salary expenses must be getting harder to sustain. However, Paul would never purchase a KIA for another reason. His Uncle had been 'Killed In Action' during World War II. He had pleaded with the KIA people to change their name but to no avail.

Their one response letter mentioned something rude about Hiroshima and Nagasaki.

While in this part of the State, he paid his respects to his Mother for a short period of time. And, afterwards, he also visited his favorite red-haired chambermaid again but, only for one night. Then, he proceeded toward Thousand Sticks, KY to accomplish his assigned mission involving more confirmation studies. The primary issue being, is there or is there not an active paranormal event going on in your neighborhood?

He was more than anxious about this trip to this part of Leslie County. In this backwoods area, there were two family sets that were notoriously dangerous. Some travelers who have ventured into their valleys have never been seen again. So, it wasn't just anxiety, it was also a deep fear of the people who lived there.

One group involved the Combs Family whose skin had turned blue because of too much intermarriage. If they didn't take a liking to you, you were destined for a quick death. It was just a matter of time before someone would squeeze a trigger or use a hunting knife.

And, the other group was the Campbell Clan. They made famous homebrew whiskey so, visitors were forced to buy some, whether they needed it or not. It is rumored in Hazard Town that this is the area where non-drinkers disappear from the face of the Earth never to be seen again by anyone.

But, before Paul ever entered the valley occupied by the Campbell's, he had already decided to purchase several quarts of their good stuff. And, he would make no jokes about wood alcohol because that's what they fed to the non-drinkers who, in some way, had pissed them off. In case, you don't know about methanol or wood alcohol, it is a poisonous liquid to drink. As little as 10-ml can cause blindness and 60-100 ml can cause a painful death unless it is quickly treated by a medical specialist.

Accordingly, moonshining is not an exact science. If the maker of white lightening makes a just few crucial mistakes, then the product can be methanol, not ethanol. One is a mood relaxer while the other is a killer. Out of all this comes a helpful warning, 'know your moonshiner' and, 'don't buy your stuff from a stranger.'

Needless to say, Paul approached both families with guarded caution and much respect. One wrong word and he would become history. Because he needed the approval of both clans for a new State Park in the area, he was forced to continue.

To the elders of both families he said, "The State of Kentucky is considering the possibility of building a new State Park in this area. I am here today to see how you feel about that. I also need to know if you have seen any ghosts in the region. What we do is to tame the ghosts and harness them for presentation to tourists by the carloads. How say you?"

Elder Combs was the first to speak when he said, "I would be inclined to favor it because of our 'blue-skin' issue. We badly need to stop marrying each other. Instead, we need to bring some eligible boys and girls into these hills and that's for certain.

I am so sick and tired of shopping over at Hazard with people staring at the color of my skin. Hell fire, I didn't do this to myself. This is our lot as a result of what our ancestors did. They are to blame, not us." Then, he yielded the floor to his neighboring family, Mr. Campbell.

Elder Campbell angrily said, "We are vehemently opposed to the building of any State Park in this region. All it would do would be to bring more Treasury agents upon us and they would destroy our property and our stills. Our life as we know it would never be the same.

Cautiously, I made this one point. "It would be good for your business, Mr. Campbell. More customers do represent more sales of your good stuff." He replied, "I know that, young fellow. But, look at it as I see it. We are already running at top speed and fermentation is a process that cannot be rushed. It's something that even God can't accelerate. In a word, that process takes one important ingredient and that is 'time'."

Paul tried to insert a new angle. He asked, "If we were to build a new park in your back yard, would you change your opinions if the Governor gave you a large share of the cash money that is thereby generated?" In this matter, both Combs and Campbell were of the same opinion.

They each said something like the following, "Hell no, and who can trust a Governor? Certainly, not we hill people. That SOB from Frankfort and the people that have preceded him in office have been trying to make us pay property taxes for many long years. That problem goes back to the Revolutionary War when our ancestors first settled this land. We were here before any Tax Collector ever took office. We want nothing to do with the likes of his highness and the people from his Palace."

Sadly, Paul said, "Well, that's two negatives against one positive. I guess that I will just have to go back to Lexington and report to my boss that the good folks of this area are against any State Park project. Before I leave these parts, I wonder if I could buy some of 'Campbell's finest". It smells too good to leave it here in an aging barrel."

The senior Campbell smiled and said, "Of course, my son. I'll be happy to help you. How many bottles will you be having, today?" I told him, "Twelve quarts in a stout box." He pointed to one of his kind and that boy went running with a big grin on his face. Making a good sale was a very important thing for the working men of his clan. And, it should be sufficient to get me out of this valley alive.

Then, Mr. Combs asked Paul if he would spend the night with the Combs family. Before, Paul could say anything, he added, "My wife is the best cook that I have ever known, please stay. I was aware of how mean these blue Combs's could be if they got their dander up but, I was also hungry for a home-cooked meal so, I said, "Thank you, I would be happy to join you and your wife.

She made steak and potatoes with poke salad and garden greens, a favorite of the hill people. And, dessert was home-churned ice cream. So, it was a meal to remember. He kissed her on her forehead and thanked her for that fine meal before leaving the dining room table as full as a tick.

He asked this question: "Mr. Combs, No other person has ever invited me to dinner and asked me to spend the night. I am truly impressed and surprised. I just don't understand how you can tolerate a guest who works for the Governor. So, why are you being so nice to me?

The patriarch of the Combs family replied, "We need fresh sperm to be injected into our young women in order to stop this damned blue skinned business. You can stay all night if you promise to try and impregnate all of the women that you can handle, okay?"

Paul grinned from ear to ear and said, "As long as I can do my own impregnating, we have a deal, Mr. Combs. Bring on the blue, one at a time and no virgins, all right? He knew that, once again, his pipes would be empty but, he didn't care. If that's what the Elder wants, then that's what he gets.

Before the first girl arrived, he wondered, "What does a blue pussy look like up close?" He and his tongue were about to found out as the first naked girl entered his bedroom. She was gorgeous beyond all dreams, a mountain girl of Cherokee extraction with dark black hair and a perfectly proportioned body. The blue skin was an added attraction for Gray. Paul said, If the rest of them look like this one, it's going to be one hard night. Tough work but, somebody has got to step up and do what must be done for the Combs's.

That second woman was also magnificent in her beauty and appearance. She could have been a movie starlet if Hollywood scouts knew what they were doing. With them, they spend too much time on the casting couch and too little time traveling.

If they had seen this woman, they would have stopped looking for any others. Obviously, Paul felt highly privileged to enter her glory hole and he worked doubly hard to see that she had a fantastic orgasm. And, all of the broads that followed were each very attractive samples of feminine pulchritude. Gray sighed to say, "This is my Shangri La. Who could ask for anything else?"

Finally, after Gray was almost totally exhausted, he called off the procession of any more women onto his bed and he tried to take a short rest before breakfast was to be served. Then, he heard a child-like cry coming from the hallway.

He got out of bed to see what was going on. She was a 98-pounder and five-footer who was not very beautiful but, she was pleading, "Please, Mr. Gray take one more woman, take me. I want a white child more than anything else in the whole World. I know that I am not beautiful like the others girls are but, I have a good heart and plenty of grit. I want to have your baby and I will be a good mother to your child, I promise you."

Paul was immediately taken by her pleading so, he said, "Come on, we will have a go at it. What's one more, give or take a few?" Although he knew that he would be hurting after this last encounter, he continued because he liked her sincere pitch.

He just hoped that one of his sperm would impregnate one of her eggs. He also asked her what her name was and she said, "I am known as Naomi Combs, the ugly duckling." He scolded her for being so hard on herself. And, guess what? Naomi gave him better sex than any of the other women did. But, he was late for breakfast because he gave Naomi a second romping just to make certain.

The breakfast feast was also a ritual, of sorts. He was served breakfast by all of the naked women that he had served during that long night. The Elder ate breakfast with him and his first question was predictable. He asked, "Paul, how was your night?" Paul answered, "Sir, it was like nothing else that I have experienced in my entire life. No matter how long I live, I will never forget last night. Thank you for giving me the opportunity to perform."

His second question was also predictable. He asked, "Which one gave the best sex?" Paul didn't hesitate one second when he answered, "Without a doubt, that would be Miss Naomi Combs who called herself the ugly duckling." Immediately, Mr. Combs became quite angry. He said, "She wasn't on the short list and she wasn't supposed to be there.

I will have to punish her for breaking my rules. We wanted you to have nothing but the most beautiful women of all our families."

Quickly, Paul came to Naomi's rescue to say, "Please don't punish her because she doesn't deserve such treatment. She should be honored for being the best sex companion of the night. I'm only guessing but, of them all, she will be the only one that delivers twins."

Mr. Combs promised not to punish her and he added, "I am proud to tell you that, when we have done this before, we have never had so many waitresses. The tradition is that whomever had sex with you last night would also have to serve you nakedly while you try to enjoy your breakfast."

Paul, said, "If that be true, where is my darling little Naomi?" Combs sent a young courier on a mission to find Naomi so that she could be a part of this procession around that dining table. When she came, she had to disrobe before serving me a date cookie to enjoy while I had my coffee. And, as she circled around the table, I gave her a loving smack on her beautiful buns. Mr. Combs smiled because he could tell that I liked her best.

Then, Mr. Combs said, "You hold the record of handling fifteen different women in one night. If I were you, I would call myself the absolute 'King of the Mountains'. Thank you so much and, you will always be welcome to do this again whenever you are in the neighborhood. Goodbye Paul Gray and thank you for your service. Gray actually hated to leave but, when he gave the girls a look in the rear view mirror, only Naomi blew him a goodbye kiss.

On the way back to Lexington in his toy car from the Pacific Rim, Paul dwelt on the previous evening and hardly anything else. In fact, he thought about Naomi and her associates too much because he almost had serious trouble avoiding other cars and three collisions. He noted that all three collisions involved young drivers and foreign cars. He swore that he would never do this again. No more rental vehicles, not ever. He would wait for his 'Yankee Tank' to finish its maintenance cycle before leaving Lexington.

When he did get home to Lexington, he gave thanks for two blessings, his safe arrival and his assignment. He said, "God, I sure do love this job. Please don't ever take it away." Then, he reported in to both Lola and Mira that he had arrived safely. Each of them wanted to spend the night but, he begged off saying that he was too tired to entertain any female company. With the plumbing job that was done by fifteen women, he didn't want to try anymore trysts until his sperm count could be restored to a higher level. After all, blood in the sperm is not very attractive to most women.

Instead, he chose to put the final touches to his Report about his visit to the Smith and the Campbell properties. He had to gently inform the Governor that he was not welcome in that part of Leslie County and, if a State Park was forced upon on the locals, their response would be a terrible rebellion.

Elder Campbell said it best and Paul quoted his words verbatim, "We have been buying up ammunition and stockpiling our bullets since the end of World War II and we are capable of defending ourselves very well. We have caves and bomb shelters to hide in so any uninvited guests will be disposed of in short order."

He also added, "We have a terrorist cell in Frankfort just in case we need to attack the Governor's Palace. You tell him to leave us be. The Campbell's and the Comb's are two tough bunches and we are plenty mean enough for that dirty bastard and his pitiful little army of Kentucky Colonels that run the State Militia.

Paul could hardly wait until his summary comments were forwarded through Mira to her almighty supervisor, our despicable Governor. And, in a way, it was a shame that Paul was stopped dead in his tracks toward proceeding with a State Park at Thousand Sticks, KY. Naomi had told him, in confidence, that there were plenty of ghosts in her area. For many long years, unwanted visitors had been killed and buried in a common grave somewhere on the Campbell property. Naomi was afraid to talk about it and she was terrified of going anywhere near those ghastly sounds. So, be it best for Naomi that our secret remains ours and ours alone.

One thing that was starting to bother Paul was his unfinished dwelling in Lexington. Why was it taking so long? Will he be forever exiled in Eastern Kentucky for long periods of time? At this point, it wasn't a big deal because all he was doing was developing new 'swimmers' for someone's eggs to grab.

Chapter Fifteen

CANDLE

GRAY WAS ALONE and he was thinking about his Father who worked as a laborer for 48 long years on the L&N Railroad. Paul admired the man greatly so, he had many regrets that he died too early at 74 years of age. He wanted his Dad to be available for a much longer period of time. He still had his Mother but that was not the same. A son mourns his best buddy always and nothing will ever change that special bond.

One of the things that he and I had in common was the love of lighting. Dad's early childhood was filled with memories of coal oil lanterns of the same type that Abraham Lincoln read by at night. When electricity finally became available to we hill folk, he was one of the happiest men in our entire County. He raved about "No more kerosene to be purchased and no more fires to be caused by those unsightly and unsafe lanterns."

But, to Paul Gray, they were anything but unsightly. He learned his ABC's using them and he felt as great as old Abe did with his similar achievements. His Mother made him read short stories and children's books every night so, he came to believe that his early successes in life were a result of reading just as Lincoln did. I stopped wanting to be like Lincoln when a politician picked my pocket on Main Street one day.

The next stage for my loving all things associated with lighting was probably the lanterns that railroad men carried and used on the job. I would sit on my front porch and watch them wave their lanterns high in all directions to send secret signals from the caboose at the rear to the locomotive up front. In some cases, the line from front to rear was quite lengthy.

I have seen loaded coal cars in Hazard that stretched for over a mile from Bluegrass Hollow to the L&N Coal Tower. I was too young to understand the code for all signals but I learned what I did know by association or identification. For example, the signal for 'break' forced most men to open their dinner pail. Nobody ever called me a dumb kid.

What followed was an innate love for beacons and signals, in general.

The highway signals which warned us that a car wreck was ahead, the searchlights that were looking for Nazi bombers in the sky, the rotating lights on our tallest buildings, the spot lamps on our police cars, the gigging lamps for hunting frogs, the lighthouses that warned ship captains about a rock filled coastline, et cetera.

So, when Paul was reading his next Case File about candles, he was reminded of all the old memories concerning lighting of all types and sizes. Paul felt very fortunate to have been born during an era where lighting and non-flammable torches became commonplace for ordinary citizens.

However, Paul was always interested in sirens of another kind. That red headed boss of his and the chambermaid at Farler, KY were beacons that were ever beckoning to him saying, "Come hither, come. He did, whenever his sperm count was high enough and, if he was in the mood.

After those pleasant thoughts went 'slip-sliding away', he turned toward serious business once again. He had been exiled to the 1000-sticks area for too long. And, he was hesitant about any more 'tip-toeing' among the blue-skinned Combs's or that Scottish clan of the feared Campbell's. In either case, you had to be extremely careful of every word that you chose to use.

When he did get out of those mountains safely, he gave his thanks to the Lord above for a successful escape from those attractive blue women and the tough moonshiners who lived next door. In all seriousness, he vowed to never again visit those two families. It is very hard work to create a baby when the woman is just going through the motions and nothing more. For the 'fifteen minus one' women, they were just taking orders from the Combs Headquarters. It was something that the Elder wanted, not what they wanted.

However, where Naomi was concerned, it was the one thing that she wanted more than anything else in the whole World. In other words, Naomi was passionate while the others were totally without passion. Clogged pipes are one problem but, totally drained-out pipes create another difficulty. The latter seriously harms the male ego. He would rather be armed for all occasions and ready for all attractive opportunities that could present themselves. In other words, he didn't like to say no to the office women of PESO.

After perusing his new case file which was about flickering candles, he decided to give 'candles' a rest for a little while. Instead, he wanted to know more about the current status of the scheme to scam the Governor. In essence, he was curious to know if his highness had taken the bait and, if so, how he had reacted to being raped by Lola. Paul wanted to know more details about the 'hook, line and sinker' event.

He arranged to meet Mira at Starbucks next morning where they could discuss such results privately without the other PESO employees hearing things that they didn't need to hear. Paul and Mira were interested in protecting Herb, Shirley, Lola and Joan for as long as possible.

When Paul broached that subject to Mira at their breakfast meeting, she just smiled and said, "Mission accomplished. All of the details are still unknown but, the First Lady of Kentucky has her husband housebound at this time. Our 'insider' at the Palace says that Governor is firmly shackled to his bed post while his wife force feeds him doses of 'Caster Oil. She said, he badly needs a cleansing and, he's getting a pretty good one.

At this time, the Lieutenant Governor is taking care of all State business. The Governor can't phone anyone or go anywhere until she decides how long his punishment is going to continue." Paul said, "Wow, I don't envy our Governor at all. Back in my Mother's time, a Castor Oil cleansing was the discomfort of the day for children who had been misbehaving. I can't remember when I received my last 'laxative-punishment' treatment but, I will never forget it. I was miserable for several days."

Paul continued, "It sounds as if the First Lady of KY might have an official announcement about their pending divorce almost any day now."

Mira interrupted to say, "Oh, I don't know about that Paul. Chances are that she has him shackled just to demonstrate who the real boss is and what he hasn't been getting from her.

I can easily envision KY's First Lady parading around the Governor's bed being stark naked while holding a bottle of that wicked laxative in her hands. That would be double punishment for a man with his high libido rating. If this 'bondage-laxative' thing works and those two get cozy again, we could be in serious trouble.

We figured her for a divorce proceeding but, we didn't count on her getting into bondage. If she becomes the First Lady, through and through, she could annihilate PESO completely. We have to think of something 'large' against her and we have to do it quickly. Put that dirty mind of yours to work, Paul. We need something sensational and we needed it yesterday."

Paul said, "The only thing that comes to mind quickly is that you could invite the First Lady over to PESO for a tour of our facilities and our modernistic forensic laboratory. Give Lola a day off because she might recognize Lola from the Governor's naughty pictures. After the tour is over, you and Joan could execute a female threesome party where she gets raped by two other females in your PESO office where photographic evidence can be documented by our hidden cameras. And, history is repeated for a second time, if you get my meaning.

The rest of us will be on field assignments while you and Joan play with Mrs. Governor. Later, we will send that final film cut to our friendly contact who works inside the Palace, insisting that she gives that CD to only his honor and to no one else. Next, we set back and watch for any evidence of the feud or fallout that will surely erupt."

Mira said, "Paul, what a wonderful one-way mind that you have. She is now holding Lola's film against her husband. And, if this plan of yours does work, hubby can hold this latest film against his wife. That stand-off should end all bickering between that pair. At least, the playing field will be leveled. And, the beauty of this plan is that I don't see how it could harm any employees at PESO. Let's set the plan in motion, shall we?" Paul responded, "Call me, if you need my help because I would sure like to screw that First Lady. She's related by marriage to a man that I despise."

Early next morning, Paul drove across town to visit the Lexington Genealogical Institute. He needed to examine pages of the 1862 Census Records so that he could trace the survivors of one Luther Muncy. He didn't look forward to this phase of the investigation because staring at microfiche records for several hours is not exactly exciting. But, it has to be done if you are trying to locate a specific person based upon their lineage information. He was searching for a descendant by the name of John Russell Muncy.

It didn't take too long to find him. John Russell Muncy, an octogenarian, was now living in Bardstown, KY as cited by the 2010 Census Records. Paul called the Muncies to make plans to visit with Mr. Muncy on the very next day. His intent was to evaluate the apparition of flickering candles which, according to hearsay, began with Luther Muncy several years back. He was hoping that old John Muncy might be able to fill in some important gaps for him.

He had high hopes that this particular octogenarian would be having a good day during tomorrow's visitation. Paul was not a man who could easily tolerate drooling spittle and senile dementia. His late afternoon siesta lasted throughout the entire night so, next morning, he figured that he was hungry enough to eat an entire horse. Clearly, he was famished so he stopped his car at Kelly's Restaurant where he devoured a super-large Country Breakfast.

After that large breakfast, he did feel stuffed but, several cups of caffeine-rich coffee kept him alert for the drive toward Bardstown, a city near Louisville, one that is famous for another tourist attraction called 'My Old Kentucky Home'.

As he drove toward Bardstown, he was noticed by some State Troopers who waved at him while they were hiding in the shade of some nearby trees. Paul felt sorry for them because they had to wear those hot trooper hats all day long in this hot outdoor sunshine. Paul thought that it was a shame but, Trooper rules forbade them to give any tickets unless they were fully attired in a complete uniform, including those hideous hats which he called 'cranial cookers'.

He arrived at the Muncy residence on schedule where he began his interrogation of old John Russell Muncy and his young wife,

Mary Ellen Muncy. He asked, "What can you two tell me about these candle sightings?" John Russell Muncy was a man who should have been structured as a woman where chatting is concerned. John never stopped talking the whole time that Paul was there. His comments about the candle apparition are listed as follows:

- "Along Route 15 in Clark County, there is an old Church and Cemetery that was built around 1780 or so. That Church was built using large oak logs and chiseled limestone stones.
- My ancestors, Luther and Madeline Muncy lived next door to the Church and the Cemetery. They made their living selling candles from their little cottage that was adjacent to the Church property.
- Madeline Muncy died in 1835 and she was buried in the Cemetery next door on a small knoll behind the Church.
- Luther was concerned about the thought of his beloved wife being there in the dark and all alone.
- Each night, he would take a lighted candle to the graveyard where he would place it on his wife's tombstone.
- He would talk to her and keep her company through the late evening hours.
- Luther continued this ritual until he died in 1855.

With all those years since Madeline's departure, Paul wondered if the Church and Cemetery were still there. Or, were they neglected and abandoned? As a general rule, log construction, crumbling mortar and thin sandstone markers rarely survive in the outdoor elements for more than about 150-years. And, 1835 was a long time ago, 175-years back, to be exact.

He asked John Russell this meaningful question, "When did you last visit Madeline Muncy's gravesite?" And, before he could answer that question, Mary Ellen chimed in to say, "I go there every Decoration Day and I haven't missed any since our marriage. Last May, it was in fine shape and the candle was still flickering. It gives off a beautiful glow in the late evening hours of dim moonlight."

Then, Paul asked, "John, can you take me to where the candle can still be seen? I will pay a discovery fee of $500 if you will serve as my guide. What say you, Mr. Muncy?" John said, "No, not at my advanced age. I don't get out much anymore but, Mary Ellen will be more than happy to take you there, if you want.

Mary, will you do that for your loving husband?" Paul was sitting on their couch with his legs spread apart ever so widely. She took a single glance at that large bulge of his crotch area while she said, "Of course, I will, my dear husband. We need that money for our expenses, to buy groceries and such."

As Mary and he left the house to get into Paul's Police car, she winked at him in a flirting way. She was not a day over fourteen yet, she was a raving beauty. And, while they were driving toward the location of Madeline's candle, she tried to reach over his computer and radio equipment to massage his penis which was growing in size at a faster rate.

However, the computers and related equipment prevented her from doing a very good job with that specific maneuver. Finally, he pulled over and parked so that she could have her way with his large plaything. The back seat of his Ford was not unaccustomed to such practice.

After she had finished with him, they drove several more miles until they arrived at the location of the flickering candle. Then, Paul extracted his big thick blanket out of his car's trunk area. He kept that blanket for special occasions like the present one. Then, he spread the blanket over dead leaves and soft topsoil for her comfort.

Afterwards, Mary Ellen would spread her legs and he could have his way with her beautiful body. She had several orgasms as they waited for midnight to reveal the optimum glow of that flickering candle. It was a bluish flame that was beautiful, just as Mary had promised. One could hardly take their eyes off of that mesmerizing glow. And, then they slept a few hours until Paul could inspect the candle more closely during the early morning daylight hours.

Gray discovered that the perpetual candle was a masterpiece of construction and ingenuity. Luther had built it using buried pipe that led from Madeline's tombstone to a small sinkhole about thirty yards away from the Cemetery property. He used his metal detection equipment and the odor trail to find the origin of the fuel that fed the candle. It was lighted by hydrogen sulfide gas that was emanating from the sinkhole site. H2S is a flammable, poisonous gas that has the odor of rotten eggs. It is found in many mineral waters and putrefying matter.

But, the most amazing part of this candle design was how Luther designed the barrel to ward off the oncoming wind or rain. This was a slam dunk as a historical site and a new State Park. He would refer to it as the all-natural 'eternal flame' of Clark County. Luther Muncy was a mechanical genius. Of this, there can be very little doubt.

As usual, Paul took many samples and lots of photographs of the area. He needed to pinpoint the area so that Herb could find the location by himself using his GPS coordinates and associated maps. They broke camp and headed back toward Bardstown to where Mary Ellen lived.

Along the way, Mary tried to explain why she didn't want to be remembered as a whore. Paul said, "Mary, you don't have to explain anything to me. How could any fourteen year old girl be considered as a prostitute? You are much too young to have that kind of reputation." Yet she continued to talk. She said, "Both John and I want a baby and you were nominated as the sperm donor, like it or not." And, Paul was more than happy to oblige.

He did Mary Ellen the equivalent of '15 women at 1000-sticks' so they both had a blast. In other words, they saw the flickering candle at least once while they saw each other as an entwined couple about fifteen times.

Paul was so impressed with his would-be-mother that he gave her all of the cash which he had in his possession and that was the tidy sum of almost $2000 dollars. As he gave her the gift of cash money, he said, "The baby bed is mine to buy."

As he let Mary Ellen Muncy out of his Police cruiser, he truly hated to leave his child-like lover. That was the tightest pussy that he had ever felt. His final words to her were, If my sperm doesn't take and you do not become pregnant, call me, and I will return to try and make you a mother once again. He gave her his business card before spinning his tires for Lexington which is roughly due South of Bardstown, KY.

Golly, he was so happy with his thoughts. To service any young lady is a nice thing but, this was a far better thing than he had ever done before. Mary Ellen Muncy wanted to be a Mother more than anything else on Earth.

At the time, Paul wasn't aware that he had just fertilized three healthy eggs within her womb. Later on, Mary Ellen would call him on his home phone to leave this message, "Paul, they are each boys and they look exactly like you.

Each of our three babies do have the largest penises that I have ever seen for babies of this age. When they grow up, I know what to expect. Girls for miles around will be impregnated by your offspring, like Father, like sons. Thank you for helping me to achieve my dream. I was born to be a good mother and you certainly gave good assistance with my favorite fantasy. Come up and see me some time. I would always enjoy another romp with you." When Paul did arrive at home that night, he played that wonderful news over and over again. He was now a surrogate daddy.

The 'eternal flame' of Clark County was a slam dunk for a new State Park but, its timing was more like a 'skunk-dump'. And, the reason for that was that the Governor was still in bondage. Our Palace mole said that he was extremely angry at all of the PESO people.

Gray knew that Clark County would lose this opportunity because of bad timing and the Governor's rage. Last year, it might have been a 'yes' but, this year, 'no way'. Both he and Mira decided to place the flickering candle on the back burner until after the political situation became more favorable. After the upcoming elections was a more favorable time for proceeding with the 'eternal flame' project.

Chapter Sixteen

SOLDIER

GENERAL JOHN HUNT Morgan was a Lexington celebrity that many writers have studied when they take a hard look at the Civil War campaigns and the history thereof. Morgan's greatest achievement in his War efforts for the Confederacy occurred when he penetrated farther North than any other Southern Force of the entire War.

He started that 1863 campaign in Tennessee, went through Kentucky, into Indiana and past Southern Ohio. He rode his one war horse, Black Bess, for over one thousand miles during that single campaign. Morgan was the one Calvary Officer that the Yankees feared more than all others combined. He achieved that lofty status because he was highly mobile and he was ready to pay the price for his strenuous efforts.

To my way of thinking, riding that one horse over that large distance was a monumental achievement all by itself. General Morgan was called a 'thunderbolt' by both his friends and his enemies because he would strike when no one expected it and, afterwards, he would vanish in the same manner, unexpectedly. He was a raider at heart and, a very good one. There were no others that were his equal at using the element of surprise and artful retreat.

However, hate and envy from both sides of the War were almost too much for him to bear. Rarely, was he praised or given any respect for his achievements. All he ever got from his jealous Officer 'friends' was either contempt or criticisms. His Commanding Officer despised him because he couldn't be trusted to follow orders.

If a superior officer told him not to cross a certain river, then that upstart rebel, Gen. Morgan, would surely cross the damned river. He was captured by Union soldiers three different times but, escaped twice. His final surrender occurred during a Union raid in Tennessee but, this time, he was executed because those Union soldiers were afraid that he would escape once again.

His brilliant mental skills and his talented leadership abilities were his own worst enemies at the end of his life. John Hunt Morgan's body remains now rest in the Lexington Cemetery and Paul Gray has visited that gravesite on many occasions. They were two men of a similar type and Gray much admired Morgan's tenacity.

Paul's current case involves a young Confederate soldier who served under General Morgan during a raid into Kentucky from Morgan's home base at Greenville, TN. And, that woeful tale occurred in June of 1864 near Quicksand, KY. It was here that General Morgan and his men fought a minor, short term engagement against the local Union militia and their paid mercenaries, Huns from both Germany and Poland.

An old log cabin belonging to the Cottrell Family stood at the site where this mini-battle took place. The Cottrell house was situated near Lick Branch and the North Fork of the Kentucky River. At the time of this specific skirmish, the house was occupied by both mother and daughter of the Cottrell Clan.

And, that was nice for Gray because their subsequent testimony was documented as provenance for what happened during the fighting. They watched through their plate glass windows as men in blue and gray tried to kill each other. It was both interesting and frightening while the two women were pondering, which side will win and, will a stray bullet kill one or both of us?

The blue soldiers were deployed along the other side of Lick Branch while the gray soldiers took refuge behind the Cottrell house or amongst the bamboo shoots that grew so profusely in the moist sand of the riverbank. Several soldiers on both sides were wounded but only, one was killed, a young Confederate.

Paul thought that the Cottrell papers of the Morgan Museum were a very good source for eye-witness details about the battle that occurred in their area. Daughter Miranda Cottrell wrote the following: "When the shooting started, several of the Rebels took cover behind our house. I could see the Yankees shooting at our cabin by watching them from under our curtains and out of our windows. Those old oak logs were the only thing between Mom and myself against those Union bullets. I am very grateful for the high strength and great toughness of those old logs.

She described the Yankee soldiers as being affected by two kinds of emotion, fear and hate. There was the fear of God in their stone cold eyes. They had killed before and they would kill again. At one time, they might have been innocent boys but, now they were hardened warriors who wouldn't mind killing anything or anyone. Somewhere along the way, they had lost all evidence of ever having a conscience.

After a long time, the Yanks ran out of ammunition and, then, they couldn't find their supply wagon. The wagon, its horses and the driver had been swallowed by a large pit of quicksand that was nearby. Without sufficient bullets or supplies, they hastily left the region, being very careful to avoid any apparent quicksand in their path.

Then, the Rebels buried their young casualty down by the willow trees and bamboo shoots that lined both sides of the river. We tried to find his grave but, a strong rain had removed all trace evidence and foot prints. That unknown soldier of Breathitt County became unknown for eternity.

After the rains were over, the Confederates left the area but, they took a different direction than the one which the Yanks had used. What we were left to observe on every damp night with clearing skies and light winds that offered plenty of dense fog was the dead soldier's haunting image. That soldier haunted us until we left the area and moved to a safer place. Mom had no use for such hauntings."

Paul really appreciated that old testimony about the Quicksand Battle which was written by the Cottrell daughter. It would be excellent background material if, a new State Park was approved by Mira and her boss, the Governor. It is extremely rare that documented proof is available for a haunting site. Usually, Gray had to deal with distorted facts or hearsay with little help from anything else.

In terms of additional documentation or written statements supplied by witnesses, there were four others that had something to say about the Confederate soldier and the relevant sightings. These four persons were each men of medicine; namely, Dr. Joseph Stevens, Dr. Donald Harrod, Dr. William Davis and Dr. Gerald Scott. In each case, their sightings were similar and this is the typical manner in which each of their sightings unfolded. All four incidents occurred at different times since 1863.

- The Doctor would be on a house call in the area.
- The Doctor would be approached by a Confederate Officer astride a Black Mare which he called Bess.
- The Doctor would be asked to help a wounded soldier.
- After the Doctor's examination of the body, he would say, nothing can be done for this man, he's already dead.
- The Commanding Officer would thank the Doctor for his service.
- The General would allow the Doctor to safely leave the area.

The final testimony about this event was documented by a young Union soldier who took part in the Battle of Quicksand. He recalled how well the Rebels fought and how the Yanks had lost all of their replacement ammunition because of that collapsible quagmire which swallowed a team of eight horses, a heavily loaded wagon and that poor driver. That's how Quicksand, KY got its name.

Fortunately, for PESO agent Gray the nineteen-year-old soldier of 1863 documented his account of the tragedy more than once. That young soldier died in 1944 at the age of a 100 year-old-Centurian. This was a haunting that Gray could easily sell to PESO management because there was more than enough provenance to support the constant demand for unquestionable authenticity.

Paul Gray had been staying in a Jackson Motel instead of driving back and forth to Lexington. He made that choice because Lexington and Quicksand were separated by so many miles. This time he wanted to do the assignment differently, get the story, complete the job and high tail it out of town without any return visits being mandated.

Because his Ford Cruiser had so many carbon deposits on its pistons and valves, he figured that the best way to clean those surfaces would be to set a new speed record on Interstate-65 between Winchester and Lexington. His intent was to reach 148-mph. He called his State Trooper buddies to warn them that he was coming.

He asked them to keep one lane open just for him. He pleaded that top priority was in the chase and that he had to reach Lexington before a certain hour. He said it was a matter of life or death and they believed him. So, Paul did lie a little bit, who in the hell cares? He got what he wanted, the record speed for that part of Kentucky. Otherwise, his return to Lexington was uneventful.

He was anxious to visit his favorite bed sheet 'Marilyn Monroe' once again. He needed a good rest and his best sleeping came when he was under or on top of Miss Monroe. He had received no urgent calls from Mira requesting his help but, for some unexplained reason, he felt that she needed him. Paul wanted to be close to her in case the Governor had been released from his bondage or, if the First Lady became overly upset about being raped by two PESO women.

Tomorrow, he would interview Miss Mira as to how that situation was progressing. They would meet at Starbucks over pastry and coffee which he would purchase. He wanted it that way because it made him feel as if he were on a date with a beautiful woman. It was previously arranged by telephone and he looked forward to seeing that red head again. He had a real desire to nibble on her ear lobes while they were snuggling at Starbucks. She liked it when he would use his tongue in that manner. She said, "It reminds me of Joan licking me elsewhere."

He said, "Good morning girl. You look so pretty this day. You remind me of the other redheads that I have cared for; namely, Clara Bow, Bette Davis, Greer Garson, Mitzie Gaynor, Susan Hayward, Katherine Hepburn, Deborah Kerr and Nicole Kidman." To which she would reply, "Wow, that's quite a list to live up to. I shall try to do them justice but, I doubt if I can."

Then, Paul quickly got down to business to ask, "Any word from our mole in the Governor's Palace?" She replied, "Since you have been over at Quicksand for so long, a lot has happened. Joan has turned the First Lady. She likes being a lesbian and I doubt if she will ever have sex with another man."

Paul grinned and said, "That depends on the man, dear Mira. Would you like to take a wager on whether or not I can shag the First Lady?" Mira wouldn't dignify that question with a response but, she did make another point when she said, "Paul, we may need your help because, at this time, things are not going in the direction that we planned."

"What about our nemesis, the Governor? Has he gotten out of jail yet?" "Yes, she let him loose and the first thing that he did when he was free of his shackles was that he raped our insider person and, repeatedly.

Currently, he seems to be in love with his housemaid and our snitch".

Paul interrupted to say, "That could work to our advantage. Maybe you ought to increase her stipend to keep the Governor away from you and my beautiful girlfriends here at PESO.

"Mira, this is your decision but, if it were me, I would stay away from that Palace and the Governor for as long as possible. Now is the best time to apply the silent treatment. And, let us hope that it lasts forevermore."

Then, she smiled and asked, "Which one of those Hollywood actresses do I resemble the most?"

Gray answered, "That would be Greer Garson and without any reservations whatsoever. He turned that question around and asked, How about me, Mira? Whom do I remind you of when it comes to Hollywood actors?" She smiled and said, "That would be Van Johnson, of course."

We were both pleased with our choices so, we strolled over to PESO Headquarters, hand-in-hand as lovers do. As we returned to our office, we no longer staged our entrance to be one and only one at a time. We barged in as if to say, "World, I am happy with this person and I don't give a damn about who might be watching. But, it was a mistake.

I could tell that Joan was angry at Mira. And, similarly, Lola was furious with me. It would take a lot of time to mend that glorious entrance to PESO. I decided that Mira and I would not make that mistake again. Perhaps, I should start Lola off with candy and flowers hoping that those little gifts might help to heal this little tiff.

Herb, Shirley and Lola seemed to be especially interested in my report on the Confederate Soldier. Herb gave me one his typical cockney chants by saying, "Great job, Mate." Shirley said, "I have always been a fan of General John Hunt Morgan. I have visited the Mill Street Museum several times. And, Lola said nothing because she had too many tears in her eyes to talk.

I thought that those tears might have been about me but, they weren't.

When the tears cleared and after the Kleenex had done its job, she asked, "Why is it that the good die so young?" I answered, "Lola, it has always been my opinion that young people make the best soldiers. They are afraid of nothing and no one. They try to do things that only heroes try and, in the process, some of them lose their life. God bless those young Patriots."

After Paul turned in his Final Report on the Soldier, he was handed his next assignment which was called 'Witch'. Immediately, he wondered whether the content or locale was similar to that which he had previously written for his Report about the 'Warlock' matter.

As it turned out, these two assignments were not similar at all. The 'Warlock' spirit was evaluated in the vicinity of Viper, KY and this 'Witch' assignment was examined at Somerset, KY, the County Seat of Pulaski County. The general location for Somerset is in the South Central Zone while Viper is located among the snakes of Southeastern Kentucky.

He was off to meet the 'Witch' of Pulaski County and, it was an interesting trip with lots of wide straight sections to allow him the test the temperament of the local State Troopers. They would ask, "What's a Police Cruiser with Fayette County plates doing in our back yard?

They would give chase but, before they could get their cars started, Paul was 'Gone with the Wind'. It was a futile effort to give chase when Gray had a lead of more than 130-mph. Today, Paul was running large, very large. He had people to meet, things to do and places to go. And, to top it off, Paul Gray was not a patient man. Not necessarily impatient, just unusually busy.

Chapter Seventeen

WITCH

NEAR THE CITY of Somerset, there is a unique grave site which has a sharply pointed tombstone. That shape signifies that a witch is buried there. And, all around that grave there is a tall wrought iron fence which is always kept locked to prevent any grave robbers from vandalizing the grave or its surroundings.

Because this grave contains a witch, it is isolated from the others, ordinary people are buried in the front of the church but, witches or warlocks are buried in the back field behind the Church. This was believed to be the initial start for segregation. Bus segregation would come at a much later date.

She was, apparently, banished from the rest of the Church membership forever. Her name on that pointed tombstone was badly weathered but, it could still be deciphered, especially with acids and portable micro- scopes.

Her name was Kathleen Rollins and she died on September 11th of 1899. She was a witch who had passed because of mysterious circumstances. The locals had a good story to tell about her, one that he could not afford to ignore. This is to say that, Dr. Gray needed to evaluate her death and the story's potential for becoming a new State Park. Paul was excited about bringing her story to life again because he had never done a witch before. Live ones, yes. But, dead ones, no.

He decided that he would bunk at the Day's Inn Motel in Somerset and drive to the sighting which was off new Highway 27 and near Clifty Road. Fortunately, he found a guide for only $500.00. His name was Coram Walker, a grisly-bearded old man who was better known as 'Gabby. But, as far as Paul Gray was concerned, Gabby was irreplaceable. His Walker Family line was traceable back to before 1880 when this drama about Kathleen first began.

Imagine the joy of finding someone whose family folklore included much knowledge about this particular witch. He felt as if he wanted to celebrate the discovery of Gabby Walker because having someone like him aboard would greatly support and advance the provenance factor for this entire project.

He asked Gabby to discuss what he knew about witches in general and his guide responded with more words than were warranted or necessary. But that was normal for Mr. Walker, a talker, not a listener. However, Gabby would provide excellent input for Paul's investigation.

As the first few days wore on, Paul became more knowledgeable of Gabby's lineage and his ability to state specifics that were not otherwise recorded or readily available. Gabby was also able to offer the loan of precious Walker documents that would greatly assist Paul's research. That would be his Family Bible, old diaries and a few novelettes or poems which contained numerous references about Kathleen, a.k.a. 'Katy'.

When Gabby talked about Katy Rollins, these are the salient points that he covered about her and her kind:

- Witches are not unique people. They are either evil or good.
- Witches do not heed all of the words from the wicked one down below. They have a mind of their own.
- Witches believe that both Earth and Nature are holy entities.
- A pentagram is the one symbol that all witches prefer.
- Witches can cast spells of these types; money, revenge, healing, good luck, protection, divorce, reversals, legal, pregnancies and so forth.

After that extended soliloquy, he asked Gabby, "How does one authenticate a witch?" He answered in this manner, "We have tests which we administer and some of those are cited as follows:

- More than two black moles on her skin demonstrates that she is a witch.
- Witches can float in water but innocent women cannot.
- Witches can't recite the Lord's Prayer without making a mistake.
- Witches cannot survive torture but innocent maidens can.
- Witches are intolerant to objects made of silver.
- Witches can resist men but, not warlocks.
- Witches cannot give birth to twins without one of the pair dying.
- Witches always eat their dessert before they eat their entrée.
- Witches are overly protective of their mates.
- Witches are control freaks.
- Witches think in a negative manner, not a positive one.
- Witches usually have blonde hair.
- Witches wipe their ass with the wrong hand.

"Tell me what you know about our own witch, Miss Katy Rollins."

"Yes, Sir, I will be happy to do so. Kathleen's mother died when Kathleen was born so she spent her early years living with her Father, Oscar Rollins. Katy wasn't born to be a witch so, her first twelve years were her non-witch years.

After her twelfth birthday, she began to show supernatural tendencies of the following types:

- She could read other people's minds.
- She was always correct and never wrong to the point that it was irritating to all others.
- She always ate her dessert first.
- She was overly protective of her boyfriend.
- She was negative about everything around her.
- She had blonde hair.
- She was a control freak about most everything.
- She never wore any silver jewelry.
- She could never recite the Lord's Prayer correctly.

These were traits that a normal twelve year-old-girl would not, normally possess.

It was about a year later when the neighbors stopped going by the Rollins Farm. And, subsequently, ugly talk among the hill people began to assume a threatening nature. This attitude on the part of his neighbors caused John Rollins to fear his own daughter so he left his farm, leaving Kate everything.

After John Rollins left the Somerset area, Katie spent most of her time in the outback, in the woods and along the river. She seemed to prefer dogs and cats over people because she was so lonely. It was observed by the few people who were lucky enough to experience a sighting that wild animals were not afraid of her and that Katy was aging far faster than normal. They assumed that she had placed a spell upon herself because a World with nothing but loneliness is much too harsh for anyone to bear.

As the years went by, neglect and loneliness took its toll. Katy sightings revealed a skinny, wild-eyed woman with long gray hair that was stringy, dirty and unkept. Her body odor was indescribable. She looked like an old hag who had lost her mind to senility. During the worst years of her personal suffering, strange things became commonplace; namely,

- Cows would fail to give milk.
- Chickens would not lay eggs.
- Young animals would drop dead for no apparent reason.
- Large snakes which were not normally seen in the area were abundant in large numbers.
- Huge owls could be easily caught by the local farmers when, normally, they could never be caught by anyone.
- And, pigs would refuse to eat their own slop.

After some time, the neighbors got suspicious and blamed Kathleen for all of their problems. Some superstitious hill person branded her as a witch and the neighborhood made plans to get rid of her. She would either leave the area or be burned at a stake.

One night, several hostile farmers took it upon themselves to carry out the usual punishment but, when they arrived at her house, they would discover only a twelve-year-old cadaver. She had cast another spell on herself before dying. Evidently, she wanted to be remembered as a youngster.

Kate was lying on her bed of white linen sheets and she was dressed in a new dress that nobody had ever seen before. She was wearing a white satin bridal dress. Her arms were crossed over her tiny breasts and she had been dead for several days as measured by the odor but, other than that, she was magnificent in her appearance.

The mysteries of how she had survived for all those intervening years, what caused her death, and how she had transformed herself from a deranged old lady to that of a beautiful young and glamorous girl were never solved. But, normal life did return to that little valley in the sense that eggs and milk were, once again, abundant. Pigs ate their slop and large snakes were no longer in evidence, et cetera.

Because of both superstition and fear, the people of that little Church would not allow Kathleen to be buried in the Church Cemetery. Instead, Katy was buried behind the Church about 100-yards away from the building. It appeared that they wanted her out of both sight and mind in the back field that was dedicated for witches and warlocks, only.

Some of the richest church members chipped in with enough money to pay for that sharply-pointed tombstone and the wrought iron fence. And, they also planted a young oak tree. They maintained that no twelve year-old-girl should be treated otherwise.

In the end, Katie got the respect that she failed to receive when she was alive. Actually, they had Katy's property condemned, sold her farm and paid for those burial expenses out of the profits from that transaction. They were not very good at philanthropic acts. They were thieves who had a conscience.

That young oak tree began to grow rapidly after Kathleen's burial. Now, there is a large limb of that giant oak that droops downward to almost touch the grave of Kathleen Rollins. Is that oak tree growth and its subsequent limb migration trying to reach out for someone who loved all growing plants and every tree of the forest?

If we could speak to her spirit down below, then we would know. If we could understand the wind as it winds its way through all that uncut grass by her fence; then we would know. If we could ride a sun ray into her long gone heart, then we would know. In any case, her story and her life make a good combination worthy of any storyteller's interest."

Paul paused for a moment before saying, "Gabby, that was a good story. You sure missed your calling. You should have been a writer or a storyteller. Promptly, he replied, "Never did I go to school, not one day in my whole life. I can't write my name. But, I can make my own way. The merchants of Somerset have adopted me and my chief activity is to beg.

I give them a few dance steps and they buy me hamburgers. It's a wonderful life.

Gray changed the subject when he said, "Gabby, tell me what I need to know about Somerset or Pulaski County. I have never passed this way so my unwritten report needs some help from you." He replied, "We are like any other small town. Which version do you want to hear about, the good, the bad or the ugly?" Paul said, "Your choice. I just love to hear you talk." So, he danced a few fancy steps before launching his artistic performance about his home place. These are the highlights that Gabby said to me.

- "We have electricity and the greatest invention that mankind has ever known. We have indoor plumbing.
- We were settled in 1798 by a family from New Jersey. But, don't tell anyone that I told you that.
- We have one of the largest man-made lakes in the World. Accordingly, we have more 'love boats' than any other KY lake.
- We get almost two-million tourists each year and that's when I eat steak instead of hamburgers. I dance for money whenever it's prime time for fishing, mostly on the weekends in the summertime.
- Just eight miles west of here, a famous Civil War battle was fought at Mill Springs, KY but, nobody can tell me who won that fight.
- If you need water, come to Somerset. We have two trillion gallons of that stuff and that flushes a lot of toilets.
- We don't have any coal but we do have the longest strip of continuous business houses, excluding Lexington or Louisville. We call it our 'strip' after what it reminds us of, that being Las Vegas, NV.
- And, for you Yankees, we are 95% white people. So, if you are black and want to be noticed, this is where you need to be."

"Gabby, that was a fine presentation about Pulaski County but, I want to give you a good tip. I don't think that you ought to say too much about that last statement. There is a lot of Afro-American people who might object to such lingo." He looked at me and grinned before saying, "I am an old man of almost ninety years of age. If I go tomorrow or the next day, it doesn't matter. Life is too short for horseshit arguments over blackness or whiteness. What really counts is the spirit that roams inside of our body.

And, another thing, I try to tell the truth so that I don't have to remember what I said to whom. Good, bad and different, that's me. At the end of the day, I am just an oblivious spectator for the parades that most people follow. I might watch or listen to their music but I won't participate. I've got more important things to do. For example, right now, I have the urge to whittle on a piece of soft cedar. It beats doing drugs or drinking too much."

"Well said, Gabby. There are a lot of people that need to hear your views on life. Especially, those people who are hooked on prescription drugs. That terrible addiction is threatening our very existence in these here mountains and that's for certain. We need to get tougher on how prescriptions are written and processed.

Give me a hand with my gear and we'll go visit with your ghost lady. The weather tonight is supposed to be ideal for a good sighting." I asked him what he knew about the Clifty area and he talked all of the way there.

He reminded me of Gabby Hayes, the cowboy movie star from the 1930's and 1940's and he even had some of Hayes's mannerisms.

When we got there, Gray took samples for Lola to examine and he positioned his cameras for the evening's guest while Gabby continued to speak about what his ancestors had said about this place. For example, he said, "This big oak tree attracts more lightning strikes that any other tree in the neighborhood. But, for some unknown reason, that pointed tombstone serves as a lightning rod to stave off any fire that would ravage the Church that Kate loved so well.

Then, he talked about the weather and what we both might expect for tonight's entertainment. He started with the fog. "Sometimes, it's so dense out here that you can't see your feet when you try to walk. Fog serves as a medium for Kathleen to make her grand appearance. The moonlight helps with the contrast and, if there are light winds to give her some assistance, she will materialize. It's a beautiful sight to watch pieces of her to come together. It sounds like snap, crackle and pop.

In my lifetime, I have danced with the ghost of Miss Rollins on many occasions. She is a good dance partner but, she always insists on leading with the dance steps. I love the way that she smiles at me, sort of special like. Needless to say, I come here a lot and I think that we qualify as spiritual lovers. My last will and testament states that I am to be buried by her side so that we can be close for all eternity."

Gray interrupted to ask, "I hope that you recorded all of that on my voice recorder. You did, didn't you?" Gabby looked puzzled as he replied, "If you mean this little gadget with the flashing red light, Yes Sir, I did."

"Gabby, this has been a very good day and I have placed all of my cameras exactly as you have instructed. The dance floor is cleared of all obstacles so let's hope for a productive evening where I will have the honor of making film history.

A ghost dancing with a live person as documented on my camera film. I feel so fortunate to be a part of all this. But, if she will dance with me, I will have to take the lead since that's the only way that I can dance and, please warn Katy that I am not a very good dancer." Afterwards, they both waited until they could hear the snap, crackle and pop sounds.

After that, the dance party began.

Chapter Eighteen

SISTER

PAUL GRAY WAS extremely happy to expound to anyone that would listen about what it was like to dance with a ghost. The PESO personnel had heard several versions of his 'Dancing in the Fog' story and, that was the case, before Lola had the opportunity to process all of his film. After the film was examined, each of the ladies was more than thoroughly impressed. And, old Herb muttered his standard phrase, "Good job, mate."

Both he and Gabby had a wonderful time dancing with the beautiful Kathleen Rollins who happily smiled throughout the entire evening. Al-though she had been unhappy in her former life, it was apparent that she and Gabby were devoted to each other. Theirs was a relationship made in the 'here and now' and within the world of spirits.

When Paul met with Mira for their morning session at Starbucks, she asked him, "What's it like to dance with a ghost?" Paul replied, "You know that I am not a very good dancer. Certainly, not as good as you or old Gabby but, I refer to it as 'slippery slope dancing'. It is like dancing on a wet, muddy surface. Whenever, you think that you have your dance partner firmly in hand, she goes slip sliding away.

I just couldn't do it as well as Gabby could because, over the years, he has had so much more practice on dancing with that lovely spirit, Katy Rollins. I was clumsy but, he was as fluid as a super cooled liquid. He's ninety years young and he didn't miss a beat."

Then, she asked, "How did you handle that situation, Paul?" "I always have my music files and my 'boom box' with me so, I selected some of that modern-day crap and we danced without touching. I still prefer ball room dancing but she seemed to enjoy the change.

Before you could say 'Booker T. Washington', both she and Gabby were doing the 'bump and grind' together as experts. Katy reminded me of you when you were doing your version of 'Burlesque'. To be brief, they were both hilarious about doing a different kind of dance, for a change."

Mira asked, "How does it feel to be the first ghostologist who was ever captured on film while dancing with a ghost?" He said, "Mira, I loved it. I am going to present that film and a technical paper at the Paris Convention this year." Immediately, she interrupted him to say, "Not unless you take me with you, you won't.

I have always wanted to do some serious shopping in Paris, France. That's where some of the most famous fashion designs come from." He held her hand while saying, "It's a date, babe." Then, they got down to serious PESO business when Paul asked, "What's the status with Mr. and Mrs. Governor?

I need for you to bring me up to date on all that's happened since I have been in Somerset for so long. All of this past week, I have had this gut feeling that everything was falling apart at the Governor's Mansion. Is that so?"

Mira answered by saying, "Yes and no. Unfortunately, the primary players have reverted to a Jungle-type behavior since I last spoke with you. His honor must be on double doses of Viagra because he has forced our insider mole to resign her day job as his private chambermaid. She told me that she just couldn't handle being raped every day and night, once by him and once by her but, frequently, by both. What should we do, Paul? I'm at my wit's end about how to handle this damned problem."

Gray mulled the situation over for a little bit and, then, he said, "Give our former mole a day job here at PESO. We could use a full time maid or she could be an understudy for Lola who is way behind on her sample analyses. You choose the position but, make certain that she gets a large pay increase. She has information in her head that will prove to be 'priceless'.

She deserves to be rewarded for all that overtime which she was forced to endure while serving as a 'sex slave' for Mr. and Mrs. Governor. By having that rape victim under our own roof, both the First Lady and the First Gentleman should think twice about doing PESO any harm.

They can't withstand much more blackmailing if they want to be re-elected, right?"

Mira, said, "That seems like a good fix but, where will they find their next sex slaves? Not here, I hope." Paul responded, "Where else but, the Legislature? Just about every one of those Senators and the Representatives own their own whore or lesbian, and those 'sex slaves' seem to be a fixture that comes with their job. You need to have a party and you need to drop a few hints that the Palace has two openings, one for his highness and one for her highness. Get Joan involved. She could be a very good party girl if you would just release her to the outside world. She needs to get over that shyness of hers.

Sadly, Mira responded, "I don't want to lose Joan. She belongs only to me and no one else." He responded, "If you and I do get more serious and, if we do go to Paris together, you will have to split-up with Joan at that time. I won't consider marrying two women when one like you is more than enough.

When that time comes, Joan will be extra baggage for you and I. Is that understood, Mira? She said, "Are you serious? Do you really feel that way toward me? He replied, "Yes." She gave him a glowing smile and a big goodbye hug before leaving for her office. He would wait another twenty minutes before he departed for the same destination that Mira had sought.

This longer delay was necessary to avoid making both Joan and Lola angry at the two of us, Mira and himself. As he waited for the passing of more time, He became a little angry at Mira because she had failed to answer his direct question about Joan becoming 'extra baggage' prior to the time when the Paris trip occurs. Finally, the twenty minutes transpired so, grudgingly, he went to work at his PESO desk.

Shortly thereafter, Herb said "Hi", as he motioned for Paul to join him at his desk to sit in Herb's guest chair and talk. Paul said,

"What's up?" Herb said, "I won't waste your valuable time. I have one question that I would like to ask and here it is, "Is my job secure?"

Paul inquired, "Why do you ask?" Herb said, "I am getting to be very near my early retirement age and I worry about you being out of town so much. When you are gone, PESO is a totally different place to work. Everyone becomes a grump when you are gone. I am afraid of Mira and I don't want to take any early retirement. Got any suggestions?"

Let's take this sensitive conversation back to Starbucks, I didn't get enough coffee so, I need a refill. And, you need to have some place of privacy for our confidential talk. You go out the basement door and I will go out the main entrance door. He told Mira a lie when he said, "I need to visit the Ford Garage for about one hour. See you soon. As he left, he winked at Joan who blushed, as she usually does.

When they both located a suitable table at Starbucks, Paul resumed his conversation. "Herb, we can cure that concern in one of two ways, if you like." "How is that?" "We need an engineer to work in the field who will ensure that these State Parks are constructed to the National Code to maximize the ghost sighting efficiency and, at the same time, offer greater safety for our clientele. Those civil engineers that currently design our structures are overly concerned about the seating, not the sighting and, good aspect angles for seeing the ghosts are of paramount importance.

And, their main objectives seem to be their passion for building high-rise hotels instead of cheaper motels. Our dollar intake for these ghost shows will be low, so our housing costs need to be toward the same trend.

This is not Miami Beach."

The other field problem relates to the fact the Governor is taking both bribes and kickbacks. He has his own Construction Company which, somehow seems to get the best jobs every time that a 'sweet one' is placed on a bid status.

This is a dangerous job. On the plus side, you can get rich by taking the Governor out of the loop. On the negative side, you may have to pack iron to keep the Governor goons from hurting you or Shirley. I don't know if you have the balls for this particular job and I don't know if you have the kind of energy that will be required. If you really apply yourself, you could retire with a 'stuffed' retirement fund. Viva Honduras.

We need cabins to blend with the nearby forests. We don't need the high rise monuments that the Governor wants. Herb, are you interested?"

"What's my second choice? You mentioned that there were two ways to get out of this panty place and still be employed by PESO."

"Herb, there are times that I need an assistant. You could tag along with me more often. Here, you would get away from the split-tails for a few days and I could use an extra pair of hands. What say you, old chap?" Herb though about it for a few seconds and, then, he replied, "I hope that you won't be offended, Paul because I consider you to be my very best PESO buddy. But, I would prefer the former offer over the latter.

My reason is that, in my entire working career, I have never had a strong enough challenge, never! I would really enjoy my final working years if I had more responsibility and greater authority in my professional life. I will drive a police cruiser and I will always wear a holster with my loaded Berretta pistol. Both you and Shirley will be proud of me, I assure you. At one time in my life, I was a young and aggressive soldier for the Green Berets. And, now is the time for me to be aggressive again. Send on those Governor goons, I will be ready."

Paul saw a killer look in Herb's eyes for the first time ever and he smiled. Privately, he thought, old Herb is a diamond in the rough. He is just the man to bring the Governor's construction empire down. Then Gray said, "Okay, Herb, let me discuss this matter with Ms. Mirren and I will get back to you, post haste.

In the meantime, take the rest of the day off and go negotiate a conditioning program at the YMCA. You need to rediscover as much of that Green Beret body as you can. You and I both know that, in the Construction business, the successful boss is the one who is the toughest. Because of your age, you will receive a lot of physical challenges from the young laborer class. In today's world, that would be the irate Mexicans. I want you to be ready when that conflict arrives.

Paul made a final point. "If I am successful in selling this idea to Mira, your new executive level job will double your salary over what you are making at the present time." Herb gasped and said, "Oh, my Lord. I could develop a stable retirement fund."

Privately, he was thinking that this change would be ideal for PESO. He would ask Mira to give Shirley a big pay raise and then, there would be a new applicant to take Shirley's old job. If, that applicant had a high enough IQ level, that is.

What Paul really wanted to accomplish was to hurt the old Governor in his wallet. He was still angry over how that SOB had damaged his Mira. His modus operandi would involve a large change in how the construction companies would pay their bribe and kickback money.

Herb would receive all the cash money that had previously gone to the Governor. And, PESO's new Construction Company would be in control instead of those that belonged to the Governor. It was a large risk but, one that was worth taking. Because Herb was so near the early retirement age and since he suffered from mellitus, he could sure use the money, no doubt about that.

Today's Social Security payments are not enough to pay for the prescription drugs that old Herb needs. And, somebody needs to adopt a citizen that is facing retirement. Herb would be Gray's first and best liked adoptee.

Before he left his PESO office for the day, he checked with Lola in her basement laboratory office to determine if his infrared photographs had been developed. He wanted so badly to examine a good picture of his dancing with that ghost lady named Katy. But, as you might expect, Lola had not yet been able to finish those photographs. He told her that he was headed for Hazard in the morning and would be absent on assignment (AOA) for a few days or weeks.

His final request to her was, I want these negatives to become top-quality prints because I plan to wrap a technical paper around them. But, he didn't mention the Paris trip. He also added that these particular pictures would be at the top of her priority list until further notice by Mira or himself.

Next, he went by his new Clay Street address to see how his make-over project was progressing. He needed some good bed rest before tackling the traffic in the morning. He was shocked by what he saw on the inside of his new quarters.

In every room and bath, psychedelic colors and bright geometric patterns existed on each wall, ceiling and floor. Those intense and distorted perceptions caused hallucinations that were so luminous, he felt like putting on his sun glasses to oppose the glare.

It was plainly hideous and, he didn't care for it at all. But, he was not about to say anything publicly because he didn't want to hurt the feelings of Mira, Joan or Lola who had worked so hard on the project. All that was needed now was a rotating glass disco ball which he assumed was probably on a back order status.

Madly, he raced to that big bed of his to inspect his bedding. Yes, those three split-tails had kept their promise to him about one thing, at least. He still had sheets of Egyptian cotton with Marilyn Monroe's imprint on the fabric. And, in this case, Mira had purchased the higher priced variety where Miss Monroe was posing in the nude.

And, the bed was so large that one wall of the house had to be extended just to receive what he called his 'monster bed'. Paul was pleased that his new big bed could easily accommodate any threesomes of the future. He boiled his cabbage down and remarked, "To hell with the incandescent paint, the associated glare and all these pink colors, I got what I wanted. Then, he forwarded e-mails to Mira, Joan and Lola saying that he really liked the way that the Clay Street home had turned out.

That was a blatant lie, of course but, he didn't want to hurt their feelings. Those three ladies had worked very hard to achieve the optical illusions that they each wanted. He decided to try it for about a year and, if he couldn't stand it anymore, then he would sell it based on the fact that Radon gas was affecting his libido. He knew that they would go along with the sale because they seemed to enjoy his lust ratio being as high as possible.

Then, Paul Gray turned to the assignment of the day, one that was called 'Sister'. It was a recurring sighting that appeared in Hazard near where Paul was born and reared. Because of the exact location of the haunting, he was hoping that the Mayor of Hazard, Mrs. Nan Gorman would agree to be a force behind the development of a new State Park inside of the Hazard City limits. At least, he hoped that she would be so inclined.

But, as Paul read through the summary for 'Sister', he had some serious doubts about this one. It would have to be built in Hazard where Commercial real estate is so difficult to acquire. Unless, he built the grandstands out and over the Kentucky River, that is. That would be an attractive site and, somewhat practical but, a dangerous one during the flooding season. At the end of the day, this apparition is going to be a hard sell for PESO management to approve.

But, before we commit to an important decision that might be regretted at a later time, let's examine the players and their part in this story. They might sway the commitment issue because so little is actually known about the French–Eversole feud in these modern times.

It all began on a cloudy day in June when five young men of the Eversole family had been to a big wedding in the center of downtown Hazard. As they left the Bowman Memorial Methodist Church to return to their family farm, they were ambushed by a bunch of men from the French Family at a point where a low gap in the mountains occurred. This is to say that they were dug-in near the village of Walkertown.

As the unexpected shots were overheard, the French riflemen knocked all five Eversoles out of their saddles. They fell on the ground stone cold dead except for the youngest, Earl Eversole. He was the luck one of the lot. He was bleeding from a head wound but, he was not mortally wounded.

He knew that the French Family would try to be thorough so he remained as motionless as possible. He hoped to avoid another bullet that would finish him off. Earl was still somewhat dizzy from the shock of being hit but, he had enough resolve to continue 'playing possum'. And, then, one of those despicable French Family members came to his side to try and add to his sorrow.

All he felt was the heavy kick in his ribs and the associated pain that followed. Fortunately for Earl, he was able to quench the pain because 'playing possum' was a deadly game. One wrong move or any deep gasping would quickly get him a bullet in his forehead and he would be as dead as a door nail.

Because his head wound was still bleeding out, he succeeded in fooling his would be murderer. Some of the blood had dried but, continuous bleeding was still evident. So, Earl waited until the cowardly bushwhacker had moved on and, was no longer in plain sight. Then, he clawed his way over that rocky soil until he reached an artesian well where fresh water was available. He drank as much of the cool water as he could because he knew that his system needed more liquids. While he was under the protection of a massive Willow tree with that artesian well nearby, he feinted.

Eventually, he awoke when the moon was high overhead and the fog was extremely dense. Someone was trying to make him swallow more water. It was another sister, Jane Morrow (Eversole) who had died in a train wreck over a year ago.

He asked, "How could this be happening? You perished in that awful train wreck where some evil vermin placed a big tree trunk over the tracks. Your train derailed and that was nearly 1000-miles from here. How did you find me and, how could you know that I have been hurt?

Jane responded, "Earl, haven't I always been at your side when you needed my help? He answered by saying, "Yes, I remember. You were my second mother after Maw passed. Hold my hand, dear Jane. I need to feel your presence."

She replied, "I can't stay with you because if, I don't get you some medical help real soon, you will die. That's a nasty head wound that you have, little brother and you have lost a lot of blood. That's how I found you. I followed the blood trail. Now, I must get you a doctor and very soon. Dr. Summers lives close by so, I'll get him to help you and we'll both be back in just a few minutes. Bye, bye sweet brother. And, she was off in a Perry County second.

Earl wondered, "How in the World is a ghost going to be able to communicate with a mortal being? How in heaven's name will Jane be able to lead him here?" This is where the fog is and old Doc Summers lives higher up on the mountain side where there is no fog tonight. How will she materialize and how will she communicate?

It will be a true miracle if she succeeds so, I might as well just go ahead and die. He went fast asleep thinking that he would never see the light of another day, not ever again. He awoke to discover that Doc Summers was working feverishly on his head wound. They were using the water from his artesian well to clean the wound and Doc Summers had everything else that he needed to repair Earl's damage in that big satchel of his, iodine, alcohol, bandages and the works.

He asked, "Doc, how did my dead sister talk you into coming to my rescue? She is a spook from the spirit World, you know." Dr. Summers replied, "Yes, but she is a smart one. She was holding out a cedar sheet with pebbles aligned to say just one word, 'Help'.

She led me to where you are by each of us holding onto a single divining rod. It would try to go limp wherever we approached water. In that manner, we found you in this dense, dark night. You are lucky to have this lovely ghost for a loyal sister.

I do believe in ghosts and I have seen this technique used before and many times in previous emergencies. Now, you be still and stop talking.

I need to fix this damage that your bullet did, Mr. Eversole. You are lucky to be alive, young man. You hold the lantern so I can finish the cleaning, the closure and add some medicine that will protect you from infections for the next few weeks.

Meanwhile, his younger sister Molly Blankenship (Eversole) awoke from a sound sleep to shake her husband Ed until he was wide awake. She told her husband that Earl and four of her brothers had been ambushed by the cowardly French Family. Earl is the only survivor and you need to bring him here where I can nurse him back to good health.

Ed Blankenship abruptly said, "How do you know about such happenings?" She answered, "You know how we Eversole girls are gifted. My sister Jane Morrow just visited me and she told me. Now hurry up or brother Earl may soon die. Take your three long poles, your Indian pony and plenty of warm blankets and bring him back to me here at our house.

Send our two sons after the other four bodies but, the main thing is to get Earl under safe cover as soon as possible. Those French bastards could still be looking for him so, take your pistol with you. Hazard is not safe anymore. This means that war has arrived because of those damned drunken French people.

Be careful with that sling-type stretcher and, don't bump him too much. It will take longer if you go slow but, I don't want that wound to start bleeding again, be gentle Hubby and, tonight, you will get your reward if you bring him home safely to me."

Blankenship and his two sons saddled three horses and one pony as they started for the gap which is not too far away, no more than about three miles maximum. As they traveled toward their objective, they debated Molly's second sight capability. But, after they got there, the debate ended. And, they would never debate their Mother's talents again.

Doc Summers was still there working in the early morning sunrise. He was about to leave but, he stayed behind to oversee the sling type stretcher loading of Earl's warm body. Earl had somehow lost the fever that he had earlier but, at the moment he was 98.7 degrees Fahrenheit. Doc suspected that Jane Morrow had cast some kind of spell because nobody loses a high fever that quickly.

Dr. Summers filled the Blankenships in on everything that happened during the night. He told the three males about Jane, the cedar sheet and the divining rod. Plus, he lectured them about the paranormal. He warned them, don't you three men ever doubt Molly Eversole again. She is wiser than you think.

So, if you harbor any wrongdoings, she can hurt you in so many different ways. It is frightening to even think about it, be good or be sorry. The three Blankenships said that they would become good citizens after they had killed eight French people. They killed four of our kind so we will kill twice as many of them. That's the way it is with the business of feuding. Losing four of the stoutest Eversoles was an unforgiveable act that would soon be violently revenged and the French Family would be the next ones to grieve.

Paul placed his summary report aside and said to himself, this one is going to be a hard sell to Miss Mira and the Palace people. He wondered how best to handle the controlling issue at this point which was how to gain suitable property rights.

If the Hazard property is either unavailable or inadequate for a new State Park project then, said Park will never be built. And that grieves me some because Hazard is my birthplace and I would like to help that old city. I recommended the old Gene Baker Motor Company building but nearby residences would have to be purchased and razed. That would not be cost attractive.

That was his final thought on the matter so, he said goodbye to his Mother and left the area to travel toward his new Clay Street address in Lexington. In the morning, he would have to present Ms. Mirren with a negative vote on the 'Sister' project.

Jane Eversole was an interesting apparition but, sometimes, an apparition will only appear at a location where it is impossible to build suitable lodging with the amenities of a parking lot and gift shop, et cetera. If he did vote for a big construction project at Hazard, most of the downtown area would be lost forever and I don't think that Mayor Gorman would go for that. And, I can't imagine Jane Morrow (Eversole) being inside of Gene Baker's Garage building. Mayor Gorman would enact a recall on my 'Key to the City" and I wouldn't part with that big bronze key for nothing.

As Paul sped homeward to his 'interesting' abode on Clay Street, he thought about Herb and Shirley being transferred to the field. They tell me that Herb has 'abs' and a new sveltely body, thanks to the YMCA gym and his intense desire to be another John Wayne. They also told him that the new agent to replace Shirley was named 'Angel' of all things. Mira said that her IQ level was higher than any other PESO employee, including you know who, even Paul Gray. He was anxious to meet 'Angel'. He would make the final evaluation of her in his new bedroom.

He had never taken a 'genius' to bed before and this could be the time when her craftiness is truly tested. He was hoping that it would be like one pit bull versus a pit cow, both equally aggressive.

Chapter Nineteen

BRIDE

PAUL GRAY WAS sitting in his favorite chair at the Starbucks coffee house where he was busy reading the latest edition of 'Sporting News'. Later in the day, he was going to visit Lexington's famous Keeneland Race Track to bet on a hot horse named 'Red Rose'.

He loved poetry so he felt a strong connection to his 'bet of the day'. One of Paul's favorite poems was penned by Robert Burns in 1796. An excerpt is offered as follows:

"My Love's like a red, red rose
That's newly sprung in June;
Oh, my love's like the melodie
That's sweetly played in tune.

The odd makers had her at 50-1 to win at Keeneland. But, Gray noticed that this filly had won her last four outings, each of them on mud at some of the lesser known tracks in Louisiana and Florida. So, it looked like the proverbial 'fix' was in.

He was planning to bet heavily using some of the PESO expense money that he had not yet spent. It was there in his wallet, doing nothing, so why not set it free? But, that was a confidential disclosure which wasn't meant for Mira's ears.

As soon as he had forgotten that little guilt trip, 'she who must be obeyed' showed up at his coffee bench for her morning treat. Quickly, he rolled the Sporting News Magazine into a tight little roll and squeezed in under his left leg, where he hoped that she wouldn't see it.

Cynically, she said, "I saw that, Paul. Are we going to the races today?" Before he could dig a larger hole to hide in, she added these words, "I heard that there is a hot little pick named 'Red Rose'. I'm going to bet my money on her.

Which stallion are you going to bet your money on?" He was speechless but, he did manage a big shit-eating grin while he asked a relevant question, "Why are you betting on my horse?" She replied, "Oh, I don't need a magazine to help me. I'm red haired and I am a woman. Red Rose is a filly and she has a dark red coat of hair. Need I say more?"

He changed the subject by asking this question, "How is Angel working out in her training for Shirley's position?" She didn't answer right-a-way. Instead, she asked, "If she could car pool with me to the race-track and back again. Grudgingly, I said, Of course, my dear but we need to leave by 1230-hours, no later."

She didn't scold him for copying her wager but she did say that our former informant at the Governor's Mansion was working out just swell at PESO. And, she added that Herb was doing great in his new field service position. Already, a bunch of dollars have been diverted by Herb away from the Governor's sticky little fingers and back to PESO where they rightfully belong.

"You were right, Paul. Herb does have the balls for this assignment. My short range plan is to re-unite both he and Shirley together again and, in the field, full time. But, first, Angel has to be fully trained by Shirley.

As she nibbled on her Danish Pastry, she added that Angel has the highest IQ score that the testing people have ever recorded. They say that she is off the charts where intelligence is concerned. And, Paul, I hate to tell you this but, her test scores out-distance yours by a large amount.

One day, that broad will own all of PESO if she plays her cards right.

In any case and, for the present, Angel is staying put. We don't need a maid to clean your men's room so try and hit the urinal more often. You will just have to forget that fantasy about you having your own little maid. Instead, I will have a tough little chat with the night crew."

Paul asked, "How's Shirley coping now that Herb is in the field so much?" "Oh, you know Shirley. She likes to be on top and in control. There are a lot of old timers who are more than willing to make her happy. Older men like to lie down and rest while she pumps them as hard as she can.

But, Shirley had better watch out because I saw her yesterday at the Salvation Army shelter stealing away two men for her own little games. I am afraid that she might catch some horrible disease and transfer it to our toilet seats. We do share the same Ladies Room, you know."

In a consoling tone, Paul answered, "The odds are very low that you should have to worry about that occurrence. Just tell the night crew to scrub both bathrooms as the military would do. Mention that, if they don't start doing their job a whole lot better, then, they get to do the next night with just one tool, a toothbrush. If that doesn't work, just change contractors. I would choose a Mexican crew if I had my way. Their work ethic is a lot better than the black bunch that we currently have to deal with now.

He was also anxious to hear if the Governor and First Lady had experienced any attitude adjustments or not." Mira said, "No, what they are pissed off about now is how well old Herb is diverting kick back funds into PESO instead of Frankfort and, in particular, the Governor's Mansion.

They both demanded that I fire Herb but, I handled it. I used only one word when I said, 'Film'. Immediately, they both hung up their telephones in a very polite manner. They have a major problem on their hands which involves the gubernatorial election of this year. If we spread our pictures around, to certain low class people in high class positions, that asshole Governor will be history. There is no way that his highness can be re-elected, not if we use our weapons in the proper way."

Paul said, "I agree but, please remember that dangerous pictures can be, in a word, dangerous. Be careful how you use them. For example, where are the naughty pictures located at this time?" She answered, "In a file folder inside my locked PESO office desk, of course."

He scolded her, "Not good enough, Mira. Put them into a new bank vault that has no obvious traceability back to PESO. Use a fictitious name if you can. I am quite surprised that our egghead Governor hasn't broken into PESO and stolen them already." She said, "That's because he isn't as smart as you are, honey."

"Let's change subjects. I don't enjoy talking about Mr. or Mrs. Governor too much. How did you like my last two e-mail attachments that I sent you regarding the 'Witch' and 'Sister' projects?" "Don't be offended, Paul but, I did like the 'Witch' write-up best. A sister who is pouring spring water over her wounded brother just doesn't appeal to me.

In my opinion, a 'singleton' sighting just doesn't cut the mustard in this business. You really need to have two or more ghosts in order to have a reasonable chance to succeed with these State Park promotions. And, any two ghosts that you locate, they need to be doing something together. In other words, I loved seeing you, Gabby and Kathleen Rollins dancing together in the fog.

I predict that, after Gabby dies and enters the spiritual world, those two ghosts will make Kentucky a small fortune for many long years. 'Witch' was a fabulous discovery, Paul. It was also a breakthrough for the scientific annals. Ghostologists will be writing articles about that pair for a long time. You have put us on the page of every paranormal textbook and I appreciate your hard work.

"Thank you, Mira. I value your opinion and we are of the same mind set regarding those two projects, 'Witch' is a better property than 'Sister'.

She winked and said, "Now, we should report to work to see and be seen before we exit the office and head for the Keeneland Race track. I think that we should leave earlier than 1230-hours, how about eleven o'clock, instead?"

Paul nodded his head in the affirmative and said, "You go first and I will follow you afterward. I'll see you again in about ten more minutes or so. She said, "Bye for now lover. I am really looking forward to seeing the horses run this afternoon and thank you for allowing me to be part of your afternoon and early evening. It will be a hot date for me, one that I will always treasure."

He watched Mira until she was out of sight as he said to himself, "With Red Rose and her red hair, I can't lose today. Mira and he were a happy couple and they were about to become happier. Sex between two lovers is almost at the top of every bucket list but, sex isn't everything. This afternoon, we will just relax, hold hands and have good time together as sweethearts or well-married couples do. There is a lot to be said for this touch and feel stuff if the involved couples are both right for each other.

While he was waiting for their late morning departure to the racing grounds, he was looking over his next assignment, know to him only as 'Trees'. What in the hell am I doing writing about trees, I am not a zymurgist. I will have a little talk with Mira about such an assignment but, first, I must finish with the current assignment on 'Bride'. Then, later on, we will argue about 'Trees'.

The setting for 'Bride' was in Rowan County and its County Seat was a town called Morehead, KY. He knew that city well since his favorite cousin Earl 'Buster' Henson still lives there. He was hoping to visit with Old Buster while he was in that part of the Eastern Kentucky. His final destination was along State Highway 60 and Interstate 64.

Like Hazard, Morehead was also famous for a feud which occurred in Rowan County during the 1880's. Buster's feud was called the Martin-Tolliver-Logan Feud or, simply, the Rowan County War. It lasted about ten years and 20 people were killed with over a hundred being badly wounded. This feud was a lot worse than the French-Eversole Feud of Perry County.

Paul kept on reading the documents in his file to acquaint himself of where he was going next and the party or parties that were to serve as his apparent apparitions. He soon read that the crux of this matter involved a lady who was about to be married but, never actually became married.

And, the emotional shock that followed this betrayal was caused by the would-be-husband, a low down scoundrel who couldn't keep a promise to his would-have-been wife. Moments before his intended marriage, the reneging groom dropped by to sing an old song which was most applicable for the given situation; namely,

"Please release me, let me go.
For, I don't love you anymore.
Leave me be, Darling, Set me free . . ."

Before the groom could sing anymore of that famous old song, the bride grabbed her father's shotgun and she shot him dead. After making certain that he was no longer of this living World, she shot once more to commit suicide. She fell in a clump over his dead body and they were together again, just as she always desired, one body upon the other.

So, in this Rowan County matter, Mira has her two spooks with many reliable witnesses from those who had attended an uncompleted wedding ceremony. In the years, afterwards, there would be multiple sightings, as well. He concluded that this incident at the house where she lived could qualify as a possible State Park.

There were some things that bothered him about this State Park nomination. One thing was that Morehead has less than 0.1 percent running water. They do have Cave Run Lake so, with the right amount of humidity, they could occasionally have the dense fog that is required for productive sightings.

He would have to very closely review the fog data for that area. And, he needed to separate truth from hearsay regarding this apparition. It helps to know someone who lives in the area for most of their adult life. In this case, that would be old 'Buster', his favorite cousin.

But, for now, he was more than ready to visit the race track and, it's already 1245-hours in the afternoon. When will Mira ever learn to be on time? Gray had hoped to have Mira all to himself, but, when she arrived, she was surrounded by all of the other ladies who worked at PESO. So, he was forced to drive that big Chevrolet Van that he detested so much. And, like his Father, he hated it because it was a Chevy, not a Ford.

So, here he was, completely surrounded by a hen party and, he wasn't even consulted. Inwardly, he was furious with Mira for doing this without talking to him first. When Mira did determine that Paul was upset, she made just one statement on her own behalf.

She said, "When was the last time that you did something to me which was similar? Did you think about my feelings when you turned off all of your radio equipment and went silent on me? That was very embarrassing to me because I had an audience with me, a newspaper reporter." Immediately, Paul was put in his place by one smart woman so, he decided to let sleeping dogs lie.

There would be other such occurrences but, who is counting or who should be counting? Nobody, should be counting, that's who. At his first opportunity, he would whisper in her ear his final statement on the subject, "This is an office party, not a 'hot' date." And, Mira would whisper back, "I'll make it up to you later, Love," And, suddenly, his World was back on track, again.

They missed the first race because of their late departure and the traffic which was awful. Each parking lot was nearly filled with cars, trucks and vans so he had to park in the rear section nearest Versailles Road. He let the girls off at the main gate but, he had to walk that long distance back to the race track by himself.

Gray didn't bet heavily until the race entry called 'Red Rose' became apparent. After he had bet two-grand on his filly, he watched the odds plummet to 5-1 where they were 50-1 during the first race of the day. Yes, it does look like the heavy betting on 'Red Rose' is nothing more than a 'fix' among the bookies and the system. But, he deduced the following, if they win, I win. And, there is no need for him to become greedy. There would be other horses in his future.

Both he and Mira shouted, "Come on, my red, red rose. Mr. Burns and I are here today to spur you on. Win, baby win and win, she did". He and Mira were both elated but, the other girls were dejected because they didn't go for the low 5-1 odds. None of them had followed the key information that was spelled out in the Sporting News Magazine.

Near day's end, he met Angel at the betting window and she whispered in his ears the following, "Paul, I want to spend the night with you because I want to thank you for getting me this swell job at PESO." He asked for a rain check because of his big trip to Morehead in the morning.

Angel was somewhat upset and, Paul could tell that she was visibly disappointed. He had seen that huffy appearance by other ladies at different times. Gray told Angel that he was very flattered and quite interested in fulfilling her offer but, it would have to be after he had returned from Morehead, KY.

He summarized by saying, "When I return from this trip, you will be at the top of my 'to do' list, I promise." She smiled and said, "I can't wait, I just can't. Everybody tells me that you really know how to please a woman. Therefore, I am looking forward to your safe return.

Paul Gray, don't fail to treat me right, please don't fail." It was obvious that poor Angel had been badly abused by those two monsters over at the Palace. He promised himself that he would be extremely gentle with Angel when the time came for them to have sex together.

His journey to Morehead was uneventful. Every time, he looked around, another 800-Foot mountain was in his path, surrounded by curved stretches, not straight ones. His pistons were falling to sleep on him and there was nothing that he could do to arouse them. Fast driving is too dangerous when the hill density is this great.

First off, Paul was reunited with his cousin, his wife and their family.

We had a rousing good time talking about our youthful experiences. I had nothing but positive tales to talk about since visiting Aunt Mina was always a blast, with good food and great stories. Mina was an excellent storyteller. Her favorite genre was about the paranormal events of her own lifetime.

But Buster wanted to talk mostly about the one bad incident of which he could never remove from his mind. This was the occasion in which our common grandmother called Buster a thief. Some cash money had gone missing while Earl was visiting his Grandmother's house and poor Buster was blamed for the theft.

Subsequently, the real robber was identified as Uncle John but, poor Buster was never seen at Grandmother's house again. Aunt Mina wouldn't let him go there, not for a barrel of monkeys. After all these years, Earl was still mad and quite hurt. He was justified in feeling that way because no one enjoys being falsely accused and no young man likes to 'lose' his grandmother.

However, Earl did sign on as Paul's personal guide for a price that was to be determined, probably somewhere around $500.00. And, they agreed to leave Buster's house early on the next morning, around 0300-hours or thereabouts.

They talked until about midnight so they both realized that they would be very groggy as three o'clock approached in the early hours of the day. But, neither one of them complained about anything. Talking with each other after all of those intervening years was absolutely nothing but prime time and, as a result, it was totally priceless.

Buster started telling the history of the local sightings over an early breakfast of eggs, sausage and homemade biscuits that were absolutely delicious. And, on the way there to the manifestation site, he continued talking about the different sightings that had been officially documented by other witnesses.

The fact that Earl was a volunteer policeman and a volunteer fireman was very helpful to Paul's needs and priorities, As a result of that situation, Gray had better access to official information than any other guide might have. Then, we arrived at our final destination of the day.

Earl began by saying, "There used to be an old house that stood at this particular spot. And, he was pointing downward toward what appeared to be an original foundation stone. The house was, at an earlier time, an old weather-beaten, four-room dwelling on this back road of Morehead.

For many long years, the house was maintained to a level that he called 'fair' condition. Also, the house was located on a beautiful knoll where you could see for miles. Buster described the dwelling as being in good shape when he first moved to the area but, deterioration ran rampant because of neglect and, since it was lying vacant for too many years.

No one wanted to live in this house because, during dark, misty nights, a woman dressed in a white linen wedding gown could be seen and heard on too many occasions. She would utter some blood-curdling screams before vanishing completely into the darkness of night.

One family did try to live in the dwelling because they were unable to afford anything else. They ignored the female ghost screaming at night until they lost two children as a result of 'unexplained' deaths. Then, they moved away from the house and were never seen again by anyone. And, the neighborhood never faulted them for moving away.

On another occasion, a migrant tramp from the railroad trains moved in because the house was vacant and, apparently, available. The railroad bum chose to spend one night in the deserted house but, he was discovered on the following day, strangled to death by a white rag. Rumors claimed that the white rag was torn from a wedding veil but, that was never confirmed because of the rag's old age and near rotten condition."

The root cause for this unusual apparition and the uncanny screaming was never unearthed. And, the three killings were never solved. It remains a cold case after all of these years. Both Paul and Earl were very tired but they waited until they could see if any manifestations would be seen on this night of wet grounds, light winds, clearing winds and limited visibility with attendant fog.

Shortly before sunrise, the apparition appeared, along with her former lover. They were strolling along, arm-in-arm and, apparently, very much in love. Then, they began to have a fierce argument about some issue before she grabbed the shot-gun and killed him. Shortly thereafter, she shouted out a frightening, blood curdling scream just before killing herself.

While they were both on the ground and motionless, they each vanished into the unknown and mysterious divide. Both bodies left behind a single drop of blood for each corpse, his and hers, without a doubt. Quickly, he gathered a blood sample for Lola to examine.

When he was finished looking at this scene of re-enactment, he asked Earl a question, "Is it always the same, Buster?" Earl answered, "No, Paul, it is not always the same. I have been here many times and these are some of the apparitions that I remember:

- *She is sometimes alone and weeping repeatedly. When she isn't crying her eyes out, she is screaming that awful sound.*
- *Occasionally, she is seen trying to suffocate some female rival. We believe that this is supposed to be the groom's mistress.*
- *She is alone and chasing little children with a noose. We think that these are the kids that she was denied.*
- *She is running visitors off her land using her terrifying screams.*
- *She is searching for some one, either the groom or his mistress.*
- *She is running away, apparently, frightened by the observers.*
- *As a runner, she sometimes just fades to black.*
- *She is, sometimes, beating on a young woman as if she is withholding information. That might be her bridesmaid who may have known about the groom's errant ways.*
- *She is sometimes making love to the best man for revenge purposes. What's 'good for the gander is good for the goose' type stuff."*

"Paul, she is not consistent in what she does but, she is very reliable on the nights when we have a dense fog. At such a time, she always appears and, whatever she brings to the table is always entertaining." "Buster, I think that you people of Morehead are about to see a new State Park, what say you old cousin?"

He said, "I hope so, Paul because Morehead is approaching bankruptcy and we could sure use any extra cash money. I packed up my cameras and the computers into my police car and we went to his home to try and recover from our reunion and last night's burden of constant chatter. Fortunately, for PESO, we did observe the appearance of a very interesting and promising example of the supernatural type.

I paid Buster two thousand dollars of my racetrack winnings for his kind and efficient services. He argued that it was too much money for guide services. But, he no longer resisted me when I told them this story about our common grandmother.

"Earl, call this a gift from our joint grandmother. When Granny found out that it was Uncle John who stole her money, she cried over and over again." She told me, "This will probably devastate poor Buster and, I had no business of accusing him so rapidly, not without appropriate facts. But, at that time, there were only three people in the house, John, Earl and me. I would like to apologize but, by this time, he probably hates me. And, I don't really blame him for hating me because I certainly deserve that hatred." Paul took the two grand and held it to his chest as if it was sacred. And, I could see the tears in his eyes. In his mind, there was only forgiveness and it was heart-warming to watch.

I gave my thanks to Buster's wife for all of the delicious food and I drove in the direction of Angel who wanted to be serviced by one Paul Gray. Isn't life grand? These ghosts aren't so bad, either. They provide some interesting entertainment. And, I enjoy working with them because they pay my bills.

And, now, it is time to argue with Mira about my next assignment called 'trees'. What self-respecting ghostologist works on 'trees'? He would royally chew her ass out at during tomorrow's meeting in Starbucks. But, tonight, I have Angel for the whole night. Wow, what a job this is!"

Chapter Twenty

TREES

JUST AFTER PAUL had returned from Morehead, he chose to ignore Angel's frantic messages from PESO. He didn't arrive in Lexington until the wee hours of the morning so he decided to be unavailable for one more day. He needed about fourteen hours on top of Marilyn Monroe and he was surprised to find out that someone had installed a 'Temper-Pedic Liner' under his Monroe sheets. What a difference that makes for a tired man who really needs his bed rest. No aches, no pains is a powerful endorsement for any mattress improvement, especially Miss Monroe's.

Paul Gray ate his daily breakfast meal of Kashi's toasted berry crumble containing additions of dried cranberries and wild blueberries.

He tried out his new Keurig coffee machine using a 100% Arabic Extra Bold blend. Damned good he thought. Someday, this little machine is going to really damage old Starbucks.

Then, he was off to his own Starbucks Coffee House where he would visit with Mira for an updating session on his next assignment. He hoped that Keurig would never kill off Starbucks because both he and Mira were becoming accustomed to this shop as a meeting place in the mornings. Paul loved being one-on-one with her in this, their private little canteen. He imagined that they were in Paris and sipping cups of coffee together in a street café near the 'Avenue des Champs-Elysees'.

When Mira arrived, she was wearing a matching outfit of red and white combinations that sent a message saying, "Look at me World, I'm alive and I am in love". She was absolutely gorgeous on this beautiful day. Her vest coat and white blouse were unbuttoned just enough to reveal the rounded cusps of her beautiful breasts. And, her skirt was plainly outrageously short, barely covering the black panties that were worn over her 'jewel box'. And, her red shoes were a knockout but, what red-blooded man could keep his eyes off of that cute little mini-skirt? He couldn't do it and, that's for certain.

When she sat down, he quickly saw a brief flash of her black panties.

Immediately, Paul thought that the black panties should be properly hidden from all public viewings so, he asked if she was cold and would she like a blanket from his car? She smiled as she said, "I wanted to impress you and to get your mind off of that Angel person. That woman is obsessed with getting you into her bed.

She says it's because you got her a wonderful job at PESO. Hell, I hired her, not you. You weren't even here at the time that she was employed." "Mira, that's just a temporary infatuation which exists because she was tortured when she served our needs at the Palace. Give it some time and she will find someone else, instead of me. It's logical that she is feeling this way towards me and, it really speaks to the issue that she is very happy in her new job with PESO."

Mira asked, "Will you promise me that you will have nothing to do with her?" "No, I won't promise anything of that nature because she knows too much about PESO and what we did while she was our insider mole at the Palace. She could turn on us and, in the process, do a lot of damage for the two of us. If Angel makes me an offer, I won't refuse her. It's just too dangerous to say, no thanks.

"Paul, I don't want you fucking her and that's final." Paul countered, "Does she belong to you, Mira?" "Not just yet but, I am trying to turn her around." Privately, he thought, there's the rub. She wants Angel for herself. "Mira, you encouraged a threesome between you, me and Joan.

Therefore, I really don't know where you are coming from or what you want at this time.

Angel is damaged goods because she was abused by that Palace pair.

Now, she needs some tender loving care that only a sensitive man can provide." Mira said, "Please, don't let us have an argument about Angel, OK? In my opinion, she isn't worth it. Her mind might be brilliant but, to me, she is a calculating whore that is trying to steal my man away from me."

"That might be true Mira but, for the present, that brilliant mind of hers holds too much information about stuff that we need to know. She needs to tell me everything that she knows about his and her highness over at the State Mansion. Such information will prove to be both helpful and, in the end, priceless."

"Paul, if you insist, I will bow to your superior knowledge of strategy or street games. But, let me warn you about something. Angel has built you up into some form of a sex God. If you do fulfill her fantasies, she will never let go of you. However, if you were to disappoint her in a few positions or if you were to suffer some form of a fake erectile dysfunction, she might leave you alone for a little while." Privately, he thought, "There's the rub again, Mira's trying to win Angel for herself."

"Mira, what you are asking me to do is for me to resign from my status as one of Kentucky's best lovers and, I can't do it, not for you or anyone. If you and I do become hitched, I will take my vows seriously and become a one-woman-husband but, not right now. If Angel opens her velvet trap for me, then I will penetrate it as thoroughly as I can.

In plain terms, if Angel will swap information which we need in exchange for sex from me, then we shall have sex. We need to keep the Governor and his wife on their toes and I am the one fellow who can do that to a remarkable degree of success, don't you agree? She murmured 'yes' but, I could tell that her heart wasn't in it.

"Let's move on to some items that are more pleasant, OK?" She said, "Fine with me but, you watch out. She is a man-trap and, I don't want to lose you to her because I do love you so very much." "Angel is just business, Mira. We need to squeeze all of the information out of her that we can. It will help Herb in the field who is currently fighting an uphill battle over contracts and we need to support him, if we can. Trust me."

She replied, "I know that and I will always try to trust you, believe me. He smiled as he received his current case file from her grasp. Then, his smile was transformed into a scowl. "What the hell is this, Mira. I told you last week over the radio that I do people, not trees.

People who have died and become lingering ghosts who are refusing to enter the bright light. It is my mission to understand why they won't leave and I also have to manipulate that reason for staying by wrapping it around a new State Park, if possible. Who sent this garbage into PESO?

Did it come from the Governor's Palace? Are they trying to make us look bad?"

"No, Paul. Neither of those two people is here involved." "Then, who is involved, Mira? I have to know who did this to us." "First, let me say this, you are in the field most of the time so, you don't have to handle complaints like I do." He interrupted with a comment, "Mira, that's part of your job description. Better thee than me, old friend."

She ignored that barb and continued, "Paul, the Indian tribes are still a force in Kentucky politics. They have banded together with a legal grievance. They make the claim that PESO is biased against them and they want a new State Park pronto. This assignment is mostly about *sacred* trees and innocent Indians, instead of people."

He answered, "Oh they do, do they? This involves my own job description and I resent this intervention. If we write a report about trees that love each other, we'll be laughed out of this business. I think that the Governor is somehow behind this but, I don't know how. He really wants to hurt us, if you know what I mean."

She replied, "Just read all of the attachments and do the job for me. Their Indian lawyer has me trapped in a corner and the PESO lawyer is demanding that I quickly eliminate his arguments about any alleged racial bias."

Paul asked "Will a historical road sign from the Foundry over at the University soothe their injured egos?" "No, Paul. That was tried already and they turned it down by an official tribal petition. They want more. They want a new State Park on their reservation and, they won't budge for any other substitutes." Paul said, "Oh hell, it looks as if I am forced to do this damned assignment, whether I want to or not."

"Look it over, Lover. You will think of something that keeps both sides happy." "In order to do that, Mira, I demand to know who sent this garbage our way." "If you must know, the topmost signature on this petition was signed by the guy who is campaigning to be Kentucky's next Governor, a Mr. Tedd Fox who has Indian blood in his background."

"Mira, that does change a few things, doesn't it? Tell Teddy that I will work my balls off to see that he is satisfied. Call your PESO lawyer and bring him up-to-date. He will need to file some important papers on behalf of PESO for a Court-approved stay.

She said, "Ok, my love but, save those family jewels for me, don't work them too hard." Paul replied, my pipes will always have some swimmers for you Mira, don't worry. When I return from the 'trees', I will call for the 'plumber lady' to unclog my pipes for me, fear not. But first, I have this trip to Boonesboro to smoke the peace pipe with a certain Indian Chief.

Before he left PESO for the day, he called his favorite genealogist, Dorothy Moore, to provide all of the information about Tedd Fox and his living relatives. He asked her to consider this to be a 'hot' job for the final data because he wanted it in his hands before his initial meeting with the tribal Chief. Dorothy answered, "On your desk in three days." Dorothy was a beautiful blonde but she, didn't waste words with anyone.

But, first comes first. This was the night that Angel would have a sleepover at his new Clay Street address. An overnight stay which she was anticipating with a passion. And, one that Paul was looking forward to with an equivalent interest. or, perhaps, even more yearning than Angel. They both had been looking toward this date with far too much interest and too much waiting. Privately, Gray thought that their first orgasm might turn out to be an virtual explosion.

And, he was excited about gaining some other much needed information, as well.

- *Who is she campaigning for? The incumbents or Tedd Fox?*
- *Is she now a mole for some agency other than PESO?*
- *Could she be trusted?*
- *Has this woman been turned by Mira? Is she forever bent?*
- *Was she working for herself or some other party?"*

She was early for her appointment. When he got there, she was sitting on his front porch swing with sweat all over her fancy outfit and her lovely body. Gray apologized and said, I was out of rare vintage wine and that wouldn't do for this great occasion with a sexy lady like you. She smiled and said, "It's OK. Let me carry some of those groceries for you but, open your front door quickly. I'm hot and I am about to become hotter."

Paul liked this pretty girl from the very start. How many other women would help him carry his groceries? None, that's how many. After we had put the groceries away in their proper storage places, I offered her a shower but she refused. She said, "Personally, I like it all slick and slimy. Back home on the Farm, we used to call it wet-belly weather. Paul, if you object, I will take a shower first but, that's not what I want. I want you as soon as possible and, I have wanted nothing else for a long time now."

I studied that hungry look and those animal-like eyes before I said, "Why don't we do Round one first? That Chinese take-out will wait until after we have finished. I want to possess that beautiful body, ASAP. That very desirous woman turned off the air conditioning, took all of her clothes off and she lunged at me and my bed. It was going to be an interesting evening, of that, there would be little doubt.

Angel pushed and I shoved with equal forces and in perfect rhythm. She didn't just lie limp like the other PESO ladies did. Hers was the wettest pussy that he had ever encountered. And, he told her so. "This is the way that intercourse should be practiced. Watch out, Angel. I think that I am falling in love with you. Then, the predicted explosion occurred. They both had huge climaxes.

After Round fifteen, when his pipes were thoroughly cleaned, he said, "That's all for tonight. I am plenty tired and quite hungry. Let's have our supper now and a sampling of that vintage wine. Angel said, "Paul, I have never had fifteen climaxes with any man before. You are such a gorgeous hunk. I can't begin to tell you how much I have enjoyed this sleepover. For me, this night is something that I will never forget." And, then she made a tactical error when she said, "Are we on film?"

He answered her by saying, "If we are, then I want a copy for myself. Sex with an Angel and what a night! I feel both exhilarated and very lucky. Privately, he was wondering where she heard about the filming, at the Palace or here at PESO. After more thoughts on that question, he finally concluded that he really didn't care where she heard about it. Among all the components in the grand scheme of things, this issue was quite meaningless and totally insignificant.

He brought it up again and said, "Angel, I would like to accommodate you but, I can't. At one time, there were cameras in this bedroom but, I had them removed during my makeover sessions which occurred after I had purchased this house and moved from the apartment. Hidden cameras are illegal and, I am too much of a policeman to see it as being any other way.

Angel agreed that Paul was not the type to stoop so low. Then, she made another critical error. She claimed that she couldn't remember where she first heard about the hidden cameras and risqué film. She passed it off as being at the Palace or here at PESO which could be complete honesty.

Paul was hoping that it was during the chambermaid phase because if, it was at PESO, someone had to have leaked the information. He made a note to have Mira watch out for what happens during the gossip sessions. Time will tell and truth will out.

Sadly, he said to himself that this lovely, smart girl could be nothing more than a mole for one of our opponents, but, which one? PESO was losing allies at a record pace. He was praying that Angel was not involved because he did believe in love at first sight.

And, since she had never experienced a marathon thrust of fifteen orgasms, she might have been vulnerable enough to make that Freudian slip. Maybe her tongue just blurted out what her neurons were trying to retain. Or, he could say that our highly intelligent Angel does have a few moments of pure dumbness no matter what her IQ level is and, that's typical for most members of the intelligentsia. He would think about when and what to tell Mira or, maybe, it was best to tell her nothing.

One thing that hurt his manly pride was the fact that Angel seemed to be pumping him for strategic information. In other words, she could be playing him because she plied more information him than he did from her? Or, was it just conversation between two agents who had only three things in common, the Palace versus PESO versus sex? They quit talking and eating before they retired for the late evening.

He woke up first and spent a few moments evaluating his file on 'trees'. Shortly, she awoke saying, "That was the best night of my life. I think that we might have created something last night." He wasn't paying much interest to what she was saying so, he said what he was thinking, "Honey, I hate to leave you but, I have got to go to Boonesboro to see an Indian Chief about some PESO business. Here is your personal key to our house so, make yourself at home. Stay as long as you like, I'll see you in a few short days or weeks. You are the best, the very best." And, he left the house leaving Angel with just one small unheard sentence, "I love you."

Then, he would awaken some dormant pistons. His engine badly needed a hard workout but, today's journey to Boonesboro, KY would take care of that problem. As he drove in that direction, he asked some crucial questions; viz.

- Why would anyone want to visit a State Park that features only trees? Hell, most of them have plenty of trees in their own backyard.
- Why would a buckeye drive all those miles to see a briar-hopper's tree? It does not compute, folks.
- Do trees have a story to tell that merits attention by our employees? How will I interview a tree?
- Is the Gubernatorial nominee, Mr. Tedd Fox, behind all of this?
- Are there enough Shawnee voters to get him elected as our new Commander-In-Chief?

It was clear to Gray that additional studies would be required before this item could be justified as a potential State Park. This is to say that he had to hit the books, the Internet and, lastly, he had to talk with the Indians. His appointment with Mr. Tedd Fox was imminent and Paul was not yet ready.

Gray was unaware that there were seven different Native American tribes that lived in Kentucky before Daniel Boone first invaded their space. They were the following: Cherokee, Chickasaw, Delaware, Mosopelea, Shawnee, Wyandot and Yuchi. The largest tribes and the most feared warriors were the Cherokee and the Shawnee. And, these two tribes were always at each other's throats.

After a lot of reading and much study, he became convinced that it might be possible to weave a central theme around the subject of 'trees'.

Provided, that the Shawnee tribe would cooperate and give him some assistance along the way. His approach to them would be, let's forget about that angry petition and, together, let's get this job done.

He loaded his gear into his car and made final plans to explore the Kentucky River area of East-Central KY. That would be near the Eastern part of the Transylvania Purchase. His precise target zone would be along the Old Warrior's Path; also known as the Wilderness Road, Kentucky's earliest land route. Reportedly, there is in this area, one very dense growth of Sycamore Trees, no pines, no oaks or any other species. These were the trees that he needed to locate in order to confirm or deny the Shawnee legend.

Just for the sport of it, he decided to paddle his rowboat from Hazard to Boonesboro. He would leave his car with his Mother at Hazard and go from there to the trees near Boonesboro Beach. Boonesboro was a few miles Southeast of Lexington. That was a journey which he always wanted to make because that's how the forests of Eastern Kentucky were decimated.

Lumberjacks would cut the trees and float them down the river to Beattyville and other cities. He also wanted to make that voyage for another reason. Bill Gorman, one of Paul's old friends, made a similar trip in the 1950's. But that was done on a houseboat. So, it was time to do it again under a more demanding setting, using only a small rowboat.

It was the season of spring flooding. So, Paul waited for those tides to arrive before initiating his grand voyage. Those large, deep floodwaters would propel him to his desired destination. Dangerous, of course, it was very dangerous. But, Paul Gray lived for the moment when a strong challenge could be conquered. I remember one comment that was made just after Paul finished his voyage. He told the reporters that he didn't have to paddle. He just steered and pushed broken tree trunks away from his small boat.

From Boonesboro Beach, he would walk due South along the Wilderness Road until he discovered those particular Sycamore trees. He needed to verify that they still existed and were thriving after all of these intervening years.

His best guess was that those elusive trees were to be found at a point which is 3-to-5 miles due South of Boonesboro. And, he was right. He found a dense patch of sycamores at exactly 2.8-miles from Boonesboro and they were magnificent. Some of those tall trees were over 100-ft tall with crowns up to about 80-ft wide.

It was now time to contact members of the Shawnee tribe. But, first, he would rent a room in Boonesboro and, afterwards, he would seek the advice of the local Madison County Sheriff. Quickly, he determined that it was wrong to assume that people with a Shawnee background would be hard to locate. They were everywhere to be found, from the sandy beach through the surrounding forests. They had shops and assorted businesses all along the highway. They seemed to have proliferated in all directions.

They were extremely fortunate not to have walked the Cherokee Trail.

The local Sheriff guided him to a suburb where plenty of Shawnee relatives were to be found. He introduced Gray to Chief Iron Eagle of that clustered group before motoring back to town. Iron Eagle recommended that Paul should speak with a Miss Meg Raintree. "Why her, he asked?"

And, the Indian Chief replied, "She is getting her Doctorate in Shawnee history over at UK-Lexington. I am certain that she can help you. He even scribbled a little 'This will introduce a Mr. Paul Gray' note for me. In that note, he wrote the following words, "If you have the available time, it is absolutely necessary that you help Mr. Gray on this matter of prime importance for the entire Shawnee Nation. Consider this to be a personal favor for both Iron Eagle and Running Fox."

I was surprised by the mention of 'Running Fox' so I asked for a clarification, "Would this Running Fox be the same man as a Mr. Tedd Fox who is our new gubernatorial candidate?" Proudly, the Chief said, "Yes, they are one and the same." Gray was pleased to hear his response because it offered huge possibilities with new and multiple opportunities for PESO.

This meant that he didn't have to worry about the Governor and his wife hurting him anymore. All he had to do was to insure that Tedd Fox won the upcoming election. It wouldn't be easy but, he did have a 'light bulb' about how it should be handled. And, in the process, he would have his own backside well protected.

He thanked Chief Iron Eagle for his cooperation and he asked him if he might do anything for him. The Chief licked his lips and said, "I could sure use some firewater, if you have any." Paul replied favorably to say, "I will send you two quarts of the best fixings that Leslie County has to offer. But, at the moment, it is located in my Peso laboratory in Lexington. I will send it to you before I finish this assignment, OK? Give me your business card and I will take care of it." Will that do?" The Chief said, "Bring it on, Pilgrim."

As he exited the home of Iron Eagle, he said, "I will do everything that I can to get you a new State Park and some increased income. He answered with a wry smile and said, "Today, the State Park and, tomorrow, the Gambling Casino." Paul was left with the private opinion that this old man with the long gray hair was playing the system to his own advantage. But, who doesn't these days?

Meg Raintree turned out to be a ravishing young woman who was still in her twenties. Even better, she agreed to serve as his guide on the investigation of her sacred sycamore trees. It would be very hard to resist her physical attributes but, it could also be bad politics to take advantage of her. So, he decided that, should she make the first move, he would not turn her down. What matter of man could turn her down, anyway? She was too pretty for that to happen. She was absolutely gorgeous.

During our first day of entering that sacred sycamore forest, she donated about two reams of paper for our common cause. She had written these papers for her qualifying research to support her PhD Dissertation.

I thanked her for her sage contribution to the case at hand.

She said, "There is more folklore to discuss. Turn on your voice recorder and I will document what you need to know. I said, "Gladly" while she continued to deliver her verbal explanation of the old myth about these trees.

"We of the Shawnee Nation refer to the sycamore tree as our 'ghost of the forest'. We do this because the long stout trunk has an exfoliated bark that separates in patches to reveal an underlying inner bark of outstanding colors. We believe that changes in the bark represent changes in life or death. When patches separate, we can see contrasting regions of white, green, cream and gray, the colors of life and death for a tree.

During misty weather, light winds, wet ground and clearing skies, we who are blessed in that way can see evil and frightening sights. It seems as if the bark is either dancing in the dark or fighting with some Cherokee warrior, our enemy tribe. After the fog has lifted or after sunrise, those images just vanish into thin air.

Our ancestors did disseminate the belief that the evil ones entered the sycamore tree forest as their sanctuary until conditions were favorable for more killing and fighting between both tribes, the Shawnee and the Cherokee.

Our own legend began with two specific sycamores that were, apparently haunted. Shawnees walked very carefully when they were forced to pass those two trees. They would lower their heads and run quickly away. It was as if they feared that the trees were going to harm them in some way. In any case, they wanted to avoid them in any way that was possible.

Birds never nested in those trees. In fact wild birds never came anywhere close to those two trees. Wild animals also avoided the twin trees. Occasionally, a dead carcass would be found up in the limbs and branches as if it had been caught and tossed.

The legend of the twin trees also involved one Shawnee maiden and one captured Cherokee warrior. The original story was dated during several years ago, when a raid was made by the Shawnee tribe against the Southern Cherokee.

The young brave fought valiantly but, he was badly wounded and, subsequently, subdued. The Shawnee tribe places a high value on courage so, because of his bravery, he was not killed. Instead, he was taken back to the Shawnee village just north of the Ohio River for healing and recovery.

During his convalescence, a lovely Shawnee girl nursed his wounds and they became madly in love with each other. Knowing that the Shawnee Chief would never allow them to marry, they decided to run away together just as soon as he was road worthy and able to ride a fast horse.

Realizing that they would both be killed, if captured, their plan was to go south through, what is today, Boonesboro proper. Then, they would cut to the east toward the big Gap and, ultimately, they would seek refuge in today's Southeast Tennessee, a wild, uninhabited land.

So, late one summer night, when the young man was well enough to travel, they quietly slipped away from their Shawnee encampment, seeking their futures together. For three days, they hurried South along the Warrior's Path because they could make better time using that well-worn route.

On the fourth day, they heard a dog barking which meant that the Chief and his warriors were catching up with them. Although, these two lovers and their horses were almost exhausted, they continued to struggle onward in the divine hope of evading their pursuers. Just as the Sun was about to set, a bad storm could be heard in the southwest and it was headed in their direction. After a few more miles of frantic movement, they found themselves on the left bank of a river that was flowing north. That would be once mighty Kentucky River.

As the raging storm was approaching the two run-a-ways, both of them knew that they were trapped. So, the lovers just clung to each other awaiting their inevitable death. When the Shawnee Chief and his followers were within a five yards of the pair, a large bolt of lightning struck.

That was immediately followed by the earth-shaking clap of thunder.

Several of the pursuing Shawnees were separated from their mounts by that bolt of electricity which also tore a huge cavity in the ground exactly where the two lovers were cowering.

No traces of the couple were ever found for the couple. And, the Chief searched the entire area dutifully after the storm had passed. He was angry. He had suffered large losses of men and horses without any hand-to-hand struggles, an embarrassing event for a 'War Lord' who was dedicated to always winning or accomplishing his goals.

At a later time, two small sycamore trees sprouted from that large cavity where the lovers had died. One sprout was stronger and larger than the other. As they both grew, that ratio did not change. All Indians who passed this way would notice their odd behavior during a wind storm. As the wind blew, their long limbs would seem to caress each other in an apparent protective mode.

It was also observed that, during the flooding season, the tallest tree would sway back and forth in a protective manner. It was obvious that the tallest tree was trying to protect the smaller tree. We Shawnees have respected sycamore trees ever since and we have given those two the names of 'Mada-Eve' which means in English, 'Adam-Eve'.

When white settlers arrived in this area, they heard about the 'Mada-Eve Legend' and they laughed at the idea of human spirits inhabiting the sycamores. One white settler tried to prove a point when he took out his axe and tried to cut down the larger tree. His axe blade bounced off of a hard knot and the axe was deflected toward his knee. He bled to death quickly giving root to the concept that the trees contained some strong poison.

The sap was a pale redish color as if it was similar to human blood.

Shortly after the lumberjack's death, another man was found at the scene and he was hanging about twenty feet off of the ground, snared and strangled by wild grape vines that were tightly coiled around his neck. A third death recorded another white man's death.

He was found sitting under the smaller tree with no marks on his body but, his face showed great fear or surprise. It was assumed that he was scared to death by the spirit within the larger tree. As a result of these three deaths, knowledgeable people just avoided both trees after that time.

In 1929, with the great financial crash of Wall Street, the larger tree just began to shrivel, dry up and die. It fell to the ground with a thundering noise that was heard for over a mile away. Observers said that the fall of that tree was accompanied by a shrilling Indian War Cry. Some argue that it could have been a shrieking sound from splitting lumber but, my Grandfather was there when it happened.

He said that the noise was definitely that of a Cherokee warrior. He had gone through too many skirmishes with the Cherokee in his past and he said that he would know that sound anywhere. My money is on my Grandfather because no one ever knew him to tell a lie.

Strangely, the smaller sycamore tree died a few months later. She fell across her Cherokee lover with a tortured wailing sound. There was no debate about this sound because every Shawnee family recognized the wailing of a widow for a dead husband or child.

He turned his recorder off and asked a critical question, "Do other sycamores act in the same manner?" She replied, "Yes, they mate in pairs just as we humans do. I have no proof to offer you but, in theory, the Shawnee firmly believe that sycamore trees have a humanistic side to their growth and behavior."

"Dr. Raintree, you are an inspiration to me. I think that I might be able to offer you and your tribe some scientific proof that trees are, indeed, similar to humans. I will have to compare data between three opposite sets before I can write a paper on this topic. But, I will share all my results with you when I finish that experimentation because you have inspired me so much.

Meg, this stuff about trees that love each other is one hell of a paranormal story. It will look good in my Final Report and, I thank you for sharing all of this information with me. Please tell Chief Iron Eagle that this is now an approved site for his new State Park. But, the gambling casino will have to be his responsibility, not mine or PESO's. In summary, he said that this has been a tale worth hearing."

Suddenly, Meg made her move. She said, "Wouldn't you like to share some 'tail' with me before we leave this sacred place?" He went back to the trunk of his car to get those treasured blankets of his while she gathered dried sycamore leaves to serve as nature's own cushion.

Privately, he wondered, "What do swell looking women see in a guy like me? I am just a guy who has a larger plaything than most men do."

He didn't know it at the time but, Dr. Raintree had a point to make. There was absolutely no wind but, the nearby sycamore trees were swaying back and forth as if they understood and approved of the oncoming tryst.

The sycamores were unable to communicate with Gray in a language that he could understand. Like every other man, he wrongly concluded that it was his great looks or his muscle-bound frame. He felt that, in this regard, he was just luckier than most men. Then, they were joined together as experienced lovers in a push-and-shove match of estatic proportions.

When they were about ready to climax, she whispered, "Paul, look at the trees. They were swaying back and forth in a vibrant mode and, they appeared to be wildly 'dancing with the stars'. When both lovers did have their orgasm, the ground did shake and, it felt like a 3.2 reading on the Richter scale. And, then he knew what Meg had wanted him to learn, the trees were having sex along with them.

Because he was a scientist, he was 'forced' to repeat the experiment several times. Each time that they had a climax, the ground would move and the trees would merrily dance. Their joint theories about 'sexy' sycamores were witnessed, recorded and validated on multiple occasions.

As an added advantage, Meg Raintree was a talented companion and he enjoyed being with her in this manner. He had never done a College Instructor before and, besides that, she was fun to be with. He ranked her pretty high on his list of conquests, from Angel to Mira to Meg.

No matter the ranking, she certainly merited return engagements and often. He told her, "We mustn't disappoint the sycamores. If they want to watch an X-rated sex show, then the least that we can do is to follow through, right?"

And, fortunately for Dr. Gray, Dr. Raintree agreed by saying, "Paul we are almost neighbors over at Lexington and I figure to be on Clay Street often, if you don't mind." He said, "Fine with me but, call ahead, please. I have to screw my boss lady on a regular basis. He took specimens, loaded his gear and he left for home base where he would, eventually, hook-up his boat trailer to go and rescue his rowboat at Boonesboro Beach.

Man, what a story. My second paper could win me a lot of favorable exposure at the Paris Convention. Who ever heard of a hillbilly policeman who was nominated for the Nobel Prize? What a complex World we live in these days!

Chapter Twenty-one

TUNNELS

P AUL GRAY WAS the son of a railroad man. Therefore, he did have more knowledge about tunnels than the typical man-on-the-street would ever know. Yes, Paul knew quite a bit about those 'holes-through-the-mountains', especially, the haunted ones.

When Gray was a youngster, he would carry a hot lunch to his Father and they would dine together at the L&N Coal Tower. Dad's primary job was to stock the steamers with coal to fuel their boilers as they proceeded through the State from Hazard to Ravenna, KY. Dessert would always be delicious but, Dad's railroad stories were tastier. As a child, Paul couldn't get enough of his Father's stories, especially the ones about baseball, the Cincinnati Red Legs and the haunted tunnels.

The nearest haunted tunnel for the Hazard Yards was the one that connected Combs, KY to Hazard, KY, which was less than 500-feet from where their lunch was consumed. Dad was a man who told beautiful stories in a brief and dry manner meaning, that they were always short and without any useless filler or kinky sex.

I enjoyed hearing good stories about bad tunnels until the time came that I had to ride through one of them. Then, I would shut my eyes and pray that the arch would not fall down and upon the train to kill me. My vivid imagination and that awful darkness of a long tunnel were more than I could handle. Back then, young Paul Gray had no interest in ghosts whatsoever. In his mind's eye, ghosts were scary things and nothing more.

Young Gray rode the passenger train quite a lot, especially during the summer, when there was no school classes to worry about. He would visit his grandmother and his favorite Aunt Mina who lived in Jackson, a gargantuan trip of more than 44-miles from Hazard. When he started his trip, he was scared about that damned tunnel and, after he arrived, he was frightened about his return trip through that same damned tunnel. In brief, he didn't like tunnels.

There were two haunted tunnels that his Father liked to talk about best. One was at the North end of the Hazard Yards. That one was hiding in plain sight if your aspect angle was from the top of the Coal Tower. It was called the 'Dewey Daniels Tunnel' in honor of an extraordinary citizen who lived and died in Hazard, KY.

The other haunted tunnel was about halfway between Elkatawa and Oakdale near Highway 52 and it was situated due west out of Jackson. It was named the Chenowee Tunnel. Because of the elevation grade, the tracks near Chenowee required pusher trains for enough power to move over and through the mountains. In other words, every single string of loaded coal cars was assigned three locomotives at the Jackson Yards, one forward and two aft.

Both tunnels were frightening but, in different ways. The Daniels Tunnel screeched an eerie sound because the track offered a tight turn with an insufficient allowance for too much sway. This is to say that the tunnel was barely wide enough to let the traffic pass without some slight contact to be made. And, if the engineer was going too fast, sway would increase and, accordingly, more contact noises were to be heard.

That metal-to-rub that the wheels made against the rails was a fearful sound. Decibel for decibel, it sounded like that of a dying man who was facing a horrible death. And, if the train's speed was excessive, loaded coal cars would badly sway to cut deep gouges in the tunnel's sidewalls. That gouging sound of dynamic wear would sound like the roar of a jungle lion prior to devouring his captured prey.

So, the roar and the scream were enough to convince many people that someone was being killed by the resident ghost that resided inside the subject tunnel. The Chenowee Tunnel offered a different sound from that which was emitted by the Daniels Tunnel.

Dry sand was blown onto the rails to provide more friction so that the helper trains did not have to work so hard in making that difficult grade.

The crunching of sand by the rotating wheels of the three locomotives constituted a weird sound in its own right. And, ghostologists likened the sound to that of a human body being crushed. It was a 'crunch-crunch' sound that frightened many persons, especially on the passenger trains.

And, to make things worse at the Chenowee Tunnel, consider the odor that is emitted when hot, wet sand is blown by superheated steam to improve the frictional contact with those rails. It was a charnel odor that reeked of burnt flesh. And, it certainly annoyed the people that lived in the neighborhood. They each were committed to the concept that a killer ghost lived inside of the Chenowee Tunnel. In its own time, the Chenowee Tunnel has been blamed for many deaths and suicides. As a result, it has become a haunted place that is occupied by several different spirits.

Some sightings have been attributed to construction problems. For example, the Daniels Tunnel had a spell cast upon it when a worker named French was killed under suspicious circumstances. Reportedly, he was knocked off of his scaffolding by a co-worker named Eversole.

French's head hit an outcropping of sandstone and he died instantly from brain damage. Detailed follow-up investigations revealed that this incident was related to the French-Eversole Feud. So, the L&N Yardmaster was blamed for placing two known enemies inside the same work location, a tunnel tube. However, that doesn't explain the sound of a crushed skull that has been heard for many long years after the 'alleged' accident occurred. Is this sound the result of a French spirit that is trapped inside of the mountain or, is it just related to rubs caused by too much sway?

The Chenowee Tunnel was affected in a similar way. Early in its construction phase, a worker was using his sledge hammer to clear the way for an enhanced sway improvement project. He lost his footing on the rock that he was hitting. Because of the fact that he had opened a critical crack, he fell to his death.

His death was also ruled as a result of extreme brain damage combined with routine chance arising from matters which he could not control. In other words, don't stand on the precipice which you are using a rock chisel on.

However, that cause of death does not relate to the fact that his screams have been heard by countless ears since the day that he died. Or, is it just a metal-to-metal rub along a very tight turning circle? To make matters worse, a Carnival Witch placed a wicked spell on the tunnel to demonstrate her power to her audience. In any event, weird sounds have been overheard which cannot be explained by specialists.

Gray folded his file on both tunnels and he wondered, how in the World am I going to wrap a State Park around a railroad tunnel? It would be ideal if it were an abandoned tunnel where there is no train traffic. However, the traffic through these two haunted sights is high so, there is very little chance that the railroad officials would allow any throughput by PESO. He decided to place both tunnel sites on an indefinite 'hold' status.

If a new State Park is to be built at some point in the far-distant future, more dedicated planning will have to done at that time, not the present. On the basis of what he knew for the present, he would have to vote 'no' for any further activity for this particular project. Tomorrow at the breakfast meeting with Mira, he would present the final summary to her as a 'negative' project. And, the bottom line for these tunnel sightings is simply stated as follows: "No French-owned railroad company would forfeit their current profit of hauling Black Gold to the marketplace which is, by the way, somewhere in that damned country called France.

He would also present to Mira two other items of concern; viz. (1) Angel the mole? (2) The 'truth' about Running Fox. Having nothing else to do, he decided to take a short siesta on top of Marilyn Monroe. To make it more interesting, he ate some chocolate ice cream. Then, he went to bed for an afternoon nap.

He was awakened much too soon by his own preferences. But, Mira was there and she was licking his face to get him out of his sound sleep, just as a dog might do. She had used her personal key to gain entrance and she had the look of pure panic on her face. After they hugged and had some small talk, He said, "What's wrong, love?"

She dropped a bombshell about Angel when she said, "That whore whom you like so much has told the Governor that we are aiding and abetting Mr. Tedd Fox, the Governor's foe in the next election." Then, Paul told Mira about Angel's recent interests, including hidden cameras and the new State Park for Chief Iron Eagle.

Gray added, "If you count those two issues, we are indeed helping the Fox campaign. And, old Governor forgets the fact that he was the original sponsor for the sycamore assignment. So, who is threatening your tenure?

She answered, "The President of the University of Kentucky told me that the Governor leaked the information to the Board of Trustees in a scheduled Board Meeting. His exact words were that, by the end of his current term, PESO would no longer exist.

Paul thought about that stupid move by the Governor. In all aspects, such foolish comments about PESO in the public domain may have just caused the old man from being re-elected. Not to worry your pretty little head, Mira. I have a plan which is in the development stage and I think it will work to solve all of your problems with the Governor.

Now is the time to release some of our sex-sensitive photographs about Mr. and Mrs. Governor. Immediately, she cried out, "How do we manage to do that?" Paul answered, "I will see that all of the information is transferred to the Shawnee Nation through a young maiden called Raintree.

She is close to both Iron Eagle and Running Fox. If anyone catches any heat for having those files, it will be the Indians, not PESO." She considered the idea for a few seconds and then she said, "That might just work because the new election is just weeks away."

Next, she reverted to her womanly ways to ask, "How well do you know this Shawnee maiden?" Paul answered, "Mira, she's just a young girl that served as my guide for the sycamore job." Fortunately, Mira let it go at that because she offered no more inquiries about that subject. Instead, she did have another question for him to answer.

"May I visit with Miss Marilyn while I am here?" "Of course, you can, dear Mira. Especially since you and the girls turned my home into a psychedelic hen house." "Oh, Paul, you don't like our little creation, do you?" "Mira, it is okay but, when is the disco ball going to be installed?"

"Honey, it's still on back order." After some more chit-chit, they made rapturous sex on top of Miss Monroe, aka Norma Jeane Baker.

During a subsequent rest period, they discussed ways to get rid of Angel, the mole who was playing both sides, PESO's and the Governor's. Paul's heart wasn't really into that subject because he had fallen madly in love at first sight. He was remembering that night that they had together while Mira was seriously dedicated to dumping her as a risk which would be foolhardy to keep as a PESO employee.

So, they struggled off and on with that subject all night long. Their night was dedicated to sex, sleep and strategy. Paul enjoyed the first two activities but, not the latter one. In his mind, he knew that Angel had to leave but, in his heart, he wanted her to stay and for a whole lifetime. For the first time in his life, he was thinking about asking someone to marry him.

Each of their connective sessions involved the image of Miss Marilyn which had been sewn onto his Egyptian Cotton bedding sheets. Mira had purchased two sets of bedding sheets. In one view, Marilyn was completely nude. In the other view, Marilyn's dress was being blown skyward by a blast of compressed steam. Talk about hot, wow! Paul considered the latter to be a creation of the highest order, a masterpiece of photography which gave him a boost whenever he needed one.

When their love-making ended, they grabbed about two hours of sleep in which they both forgot all about Angel and that associated aggravation. But, like all nagging problems, they reappeared next morning. He bade Mira goodbye so that she could go home to Joan, her other lover, get a shower and change her outfit. Mira didn't want her girls to notice that she was wearing the same dress for two successive days.

In between preparation for Starbucks and, subsequently, a day's work at PESO, he decided to make a short list of how they might get rid of their mole and double agent, Angel. These are the best items that he could come up with:

(1) *PESO could hire a Mexican assassin but, Angel did not deserve such treatment.*

(2) *PESO could send Angel on a World Cruise but, that would be $20,000 that was badly misspent.*

(3) *PESO could transfer Angel to the MPD but he didn't want his former Captain to be anywhere close to her.*

(4) We could terminate Angel using the information that we already have but, could we prove those facts in court?

(5) We could hire a detective to follow Angel and obtain more evidence against her.

(6) We could expand to Texas where that Governor wants his own PESO organization. And, Angel would be safe in Texas.

(7) Or, PESO could just wait until after the elections because one-half of her money would disappear when Fox does win the election.

Gray would present these seven possibilities to Mira over their coffee and snack meeting at Starbucks this morning. He would pressure her strongly to adopt his favorite, solution number (6). That method of choice for the ousting of Angel appeared to be the one with superior good taste. A lot of priceless information had been obtained from Angel when she was at the Palace so she still had his respect. And, of course, Paul did not want to see Angel hurt by anyone or anything, not now. He adored the woman.

It was not a hard sell. Mira went for number six solution in a big way. She said that she would be making a telephone call to Austin, TX this very morning. If that didn't work, we both agreed that solution number Five was our backup plan. That settled that.

Then, he would tell her that he had no intention of trespassing on L&N property and why he felt that way. Temporarily, she agreed to place the 'tunnels' file into her cold case file. And, that usually had the same effect as putting something through the shredding machine. Personally, he hoped that those two tunnels would never be heard from again as probable candidates for new State Parks.

And, for the son of a railroad man, that's really saying something that is entirely atypical. Usually, a railroad family will support anything that could cast the Railroad in a better light. As a rule, we were sick and tired of being called 'railroad trash' by the overweening citizens of Hazard. And, Paul, as a young student, was mindful of all the girls that said 'no' to his request for a date. The wealthiest ones were in the coal business and his Father forbade any contact with those arrogant girls. He said, "Those gals are not the marrying kind.

Next, they would both retreat from Starbucks in tandem fashion as per usual. She would go first and ten minutes later, he would follow. This time, when he arrived at his desk, he discovered some evidence of how Angel was stealing confidential information. On top of his desk was a file copy of 'Trees'. That one was about Indian ghosts and sycamores, remember?

And, the file was badly disheveled. The sheets were spread apart while Mira had always stapled them together. Clearly, someone had removed Mira's staple and spread the pages apart as if they had been to the copy machine. Probably, she was trying to offer evidence that PESO was supporting stories that supported the Fox tribe.

Gray said, "To hell with Angel and all of that associated spy business." That side of her character was not what he wanted in a wife. He was running behind schedule and he needed to be reviewing his next case file. But, mainly, he wanted to be somewhere else. Someplace where people don't play so many games would be nice, so very nice.

Perhaps this trip would be what his tired soul needed. It would require him to visit Vanceburg, KY, the County Seat of Lewis County. Vanceburg is situated on the Ohio River near the top boundary of the State. Adjacent Counties are two, Adams and Scioto which are in Ohio just across the big river from Lewis County.

One of the most famous citizens from that part of the State was Meriwether Louis of the famed 'Lewis & Clark Expedition'. He was excited about going there because it would be the first trip to that part of the State and he enjoyed looking at new things, mostly women. He packed his gear into his Cruiser and he left Lexington in a rainstorm.

He would call Mira later to inform her of his position and his mission.

She liked to keep track of his movements because he was such a dangerous driver. Deep down, Mira did not want him to hurt himself because she had big plans for his undamaged body. And, don't forget, she was talking about some serious shopping in Paris, France.

He would tell her that he was on the road to Vanceburg and places generally northeast of Lexington. Additionally, he asked her not to leave sensitive information on top of his desk, not when Angel was known to be prowling around.

What he would not tell her was how depressed he was over the political side of his job. He was sick and tired of fighting the Palace antagonists that were currently doing battle against PESO. He didn't want her to feel the same way that he did so he remained silent about that subject. Redheads are easy to tip, one way or another, because they are so high strung. So, today, he would not be one of those people who would add to Mira's list of problems.

Paul was supportive of Mira's goals more than anyone else. Therefore, he needed to help her, not to add to her workload. He was speeding at over 100 miles per hour but, he took time to smile. He was proud of himself because he had just spared Mira from some additional grief. And, at the same time, he was helping Angel to get away with whatever she was doing to harm PESO. Isn't it strange that Paul was just as guilty as Angel was, if you boil the cabbage down, that is.

Chapter Twenty-two

IRISHMAN

WHILE ON THE way to Vanceburg, Gray called Mira to see how she was doing and she said, "I wish that you were here, I miss you." He said, "I long for you too, Babe, why do you think I called?" After the small talk was over, he asked her if she had yet decided on how to deal with Angel and her double dealing.

"I think that the Texas Branch of PESO is the best way to handle this, especially since the Governor 'down under' is so interested. I called him this morning and he said, "The ball is in our court." Ultimately, you and I will have to visit Austin, TX for a formal presentation of what we do and how we do it so well. That presentation will have to include financial details which I will cover but, I shall leave the technical matters to you."

"That's good Mira. Perhaps, we will get some resolution on that pesky little problem about Angel sooner than expected. What about the ousting expose of the Governor and his First Lady? Any thoughts on 'how and when' we drop that little bomb?" She replied, "Have you ever considered printed photographs being dropped from an airplane?"

Paul answered, "No, it's too easy to identify an aircraft in this day and age. Before the Shawnees could ever finish the job of dropping our little bomb, the Governor would have his own airplanes on their trail. Either that or the State Police would be wherever the Shawnees might try to land. Mira, the problem is that each plane is numbered for identification purposes and that serves the Governor's interests, no ours."

She said, "If you feel that way then, it's a 'no' vote for TV and radio coverage, isn't it?" "Yes, it is my dear. However, mass mailings from all over the State of Kentucky at exactly the same time would do the trick. Each photograph should be placed in an innocuous brown envelope and mailed to every Church in Kentucky. Tonight, I will call Chief Iron Eagle to solicit his help in playing a little 'post office scam' with me.

She, like the tigress that she is, said, "What are you going to use for a return address?" Paul replied, "I was thinking about something totally inoffensive like the 'Re-elect or Not Committee'. What do you think, Mira?" She responded, "Sounds like a winner to me, Paul but, you had better hurry because the election date is drawing nigh."

He responded, "Have you got the photos finished?" She reacted in this manner, "Yes, I printed them at home on my computer to avoid leaks through Angel." He replied, "Good, I will call you tomorrow about Iron Eagle's reaction to our plan. Hopefully, the Chief might be able to help us with our distribution problem. I believe that he will help us and our plan because Iron Eagle wants Running Fox to be elected. Otherwise, there will never be a Casino on his reservation.

She inquired, "What's our distribution problem?" Jokingly, he responded, "We need about 5000 Indians to lick a lot of stamps and to send those brown envelopes to the Pastors of every Church in Kentucky."

"Oh, Paul, you think about everything that is important to PESO. I don't know what I would do without you." He said, "Never mind that as long as you don't forget what to do with me." They both laughed and they hung up their phones. Then and there, they had set their devious plan in motion.

From here on out, their success depended on the old 'snail mail' system and the hard shell Christians of the entire State. Or, from another viewpoint, how badly the Shawnees wanted a new State Park and Gambling Casino. With the insider information that Paul Gray had, he was ready to bet everything that he owned on Fox as the winner and the next Governor. Paul would call his bookie tomorrow to see if the election odds were worth the risk.

Vanceburg turned out to be a big disappointment in size, population and hydrology. For example, the city itself included about 1800 people at the last Census and, it was small, just 1.2 square miles in area. Surprisingly, there was no running water in Vanceburg. So, the requirements of a dense fog for quality ghost hunting was a major problem, to say the very least.

Gray would have to import large quantities of river water from the Ohio River and, he would have to refine that water if quality sightings were to be evident for the Vanceburg Ghost Park. It was workable but, it would be very expensive with the atypical requirement for a dedicated Water System. Water is critical in the paranormal business because a precise specific gravity is mandated for optimizing the optical clarity that is needed to properly resolve a ghostly image.

He rented a room at a friendly-looking bed and breakfast operation.

Hoping all the while that another red headed widow would appear, like the one at Farler, Kentucky. But, so far, none had surfaced. He would wait until the morning to see if any spare feminine pulchritude existed in the small town of Vanceburg.

If he had found none by ten o'clock in the morning, he vowed to go to work with a heavy weight of disappointment on his mind. Ten AM came and went so, sadly, he went to work with his clogged pipes being totally ignored by the entire female population, all 976 of them.

He visited the local barber shop to determine if anyone knew anything about the ghost that was pestering the town. It was a single-chair-shop where two men were waiting for a haircut while another was in the chair getting his hair trimmed.

When he loudly announced his purpose in visiting Vanceburg both customers who were waiting for a haircut vacated the shop and quickly so. The cantankerous old barber was quite angry about losing two of his best customers because of 'fear fright'.

He told Paul that he would have to reimburse him for his loss of income and haircuts, in this part of the country, were still $8 per head. So, Gray had not yet said "Hello" and he had already spent $16 smackers. He smiled and said to himself, "This old bird is different kind of cuss. I will have to watch this one very closely.

When Paul paid for the loss of income, things settled down somewhat. Gray then asked, "Who can I talk to about this Vanceburg ghost that I keep hearing about?" The barber stopped trimming and he said, "That would be me, sonny. Just wait until I finish this man's hair. Then, I will close up the shop and we will go across the street to Miss Molly's Restaurant for a few cups of good strong coffee. Then, I will tell you all you need to know about my McArdle ancestor."

While he was waiting, Paul began to read the magazines that were available in the Barber Shop. That experience was like a time warp. Their average age was five-to-10 years old. But, he wisely decided not to say anything bad about McArdle's Shop, not just yet. The one article that caught his eye was entitled "Will Obama Be Good For Our Nation?" Paul knew the answer to that question but, he didn't have an opinion to express, not here and not now.

Paul would wait until he could get from McArdle what he needed most and that was background history on the McArdle Ghost, the Irishman. He would not allow old magazines to interfere with his personal goals. That would prove to be unwise because 'cantankerous' was the key word when describing this old barber.

The old man locked the doors of his barber shop and the pair went to see Miss Molly about some Java in the morning. When he first saw Molly, he was tempted to ask, "Where were you last night when I needed you so badly?" But, he held back from saying anything naughty. First, he wanted input from the barber. Naughty would come later because Molly had all of the right equipment in all of the right places. Her *derriere* was of considerable interest to him.

And, McArdle stood firm when he said, "I don't talk on an empty stomach." So, Gray bought him a country breakfast, a feast of too much and everything. Surprisingly, McArdle ate the whole thing and he burped loud enough for everyone in the Restaurant to overhear. Privately, he thought, "They don't make characters like him anymore."

Paul sipped his strong coffee and said, "All right Mr. 'Barber-Man', you have the floor. What do you know about the Vanceburg Ghost? The old man said, "To start with, let's discuss the terms of payment for my knowledge.

Is that all right with you, city slicker?" Paul said, "How about a Century note for today's interviews?" The old man almost choked on his coffee. He took too much at precisely the wrong time. He said, "That will be all right for starters. I will want more if this gets to be a lot of work, OK?"

By this time, Paul was getting to be a little upset but, he bit his lips and said nothing. This old bird was giving him the hustle but, he was patient. He needed McArdle more than McArdle needed him so he felt that patience was what he needed to have."

I need a guide to the location where this apparition was first observed.

And, that usually carries a price tag of $500.00 and, that, Mr. McArdle is all that I am allowed to pay. The old man swallowed a larger gulp of hot coffee and he spit it out to avoid choking. Quietly, he murmured, "That will be acceptable for me and my services. However, I am not going to cut your damned hair for nothing. That will cost you extra."

He paid the rascal $600.00 cash money from his large roll of expense money but, he made certain that Molly had witnessed the whole transaction. He would be paying her later from the same roll so it was vital for her to see that he was not a typical customer off the street, not by a long shot.

The old geezer began with these words, "My name is Able McArdle and the ghost that you are looking for was an ancient ancestor of mine. His name was Ted McArdle. Ted could out drink and out fight any man in town. He was also known for beating up the Shawnee Indians that lived in this area. And, it was the Shawnee Nation that got him into more trouble than he could handle."

One night, a hunting party was organized by Ted and nine other liquored-up Irishmen. Their plan was to go into the woods and pick a fight with the Shawnee tribesmen. The two opponents, Irish and Indian, soon engaged each other in mortal combat and very serious fighting was the end result.

The Shawnee far outnumbered the ten Irishmen but, the kill rate was about two-to-one, favoring the Irish. After the nine white men were killed, Ted was finally overcome and captured as a prisoner. They valued Ted's heroics so much that they took him back to their encampment for all of the tribal Indians to admire and respect.

He was to be on display for five days. During that time they would fill him with all manner of food and drink. At the time, Ted didn't understand why they were treating him like royalty. But he would soon find out why they were being so nice.

After the fifth day, the Chief said, "Here stands a fine warrior of the white man's clan. He fought a good fight and he was still fighting very well at the finish when we finally overpowered him. Now, in honor of his brave spirit within his body, we will witness how well he handles being burned alive at our stake.

If he cries as a child would do, his soul will go to the wicked one down below. If he dies like a great warrior should, his spirit will go into skies above and he will live forever with the greatest God of all Gods. Braves of my Tribe, make him ready for this ceremony. We are ready to send this one to the wicked one." The Braves roped him in four directions and they forced him toward the big stake area.

"Able, how did he handle his ensuing death?" The old barber said, "Like the great warrior that he was. He confronted all of the flames without a single cry of pain. But, he did manage to curse the Indians bitterly. He also told them how it would be when more of his Irish brothers would come here from Ireland to conquer you savage beasts, to seize all of your land and to rape all of your women. That day is soon coming, and there is nothing that you can do about that, Chief.

Then, he cast a spell on everyone in the Chief's Tribe. That spell would send every member of his tribe to the wicked one down below after they died. This infuriated the Indian Chief so much that he threw a spear into Ted's ribs and my poor relative began to bleed profusely. The final words out of his mouth were, "I beat the flames, you dumb ass."

Paul said, "That is a very good story. How much of it is fable and how much is fact?" The old geezer was upset at the words that Gray chose to use. So, he answered him in this way, "As far as I am concerned, it is all fact and no fiction. It's exactly as my Father said to me and his Father said to him, et cetera.

If you want further proof, we will have to visit the actual site where all this occurred. We will have to hope for some fog to be drifting across the place where those damned Indians killed my poor ancestor so many years ago." Paul smiled and asked, "Can we leave before twilight ends?"

McArdle said, "That's a deal, Sonny. I'll go cut a few hairs and we'll meet at my place around 5PM, okay? He left and all across the street he was spitting very angrily. Paul figured that Able was still mad about that 'fact versus fable' remark of his.

Then he went over to where Miss Molly was standing by her cash register. He needed to pay for his morning feast, the good strong coffee and the use of her table for official PESO business. They settled on a bill of $100.00 as the total price for everything.

Next, he started flirting with Molly because he was beginning to feel the pain of stone ache which was caused by his clogged pipes. After a few words, between them, Molly asked for someone named Sally to leave the kitchen and work the tables. Her little sister was gorgeous and they both resembled twins. Molly told Sally, "I have a hot one that wants a 'nooner only sooner'. If I am not back in thirty minutes, close the Restaurant and join us upstairs.

Paul was delighted to have a threesome possibility with two lovely sisters. In his opinion, that planned event was certainly more palatable than gnawing on an over-fried and greasy 'Vance-burger'. He would spend most of the afternoon taking on one sister at a time.

While he was with Sallie, Molly would help him out by licking certain erotic regions on Molly and vice versa. He couldn't count all the climaxes that the two sisters had but, by the time that 4 o'clock rolled around, they were both beaming with pleasure. He left them with a huge tip because they were so good at giving sex.

Around four, they fixed him a free steak dinner while he waited for McArdle to cross the street again. Able had very few teeth left so they fixed him a soft sandwich and some mashed potatoes at no cost whatsoever. As the Sun began to set, they left for the location down near where the Ohio River meets the sandy beach of Vanceburg.

On the way there, Able said, "That is a lot of horses under the hood of your Police Car. What's maximum speed that you have driven with this machine?" Paul said, "About 150-mph without any vibrations of any kind." The old man was quite impressed as he exclaimed, "That is some chase vehicle. None of the kids around here could out-run this car even with their hopped-up California kits."

Later, Able took Paul and his equipment deep into the piney woods where the sightings were supposed to appear. He installed his cameras in a fifty-foot circle as directed by Able. And, they waited and waited but, nothing happened.

Paul became a little bit upset so he asked Able, "When can we expect some action?" Able answered, "Not until after we get some more river fog in this area. When the river fog becomes denser, we ought to see something more interesting. River water is different from freshwater or rainwater, it takes longer to materialize any apparitional outlines or recognizable features. Paul was elated because, if Able is correct, I might not need a Water Plant, after all."

Able continued, "The critical variables are all correct. Those being the clearing skies, the light winds and the wet ground. All we need now is a proper visibility index for Ted McArdle to come and pay his respects."

Able smiled and said to himself, "This city slicker is going to be surprised and, hopefully, quite pleased. He may even mark his laundry."

After about another hour and a little after three o'clock in the morning, Ted McArdle made his ghastly but, grand appearance. He was tied to a long tepee pole with Indian warriors dancing around him. Two Indians were beating their drums and, in the background, another was playing the eerie sound of a reed flute.

Paul could feel the hairs on the back of his neck standing at full salute in honor of this frightening scene. But, the main attraction for this probable new State Park theme was the cursing. No one curses like a drunken Irishman so the Shawnee maidens had to have fed him lots of Kickapoo Joy Juice. They believed that their moonshine whiskey would cause him to burn from the inside out.

Ted was angry and he was cursing as loudly as he could. Able interrupted to say, "Watch closely, Dr. Gray because this is where it gets to be very interesting and quite different from most other hallucinations." Then, one Indian Brave grabbed a burning torch and set poor Ted on fire. At that point, poor Ted really began to rant and rave.

Thereafter, a blue glow covered Ted's body. And, ultimately, he exploded with a very loud 'popping noise'. This was followed by a charnel odor that was very difficult to breathe. Paul covered his face with a handkerchief but, that proved to be insufficient for the problem at hand.

After a bit, the whole scene faded into black. Ted had disappeared as quickly as he had first appeared. Paul examined the area for any evidence of a burn but there was no lingering evidence of such. He said, "That was really a good show. I almost shit in my pants. And, I do hope that one of my cameras caught all that action on film." Able laughed and said, "No other camera has been successful in capturing that image, not ever." Paul defended his equipment by saying, "I have the best night vision cameras that money can buy. Let's hope that they do succeed because I need those images to help sell this project.

Then, Able got all stiff as he said, "Mister, I want an apology." Paul asked, "About what?" Able was getting angrier as he replied, "For that damned 'fact or fable' talk that you made yesterday morning at the Restaurant." Paul said, "I didn't realize that you were so sensitive about your ancestor, Ted McArdle." He apologized as graciously as he could. And, then, they shook hands and became the best of friends again.

Able asked the obvious question, "How did you like our picture show?" Paul Gray shook his head and said, "This is not a good show for young children to watch but, it sure got my attention. Furthermore, I have to say that it could be our best State Park ever."

Then, Able stiffened again and he said, "This here is sacred soil for my family and I own this property for several miles around. So, I might not want to sell. Tell your Governor that my price will be pretty substantial. I might even break the bank on this one." Paul laughed as he said, "I wish you success, Able. Then, I can get my hair cut by a barber who is, on the side, a multi-millionaire. Let's both look forward to that, shall we?"

They gathered up Paul's gear and they headed back to town because Able had a full day of barbering ahead of him. It was early Saturday morning and there would be a square dance in Vanceburg tonight. So, the men would want to look as pretty as they could.

Therefore, Abel asked him to put the 'pedal to the metal' and he did just that. Paul was driving at maximum speed over those rural roads of Lewis County when he asked, "Why do the Shawnee seem to prefer an Irish person?" Able answered by saying, "One reason is that the drunk Irishmen loved to fight and the Shawnee loved to win." Dr. Gray asked, "Is there any other reason?"

Able said, "The favorite color of the Shawnee is blue and only an Irishman can drink enough Kickapoo Joy Juice to provide a blue glow and a powerful alcohol-related explosion." Then, both men laughed loudly and in unison.

When they did arrive back in town, it was still dark. "Able thanked him for the ride of his life. That Police Cruiser of yours has the most horses that I have ever ridden in all of my doggone days." After Able was safely inside of his barber shop and, when his upstairs ceiling lights were turned on, he motored across the street where a candle was still glowing in the window.

This was a signal which meant that both Molly and Sally were ready, willing and capable of resuming our threesome. He sighed and said to himself, "What a great way to end such a good night. I am the original 'gifted man' and I thank God that I can still make women so happy. I am very blessed. I just pray that it will last until my nineties are over."

Chapter Twenty-three

PIANO

DR. GRAY SAID goodbye to both Molly and Sally and then, he paid his B&B Bill for a room that he hardly used at all. He was much more comfortable at Molly's place so he stayed there instead. He didn't get much sleep but he was used to that kind of nights. He pointed his front bumper toward Lexington and off he went. He was happy that Vanceburg was in his rear view mirror and he looked forward to his next assignment from dearest Mira.

The, he reviewed his present case. These were the thoughts that kept running through his mind:

- Able's dream about inflated real estate prices was not realistic. The Governor would just condemn his property and do his evil work. Paul didn't want that to happen to his new friends, both Able and Ted McArdle.
- What the cameras might resolve was a major concern. If Lola could do her magic with that infrared film, his opinion might change because that scene could be sold to almost any agency. It was high on his list of scary things.
- Imagine what might happen if 2000 citizens from Ohio came to little Vanceburg at the same time. Vanceburg would be overrun and devastated by sheer numbers.

- The city area was just 1.2 square miles. Therefore, the buckeyes would overcrowd the locals. This would mean that the new State Park would have to be built in the country and on McArdle property which PESO cannot afford to purchase.
- If Vanceburg were to suddenly get larger by annexation, a new State Park might be feasible but, in this case, Able McArdle would suffer from his unfriendly condemnation proceedings.
- The McArdle project would yield an X-rated Park where young children were denied admittance. And, Paul wanted only GP ratings for all of his Projects.
- And, the final issue was the river water. Evidently, he had made a crucial error with his plans for a dedicated Water Plant. He would monitor Lola's pictures and then decide.

For the present, he would recommend that the Vanceburg Project be placed 'on hold' for an indefinite period of time. That's a pity too because Ted McArdle did put on a great X-Rated show, perhaps the best that he had ever seen from the World of Paranormal activity.

Paul was more interested in how the political race was developing. Meg Raintree had called to say that Chief Iron Eagle would be happy to apply those stamps and to send out the bulk mailings. The photographs of Mr. and Mrs. Governor did cover the entire State so back-tracking of the return address would be difficult, if not impossible.

For successive Sundays, prior to the election date, all Baptist sermons in hard shell churches would harp on a single topic; namely, "Sin and corruption by the Governor and his wife." That sort of behavior requires each member of my Church to vote for Mr. Tedd Fox as our new Governor.

About one month ago, Paul had called Lola to make sure that all facial recognition patterns had been properly de-pixeled, except for those of the Governor and his wife, of course. In that way, all observers of those damaging photographs were looking only at bodies, not at any of the PESO faces. She assured me that this had already been done.

Up until this time, the PESO plan to displace the incumbents at the Frankfort Palace was looking very promising. And, he hoped so because Running Fox seemed to be a much nicer person. But,

Kentucky politics still suck. The greatest challenge for the Fox administration would be those gambling casinos, how many and where located. Ironically, those same Preachers that helped Fox would also be strong supporters of a 'No Gambling' movement.

He tried to make better speed on his return trip to Clay Street but, those same mountains that slowed him down on his initial trip to Vanceburg had not moved anywhere and, if anything, they seemed to be even larger than they were previously.

After he left the Mountain Parkway, he fired his engine up to its maximum rotations to play the game of 'bait' with all of the State Troopers that were on patrol at this time. When Troopers see one Police Car going at about 140-mph, they usually follow to see if the driver needs any backup. Or, they just try to catch up with that driver and make a race out of the situation. But, race or backup, Paul liked to win and, with the head start that Gray had, it was usually 'no contest'.

If they cannot catch the lead car aka 'bait', they always take their hats off to salute the lead driver. It's a ceremonial thing between policemen that only they know or appreciate. On this day, there would be four bald heads to be seen because they just didn't feel like getting involved. And, like Paul Newman or A.J. Foyt, Gray was an excellent driver. Every Trooper on the 'Winchester Run' would know that for certain.

But the problem with this process was that one of the losers in this chase would always call Mira to say, "Gray's back in town. Please see if you can talk him into driving slower. None of us on I-64 duty can catch him."

Accordingly, Mira would be alerted to his return and she would be sitting on his front porch swing at his Clay Street address when he arrived at home. City traffic would always slow him down just enough so that she could win her own race with him. The advantage went to Mira because Peso Headquarters was closer to Clay Street than he was.

And, she liked beating him in that fashion. But, she absolutely drew the line at racing against him on New Circle Road or the Interstate Highway. He was much better at the racing business when straight stretches were involved. They hugged on the porch and they went inside where they would talk business or have fun playing with each other's body.

After the chit-chat was over, he would ask about the status of those 'doctored pictures' for the Governor and his Wife. Mira told him that the first photograph had made its way onto the late-late-night TV screen. It revealed Angel being spanked by the Governor's wife with a ping pong paddle while Angel was giving the Governor a pretty good blow job. She had made a copy for him to study and he studied it very carefully for several seconds.

Then, Paul said, "Wait a minute, Mira. Something is strange about that TV picture. That's not one of our original negatives because we have a micro-marker on all our negatives and, here there is none." Mira interrupted to say, "If not us, then who?" Paul mulled it over in his mind and said, "I think it was taken by Angel herself."

It couldn't have been the incumbents at the Palace since that would amount to political suicide for any of their re-election desires. Only she had access to the Palace bedroom for that kind of photography. Therefore, Angel had both the means and the opportunities."

Mira asked, "Yeah, but, what is her motive?" "If she really wants Texas bad enough, then her motive could be 'payback', revenge or perhaps she is just 'burning her bridges behind her'. He added, "You and I had better watch Miss Angel more closely.

For someone to bite the hand that feeds her such large sums of money, she is more than weird, to say the very least. At this rate, Angel should volunteer for the Texas position any day now. If we are lucky, we may have killed two birds with one stone. Why don't we grill her severely, if and when, she asks for the job in Texas.

Mira changed the subject when she said, "What's next, dinner at the Golden Horseshoe Restaurant, Miss Monroe or both?" Paul answered,

"Why don't we do our favorite act near Marilyn first and, afterwards, we each will have a big steak to celebrate our mutual love for each other.

Traveling around rural Kentucky too much can lead to a very poor steak intake. But, thank God for the Golden Horseshoe Restaurant. They have never disappointed me with any of their fine offerings." Mira grabbed his hand and led him into his bedroom saying, "Sounds like a good plan to me Lover."

Mira had planned to stay the night as evidenced by the second dress and matching shoes to confuse the other girls at PESO. And, that was also a signal that she wanted her full share of orgasms, if Paul was up to it, that is. She knew that he was very tired but, Mira didn't know about Molly and Sally back at Vanceburg.

He felt that his gonads were almost empty but, he would try to do his best to please her because she was a cute little redhead who deserved nothing but the best of fine treatment. Together, they did their best and Mira did climax so, the enticing steak in downtown Lexington was next on the list.

Next morning, she showered first but, his pipes were finally emptied after he entered the shower enclosure, not on Miss Monroe. She exclaimed, "Now Paul, this will be our last quickie because I will be late for work if we keep doing this."

He made his last semen discharge to be one of his best before he felt truly exhausted. He collapsed on top of Marilyn and fell fast asleep while Mira pampered herself with sufficient cosmetics for the workplace. On her way out of his house, she kissed his wet forehead without awakening him.

Paul Gray was a delinquent from work on that day as he slept until about one-PM. However, Mira had left his next assignment on the kitchen table. He smiled and said, "That was very kind of her. I really needed that extra rest."

He thought, "That redhead sure gave me a pretty good workout last night. And, now, I can study this new assignment in the comfort of my own little house. That's living 'high on the hog', dear friends. But, when he did give the File a quick read, he was pissed."

It was another investigation about things, instead of people. Mira stayed here last night for two reasons. It was evident that she badly wanted some male sex. However, she also knew that I would make a big fuss about this new task if it had been presented to me while I was at my PESO Office.

Because Mira didn't want my negative reaction to be so public, she placed it on my Kitchen table while I was napping. How clever that woman is, she can read me like an open book. Paul had some more Keurig Extra Bold Coffee and, then, he took a second look at the submitted manuscript.

This assigned case was about a piano which defied the limiting laws of perpetual motion. That would be impossible since Mother Nature isn't geared that way. But, his engineering background advised him that it was worth a trip to Paintsville, KY to search for provenance. Miracles never cease and, if this be true, it just might be a fabulous new discovery. Imagine a piano that plays old music constantly. But, personally, he had doubts, huge ones.

Johnson County was still a 'moist' County where whiskey was concerned. The County people had voted to remain 'dry' but, the City of Paintsville was still wet. So, when Paul arrived at Paintsville, he went straight to a bar where he had high hopes of learning more about the so-called 'Player-less Piano'.

After several drinks with different customers, Paul finally found one man who seemed to know what Gray was talking about. And, of course, he would tell Gray everything that he wanted to know in exchange for additional free drinks.

This man was a dwarf with lots of gray hair on his head and, an untrimmed ugly beard on his face. But, otherwise, he seemed to be a reasonable sort of guy. George Huff, the dwarf, began by saying, "Once upon a time and long, long ago, before pausing as if to be organizing his thoughts or awaiting another shot of whiskey on the rocks. With so many pauses and too few facts, Paul wondered if he was being played.

Immediately, Paul began to worry if little George was able to deliver what Gray really needed but, he was willing to listen patiently for a little while longer. He visited the men's room to bleed his lizard and, on the way back toward their booth, Paul told the barkeeper to keep the drinks coming until he lifted his left arm high and straight. He said in a low tone, "Feed little George whiskey but serve me ginger ale on ice."

Crazy George continued, "Up, on Little Fork Creek, lived a tight-fisted farmer named Edna and Don Harrod. He sold timber and cattle in addition to fresh garden vegetables. In fact, Don H. was considered to be a wealthy man for that day and age. Some people would say that Harrod knew the thickness of a penny as well as its diameter.

Gossip also said that Don and Edna weren't getting along very well and that there were other women of interest to Don. One day, the housemaid and care giver, Sarah Collins was dismissed by Edna to go and get a doctor because she wasn't feeling very well. As Sarah was leaving the house, Don intercepted her to say, "She isn't sick, she just wants attention. Go back to the house and tell Edna that I will be there shortly."

He didn't get there in time to help his wife. When he did arrive, Sarah was sitting on the front porch saying that Edna had died and, painfully so.

Don asked Sarah this question, "If she is supposed to be dead, then who is playing her piano so loudly?"

Sarah said, "I don't know how to turn it off and it's been playing continuously since your Edna passed. The Legend says that Don was also unable to turn that blasted sound off. It just played and played both day and night. Finally, Don left for the timber camp which was about two-miles away to try and avoid that awesome noise which plays without any player or power of any type.

He lived at the saw mill as much as he could because he wanted no part of that cabin which he and Edna had occupied. That worrisome sound and his guilty conscience finally drove old Don as crazy as a bedbug such that he had to be placed into a mental asylum over at Lexington. Eventually, Don would die in that horrible place.

After some time had elapsed, Edna's oldest sister from Ohio came to Paintsville, demanding that Edna's body be exhumed and that an autopsy be performed on her sister's body for an official cause of death determination.

Penelope convinced the local sheriff and a friendly judge that her request was a worthy one. And, if murder was involved, Penelope would inherit the entire property and all of its assets or liabilities. The official cause of death was determined to be a classic one involving arsenic poisoning. Evil Don Harrod had been feeding Edna Harrod addictive doses of arsenic laced with laudanum over a period of several months prior to her untimely death.

George Huff said that the most remarkable part of this story was when Penny first entered her sister's bedroom, the piano stopped playing and that music was never heard from again. George reckoned that the music was some weird way that Edna was trying to contact Penelope for her help and assistance. And, Penelope did say that she heard those musical notes all the way from Ohio.

Paul asked Mr. Huff if the piano was still available for examination. He answered, "No, everything went northward to someplace in Ohio after she sold her next-of-kin property in Paintsville." Paul was very disappointed by the fact that he would be unable to examine the actual piano. So, he raised his left arm, paid their drinking bill and gave the dwarf some extra spending money.

Soon afterwards, he left Paintsville for the big city of Lexington. While driving, his thoughts were not about losing another State Park possibility but, instead, a lovely story that he would someday write. Edna's bad luck would become a short story for women to lament over.

After entering IH-64, he led a parade of five different Trooper followers who would each have to tip their hats before slowing down and giving up their race. And, most certainly, one of those Troopers would inform Mira that Gray was back in town. He drove straight to his Clay Street address so that he could write his final report on the 'Piano Job' without being disturbed by anyone.

He was sad that he was unable to meet with Edna while she was still alive and playing that Piano so profusely. He wondered if Edna was a good piano player or not. Did she play for pleasure or was she of the concert class? In any case, his interest was, as a short story writer, not as a State Park candidate.

Next, Gray would play his computer disc that featured Mira and Cher before crashing on top of Miss Marilyn for some much needed rest and relaxation. He went to sleep thinking about how many women would show up at Starbucks on the following morning. He smiled, and, with a big shit eating grin on his face, he fell asleep.

Chapter Twenty-four

RUNNER

PESO'S LEAD INVESTIGATOR was sitting at his favorite table in the Starbucks Coffee Bar as, not one, but, five lovely ladies came to partake in those delicious Danish treats. Paul just loved the image of having five females at his one table. He was the envy of every man in the Restaurant and, especially, the college students who were anxious to find their own Mrs. Robinson.

Imagine the joy of having five lovers to be with him at breakfast. Imagine also that each of these five ladies had spread their legs for him. Who needed ectasy? For him, ectasy was being at work where he could examine each feminine sample that surrounded him.

A ratio of 5:1 is defined as a bachelor's dream. It made him so happy that he was pleased to purchase their morning treats for them. After all, his evening's treats were provided by the ladies, not by him. While they ate, he just gazed at this beautiful abundance of feminine pulchritude. He did sip his strong, bold coffee but, mostly, he just enjoyed the panoramic view.

Mira was on his left and Joan was on his right and both of them were rubbing his big plaything under the table. What a morning to remember.

He was left with two thoughts, who staged this audience and would they be interested in a proposed six-some?

He said to himself, "Paul Gray, you will never change. What would you do if all these ladies said yes? If his pipes were cleaned, he would run. But, if his pipes were full, he would have them, one at a time. But, his internal measuring gauge told him that he had better get ready to run because his semen level was too low for any large action at this time.

In this manner, Paul was introduced to his next assignment called 'RUNNER'. Once again, Mira had chosen the title just to aggravate him. His position was that the title should be chosen by him after his Final Report is finished. He was old fashioned and a product of the old school of journalism; end it, then name it'.

Then he rationalized, Mira has the final say on titles so, why worry? A 'rose is a rose' if you get my drift. So, he elected to give it some time because it is entirely likely that Mira had the right title for this new assignment.

All of the PESO gals had left for the Office but, he still felt some stiffness in his middle leg so, he waited until that softened. While he was waiting for that to happen, he paid the waitress his bill and he read the summary section of the 'Runner'. He became more interested in the case when he noticed that he would have to visit two of his favorite places, both Jackson and Hazard.

As his interest peaked, he called Mira to say that he was more than interested in 'Runner'. Accordingly, he was already on his way to Hazard for conformational purposes. He asked her to call her friendly Trooper to warn him that Gray was headed east on IH-64. Would he like to try and catch me without using road blocks?

Then Paul said, "I will buy a keg of beer for the Trooper that can catch me on today's run." The hell of it was that no Trooper was to be found at this time. So, not one Police Cruiser would chase him today. On that basis, he concluded that it must be doughnut time over at Jerry's Restaurant in the city of Winchester. Or, perhaps, Mira did not make the telephone call that he had requested. She is starting to show a pretty thick 'mothering' streak toward him and his driving antics.

After he arrived in Hazard, he went straight to the archives section of their Coal Building Headquarters to check the Sheriff's records on why the 'Runner' was running. The young marathoner's name was Ed Clemons, a cousin to Paul's Uncle Bige who lived up on Noctor way.

It turns out that young Ed had killed two men in a Hazard bar, Dixon's place on Main Street. Ed and his victims were drunk and disorderly so a fist fight followed. Ed Clemons was physically the strongest man in town so, one or two jaws were easily broken and, subsequently, both deputies died as a result of their injuries in that viscous fight.

Clemons said that he didn't remember anything that happened in Dixon's bar. However, he did remember being arrested and being taken toward the Hazard Jail. On the way there, he was able to knock a deputy completely unconscious and, as the deputy fell to the ground, Clemons started running toward Jackson and Noctor where most of his kinfolks lived.

When Ed Clemons arrived at Jackson, he had already run a marathon of more than 44-miles, the exact distance between Hazard and Jackson. Unfortunately for him, he could also hear the Sheriff and his blood-hounds who were in close pursuit. They were in the near distance and they were gaining ground.

The Hounshell Family in Jackson donated food, ammunition and an old double-barreled shotgun before sending him away and toward the South Fork of Quicksand Creek. Clemons had plenty of cousins in that area. They could take care of him and hide him from that damned Sheriff and his Posse from Hazard of Perry County.

Their legal logic told them that the Hazard Sheriff had no jurisdiction in Breathitt County and they were perfectly correct. But try telling that to an enraged man who had recently lost two of his best deputies and close friends. In truth, no one would try to stop a Posse where each man carried a loaded gun that was pointed at their heads. From their point of view, they wouldn't stop until the 'Runner' was in custody or dead.

John Hounshell gave Ed Clemons one piece of good advice. He said, "Ed, run in branch water as far as possible to confuse the hounds." But, he had to emerge from the water at some point and that's where the dogs picked up his scent, one final time.

Ed Clemons ran up the stream, through the gap and down to the road which led to the South fork of Troublesome Creek near Quicksand, KY. After running two more miles down that road, the Posse caught up with him.

The Perry County Sheriff did ask for Ed to surrender but, the half-crazed 'Runner' felt that he would rather be shot with bullets than to be hung by the neck until dead. He emptied both barrels high over the heads of the Posse members and turned flush with them so that they could have a clean shot right toward his heart. Every member of the hunting party emptied a volley into his chest and he was instantly dead before he hit the ground.

John Hounshell said that he received details like that one from a 'friendly' member who had joined the Posse at Jackson. John had placed him there as an impartial observer to keep him informed as to whether Ed Clemons got a fair treatment or did not. The Breathitt County representative on the Posse said that Ed Clemons died humanely and was treated with respect.

As the Sheriff doubled back to Jackson, he told the Hounshells this.

"I might not have worked so hard to catch this man but he did kill two of my best deputies. And, I have to tell you this, that Ed Clemons turned out to be the strongest 'Runner' that I have ever seen. He could have won that New York Marathon with ease. But, I gather that New York 'shitty' was of no interest to him. Not his cup of tea, so to speak.

About six months later, the people who lived in that area where poor Ed died began to hear the terrified sobbing of a desperate fugitive running down the road with several bloodhounds baying in the breeze. An angry Posse was also in full pursuit.

Supposedly, that scene is always re-enacted on damp nights when light winds are blowing and the willow trees bend low enough to touch the shoulders of the nearby road. He called Herb and asked him to look into all of the construction problems around Quicksand, KY.

Depending upon what Herb might find, the Jackson and Quicksand area might have a new State Park in the very near future. He cautioned Herb to take plenty of soil tests because Quicksand is still quicksand. He wanted to finish the 'Runner' assignment by himself but, he was being re-called to Lexington on an emergency basis regarding some hush-hush problems about the Governor's campaign.

It seems that some person has lodged a formal complaint about the issue of professional ethics. Mira is upset and scared. Therefore, she feels threatened. And, when she is in this frame of mind, she calls for her own 'Dr. Who' and guess who that is.

He was happy about being re-called to Lexington because he had not seen his girlfriend Mira for several days now. When he arrived at his Clay Street address, her car was there and she was inside, fast asleep on top of Miss Marilyn. He was happy that he had given her a personal key so that she could come and go at her own convenience.

Paul chose not to awaken her because turn-a-about is fair play. She rarely sleeps during the day time so this is special. Mira had to have been wiped-out for her to fall asleep so early in the day. He knew that Mira would not sleep forever so he sat in his favorite chair to observe her breathing pattern.

Once in a while, she would whimper a little bit but there was no crying or screaming so, he still did not awaken her. He just kept on watching her breathe. She was so beautiful. Then, there was more whimpering. It was obvious that she was having a bad dream.

Just as he was about to halt the dreaming, she awoke on her own and without any assistance from him. She took one glimpse at him and whispered, "Hello, my dearest one. Thanks for coming home to help me." That warm greeting broke the silence ever so nicely. He asked, "Bad dream, Babe?" She said, "Yes." However, Mira offered no details so he would have to wait until she was ready to talk about her current problem.

He went to the fridge to get her some cold water over a lot of crushed ice. He was aware of how she liked real cold water in the mornings just after she got out of bed. After she had finished with all of that very cold water, she started talking about why she had recalled him when he was about one-half finished with his assigned field case called "Runner".

She apologized about her interference into his business but she added, "I need help that only you can provide, my street-wise and very intelligent lover boy." So, at that point she came out with what had happened to her and PESO while he was at Hazard and Jackson.

She said, "Angel has brought a legal suit against PESO and the Television Station over that photograph of her and that big ping pong paddle." Paul interrupted to say, "Why sue us? We didn't take that picture. And, I thought that much was understood already."

Mira asked, "What should we do?" He paused for a few moments before answering that challenging and interesting question. He mulled over the different possibilities for that particular issue and he had no specific suggestions to make at this time. He promised to make some phone calls on her behalf. He said, "Tomorrow, dear love, I will have an answer for you. But, it's too late now for business calls."

Why don't we just cuddle up and give each other a little southern comfort until tomorrow when I make some phone calls to a few of my high class friends in low class positions? That problem won't go away overnight so we might as well make the best of it.

Her eyes looked inviting as she said, "I brought some extra clothes and they are in your closet. I was hoping that you would make me an offer that I couldn't refuse. Then, they had serious sex off and on again for the balance of the night.

Next morning, after they ate their Kashi cereal and fruit mixture that was washed down by Keurig Coffee, he started the day's conversation about their current law suit and today's first order of business affairs. He said, "Mira, last night was precious and I wanted it to last forever but, you need to go to work, as per normal. Tell no one that I am here. As I said last night, I need to make some critical phone calls to sort out how we are going to proceed in fighting this complaint of Angel's."

She said, "Fine with me, love. You are the street fighter, not I. So, I will do as you say." Then, she went to the closet to choose between several different outfits. Then, it hit him like a bolt of lightning, "She's planning to stay for quite a few nights, not one. Oh, my bachelor days are about to end. In Lexington, that is."

First, he called a new friend of his, a Richard Stevens that was the new editor of the Lexington Herald. The previous editor, Don Mills had left the newspaper to head up the election committee for Tedd Fox. Paul hated to see him leave the newspaper but, this was what he wanted and one would have to search pretty hard and far to find a more capable man.

Fox was sure to win the Governor's chair now that he had Mills supporting him.

In our telephone interview, Stevens told me that, for a picture like that to be published, all three participants would have been required to sign a single disclaimer stating that they would not hold anyone responsible for legal recourse in the event that things went haywire. That, they and they alone, are totally responsible for each and every copy of the subject photograph. In other words, this sort of legal gumbo was required for the protection of the TV Station from the Federal bureaucracy.

Because of the absence of any PESO micro-markers, that photograph is not one which was produced by your cameras. That leaves just three persons who would have been forced to sign that disclaimer; viz. the Governor, his wife and our Angel. And, you will find a copy of that disclaimer somewhere inside of the TV Corporate Offices. It won't be found in the Governor's Mansion because they would have destroyed their original documents by this late date.

Stevens also said, "You should have your Peso lawyers to obtain a warrant to search the TV Station to discover a legal copy of that signed disclaimer. Almost any Judge will sign that order because you are now being sued. That makes you a definite link of this legal chain. Find that piece of paper and you should be excused from further litigation."

Paul thanked Stevens for his advice. He said, "I owe you one, good friend." Then, he called Mira to ask her to get the lawyers in motion. Unfortunately, she was in an important meeting and could not be interrupted. He asked Joan what the subject was and she said, "Safety" so, he hung up the telephone. Now, he understood exactly why he loved working in the field so much.

Next, he would take notes on how to deal with Angel and her harmful intent.

- Write Angel up for misconduct and fire her lovely ass. Neither you nor I can withstand a traitor like that amongst our midst.
- Sever all of her contacts at TX. She would be the type to land on Governor Jerry's doorsteps to volunteer for the position at Austin, TX.
- Silence that bitch as soon as possible.
- I will call Herb to ask him to stand guard at PESO for a few days. It won't hurt to have a couple of men around the premises for protection purposes. Our new Herb has abs, packs a gun and a hunting knife in his new position as head of field operations.

- At the last qualification, Angel scored highest on the firing range so you have to start packing iron until this matter is closed.

Next day was a very busy one for poor Angel around the PESO Headquarters building for example,

- Human Resources read Angel her rights before terminating her.
- Security escorted her to the PESO parking lot where she was arrested by the Lexington Police. His old boss was there and he remarked to Paul the following, "I am going to enjoy this one, Gray. Got any more like her?"
- She was incarcerated on the grounds of espionage and the 9/11 Terrorist Act.
- Her weapon, badge and ID were taken from her.
- Her PESO car was impounded for subsequent searches.
- She was not allowed to take anything from her office desk.
- And, her apartment was search by detectives of the Metropolitan Police Department.
- Officially, Angel was being treated as a non-person. Now, she was nothing but a number in the Police files.

That had to be the most unpleasant day in Angel's entire life. Mira left nothing behind in her attempt to cast Angel aside as a former employee of PESO. In a word, her treatment was 'brutal'. In a way, Paul felt bad about the ruckus but, she did sue PESO and that was a very stupid move. Mira would tolerate none of that bullshit for her little group.

Next, he and Herb would have to worry about Angel making bail and, perhaps, causing PESO additional damages. Paul Gray would be Mira's protection and Herb would protect Miss Shirley whom he loved so deeply. Both Lola and Joan were under 24-hour police surveillance.

On that basis, every possible precaution had been taken to save life and to prevent any illegal activities. Paul had better security for his new home with more lights and additional motion sensors. He had asked Mira to be a live-in until this frightening vendetta was dealt with properly. If Angel did come his way, he would be ready for her and any of her meanness. She would not hurt his Mira, not on his watch.

But, what did happen just overwhelmed everyone. It came out the blue as being totally unexpected. She made bail and she was obviously seeking revenge for those who had ruined her life. Somehow, the Governor and his wife had forgotten to remove Angel's name from the approved Palace Guest List. So, she still had the privilege of coming and going whenever she felt so inclined.

Accordingly, Angel showed her 24-hour pass and flirted with the Mansion guards by saying, "After I do the old fart, I'll come back here to your guard station to give you boys the best blow job that you ever had."

Naturally, the young guards looked forward to that with great expectations.

Then, she made her way to their Master Bedroom and used her own personal key to enter inside where she killed both the Governor and his wife while they were sleeping. One Palace Guard that was on post and stationed down the hall, heard the two gunshots and he made his way to where Angel was standing while the other guard was calling for backup. She made no effort to shoot the guard but he emptied his revolver into that pretty lady's chest. What a waste of such beautiful flesh.

The story of the 'Massacre at the Mansion' made the news highlights all over the Nation and Richard Stevens got all of the exclusive interviews. Paul's debt to Richard was more than fulfilled. For once in her life, Angel got more attention than she could ever want. Now, she was both famous and dead.

The other aftermath of her rampage was that Kentucky got a new Governor. It was easy for Running Fox to defeat the Lieutenant Governor after Angel had turned the re-election into a meaningless activity. Tedd Fox won the election by a large number of votes. Supposedly, the margin of victory was the largest difference that Kentucky had ever experienced. So, a large majority of the hard shell Baptists must have shown up and voted for new blood in the Governor's chambers.

And, to top it off, Paul Gray made a lot of money because the bookies did not believe that a Shawnee Indian had any chance of ever becoming the next Governor of Kentucky. In order to arouse less suspicion, he placed all of his bets in his Mother's name. The odds were very favorable so he ended up with a $100,000 slush fund for his mother to manage.

She would really enjoy the management of all that new money. And, nobody managed money better than his Mom. The scheme would work if she could keep her lips together at the Bowman Memorial Methodist Church. I reminded her that 'loose lips sink ships' but, I still kept my fingers crossed.

Chapter Twenty-five

ROADS

BECAUSE THE DANGER of Angel had become history, he decided to visit his nearest relatives at Slade, Kentucky which is not too far from his Clay Street address in Lexington. He wanted to visit one of the most serene places on Earth, Natural Bridge State Park.

After all, one of his favorite cousins was the Chief Forest Ranger for that State Park. His name was Clarence Henson and he had not seen him for many long days. The first reason for making this little stopover was that Clarence's wife made the best hamburgers that he had ever tasted. But, the second reason was to talk with Clarence and to count each other's wrinkles on our opposite faces.

Clarence was older than Paul so he always won that so-called wrinkle contest. Why would two grown men count wrinkles? If you tell me why, then both of us will be properly informed. On the other hand, I don't want to know why we are the way we are. That would spoil all the fun and, sometimes, not knowing about everything yields more pleasure. It was Sunday and he spent most of the day with his cousins.

Later, on the same Sunday afternoon, PESO's best field investigator was back at his home address in Lexington. He was looking on his kitchen table to see if Mira had left him his next assignment. He knew that it was about 'Roads' but, beyond that, he was uninformed.

Everyone had been calling in from the field to schedule a meeting with the newly-elected Governor Tedd Running Fox. This handsome young Governor was almost Kennedy-like so, his career in politics would take him a long way if he didn't screw it up the way his predecessor did.

An investigation by a Committee of Impartial Legislators (CIL) was formed and it was quite similar to that for the Warren Commission of a few years back. They cleared all members of PESO from any suspicious activity concerning Angel's death.

Their official opinion was that Angel had acted on her own and without the assistance of any outsiders. They also determined that the TV photo was taken by the Governor and/or his wife because no signature of Angel's approval was ever found on the documents at the TV Station. There were signatures by Mr. and Mrs. Governor but, none by Angel herself. Basically, the former Governor and his wife had taken that X-rated picture without Angel's knowledge or approval.

Evidently, some clerk at the TV Station had assumed that, because the Governor owned the Station, everything would be all right. In his eyes, the paperwork had to be correct and fully acceptable for subsequent processing. The moral to that story is simply this: Never assume that a politician does anything correctly.

In retrospect, poor Angel probably viewed her career to have been destroyed by those two people that she killed. In truth, she had decided against living in Austin, Texas where it's too hot in the summer time and too cold in the winter season. She had also done some quality research on the tarantulas, snakes, scorpions and roaches. Therefore, she had lost any interest in living down under.

And, she had worn out her welcome at PESO. Unfortunately, Mira was not allowing any love fests between Paul Gray and Angel. Each time that a spark seemed to exist, Mira would send Gray into the field and, gradually, the attraction became somewhat distant. However, her diary spoke many pages about the love of her life, one Paul Gray.

Her diary also told the story that the Governor was, in fact, going to shut PESO down within three days. So, being loyal to her new lover, she decided to put an end to such utter nonsense. She planned the execution of PESO's sworn enemies with meticulous detail. The diary was sufficient proof that the CIL needed to pronounce her as being guilty of premeditated murder.

However, the Palace Guard who killed Angel was named Sam Raintree, an older brother to Meg Raintree. And the autopsy revealed that Sam put a bullet through his only son. Yes, Angle was pregnant with his offspring. She was right when she said, "We may have created something very special during their night of passion." They took DNA samples from everyone because they had to rule out any influence by the Governor. And, Paul's protein sample was sufficient to prove that he was the one who had made her pregnant.

As a result of that unfortunate circumstance, Sam Raintree would always be a 'person of interest'. And, if Paul got any evidence toward that end, he would take Sam into the forest and kill him as brutally as he could. He would never commit murder on Angel's behalf but he would revenge his unborn son and what man would do otherwise?

Gray decided to take a wait and see attitude about this new Governor and the 'Indians' that surrounded him. He also concluded that Running Fox might or might not become a good Governor. But, he also had a strong notion that Fox and Iron Eagle wanted the casinos too much for his own comfort zone.

He and Mira would have to continue to protect their backsides because no one else would lift a finger to help them. Later on, he would explain to Mira what his feelings were and why the two of them should run a tight ship with guarded caution.

When it comes to gambling houses, Fox's best advisors were the Coushatta Indians who worked their thriving casino near Lafayette, LA.

They were a pillar of strength and good honest people who loved their main source of money.

Rumors were rampant about this new alliance between the two tribes, the Coushatta and Shawnee. So Paul wore his police uniform and pointed his police cruiser toward the Lafayette region. He wanted to see if he could pry some inside information from the Coushatta Indians about the Shawnee Indians.

He told Mira that he needed to learn more about who they were going to have to deal with in the future. Privately, he was consumed with this question. Is Meg Raintree involved? He fervently hoped that she was not a part of all this terrible tyranny.

About all that he could come up with during his trip to the south was that the Raintree family was badly bent and deeply involved. They said that Sam Raintree was their greatest concern. They called him the 'killer of the north'. And, Paul smiled to say, Looks as if I will be able to avenge my son's death, after all. And, Paul began to remember all of the torture tricks that he had learned during the time that he was in the US Army. Those things are never completely forgotten.

Next, he turned his attention to the new case file that Mira had placed on his kitchen table. She had attached a 'POST IT Note' on the file folder which made this point: "If Kentucky has more miles of running water than all other states, what about the roads that are running adjacent to all that water and fog? Paul, I think that we might be currently missing an important source of paranormal activity. Look into this for me, OK? I call it 'Roads'."

For 'She who must be obeyed,' Paul Gray would gladly go visit Hyden, KY once again. But, for any other requestor, he would flatly refuse them. Leslie County was not a five-star location for him. With one exception, of course, they did make excellent moonshine and this time he had two patrons.

He would bring some of that clear liquid home for both Mira and Iron Eagle. Mira was on his list for buying that bootleg whiskey because she liked it so well. Mira always said that it was the smoothest blend that was obtainable. Chief Iron Eagle was on the list for another reason. Gray felt that Iron Eagle was his only confidant inside the Shawnee tribe that he could trust. So, Iron Eagle needed to be rewarded from time to time with free firewater. He was on the road to Hyden, KY and he felt invincible, alive and full of piss and vinegar as the old saying says.

But, for the present, it was time to determine if any Troopers on I-64 were up to the challenge of practicing for high speed chases. Gray was badly disappointed with his poor timing. There had been a bad collision and all lanes were closed except for one very congested lane. So, today, Paul Gray would drive well below the speed limit. He passed that 8-mile stretch at an average speed of 2-mph.

To a man like himself, that was a personal embarrassment and each of the Troopers knew exactly how he felt. So, all Troopers who were directing traffic looked inside his cruiser, bowed, took off their hats, laughed and bade him 'God Speed'.

He was infuriated by their mocking behavior and he said to himself, "On my return trip, I will try to exceed my record of

152-mph. Then, these cops won't be laughing at me, no way. As each Trooper lifted his hat, Gray turned up the volume on his speaker systems to let Roger Miller sing for the occasion at hand. He played an old tape which delivered this same excerpt over and over; viz.

"I'm a man of means, by no means
I'm King of the Road".

He would, once again, have to thank Lola for her little adaptation for his tape player. It had come in handy on several occasions. He also would like to add that Roger Miller was one of the greatest singers that had ever marched down the crystalline path of stardom. Otherwise, his trip toward Hyden was uneventful.

At the time, he was comparing Hyden to Vanceburg in terms of size and population. His reasoning was that, if Vanceburg's smallness was a factor, what chance would Hyden have for a new State Park?

- Vanceburg = 1731 citizens in an area of 1.2 square miles.
- Hyden = 365 citizens in an area of 0.8 square miles.

What on Earth was Mira thinking about? Then it hit him. Mira didn't care about ghosts on this trip. She was merely interested in proving her theory that roads could have haunted sites if they were running alongside of rivers or creeks. In addition, Mira must be completely out of Leslie County's best sipping whiskey.

Otherwise, he had no clue why she had sent him to this mountain village in search of ghosts. Another huge problem was that both Hyden and Vanceburg had zero amounts of running water. He deduced that she must have become interested in certain road hauntings which had been reported in the Leslie County area. Oh, what the hell! She who must be obeyed shall be properly served. Of that, he was completed convinced.

As he entered Hyden, he checked in with the local Sheriff as a professional courtesy. He didn't want some fellow law officer to be angry about outside influence from Lexington. He introduced himself again and informed the Sheriff that he was here about the Johnson property along Dry Gulch in the rural part of Leslie County. He needed some guidance as to where the Johnson property was located; i.e., he wanted the GPS X-Y coordinates for that region.

The Sheriff started laughing and said, "You mean to say that you are ghost-busting again, correct?" And, for conversational purposes, Paul went along for the ride. Gray said, "Yes, that's it Officer. I have been told that the old Johnson Property has a ghost who can lock down the wheels of any automobile. I want to see what that damned road ghost can do against all of my Ford's horsepower."

The Sheriff replied, "I heard about you PESO people. One of your girls killed our Governor, didn't she?" Gray quickly answered, "Yes, she did but, it was a justifiable hit." He said, "Oh, I don't care about that. As far as I am concerned, that Governor was a lying, cheating bastard who deserved a bullet with his name written all over it.

If Hyden was the State Capitol, he would have been assassinated a long time ago. Up here in these mountains, there are several people who would have taken him out if she hadn't done him in already." Paul was starting to admire this tough-guy Sherriff, more and more.

We enjoyed some coffee and doughnuts together while I explained my current assignment and the PESO mission. He lamented, "I don't understand how you could have left the MPD for your present job. I realize that a guy has to earn his living in any manner that he can but, for me to be a ghost hunter, no way man. I don't look for them. I dodge them, if at all possible.

Have you found many ghosts, Dr. Gray?" Paul responded, "Not many. I would say less than thirty or so. And, that number is misleading. It might seem small at first glance but, if we build new State Parks around them, think about the increased revenue for the State's vault." He interrupted to say, "Or, for the Governor's pockets, you mean to say. Promise me one thing, Gray. Keep all of your parks in Perry County, if you can. We don't want for you to be building anything like that here in Leslie County. We have enough physical problems without worrying about the spiritual ones."

Sherriff Jones gave me the X-Y coordinates that I needed to locate the 'road ghost' that Mira wanted to evaluate. The one that is, supposedly able to snare the drive wheels of any vehicle. I had not bothered to tell him that my Cruiser is blessed with a four-wheel drive system and a super-sized transmission. But Jones was kind enough to give me some very helpful suggestions; namely,

- *"Don't go there until well after midnight.*
- *Be there when it is extremely dark.*
- *Wait until zero visibility is available.*
- *Drive your car very slowly as if it were a horse buggy.*
- *When the road ghost locks you down try to spin your wheels.*
- *If you over-spin, the odds are not in your favor.*
- *People break the axel shafts if they gun their motors too much.*
- *That area has been nick-named as Johnson's Horror Hold.*

And, another thing, here is my business card with my private telephone number but, don't call me about a wrecker truck until after breakfast is finished. I don't do rescue missions at 0200-hours anymore. I need my sleep. Are you a betting man, Dr. Gray?" "That depends on the bet, Sheriff." Jones said, "I will bet you a Century note that you will break an axle on that Ford of yours while you are attempting to get released from Johnson's Horror Hold."

Paul responded, "Your bet is on, Sir. And, here is the $100 to seal our wager. I'll see you in the morning if the weather is right. And, I won't be in need of a wrecker truck." He laughed and jokingly said, "Want me to order you an axle now or tomorrow? I can get you a good deal at my brother's parts store."

"What you can order for me is eight quarts of Leslie County's finest moonshine whiskey. I promised my woman that I would bring some home to her and I don't know my way around these here parts. I'll pay cash money for whatever source you might recommend. Jones agreed to get him two cases of the premium blend and, at an attractive price of just five dollars per quart, the going rate between two police officers. Whiskey that good was certainly worth more than five bucks a quart. He handed the Sheriff a fifty dollar bill for his time and trouble.

Gray left to find a suitable motel in nearby Hazard where he could visit with his mother until zero visibility arrived. According to the television news, the weather should become ideal for his mission in about two more days. He would gladly accept that brief delay because it was nothing as compared to some of the longer waits that he had endured at other apparition sites.

Until then, he would visit with his mother to eat lots of his favorite side dish, soup beans with additions of pork meat. He was also curious how well she was doing with her money management fund. She was happy to see him and she reported that she had already earned about $3200.00 in interest. But, she was happiest when he told her that she could keep the interest for herself. That woman could talk the People's Bank & Trust Company into almost anything.

At night, Paul would try to locate some of his old girl friends. Or, he would hang out at the 'Dixie Drive In' to flirt with some of the young girls that were looking for a workout with an older man. Gray did find one that was hot and ready for some action.

So, they trash talked for quite a while. But, he just couldn't follow through. She was jail bait and, some man's charming daughter. He paid her handsomely for her companionship but, nothing else really happened. Her name was Angel and, for me, that name made a big difference. This is to say that she brought back too many bad memories.

The following evening, Paul decided that he would make his move since the weather was perfect to accomplish his objective. Skies were overcast so there would be no moon or stars and nothing except pitch black conditions.

But, before Gray reached his final destination, he pulled over to the side of the road to attach his snow and ice chains which he used during the winter season. He installed them on all four wheels of his powerful Ford Cruiser because he had every intention for winning that gambling bet with Sheriff Jones. Why take any unnecessary risks when there is money to be made?

Besides that, Gray hated to lose any bets to anyone, period. Paul worked with some difficulty in the total darkness but, he did have two emergency lanterns of the kind that railroad men use in pitch black conditions.

After the chains were tightly installed and inspected, Paul proceeded at about one-mile-per-hour until he reached the exact GPS location that he was seeking. Then, he stopped the vehicle to take some pictures of the 'before' scene. Later, he would take some of the 'after' scenes as well.

Suddenly, he felt something snag his chains where that applied force was acting against him and, in the opposite direction of his desired motion. Thereupon, he steadily applied his gas pedal to the metal until one or more of his chains were broken. Then he locked the emergency brake before getting out of his vehicle to see what was going on at the road surface or beneath his vehicle.

He moved his lantern around until the obstruction was better defined. One of his chain links had snagged a rock that was protruding from the ground at an angle of about 20-degrees. It appeared that the rock was pivoting about its own axis.

When the front axle went past and over the rock itself, the rock edge would be rotated and elevated like a wood screw to catch the rear wheels as the vehicle kept moving forward. If anyone was going down this road at high speed, considerable damage would be done to their car or truck.

But, at one-mile-per-hour of snail pace, there was no damage to his cruiser, only his chains were disabled. He removed those chains and slowly backed his car up to take full advantage of the rock's pitch profile. It was like an auger which had two motions that were active, counterclockwise to extend upwards and clockwise to lower downward.

This old mystery was properly solved and there would be no new State Park in Hyden or this part of the forest. All that was really needed was some selective repair by the State Highway Department. They needed to extract that auger-shaped rock and to replace it with concrete or asphalt.

He sprayed the rock with red paint as a marker before leaving to meet with Sheriff Jones to collect his $100.00 wager. He declared himself to be the winner because he had not broken any axle shafts during the night. He was certain that Sheriff Jones would argue the point but, he wondered what he might do or say.

As he expected, Sheriff Jones did try to 'weasel' on the wager. He argued that too many reliable witnesses had experienced the 'Johnson Horror Hold'. And, accordingly, these good people could not be wrong. He was confident that Paul Gray was trying to 'weasel' on him, not the other way around.

So, the two of them went to where the red paint was. When Paul told him to jump on the red paint, his body weight caused the stone to move and Jones's momentum turned him sideways by an inclination of about sixty-degrees. He was discombobulated, to say the least. All he could say was "I'll be damned".

Fortunately, for Gray, the Sheriff didn't even notice the tell-tail chain marks that were on the ground. But, Jones continued to complain. People have spread the word about this haunted road since 1890. How could all of them make such an error in judgment? Paul answered by saying, "Sheriff, those people were just wrong, that's all. This auger-shaped rock could be classified as a unique geological formation but, it is not a ghost and this is not a haunting site."

But, Paul let Jones keep his $100.00 bill because the GPS location and all associated forewarnings were priceless. Without that kind of help, Paul could have been stranded in Leslie County for days, maybe even weeks. And, what sort of red-blooded American would want for that to happen?"

He said to himself, "Let them keep those 365 people because Paul Gray will never become number 366 and the next census would not change by 0.27 percent difference. He grabbed the two boxes of moonshine and burnt rubber leaving the image of that lonesome town in his rear view mirrors.

And, except for Mira's whiskey, he vowed to never again enter that village of Hyden. He would ask her to sip these four quarts, in lieu of swallowing large gulps. It was either sip or else she might have to go to Hyden and get her own booze.

Chapter Twenty-six

WARNING

THE FUNERALS WERE all behind him now or, at least
Paul Gray hoped so because funerals were never his thing.
The Governor and his wife were given elaborate sendoffs which they
did not deserve. And, poor Angel was treated as an assassin or worse.

Had it not been for Mira and the team at PESO, Angel would
have had no decent funeral at all. Perhaps, a pauper's grave at best
but, no more than that. We all chipped in and paid for a very nice
cremation ceremony.

Her legal Will and personal papers had stated the wish that her
ashes be buried near her mother's casket. No one except PESO
personnel attended her funeral and, greater grief occurs when there
is no next of kin. That's one side of Angel's character that Paul never
expected. Paul figured her to be the popular type but, instead, she was
actually a very lonely person.

In a twisted sort of way, he was grateful that they had that
all-nighter together. It was, probably, the best sex that she had ever
experienced in her entire mature and professional life. Angel was a
beautiful broad but, she deserved a better ending than she received.

Sam Raintree was a dead man walking but, he didn't know it
yet. Paul swore over the ashes of his 'common-law wife' and his
unborn son that they would be revenged. An 'eye for an eye' was the

applicable creed. And, that 'killer-from-the-north Shawnee' would soon be terminated and sent to the wicked one below.

Paul would always wonder if that crash of hers was a function of her extremely high IQ. He reasoned that the smartest chicks are the hardest ones to predict since you never know what to expect from them. Actually, Paul Gray conceded that her last moments on Earth were heroic in one way. She went in the one direction that would best preserve PESO and its future.

So, as far as he was concerned, Angel did each of the people at PESO a favor that was immeasurable. That favor was above and beyond the call for normal duty. Three more days and they would have been disbanded as a PESO group according to what the Governor had already planned.

She was an unexpected assassin but why was a killer like Raintree working as a Palace guard? He was there to kill the same pair that Angel killed and, of this, Gray was certain. It was Running Fox's back-up plan for winning the election. And, the Indian mind is famous for getting rid of the competition.

Paul said, "Enough of this awful grief and funeral talk. I am ready for my next case and I don't care where it is located. He had to get away from his sadness, a lost lover and an unborn son. Mira must have recognized that Paul was in denial about Angel's departure because his next case was in Perry County, his favorite haunting site.

That made him a happy camper so he packed his gear and headed for his home town of Hazard. And, this time, he would drive the official speed limit. He was still emotionally drained and, accordingly, unfit for high speed racing with the State Troopers or any other drivers.

Like it or not, he would for, one day only, allow the Chevrolets to pass him by. Through all of Paul's entire childhood, his Father would allow no Chevys to pass his Ford vehicle. And, now, it was 'like Father, like son.' His was a Family of dedicated Ford drivers and racers. He couldn't help it because a shrink would say, "His Father is to blame."

The DNA results were back from Chapter Nineteen (Brides) and Chapter Twenty (Trees). The results were astonishing because they support the theory that reincarnation is the controlling reaction after death. The drops of blood that were left by the Brides, indicates that they are being transformed to beetles. And, the sycamores are being morphed into grasshoppers. The math that covers this new theory is given as follows: For example, consider the DNA equality that exists for the Chimpanze(C) and the human body (H) comparisons.

$$(C) = 0.94 \ (H)$$

This leads to the conclusion that the Chimpanzee DNA is 94% of the human DNA with just six percent difference. And, since the monkey is lower on the food chain that we humans are, reincarnation fits. For the grasshoppers (G):

$$(G) = 0.33 \ (H)$$

And for the beetles (B):

$$(B) = 0.16 \ (H).$$

This new discovery about DNA and reincarnation is to be included in the Paris Convention paper where Gray is scheduled to give an invited lecture. DNA will add a little 'spice' to his contribution for the sum of total knowledge.

In addition, he would use redaction techniques to try and demonstrate that some ghosts serve a greater purpose after their death than they ever did during their entire life. He had high hopes that this field case would be a perfect example of ghosts that give a cautionary advice about an impending death. He called them 'warning' ghosts.

In other words, these kinds of ghosts gave official notice that the Grim Reaper was about to make an unwanted appearance in Perry County. No one wants to die so, to receive a warning in advance, that is frightening to say the very least. But, Sheriff Jack Horn had documents for many such warnings that dated back to about 1865. In this instance, sufficient evidence had been given to the Sheriff's Office by Mrs. Tabatha Herd, a care-giver in the area.

At that time, Mrs. Herd, a widow, was taking care of her daughter, Matilda who had been sick for the previous two weeks. Tabatha's first warning came one night when she was almost asleep. She heard someone enter the house and, because Matilda was fast asleep, she chose to investigate the matter.

Tabatha got out of her bed to see who the uninvited guest was and what he or she wanted this late at night. She was more than scared so, she carried one of her dead husband's pistols with her as she continued her stealthy approach.

As she opened her door to take a peek, she saw a lovely young girl in a long white dress that was about Matilda's age. She entered Matilda's closet to remove a white dress which she folded over her left arm before leaving the room. When Tabatha heard the downstairs door open and close, she felt some relief that no real harm had occurred. So, she went back to bed for some much needed slumber.

On the following night, that girlish figure returned to execute the same procedure as before. Again, she would take a white dress from Matilda's closet, fold it over her left arm and vanish out the front door.

This time, Tabatha became convinced that the apparition was trying to tell her something but, what?

She became certain that the images were not a dream, not imagined and, by no means, one of her daughter's friends. She also decided that she would keep quiet about all of this since she did not want to upset her family, unnecessarily.

She did speak to the Sheriff about these sightings and he documented the events in his Sheriff's log. He advised her to determine where the ghost goes after she leaves Tabatha's house. But, he did warn her that, perhaps, Matilda was about to die. He said that he had numerous documents from the past where, in each case, the Grim Reaper was involved as the end result. She cried several tears and, the police officer comforted her with an old saying, "Fore-warned is Fore-armed."

On the third night, Tabatha was seeking more evidence so she stayed awake should the apparition choose to re-appear. She was going to follow the frightening spirit that was stealing white dresses from Matilda's closet. Around midnight, the unwanted guest showed up again. She entered Matilda's room, removed another white dress from the closet, folded it over her left arm, descended the stairs and left by the front door.

This time, Mrs. Herd watched the scene that unfolded after the ghost had left her front porch. The bright moonlight was just perfect to reveal everything that happened as the ghost went across the road and entered that little white Church which was standing just beyond the road.

After a few seconds, at most, the ghost emerged from the side door of the Church and vanished into the Cemetery which was behind the Church building. She just disappeared among all of those tombstones. Then, all became quiet and lonely as if nothing had happened, nothing at all.

Early next morning, Matilda died. Her funeral service was held in the Church with the Reverend John B. Thackenbush presiding. Her interment was amongst the tombstones out back. Matilda had requested to be buried next to her maternal grandmother who had been a garment maker for her entire life. That woman sewed and mended clothing until she died at the age of 94 years old. And, she also made exquisite quilts. Her name was Elizabeth Hounshell and she was a marvelous person to know.

From Paul's point of view, Elizabeth was the warning ghost who gave three warnings that the grim Reaper would soon visit the Herd Family. It was Elizabeth's cautionary advice which warned that Matilda's time on Earth was limited.

For his Paris lecture, Gray would build the argument that 'warning ghosts' do serve a most valuable purpose in getting the family ready for what is to soon follow. Or, as Forest Gump might say, "Death is like a box of chocolates because one never knows what to expect next, recovery or not?

With warning ghosts like Elizabeth to warn us, we do know what to expect, right? That is a blessing because it gives us more time to prepare for the inevitable. The bottom line being that no one gets out of this World alive.

Enough said about that madness concerning how a person exits the living World. Gray was perfectly satisfied to deal with his own death as long as it occurred at a much later date, say 100–years from now. For the present, Mira had sent him on a hot trail which involved another example of what warning ghosts can do for mankind. This apparition occurred in Bell County, Kentucky, not too far from the County Seat of Pineville.

And, Paul was happy to do what Mira wished because Miss Monroe would witness a most enjoyable 'payback' whenever he did arrive back home in the Fayette County area. On the way to Pineville, He became aware of more interesting facts about Bell County, KY. The adjacent County list was uniquely unique. As noted by the following point of interest:

- To the North was Clay County, KY.
- To the Northeast was Leslie County, KY
- To the East was Harlan County, KY
- To the Southeast was Lee County, VA
- To the South was Clairborne County, TN
- To the Southwest was Whitely County, KY
- To the Northwest was Knox County, KY

This reminded him of the Four Corners Monument that identifies where Colorado, New Mexico, Arizona and Utah come together. They share a 'plus' sign that is separated by an included angle of 90-Degees. But, their Monument also aroused his loyalty to dear old Kentucky. He asked, "Why don't we have a Seven Corner Monument at Pineville that features seven directions that are separated by 51.4-Degrees? Someone in the new State Park systems should do something about this terrible oversight. Right now, it's left to Special Agent Paul Gray. Anyone want to take up that particular challenge?

Suddenly, Paul was alerted to the disturbing fact that he could spend the rest of his life searching for an elusive warning ghost. Supposedly, these ghosts were a beautiful woman and a little boy that was both dressed in pristine white clothing. Why do ghosts seem to prefer the color of white? Is it for purity or is it for enhanced contrast?

But, once again, Paul was reading more things into the story without listening to Mira's summary statements first. He decided to listen to her presentation because it might save him some valuable time in the long run. He had seven directions to go out of Pineville and he didn't know where or how to begin his initial search.

He listened to Mira's sexy voice again and again but, that didn't help him very much. Then, his own intelligence kicked in while he had another light bulb experience. He did a 360-turn and headed toward the Hazard Airport where he would rent an airplane and do his own aerial search. His required flying time was almost history and his Pilot's license was almost expired.

As a result, he had to pay the airplane's owner a higher rental rate than was normal. That pissed him off but, what could he do? He needed an airplane and he needed it yesterday. He was looking for a landslide zone in one of seven possible directions. And, an aerial search would represent the fastest method to find what he was trying to find.

He did an exponential search pattern starting at the Pineville area and, within an hour, he had located the exact area where he would do his research and interviews. It was about five miles east of Pineville and toward Harlan County where the rich coal deposits was situated.

He took as many photographs as possible and that proved most difficult with the winds misbehaving and an airplane which was so affected by steerage. He also scribbled detailed notes concerning his compass headings and, of course, he pinpointed his GPS data. He was confident that he could find his destination by land, even it was after daylight hours.

With everything in place for a proper characterization, of 'warning' ghosts, also known as 'good' ghosts, Paul returned his over-priced Piper Cub to its resting place at the Hazard Airport. He vowed never to fly that flight pattern again.

Those air currents are just too dangerous for these mountains of Southeastern Kentucky. With a light Piper Cub airplane, one wrong move and you are splattered all over the mountainside or, impaled on one of those jutting rocks that decorate the entire area. Needless to say, Gray was grateful that he had finished a tricky flight pattern successfully.

With the information that he had obtained from his aerial search, Paul drove his car right to the applicable area without any problems. Then and there, he started his research and his interviews of the neighbors who still lived in the area.

At one time, there was a line of ten small coal mines that outcropped near a watery branch that was due east of Pineville. These coal pits were owned by Buchanon Coal Company but, they were never developed commercially. Instead, Ike Buchanon left them open so that the inhabitants of the region could dig enough coal to survive the cold winter season. Ike was a philanthropist but, moreover, he was a nice man who was sensitive to the needs of other people.

These small coal pits were worked by the locals until about 1955 when some of the neighbors claimed to have seen a beautiful woman, dressed in white, inside those coal mines late at night. Other workers also reported that they saw a small boy, also wearing white clothing, inside the mines.

He asked himself, "Why do ghosts wear so much white clothing? Is it because of purity or enhanced contrast? Paul assumed that he wouldn't know the answer to that question until he became a ghost himself. And, he was in no hurry to become one.

One witness swore that he saw lanterns that were inside the mines but, when he tried to investigate further, both ghosts just disappeared and the lanterns were instantly extinguished. The nearby villagers were a superstitious lot so they abandoned their little pits for a brief period. In their minds, these small pits were a haunted place.

Mr. Buchanon was a benevolent man so he supplied them with coal until this superstition could be better understood. Needless to say, his coal trucks were a welcome sight for the local residents. Buchanon was happy to help them because his coal tunnels for his large mines had been originally built on their property. In a way, he was making amends.

It was not known if this paranormal event was driven by two warning ghosts or not. But, in a few weeks after those farmers had stopped gathering their small amounts of coal from those pits, a strange thing happened.

One side of that mountain imploded and collapsed into a heap of dirt, rocks and broken trees to a depth of 100-feet in all directions. Fortunately, not a single person was harmed in any way whatsoever. Had any of the men or women been gathering their coal, they would have buried alive by that terrible upheaval of dirt and debris without any chance for survival.

Paul, like all of the people of the valley, was left with the belief that the miners were dutifully advised by a pair of 'warning ghosts'. There was no other plausible explanation for the observed devastation that he first observed during his Piper Cub flyover.

Later on, Paul would check out of his Pineville Motel and drive home toward Lexington as quick as the traffic would allow. He was hoping that Mira might be there at his Clay Street address so they could have a wonderful date together, a little romp and, perhaps a good steak at the Golden Horseshoe Restaurant.

He was also wondering how Mira might react to his new bedroom sheets. This time, his theme was about Dolly Parton, not Miss Marilyn.

He had a nude, full-size Dolly Parton image sewn into the bottom cover sheet.

Perhaps, Dolly's two large breasts might be too uncomfortable for Mira to sleep on because he had encapsulated plastic bottles of chocolate syrup and silicone nipples for Joan to nibble on. The bottles and chocolate syrup were inserted where Dolly's tits were located. He provided something for Joan to enjoy because that would guarantee a threesome to exist.

In recent times, Mira never seems to visit him without also bringing Joan along. Does that mean that both Joan and Mira are being converted from the Lesbian inclination? Then he said, "You know something, threesomes are beginning to lose their luster for me."

I am beginning to think that when we do go to Paris, France as a married couple, Joan will surely want to go with us. And, I do not want that to ever happen. So, which lovely Lady should I marry? Please take a guess. I could use some sage advice.

About The Author

D R. CHARLES HAYS was born and reared in Hazard, Kentucky during the Great Depression of 1929-1941. He has strung columns, written short stories for magazines and authored six books as a personal hobby over the years. This novel, Paranormal, represents his first attempt to be a published book author. His career includes service as an internationally renowned metallurgical engineer. Additional accomplishments are comprised as follows: a novice reporter for the Hazard Daily Herald, a 0.310 batting average as a professional baseball player, US Army soldier for the Korean Conflict, worked on the Apollo Moon Missile, wrote more than 100 papers for arbitrated Journals, Chief Editor for an International Magazine and an Honorary Fellow for two Engineering Societies. He now lives in Texas where he continues to write in retirement. He is a widower who has two wonderful children, Brenda R. Hanzik (Hays) and Charles C. Hays of the highly respected Jet Propulsion Laboratory.